Pat,

Thank you — you do for us.
Keep standing for
Blessings!
Phil
Proverbs 22:6

9-6-2014

9-16-2014 PC

# Then Sings My Soul

*a novel*

## Philip D. Smith

WESTBOW
PRESS
A DIVISION OF THOMAS NELSON
& ZONDERVAN

Copyright © 2014 Philip D. Smith.

All rights reserved. No part of this book may be used or reproduced by any means, graphic, electronic, or mechanical, including photocopying, recording, taping or by any information storage retrieval system without the written permission of the publisher except in the case of brief quotations embodied in critical articles and reviews.

WestBow Press books may be ordered through booksellers or by contacting:

WestBow Press
A Division of Thomas Nelson & Zondervan
1663 Liberty Drive
Bloomington, IN 47403
www.westbowpress.com
1 (866) 928-1240

Because of the dynamic nature of the Internet, any web addresses or links contained in this book may have changed since publication and may no longer be valid. The views expressed in this work are solely those of the author and do not necessarily reflect the views of the publisher, and the publisher hereby disclaims any responsibility for them.

Any people depicted in stock imagery provided by Thinkstock are models, and such images are being used for illustrative purposes only.
Certain stock imagery © Thinkstock.

ISBN: 978-1-4908-3590-7 (sc)
ISBN: 978-1-4908-3591-4 (hc)
ISBN: 978-1-4908-3589-1 (e)

Library of Congress Control Number: 2014907811

Printed in the United States of America.

WestBow Press rev. date: 5/13/2014

This is for you Pam
You will never know how much you truly mean to me

# 1

Part of him wished he hadn't promised his sisters he'd take them swimming today, seeing as it was the first day of his adult life. He should be with his friends at the Cue Spot, playing some eight ball and bragging about his future conquests, both sexual and financial. The excitement of graduating high school and a six-year-old's chocolate moon-pie eyes had obviously gotten the best of him last night.

Bobby reached down and grasped the hand of his little sister. Jonda eagerly squeezed her big brother's long fingers, anticipation and excitement whooshing through her tiny digits. He tried to do the same with Sarah, but she being a grown-up fourteen, rebuffed his paternalistic offer. It was the first day of summer vacation, and the three siblings were tromping to the local swimming hole.

"I'm gettin' pooped. When we gonna get there? You guys walk too fast." Jonda looked up at her brother.

"No, we don't, Short-Stuff. We can't help it if your legs are too short," Sarah piped in.

"Bobby, she called me Short-Stuff again, and Momma told her not to!" Jonda skidded to a stop on the concrete roadway and jerked her hand from Bobby's. With a high-pitched huff that sounded like an upset sea lion barking at food-waving tourists, she crossed her arms and stamped her feet.

"Come on, Sarah. Leave her alone. You know she doesn't like that name." Bobby pulled Jonda's hand from her wooden-Indian pose and forced her to move again.

The trio tramped out of their Garden City neighborhood, veering east onto the grass shoulder of the always-busy Quanah Avenue. Bobby readjusted his walking, placing himself nearest the traffic and Jonda between him and Sarah. They skirted past a couple of tiny, crowded diners and soon found themselves beyond the bustle and beside the huge Texaco tank farm.

Bobby surveyed the far side of the avenue. It was much the same as the area they'd just passed, businesses humping to stay ahead of the competition interrupted here and there by mom-and-pop cafés or open-air hamburger stands whose only advertising was the wafting smell of grilling meat and deep-fried potatoes.

Beyond the busy street lay Lookout Mountain. The heavily treed apex was pinioned by a towering radio antenna. Bobby chuckled to himself. Lookout Mountain wasn't really a mountain, not even what most would call a big hill. But for people living around Tulsa, it was the closest thing to a mountain they'd see. Bobby's eyes drifted to the base of the hill and settled on the Frisco railroad yard. Even from the long distance, he could see the movement of numerous slow-moving freight trains. Somewhere over there, their brother, Josh, was working as a brakeman, no doubt sweating even more than Bobby was.

Despite the traffic rushing past them, the massive, gray-colored oil tanks evenly spread out over acres of green pasture instilled a quieting effect on the area. Bobby released his sister's hand and raised his right arm. With his left hand, he pulled the short sleeve of his cotton shirt to its fullest extent and wiped the pre-noon sweat beads from his forehead with the thin fabric. *Gosh, it's already hot*, he thought. *And it's only May!*

Jonda interrupted his thoughts. "Hey Bobby? Would we get drowned if one of those tanks broke and all that oil came out?"

"The tanks are not going to break, so don't worry about it."

"But what if they did? We couldn't run away cuz if we did, we'd get runned over by the cars. I bet we'd drown."

Sarah tried to help, "Jonda, we're not going to drown! The tanks are perfectly safe. Besides, they may not have any oil in them right now."

"How do you know? I bet they're loaded with oil. Enough to cover us clear up to here." Jonda stood on her tiptoes and pointed above Sarah's head.

"Well, at least it won't be over my head," Bobby laughed. "I'll live through the flood."

"Not if somebody lights a match," Jonda said in earnest. "Then you'd burn up faster than we'd drown. Ain't that right, Sarah?"

"Good grief, Short-Stuff. Don't you think if Bobby burns up, we would too? Seeing as how we'd be covered with the junk too."

"Oh," Jonda muttered, apparently stumped. She was quiet for several seconds, then turned toward Sarah and swung at her with her fist. Sarah easily avoided her sister's haymaker. "I told you to quit calling me Short-Stuff, and I really meant it! I'm tellin' Mom when she gets home tonight."

Bobby grabbed the four-foot girl by the shoulders and twisted her around until she faced him. He glared into her dark-brown eyes, trying his best to act angry. Jonda stuck out her lower lip and blew a wisp of air into her daisy-colored locks. She always did this when she lost her temper, which was often.

Bobby ground his teeth, still trying to control his whimsy. He glanced above the little girl's golden head at Sarah who promptly rolled her eyes and shook her head; apparently she didn't see the humor in it that he did. Sarah was totally different from their younger sister. And it wasn't simply that Sarah's hair was dark and she was rather big-boned like Josh. No, it was more than that. Sarah was a serious girl and had been since she was a child -- well, at least since Dad died. On the other hand, Jonda was ornery clear to the marrow of her skinny bones.

"You know somethin' Bobby?" Jonda stated matter-of-factly.

"Everybody's always sayin' that you and I look alike. But we don't. My hair's lighter than yours. Your hair is browny lookin' and mine's yellow. Plus that, your nose is a lot more pointy than mine is."

"I don't really care whose hair is blonder right now or if my nose is more pointed than yours. What I do care about is that you don't try to hit Sarah again. Because if you do, we're going to turn around and head straight back home. Do you understand?"

"But she called me a name!" Jonda whined. "I hate that name, and she knows it!"

"Sarah won't call you Short-Stuff anymore. Right, Sarah?" Bobby pleadingly glanced at his other sister.

"Whatever," she answered. "Can we go? I'm burning up." Sarah switched the beach towels she was carrying from her right shoulder to her left.

"Do we have a deal then?" Bobby returned his attention to Jonda.

"Okay," she stated nonchalantly. She then turned, and marched down the street, leaving her siblings behind.

"See what I get to put up with this summer?" Sarah piped.

"It could be worse, Sarah. She could be a little brother."

The trio continued walking in the high grass next to the tank farm. On the far side of the street, they passed Howard Park. Bobby looked through the pecan orchard at the baseball field and saw it was empty. No sandlot game going on. No semi-pros practicing. That was unusual. Normally, somebody, usually kids, was on the red-dirt infield playing work-up or 500.

The siblings crossed Twenty-First Street and headed into downtown West Tulsa. The brick buildings loomed huge to the pedestrians, but Bobby knew they were nothing compared to the giant buildings across the river. They passed Ozark Drugstore and, of course, Jonda wanted to go in and drink a malted. They ignored her.

"Okay, you two," Bobby stated. "Remember, this is where we're supposed to meet Josh this afternoon. We have to be here no later than four or he'll leave us, and then we'll have to walk all the way home." Bobby and the girls stood on the corner of Seventeenth and Phoenix Avenue. The building he was referring to was the Cameo Theater, a beautiful red-brick edifice that featured balcony seating and a bright-red curtain with gold tassels hanging from the top. It was Bobby's favorite place to take Maundi, his girlfriend. He smiled deeply as he thought about all the good times he'd had inside that building the last couple of years.

"Why can't Josh pick us up later so we can go see a movie?" Jonda asked.

"Because Josh gets off work at four and he's going to pick us up on his way home. There's no way he'd go home and then come back and get us. Plus that, like I told you, I'm broke. You got any money, Miss Priss?"

Jonda shrugged her shoulders and held out her hands, palms up, to show her penury. She looked like a little doll in her white pinafore blouse and pink pedal pushers. She wore her golden hair short with bangs overlapping the brows of her deep-brown eyes, but not so short that anyone would mistake her for a boy. Jonda was definitely all girl but in a feisty, feral kind of way.

Suddenly, Jonda's face steeled. Bobby watched as her jaw tightened and her brow creased. *Oh no,* he thought. *Here we go again.*

Exactly as before, Jonda crossed her arms and stuck out her lip. She tapped her bare right foot as if making time with a Glenn Miller tune. "My name is Jonda!" She stomped as she spoke. "That's J - O - N - D - A. It's *not* Miss Priss, and it's *not* Short-Stuff, and it's *not* Ornery-Britches, and it's *not* Blondie, and it's *not* Sissy! My name is *Jonda,* and I like my name! I was named after my daddy."

Bobby had to put his hand across his mouth to keep from laughing out loud. He noticed Sarah had turned away from her Vesuvian sister, her hand also hiding an upturned mouth. He reached forward and patted his little sister's back.

"I'm sorry, Jonda. We don't mean anything by it. But you have to understand that nicknames are terms of endearment. We wouldn't call you those things if we didn't like you."

Jonda uncrossed her arms, placed her hands on her hips, and stood quietly for several moments. Bobby could tell her brain was zooming a hundred miles a second. She looked up at her big brother, the corners of her mouth slowly, devilishly curving upward. "Is that why Sarah doesn't have any nicknames?"

"Good grief, Munchkin. Let's go swimming!" Bobby proclaimed, pushing Jonda toward the street.

"I'm *so* glad I've got a full-time job. Pumpin' gas and cleanin' windshields is a piece of cake compared to this," Bobby mumbled to himself as he trailed the two girls.

Bobby spread the threadbare towel on the sand and plopped onto it, extending his legs in front of him and propping himself up on his elbows and forearms. He then surveyed the swimming hole, which was, in reality, nothing more than a sandy pond of backed-up water located a few score yards from the river. Rain and the resultant rising river periodically replenished the popular swimming area.

There was not a pretty girl in sight. He sighed. All the best-looking girls swam at the fancy swimming pool at Crystal City Park, which was large, rectangular, and its chlorinated water was as clear as the Mediterranean. It was supposedly the largest swimming pool in the state of Oklahoma. It also cost ten cents per person to swim there. He silently swore that with his first full-time paycheck, he was going to take Sarah and Jonda to a real pool. Shoot, he might even buy them both a brand-new swimsuit.

They'd been swimming less than an hour, but already he felt worn out. After relaxing in the water no more than five minutes, Jonda talked him into letting her straddle his neck and join a dozen others in a game of chicken fighting. This quickly deteriorated into outright roughhousing with the tiny Jonda constantly getting the worse end. Time and again, she was ripped from his shoulders and dunked in the tepid water by older, bigger girls and boys. Gamely, she refused to quit. Jonda would resurface, shake the water and disgust of losing from her face like a dog coming in from a summer shower, and rejoin the futile battle. But as time went by, Bobby could see her little arms weaken. It took her longer to recuperate and climb back onto his shoulders. Finally, after a particularly nasty fall, Bobby grabbed Jonda's wrist and abruptly left the fray. Sister in tow, he waded to the shallows where Sarah floated on her back, leisurely swaying her arms in the water to keep afloat and humming a jazzy tune.

Sarah seemed not to notice as Bobby squatted next to her. "Sarah, I need your help."

Sarah continued her watery trance.

"Come on, Sarah. We're playin' chicken fights, and we haven't won yet. Not even once. Jonda can't help it, but she's just too little."

"It's not my fault if you can't keep hold of my legs!" Jonda protested.

Flashing his little sister a shut-up glare, Bobby returned to Sarah, "Sarah, please! You know I hate to lose and besides this is makin' us look bad." Finally acknowledging their presence, Sarah opened her eyes and giggled, "Don't you mean it's making *you* look bad?"

Bobby knew then that she would join his team. He grinned at Sarah as she righted herself and began wading towards the contest. Bobby took a last look at Jonda, warning the already crossed-arm girl with his eyes to stay in the shallows as he turned and followed Sarah.

"Good grief, Bobby!" Sarah exclaimed after bobbing up. "No wonder Jonda never won. You don't have any footwork."

"Don't blame me if you got knocked off. I'm still standing," Bobby defended.

Sarah pushed her long black hair from her eyes and sloshed towards her brother. Moments earlier, she'd lost her first tussle with a red-headed, freckled boy whose skin was rapidly turning the color of ripened strawberries in the afternoon sun. "Listen Einstein, chicken fighting is a team game. We've got to work together. You've got to move your feet every now and then to help me."

"You listen, kiddo. I've never, ever been dunked. Ever! I'm supposed to provide an unmovable base. It's your job to pull the opponent off, not mine."

"Well, *O Mighty Unmovable Base*. While your genius tootsies are jammed firmly in the sand, the people we're fighting are getting beside us or behind us, which gives them a heck of an advantage. You see, *O Brilliant One*, I can't fight very well if I have to twist around all the time while you just stand there! Are you getting any of this? Any of this sinking in?" Sarah tapped her forehead several times.

"Fine, we'll try it your way. But if I get dunked, you may have to walk home."

"I may want to walk home anyway after being with you and Ornery-Britches all day." Sarah crawled back onto her brother's shoulders, and the duo splashed into action.

Quickly, the tide turned. With Sarah barking orders at her athletic brother, instructing him to turn left, right, or completely around, she began dismantling the competition. Her powerful hands and arms, made strong by the many years of grueling household chores, pulled and pushed the others from their mounts with seeming ease. Bobby was having fun wheeling and juking at the slower couples. Sarah was much heavier than Jonda but remarkably, he mused, not nearly as heavy as he'd anticipated. Her compact body seemed tailor-made for chicken fighting, and she exhibited a ferociousness Bobby had never seen. He could hear her grunting, snarling, and then laughing excitedly as their foes crashed into watery defeat. When they again met up with the carrot-headed boy and his ride, the enemy tried the exact same offensive movement. Sarah yelled for Bobby to turn right to prevent them from being flanked as she reached over and looped her entire arm around the surprised boy's neck and skinned him from his mount as if she were peeling a just-bought banana.

## Then Sings My Soul

The contest was over! Bobby and Sarah stood over their defeated foes and watched as their adversaries waded or swam away to rest on the beach or play tag with their friends. No one else challenged them. But no one proclaimed them the champions either.

Bobby, with Sarah still perched on her throne, waded towards Jonda who was having a splash fight with three boys her age. She was winning.

Bobby knelt in the shallow water allowing Sarah to climb off. Heading towards Jonda, Sarah turned and beamed at her brother. Bobby acknowledged her I-told-you-so-look and nodded his approval. Suddenly, he realized how utterly exhausted he was and decided to relax on the shore.

"Well, looky here if it isn't the Garden City girly boy. Little ole Bobby Braun's come to West Tulsa to relax and recreate with the little kiddies."

Bobby turned towards the voice. The young man hovering over Bobby laughed while narrowing his eyes; Bobby noticed his open mouth was missing an incisor. Despite his fatigue, Bobby chirped, "How's it goin' Gibbo? I see Harpo and Chico's with you too. Tell me something, do they stand behind you when you take a leak?"

Gilbert Ross's demeanor abruptly changed from hilarity to solemnity. He slid his right foot back as if assuming a boxer's stance, but instead of baring his fists, he placed his hands on his hips. Bobby countered the hostile move by rising to his feet, preparing himself for anything that might happen. Gibbo was not a nice guy. Bobby knew this and figured his chances at getting out of this situation without a fight to be no more than ten percent.

Gilbert Ross was the leader of the infamous West Tulsa Star Gang. The two hooligans with him were the Delaney brothers, George and Vernon. Despite the warmness of the day, the three were wearing their gang uniform: blue-jean pants cuffed at the bottom, solid white tee shirt, and a black leather jacket, collar up, with a broad, five-pointed red star appliquéd on the back. The gang terrorized West Tulsa and frequently spread havoc in both Garden City and Red Fork. Bobby personally knew many members of the Star Gang; he'd gone to school with them most of his life. At least until one by one, they quit school.

Bobby had known Gibbo Ross since first grade. They were the same age. Gibbo, a good athlete in elementary and junior high school, started on the school's basketball squad and played shortstop for the Westside's Pony League team, while Bobby pitched for the same team. Bobby thought they were firm friends up until Gibbo dropped out of school after his tenth grade year and joined the Stars. His rise to the top echelon of the gang had been meteoric and fueled by a ruthlessness and daring even the older members couldn't match. Bobby rarely encountered his old friend anymore and when he did, it was as if the two had been life-long enemies.

"I guess you and the other sissy boys graduated from good ole Webster High last night?" Gibbo mouthed. "Sorry I wasn't there, I had to whip a couple o' punks and spend some quality time with a cutie out on the Line."

Bobby opened his mouth to retort, but fought back the urge. Gibbo was, no doubt, out causing trouble last night and might even have beaten up a few people. But there was no way he'd ventured to the Sand Springs Line, at least not in his Star paraphernalia. Sand Springs lay north of West Tulsa on the other side of the winding Arkansas River and was patrolled by a group of ruffians known simply as The Liners. They were as mean and as numerous as the Stars and didn't cotton to anyone crossing their territory in rival jackets. Gibbo was definitely lying about the girl, and Bobby knew it. And he was pretty sure Gibbo knew that he knew it.

"Whatcha gonna do now? Now that you're all educated? You gonna go across the river and get ya some fancy job in one o' them buildings?" Gibbo, his eyes never leaving Bobby's face, pointed east towards downtown Tulsa.

Bobby shook his head, also without breaking his gaze with Gibbo. "Na. I like where I work. I've been hired full-time at the gas station."

"You don't say!" Gibbo exclaimed, feigning excitement. He turned towards his companions and snickered. "Did ya hear that, Vernon? Mr. Braun here's got a real job."

"Ain't that sumthin'?" Vernon Delaney mumbled.

"Yeah, ain't it though." Gibbo turned back to Bobby. "I guess you know what that means, don't cha?"

Bobby tilted his head slightly. He had no idea what Gibbo was getting at, but he knew whatever it was; it wouldn't be good.

"You mean you haven't heard?" Gibbo continued. "The school counselor should have informed you. I guess I'll have to do it for her."

Bobby's eyes narrowed and his jaw clenched. He balled his lowered fists. He knew the Stars were through playing with him and were about to make their move. George and Vernon quietly fanned out on either side of their leader. Gibbo edged closer.

"You see, Mr. High School Diploma, anytime a guy graduates from good ole Daniel Webster and gets his first job, he's expected to pay us half of his first paycheck. It's kinda like a welcome-to-the-neighborhood fee."

Bobby knew the Stars were trying to bully him, just trying to see if he would cave. He thought about ignoring the demand. Instead he chose to laugh in Gibbo Ross's face.

Gibbo flashed crimson. His cheeks puffed out; his eyes bulged. He looked like a locomotive engine with clogged steam valves. Gibbo lunged, grabbing Bobby by his bare shoulders. "You stupid punk! I'm gonna learn you right now not to ever mess with the Stars!" Gibbo raised his right fist. Bobby rocked forward and pushed Gibbo hard in the chest, knocking the gang leader backwards.

The Delaney brothers charged their victim, but Bobby was ready for them. Kicking George in the stomach with his bare foot, he felt the wind whoosh from his foe's abdomen. Bobby instinctively ducked as

Vernon threw a looping punch at his head. Countering with a chopping right to the jaw, Bobby dropped the already off-balance bully to the ground. He then turned towards their rising leader and readied himself for the inevitable attack.

"Bobby! Bobby! Hurry, it's Jonda!"

Bobby forgot all about the Stars. Sarah's shrill, shrieking voice signified trouble. Serious trouble! He sprinted between a gaping Gibbo Ross and a still-down Vernon Delaney and raced down the beach. Sarah stood in knee-deep water, weeping and frantically pointing towards the middle of the swimming hole. Bobby grabbed Sarah by the shoulders.

"I told her not to go there," she gasped. "I told her not to, but she did it anyway."

"Where'd she go under?" Bobby yelled. "Sarah, quick! Show me where she went under."

Sobbing, Sarah pointed to an area only a few yards away. Bobby took two steps and dove into the brackish pool.

He swam close to the sandy bottom with his eyes wide open, scanning all directions for any sign of white limbs, yellow hair, or a pink bathing suit.

He saw none.

He emerged, gasped more air, and dove again.

He began waving his arms in a futile attempt to feel her in case his eyes were deceiving him. Nothing.

His air was running out. He would have to go up for more. Desperation seized him. He realized there was no way his little sister could hold her breath this long. He could feel tears flooding his eyes, mingling with the brown, filthy water of the Arkansas. His lungs burned. His arms and legs began to ache. He kept looking.

*There she was!* Through the floating, drifting silt he could see in the distance her tiny lifeless form lying face down on the bottom. All hope evaporated at the horrible sight. Jonda's pale arms and legs splayed from her pink-covered torso and listed aimlessly along the disturbed bottom as if she were a limp sea star. Bobby could see his sister's golden strands waving, fluttering like the hair of a mythological Greek nymph.

With fire searing his lungs, Bobby rocketed toward his sister. He wrapped his arms around her little body and hugged her to his chest as he quickly pushed upwards to the surface.

Bobby didn't wait until he got Jonda to the safety of the beach before he began hitting the middle of her back. With his open hand, he smacked her twice as soon as he topped the water, hoping and praying she would instantly awaken; then several times more as he waded to shore carrying the small unmoving form like a first-time mother would a newborn.

Tenderly, Bobby laid Jonda on the sandy beach and swabbed her mouth with his index and middle fingers, looking for anything that might be blocking her air passage. It was clear. He turned his sister onto her back, placed her head sideways, and with the heel of both hands pushed the tiny area directly below her sternum.

"I think you're supposed to blow into her mouth too!" Sarah pleaded as she stood beside her brother, wringing her hands and raising and lowering her sand-caked feet.

"I don't know how to do that!" Bobby exclaimed.

"Well, at least try it! What could it hurt?!" She screamed.

By now over a dozen people, mainly kids, gathered around the unmoving Jonda. Bobby scooted towards Jonda's head. She was already turning blue. If he didn't do something, and do it quick, she would be gone.

His mind raced to the night Josh had told the family about the life-saving class the railroad had made him take. Bobby swallowed hard and decided to try.

He squeezed Jonda's nose tight and blew hard into her mouth. He paused and did it again. Then a third time. He stopped for several seconds to see if she was responding, then repeated the process. Seeing no improvement, Bobby again focused on her stomach and gave her three sharp pushes.

Suddenly, Jonda lurched upwards and vomited dirty water, mucous, and a smattering of what appeared to be blood all over Bobby's legs. She gulped a mouthful of fresh air then alternated with bouts of coughing and gasping. Bobby smacked her on the back several more times to help her expel the rest of the unwanted water from her lungs. He turned and looked at Sarah. Relieved, Sarah just exhaled deeply and laid her hand on her big brother's shoulder.

Bobby turned his attention back to Jonda. Someone had spread a blanket beside them, so he laid her onto it. With a face which was a darkening blue only minutes ago, Jonda's color was already returning, quickly regaining its normal pinkish hue. Her breathing consisted of short staccato wisps, but Bobby felt sure this was due to the trauma and not a lasting effect. Jonda slowly, hesitantly, opened her eyes as if she'd been in a decades-long coma. Her dark orbs searched the hushed crowd hovering above her until they finally found her brother's. Realization of what had occurred flooded her face and she began to cry. Bobby gently wiped the tears from his sister's face and stroked her shimmering, golden hair. He smiled deeply, and said, "Sorry Munchkin, but you do look just like me." Jonda returned his smile and closed her eyes in rest. Bobby couldn't remember the last time he'd been so happy.

\* \* \* \* \*

Everyone said you eventually got used to the squealing and screeching of metal on metal. The old-timers even went so far as to say it would someday sound like a soft, mellifluous melody and that after long, exhausting days it would serenade your subconscious as you drifted into a restful, pleasant sleep.

Josh wasn't so sure. After three years on the job, the cumbersome movement of the lurching freight trains still sounded like overweight giants on ice skates performing Olympic jumps and pirouettes on thick, rusty sheet metal. There was nothing soft, and definitely nothing mellifluous about it. It was shrill, loud, and shot through your head like a first-year teacher pressing too hard with the chalk as she wrote the daily lesson on the blackboard. Oh well, he shrugged as he uncoupled the last of the boxcars on the mile-long train. The noise was about the only thing he didn't like about working for Frisco. The pay was good, the hours okay, and he was allowed to work around his baseball schedule.

Josh stepped back and extended his arm at a slight angle, signaling the engineer to proceed. As the red train chugged methodically past him, Josh automatically read, for the ten thousandth time, the huge white letters of his employer's name painted on the sides of every single car they owned. He looked at his watch, saw that it was 3:54, and headed for the terminal. By the time he crossed the myriad tracks, maneuvered in and out of the empty boxcars on the side rails, and skidded down the seldom-mowed grassy slope, it would be right at four o'clock -- quitting time.

"Whew! What a day! I didn't think it was ever going to end."

Josh nodded at the tall, bony man catching up with him. "I know what you mean; the first really hot day of summer is always a long one."

Lonnie Corlett, a fellow brakeman, pulled a red patterned kerchief from his overalls and wiped perspiration droplets from his brow. He exhaled as if out of breath.

"Whatcha got planned for the weekend? The movies? Crystal City? I still can't believe you talked them into letting you off every weekend of the entire summer. How'd you do it? I might wanna try it."

Josh's mouth turned up slightly as he chuckled. "To start with, I'm not off *every* weekend, only when we have games."

"Which is pretty much *every* weekend, ain't it?" Corlett interjected.

"Okay, maybe you're right. I'm off most weekends. But I also have to work in the yard all day long instead of making my usual jaunts to Joplin."

"Hey, I'll trade ya. I'll work in the yard in exchange for being off every Saturday and Sunday. I'll do that any day!"

"You coulda had the same deal, Lonnie. You shoulda come out for the team." As soon as the words left his mouth, Josh felt bad about what he'd said. The man to his left was wearing glasses with lenses as thick as the bottom of a Coke bottle.

Instead of being offended, Lonnie just laughed. "Come on Braun, you know I can't play baseball worth a dang! That stinkin' white ball's too little. I played a lotta sandlot when I was a kid, but I never was no good. In fact, if it hadn't been for Fatty Johnson, I'd o' been the worst player on the Westside. You're just lucky God gave you a pair o' good peepers. But you know me; I'll be at pert near all the games. At least when I'm off," he added with a grin.

"I know you will Lon, and we really appreciate it. And you're right. I guess I am pretty lucky."

Josh stuffed his hands into his overalls, fingering his pocket watch. Was he lucky? He didn't think so, he smirked inwardly to himself. Here he was almost twenty-one years old with only a tenth grade education, working like a dog for the railroad and still living with his mom. How lucky could one guy get? He squeezed the ancient watch. Tears banged against the doors of his eyes. Bitterness again seeped into his mouth. He thought about his mom working two jobs to make ends meet, about their too-small house that needed painting and a new fence. He had some money in the bank, a pretty good stash actually, but his mother wouldn't accept it for keeping up the house. She felt that it was *his* money, and he'd need it when he got married and wanted a place of his own. She wouldn't even take his five-year-old Chrysler to church, preferring to make Bobby drive Dad's old 1936 Chevrolet sedan.

*Dad.*

*Things wouldn't be like this if Dad were still here. Mom wouldn't be working two jobs. Heck, she wouldn't be working at all! They'd have a nice house and a nice car, and he would probably be playing big-time baseball right now instead of managing a dinky semi-pro railroad team.*

As if reading his mind, Lonnie asked, "How's the team gonna be this year? Is your little brother gonna play? He's got quite a wing on him if I do say so myself."

"Yeah, Bobby's going to play. He started throwing to me a couple weeks ago, and I think his arm is stronger this year than last year."

"Good grief! You guys'll probably never lose then. I ain't ever seen anybody throw the pill as fast as him."

Josh nodded his agreement. There was no denying that Bobby could bring the heat. If only he cared a little more about the game and put in some real practice, Bobby could be unbelievable. *Fat chance of that!*

"Who's gonna play shortstop now that Julius has moved to Meeker?" Lonnie continued.

"It's funny you ask," Josh perked up. "I've got a meeting this evening with some college boy who says he plays ball up in Kansas and is lookin' for a summer team."

"College boy, you say. Why would a college boy want to play for the railroad team? All them highfalutin college players usually join one of those teams with the fancy unis across the river. What's he comin' over here for?"

"Seein' as how we whup those eastside teams on a regular basis maybe he wants to be on the winning side for a change," Josh chuckled. "What we really need, though, is another pitcher. Bobby can't throw every game, you know. He's gotta have some help and Ray Burris turned forty this winter. He's not even for sure he's gonna play. He didn't do that well last year anyway."

Lonnie slowly shook his head. "Whatever happened to the days when a pitcher could throw every day? Now-a-days, it seems like they gotta rest a day or two before they're ready to climb back onto the mound. Are guys just not as tough as they useta be? No offense to your family, Josh. I mean in general. It just seems to me that ballplayers are gettin' kinda soft. I heard that Satchel Paige, the Negro pitcher, useta pitch two or three games in one day and then turn around and do it again the next day. I don't get it. Why can't our boys pitch like that?"

"Come on Lonnie, you can't compare a semi-pro player to Satchel Paige! He's one of the greatest to ever toe the rubber. I saw him pitch when I was a little kid, and he's the best I've ever seen – by far!"

"He ain't as good as a real Major League twirler. No way! Dizzy Dean or Bob Feller would pitch him into a hole. If he's so good, why wadn't he the first darkie to play in the Bigs? Answer me that!"

"Maybe because he's about sixty years old!" Josh felt his voice rise. He really wasn't angry; he just liked to talk about stuff like this more than anything.

"Oh, he ain't no sixty. Fifty at the most," Lonnie replied.

"Okay then, fifty. You know any other Major Leaguers still chunking the cowhide at fifty?"

"Yeah, but he ain't doin' that good. I think the Indians just picked him up as a novelty act.

"What do you mean, Lonnie? He helped the Tribe win the World Series in '48, and now he's pitchin' for the Brownies. And he's doin' it at over fifty years of age," Josh said. "Now I'll admit I've never seen a Major League game in person, but I remember watching Paige pitch with the Monarchs when they came to Tulsa on a barnstormin' tour and I'm here to tell you he's the fastest I've ever seen, white or black."

"I didn't say he wadn't good, I'm just sayin' he ain't as good as Dean or Feller."

The two brakemen ambled down the grassy slope. Lonnie didn't see the tip of a rock protruding from the ground and stumbled over it. Josh reached out and saved the flailing man before he crashed to the earth. In the process, Lonnie knocked Josh's cap from his head with one of his waving arms. Once Lonnie regained his balance, Josh bent down and retrieved his cap.

"I think you need a new cap, Josh. That one's gettin' mighty worn. Besides, why do you wear a Cardinals baseball cap while you're workin'? Didn't they give you any Frisco caps?"

"Yeah, they did, and I wear them most of the time. I just like to wear this one now and then. You do know they tried to sign me two years ago."

Lonnie nodded. He knew. Everybody knew that Josh Braun had turned down a St. Louis Cardinals baseball contract to stay and help his mom. But he'd heard it was just to play in the minor leagues, not the Bigs.

"And who knows," Josh continued. "I might have made the Majors by now. They were going to start me out in Double-A ball. Besides, I like the Cardinals. I liked 'em before they ever offered me anything. They were my dad's favorite team."

"Heck, most everybody around here likes the Redbirds," Lonnie added. "They're the only big-time team in the West."

"Hey Josh, somebody told me that if you'd o' signed with the Cards you were gonna get to play for the Oilers. Is that true?"

"Nah, the Oilers are in Cincinnati's farm system. I would have had to gone to Houston and played with the Buffaloes."

"The Texas League?"

"Yep."

"Well, shoot fire! They play the Oilers all the time. We could've all come and watched you play."

Josh lowered his head, nodded.

# 2

"Cora, I know you're on your dinner break, but we could sure use some help taking orders. They must've let the boys off early."

Cora Braun smiled, nodded at her boss, Don Porter, and swigged one last gulp of her lukewarm coffee. She pushed the half-full mug away from her and stood up from her usual stool at the end of the long counter of the DX Restaurant. Turning, she adjusted her mussed hair and surveyed the room. The dining area of the Sunray DX Restaurant was expansive with stools along the counter and lots of tables. At the moment, most were filled with dirty, hungry refinery workers talking excitedly while they waited for their meals to be brought out. The restaurant was located at the refinery entrance and fed hundreds of workers every night. When a unit at the refinery was down and extra workers were brought in, the restaurant stayed open twenty-four hours. *Thank goodness that hadn't happened in a while,* Cora thought.

Cora took a deep breath and exhaled, smoothing the skirt of her white cotton dress as she removed her pencil and pad from her pocket, and walked to a table of four. Unlike the rest of the clientele, who mainly wore coveralls, the men at this table were dressed in white shirts and ties. One even sported a suit coat. They worked in the refinery office. She immediately recognized three of them; she had never seen the one wearing the full suit.

"Evenin' gents, what're ya havin' tonight? The roast beef is lookin' good."

"Hi Cora, how's my favorite waitress?" a short, burly man with a bald dome beamed at her.

"If you wanna know the truth, Bill, I'm pretty tired. My feet and calves ache, and my hair is a floppin'. But, I get off in an hour, so I'll make it."

"Hey! I think your hair is downright gorgeous. I love your long golden hair. I just wish you weren't wearing it up in a bun. Your hair reminds me of sweet-smelling straw tumbling from the bales of a flat-bed truck during hay season."

"Wow! Aren't you the poet, Larry. You'll have to write my Christmas cards next year," Cora said to the equally rotund and equally bald man sitting next to Bill.

A tall drip of a man with thick black hair perfectly cut and shaped atop his long narrow head chuckled at the poet, "Larry, how long did it take you to think that up? I bet you've been sitting around working on it for days."

Larry leaned back in his armless chair and laughed out loud. "Actually, I read it in *Reader's Digest*. It's pretty good though, ain't it, Tommy?"

"Okay, enough friendly banter. What's it gonna be?"

"I'll have the special," Bill spoke up. "It is open-faced, ain't it? With lots of mushrooms and brown gravy?"

"You betcha," Cora replied. "Just the way you like it. Roast beef piled high on two pieces of Wonder Bread and smothered in thick brown mushroom gravy."

"Sounds great!" Bill wet his lips.

"I'll have the same," Larry said.

"Make it three," Tommy added. "Of course, we'll all have iced tea."

"I think I'll break the string and order chicken-fried steak with cream gravy and home fries," the stranger spoke up. "And I prefer coffee -- black."

Cora jotted down the orders on her pad, knowing the four men were watching her, which was not unusual. What else would her customers be looking at? Certainly not the myriad photos of oil wells, drilling equipment, and tank farms plastered seemingly on every inch of the diner; everyone present had seen them a hundred times. Except this time was different; she felt uncomfortable. But it wasn't Bill, Larry, or Tommy that caused her uneasiness. It was the new guy, the well-built, well-dressed man sitting with his friends in their rumpled shirts and loud neckties. Despite not wanting to, Cora glanced at the man while finishing the order. He locked onto her with his brilliant blue eyes. She found herself momentarily mesmerized by his forceful stare before she could break away. He continued staring. Cora did not like it.

She glanced at his hand. No wedding ring. *At least he isn't a scoundrel,* she thought, as she turned to walk away.

"Oh my goodness, Cora," Larry exclaimed. "We forgot to introduce you to our new boss."

Cora did an about-face.

"Cora, this is Robert Cornwell. He's the new assistant refinery manager."

"Nice to meet you Mr. Cornwell," Cora half whispered. "I hope you like Tulsa."

"I really haven't seen much of the city yet. I just flew in from the coast last night. I'm currently staying downtown at the Mayo."

"Well, there's not a hotel in Tulsa better than the Mayo, so I'm sure you'll be comfortable."

"Quite," Cornwell replied. He stood and stretched out his hand.

His grip was firm. Too firm, Cora thought, for shaking hands with a woman. She broke away as quickly as she thought polite. Cornwell stood before her enveloped in confidence and downright cockiness. Cora had to admit he was quite a specimen. His cropped hair was jet black, as was his neatly trimmed mustache. Cornwell's dark hair, combined with athletic shoulders and a narrow waist, gave him a remarkable resemblance to Clark Gable. Cora estimated his age at around forty, perhaps a little younger.

"Do you go by Bob?" Cora asked.

"Robert will do fine. I've never much liked shortened monikers. In my position, I can't afford to be too casual."

"Okay Robert," Cora tried to sound jovial. "I'll have your food out in a jiffy."

Cora clipped the order slip onto the rotating carousel and watched Beano flip it around and silently mouth the order as he removed it. She padded to the end of the counter and poured the new customer's coffee into a white DX mug. Next, she retrieved three tall glasses from the shelf, placed them on a round tray next to the steaming mug, and scooped ice into them. She placed the first cooled glass under the long, cylindrical teapot and began filling it.

Cora checked her watch. One more hour and she could go home to her four kids and comfy house. *Kids,* she thought. *How fast they grow up!* Josh, her oldest, was a man and Bobby, her second, had graduated high school only the night before. Then there was Sarah and Jonda. They were still kids, even if Sarah thought she was all grown up. She checked her watch again. Fifty-nine minutes to go, she sighed. The restaurant really wasn't that bad a place to work. She'd been there over six years. Most of the customers were nice, and the tips were good. She didn't like the hours. Coming in at eleven in the morning and working until eight-thirty at night wasn't exactly a prime schedule, but it was the hours Don, the manager, had always given her, and it was the best hours for tips. Her days off were Sunday and Monday, which she'd gotten used to, but again, she'd rather have been off both weekend days.

And there was her other job, her part-time domestic job. In addition to waiting tables, Cora worked across the river for the Lamberson family eight hours on Monday, her day off from the restaurant, and three hours on Wednesday and Friday mornings. It wasn't bad work: cooking breakfast, cleaning, dusting, doing the laundry. However, combined with her regular job, it made for a long week, especially when you were forty-one years old.

Cora placed the third glass under the spigot and watched the brown liquid rush in. *Was she really that old? How had time disappeared so rapidly? It seemed like only yesterday the kids were all little and John was still alive.*

The thought of John filled her with melancholy. *Had he really been gone almost seven years? Would she ever get over him?* A tear escaped and streaked down her cheek. She quickly wiped it away and picked up the heavy tray.

"Here's your drinks, gentlemen." Cora maneuvered between each man, setting an already sweating glass in front of them.

"And last, but certainly not least, here's your coffee, Robert." Cora reached across his shoulder and placed the mug on a paper coaster.

Cora suddenly jerked upright, her body went rigid.

"You okay, Cora?" Bill asked, concern etched on his face.

"Uh, uh, . . . yes. I'm fine," she replied backing away from the men. Cora hurried to the counter, set the empty tray down, and covered her face with both hands. She dared not look at her customers for fear that he would be staring at her. And she didn't want to look at *him*, ever again.

Cora closed her eyes and inhaled deeply. Surely she was wrong. She had to be mistaken. But she knew she wasn't. Cora knew what had just happened was not her imagination; nor had it been an accident. She felt anger entering her body. Her face reddened with fury and disgust as she squeezed her fingers into her palms and banged her fist on the counter top.

"Cora? Cora, are you alright?"

The voice was Don Porter's. He stood a few feet away, his hands on his hips. He appeared more concerned than upset.

"I'm fine, Don. I'm just getting a headache."

"There's some aspirin in the register. I'll get it for you if you want."

"No, no. that's okay. I'll be fine. I'm more tired than anything," she attempted a smile.

"Aren't we all," he muttered as he turned and walked away.

Cora slid around the end of the counter and bent down to the shelf where she kept her purse. She peeked over the counter at the table. Cornwell sipped his coffee in slow, measured movements and, just as she thought, just as she knew, stared directly at her. As he lowered his mug, the corners of his mouth turned up ever so slightly. *He's mocking me,* she thought. She looked away. *He's mocking me because he knows I won't; I can't, do anything about it.* Cora visibly shuddered as she ground her teeth. Mr. Robert Cornwell, the new assistant manager of the Sunray DX refinery, in town less than one day, had just pinched her rear end. And, he'd done it with impunity.

Cora reached behind her purse to where she kept her Bible. She picked it up and held it to her bosom. With eyes closed, she mumbled, "Lord, forgive me for what I'm thinking right now and help me to not hit that man right in the nose. I can't afford to get fired."

\* \* \* \* \*

Francine Fitzsimmons handed Cameron the porcelain sugar bowl. She watched in disgust as he spooned teaspoonful after teaspoonful of sugar into his tea. She turned away after the third heaping. She couldn't help it; she didn't like watching people overdo anything – especially food. Francine opened her mouth to chastise her boyfriend then changed her mind. It wouldn't do any good. Cameron VanDeaver, her boyfriend of almost two years, the man she dreamed of marrying and settling down with, was completely and totally stubborn clear to the marrow of his bones. A quality she used to admire, in fact, found endearing. Why? She really wasn't sure.

"How was your day," he asked not noticing her disapproval.

"It was fine. I helped Irma with her duties around the house, took Brutus for a walk, and took a long, hot bubble bath."

"It must be nice to live a life of ease," he said.

"Yeah, right. Yesterday was the last day of school, and I start my summer job on Monday. I don't believe relaxing on the only Friday I'll have off for the next three months is exactly taking it easy."

Okay, I give. As usual, you're right," he reached out and sat his half-full glass of tea-flavored sugar onto the coffee table.

Francine shook her head. "You're impossible," she mumbled as she placed a wooden coaster under Cameron's tea. "Mom will kill me if a water stain gets on her fancy table."

"Sorry, guess I forgot I'm not in the dorm."

"You know how she is about this house. She thinks it's a museum instead of a place to live."

"At least she lets you swim in the pool," Cameron laughed. "My mom gets upset every time I have friends over."

Francine nodded her agreement as she sipped her tea. Cameron had just finished his second year of college at Kansas University, while she had just graduated prep school.

"Okay, tell me again why you don't want to work for my father this summer and meet a lot of big-time attorneys while making a pretty good chunk of money? Uh, I forgot," Francine quipped.

Cameron pulled his finger from the tea, stuck it into his mouth, and popped it from his puckered lips. He wiggled his wet lips back and forth the way a bunny does its nose.

Despite not wanting to, Francine's frown cracked.

"I told you," Cameron replied, his eyebrows raised as if doing a Groucho Marx impression, "I've decided not to pursue law. I'm going to get a business degree and work for one of the oil companies. That's where the real money's at."

"That's where the real money *used* to be at. The oil business is drying up around here, literally and figuratively. Besides, a lot of the oil companies are moving to Houston and surely you don't want to live down there?"

Cameron shrugged. "I don't know. It's warmer along the Gulf."

"Whatever," Francine threw up her hands. "I know I don't want to live there."

"Oh," Cameron whispered.

Francine knew she'd gone over the line. She and Cameron had never spoken about the future. Marriage had never, not even once, come up in a conversation. Their relationship, although sometimes quite passionate, had never entered the "us forever" stage. Francine always figured it was because she was still in high school and Cameron was busy with college. But who knew? Maybe she wasn't in his future plans? Or, more likely, Cameron hadn't even thought about his future plans. She decided to change the subject. "By the way, who did you say you were meeting this afternoon; some railroad guy who runs a ball team?"

"Yeah, it's the Frisco semi-pro team. They're looking for a shortstop and, if I do say so myself, I'm the best around."

Francine shook her head. "I don't get it. You play baseball all spring at KU against the best college baseball players in the country and now you want to play all summer for some rinky-dink semi-pro team with a bunch of losers from the Westside? Aren't there any teams around here? What about Kip Friedman? Doesn't he have a team?"

"Yeah, but they're pathetic ballplayers. Those 'losers from the Westside' are actually pretty good. Just because they're poor and wear cheap uniforms doesn't mean they can't throw and hit a baseball."

"What about your amateur status? Won't playing semi-pro ruin your eligibility?"

"Not if I declare myself an amateur and don't accept any money for playing. Coach said a lot of guys do it every summer."

Francine rose from the divan, walked around the huge carpeted parlor. From the oversized picture window, she studied the vast manicured lawn dotted with cherry and dogwood trees. The dogwoods were still blooming despite the recent hot temperatures.

"Why are you wasting time playing baseball anyway?" she blurted. "It's a boring game and there's no money in it."

"Is money the only thing you ever think about?" Cameron snapped back defensively, the humor gone from his face. "I personally think it's a great game and you know that. Go tell Joe DiMaggio or Stan Musial there's no money in baseball."

"Yeah, but how many Joe DiMaggio's and Stan Musial's are there in the . . . ?" Francine abruptly stopped. Her eyes bulging, understanding setting in, she turned and placed her hands on her hips. "Oh my goodness," she stammered. "You want to be a baseball player! That's why you changed from pre-law to business. That's why you want to play summer baseball with a bunch of guys who only take baths once a week and only shave every other. That's why you don't want to work for Dad. You want to play baseball!" Francine laughed.

She could see Cameron's jaw tighten; his left eye twitched. He was trying to control his anger. "I didn't say I was the next Joe DiMaggio *or* Stan Musial. But I might be the next Hank Greenberg."

"Come on," Francine lightened her tone. "Unless you're a star, you don't make beans. Have you forgotten my dad played in the Majors? He sure didn't buy this house with his baseball salary. This is all lawyer money." She extended her arms and did a three-sixty as if trying to hug an elusive three hundred-pound man.

"Francine," Cameron said evenly. "Your dad played in the National League less than a week. He was called up from Double-A because the Giants' catcher and his backup were both hurt in a car accident and the Triple-A catcher was down with the mumps. Other than that, he never played above Double-A."

"Thank you very much," she grinned. "That's my whole point. How many players even make it to the Majors? And you want to gamble your entire future on the chance that you *might* make it, when you could become an attorney and someday buy a house like this?"

"Maybe I don't want to practice law," Cameron softly answered.

*Then Sings My Soul*

"Fine. That's okay with me," Francine's voice rose an octave higher. "Be a doctor like your father. You don't have to be an attorney. You're the one who said you didn't like the sight of blood. Be a pediatrician and dispense penicillin all day to screaming kids or go into podiatry and discover a cure for smelly feet. But *don't* be a baseball player. That's what the poor boys try to do."

"Baseball players do better than you think," Cameron insisted.

Francine could see her tirade wasn't getting through. He was digging in so she tried a different approach. Sitting down next to him, she grasped his hands in hers and gazed into his eyes. Seeing the passion in those deep-blue eyes, she again realized why she liked this boy so much; that is besides the fact that Cameron was tall, dark and handsome. "I'm not trying to be mean, Cameron. I'll back whatever you do. I just want you to really think about what you're getting into. Think about the professional players here in Tulsa; the ones who play for the Oilers. Do you really want your business apparel to be those awful looking pajama suits with stripes down the side? Do you want to sign autograph after autograph for dirty little urchins who sneak out of school to watch a doubleheader? Do you want to live in a duplex and wash your clothes at the laundromat the way most Oiler players do? Why can't you simply play baseball for fun?"

Cameron sighed.

Francine thought it was a good sign.

His lips parted as if he were about to say something. He closed them and attempted a smile. Finally, he spoke. "Francine, I know you don't like baseball. You never have. And perhaps you're right. Maybe I don't have a future in it. But let me give it a shot this summer. One other reason I want to play with the Westside boys, a reason I didn't tell you, is that there are a lot of pro scouts who come through Tulsa and watch these semi-pro games. Perhaps, one will notice me."

Cameron got up from the sofa. He stuck his hands into his pants pockets and walked to the same window Francine earlier had peered out. Francine remained on the couch watching him. He stood silent and unmoving for over a minute.

Cameron *was* a true dreamboat. With blue-black hair, broad sloping shoulders, and long athletic legs, he was any girl's fantasy come true. Francine met him during lunchtime while doing research for sophomore composition class in the library of Lansing Hall. He was a senior. A senior and the quarterback of the football team and vice-president of his class.

He introduced himself and asked her if it was her first year at Lansing, which it wasn't. Nevertheless, the ice had been broken, and the two talked the entire lunch period. Cameron walked her to class, asked her out, and they'd been together ever since.

Cameron turned away from the window and faced her. He bit his lower lip with his immaculate teeth and looked Francine over as if deciding whether or not he would buy her. Out of the blue, he asked: "Have you done something to your hair?"

"No, it's the same old dishwater blonde it's always been."

"I like your hair," Cameron said without smiling.

"Really?" Francine jovially replied. "I always thought it was my curvy figure."

Cameron laughed. "I like you on the skinny side. That way, I don't have to worry about you getting fat when you get old. I'd much rather have a skinny, old wife than a fat one."

Francine paused and looked directly at Cameron. Now, he had made a comment about the future. *Who knows,* she thought. *Maybe this was going to be one of those summers a girl remembers for the rest of her life.*

# 3

"Hurry up Josh, the food's almost ready."

"Just about done Sis, I'm putting the silverware on the table now." Josh said to Sarah without looking at her. She was busy at the stove preparing the evening meal, which she did nightly. With their mother working almost every single day and night, household duties had fallen to Sarah, being the oldest girl. The fourteen-year-old did all of the cooking, most of the laundry, and made sure the house was swept and dusted. It was Josh and Bobby's job to keep the yard mowed, the cars running and help their sister by setting the table and doing the dishes. Tonight it was Josh's turn to set the table and afterwards Bobby and Jonda would wash and put away the dishes.

Josh stood at the kitchen table only a few feet from Sarah. There was no fancy dining room table, as there was no dining room. The narrow kitchen with a single row of homemade cabinets, a sink, cook stove, and second-hand table was it. The Braun family lived in a tiny two-bedroom frame house with the two girls occupying one bedroom and Josh and Bobby the other. Their mother had converted the screened back porch into her sleeping room. A single bathroom serviced all five. Mornings around the Braun house were hectic, to say the least.

Josh held a fistful of spoons, forks, and butter knives, which he clumsily placed around ceramic plates. Most of the plates were chipped, a few cracked. All showed signs of age and constant use. Josh made a mental note to buy his Mom some new cups and plates for her birthday in July.

"Come and get it while it's hot!" Sarah exclaimed. She carried the heavy cast-iron skillet to the table using both hands, a wall of steam shrouding her face as if she were walking down a foggy London street.

"What're we havin'?" Jonda asked as she plunked into her usual chair by the window on the far side of the table. Bobby sat next to her and leaned towards the sizzling food.

"Looks like macaroni and cheese to me," he said.

"Again?' Jonda sounded disappointed. "We just had that Tuesday night."

"Well I'm sorry," Sarah retorted. "But that's about all we've got right now. Momma doesn't get paid again until next Monday. Besides, I cut up a bunch of weenies in it so it's not the same as we had Tuesday."

"Oh wow! We get to eat weenies in our macaroni and cheese. I'm impressed."

"Knock it off, Short-Stuff," Josh said. "Sarah does the best she can. I could have stopped by the Big Store and bought some hamburger meat and buns, but I thought you wanted to go to Crystal City tomorrow?"

Jonda's eyes got big. She looked like she'd just unwrapped a Shirley Temple doll for Christmas. "I forgot all about the amusement park!" she exclaimed. Jonda pushed her plate towards Sarah, "Macaroni and cheese, please."

Sarah dipped a big spoonful onto Jonda's plate and added a helping of green beans.

"I didn't ask for any yukky beans," Jonda complained.

"Well, you got 'em anyway. Mom said to make sure you eat some vegetables."

Jonda squinched her face up at her sister. "Yeah, but ain't macaronis a vegetable?"

"Not hardly," Bobby jumped in. "I think they're in the starch family.

You know, like mashed potatoes and French fries and hash browns and stuff like that."

"What's wrong with the starch family?" Jonda ignored her sister and looked at her brother. "I think I like the starch family." She took a big bite of her food.

"There's nothing wrong with starches," Sarah said. "It's just that little girls need their vegetables too. Would you please at least act like you're chewing your food before you swallow it?"

"Is there a vegetable family?" Jonda asked. "I do chew my food. Quit acting like you're my mother."

Josh and Bobby glanced at each other and shook their heads. They'd witnessed this conversation a thousand times.

"I guess there is," Sarah answered. "There's also a meat family and a dairy family and a bread family. And if I *were* your mother you'd probably be eating your supper at a long table with a bunch of other kids at the orphanage over in Sand Springs."

"Why do they call them families? Do they have a mom and dad and kids?" Jonda took another even bigger bite of macaroni. Several noodles protruded from her closed lips.

"Quit acting silly, Jonda," Sarah pleaded. "You may think you're funny, but you're not. Eat your green beans."

Jonda puffed out her cheeks. She looked from brother to brother. She pushed a noodle out from her lips then sucked it back in with a swoosh. Despite trying not to, Josh and Bobby chuckled then burst out laughing.

Sarah shook her head at her brothers. "You two don't help a whit. You just feed her goofiness."

"Come on Sarah, lighten up," Josh said. "How can we not crack up at her. Look at that face."

As if ordered to do so, Jonda flashed her older sister a wide-open toothy smile and tilted her head as if posing for her senior picture.

"All I see is a spoiled brat who's got you two wrapped around her finger. She doesn't fool me."

"Sarah, just think of it as practice for when you have your own family," Bobby said.

"If I have a child like that one," Sarah nodded at Jonda. "I'll give it away to the first person I meet on the street."

"You'll feel differently when you have your own. You and Jonda are around each other too much is all," Bobby smiled and winked at Sarah.

Josh inhaled and blew the air out his mouth as if blowing out birthday candles. He paused several moments before speaking, "Sarah," he began. "That was a fine meal. I'm simply amazed at your culinary expertise. I do believe putting weenies into the macaroni was a stroke of genius."

"Good grief," Sarah muttered.

"Say, Josh," Bobby said. "Did you get to talk with that hotshot shortstop from across the river? Did he actually show up? Does he really want to play with us?"

Josh perked up. "Yeah, we met at Pennington's Restaurant over in Brookside."

"Is that the drive-in on Peoria Avenue?" Sarah asked. "I've never been to it."

"Yeah, that's the one. It smells like a good place to eat, if you've got the money. The foot-long hot dogs and Black-Bottom Pie looked especially good. All I had was a Coke."

"I love chocolate pie! Let's go there some time," Jonda nearly shouted. "How 'bout tomorrow?"

"Okay, we can do that," Josh said. "We won't be able to go to Crystal City, though."

"How 'bout some other time, but not tomorrow," Jonda quickly changed her tune.

"Okay, it's a deal," Josh said, a paternal smile on his face.

"Well?" Bobby sounded impatient. "What did Mr. Studly Player have to say?"

"Mr. Studly Player's name is Cameron VanDeaver and he, at least, looks like a ballplayer. He carries himself well."

"Where's he played before? Who'd he play for last summer?"

Josh took a swig of tea before answering his brother. "He's a college player. Plays up in Lawrence."

"College player? Kansas? He must not be too good. Nothing against Kansas, but most crackerjack players go straight to the pros. What's his problem?"

"I think he's playing in college because his dad's a doctor and wants him to get an education. I can understand that."

"Me too," Sarah interrupted. "That way if he doesn't make it in baseball, he'll have a career waiting for him. Sounds down-right smart to me."

"What does Crackerjacks got to do with baseball?" Jonda asked.

Everyone ignored her.

"So? Is he on the team?"

"He'll be at practice Sunday," Josh rubbed his hands together as if he were cold, which he wasn't.

Sarah rose and pushed her chair under the table. She picked up her plate and glass, turned and walked to the kitchen sink. "Jonda, help me clear the table, please. I think everyone's finished. You and Bobby need to get the dishes done before Mom gets home."

The girls began piling the dishes in the sink. Josh and Bobby remained at the table sipping their iced tea. Josh swirled the tea in his glass and watched as the slowly disintegrating ice cubes bounced against each other like bumper cars at an amusement park. He wanted to broach an emotional subject with his brother but didn't know where to begin. He realized he needed to tread lightly. However, that wasn't his style.

"Bobby?"

Bobby looked at his brother. His face flexed taut. *Here it comes,* he thought, fully expecting a million questions about the swimming hole, Jonda, and the near tragedy.

"Bobby, tell me again which of the punks from the Star gang roughed you up."

"None of them actually *roughed me up*." Bobby answered with a defensive tone. "The ones who *tried* to mess with me were the Delaney brothers and Gibbo Ross."

"I thought Gibbo was your friend?"

"Used to be. That was a long time ago."

"Seems to me you guys were playing ball together not two or three years ago."

"That *WAS* a long time ago." Bobby's voice took on an edge.

"Whatever," Josh waved it off. "It's not important. The thing I don't understand is why you were lounging on a soft cuddly blanket under a big shade tree while your little sister, the main one you were supposed to be watching, was gulping down most of the Arkansas River."

Josh could see Bobby's neck stiffen. His jaw tightened. *Too bad. Bobby screwed up and he needs to realize it so it didn't happen again.*

Jonda turned and yelled from the sink. "It wasn't a blanket he was laying on, Josh. I told you that, already. It was one of Mom's beach towels, the yellow one. You know, the one with sea shells all over it."

"Shut up, Jonda," Sarah hissed. "Nobody cares about whether it was a towel or a blanket."

Jonda shrugged. "Just tryin' to help," she mumbled.

Bobby ran his hand through his blond locks. Josh thought he looked tired, drawn. He hadn't noticed this before. Bobby hoisted his arms in the air as if surrendering to the enemy and shouted: "Okay, okay, you win. I almost got my sister killed! It's all my fault. I should probably be arrested. Or even shot. I know now that I should have been holding her hand the entire time she was in the water. I forgot that a seven year old isn't smart enough to stay out of the deep water, and I forgot that her big sister can't be bothered to help out, and I forgot . . . " Bobby leaned halfway across the table and glared at Josh, ". . . I forgot that I'm not the almighty, perfect Josh Braun; the man who does absolutely nothing wrong . . . ever!" Bobby sprang to his feet, knocking over his chair. He looked at his sisters as if wishing they would say something in his defense. He turned and stomped out of the kitchen, through the front room, and out the screen door, almost bumping his just-arriving mother off the porch.

"I hope you're proud of yourself," Sarah stated, glaring at Josh.

Jonda walked to the front of the table and peered into the empty front room. She looked back at Josh. "For your information, I'm only six. I won't be seven for three more weeks."

\* \* \* \* \*

Cora thought it wise to say nothing to Bobby. He was obviously upset. He hadn't seemed to notice that he'd nearly knocked her off the small porch while flying through the screen door like a fireman rushing to a three-alarm blaze. She paused at the threshold and watched her son, arms akimbo, pace up and down the fence line of their front yard. Sinbad, Jonda's yellow Lab, followed the distraught teenager back and forth, back and forth, as if the two were on guard duty at a top-secret atomic installation. Not knowing what to expect, Cora turned and entered her home.

She laid her purse and Bible on the end table by the long, over-stuffed couch she and her husband had bought two weeks before he'd shipped out. Cora had been so proud of her new couch. She'd called her mother and both her sisters the day it was delivered and begged them to come over and see it. It was the first, and only, new piece of furniture they'd ever bought as husband and wife. Everything else they owned had been hand-me-downs from her mom and dad or purchased at the used furniture store in Sapulpa. The arms were now threadbare, the once golden cushions worn and sagging. The tiny blue and pink flowery design of the fabric she'd thought so pretty had lost its luster.

Cora sighed. Most days her life resembled the old sofa. The luster had gone out of her life also. She felt old and tired, but mostly tired. She thought about the incident at the diner and believed she'd made the right decision. Despite being asked several times by Don Porter, her boss, and the other DX waitresses if she was okay, Cora had said nothing about Mr. Robert Cornwell and his rude hands. She merely told everyone she was pooped, which was true. She was an adult woman; she would handle Mr. Cornwell in her own way. She simply would not ever again put herself in a situation, either physical or verbal, where he could take advantage of her. Cora thought and prayed about it the entire drive home and felt at peace with her decision.

"Hi Momma, have you eaten supper yet?"

Cora mustered a smile at the little blonde head bobbing out from behind the entryway to the kitchen. Behind her youngest, Josh sat at the table, head down. "I ate at the diner, honey. But thanks for asking."

"Sarah fixed macaroni and cheese and green beans and I ate a whole lot of green beans."

"Liar," came a female voice from somewhere beyond Jonda.

Cora thought she heard a chuckle emanate from the table. She walked over to Josh, squeezed his shoulders and kissed the top of his head. "How was your day, Son? Thanks for picking up the kids at the swimming hole."

"Momma, you wouldn't believe what happened to me when I was swimmin'," Jonda blurted. "I almost got drowned. I would have 'cept Bobby saved me. Really, he did and I ain't lyin'."

"Jonda, honey, don't say ain't. It's improper usage."

"Get over here and get to drying," Sarah said from the kitchen. She had begun washing the dishes; the dishes Bobby should have been washing.

Cora turned to her silent son still sitting at the kitchen table. She pulled out a chair opposite him and sat down.

"I don't know whose tea this is, but I think I'll drink some of it," she said as she lifted the half-empty glass to her lips.

Cora drank twice from Bobby's glass of tea before saying anything. "You and your brother have a row?" she asked without looking at her son.

"You could say that," Josh answered.

"Wanna tell me about it?"

"Not really," he said, looking across the table at the empty chair beside his mother.

"Did it have anything to do with your little sister?" Cora asked.

"You could say that. Mom, Jonda almost died today. She almost drowned because Bobby wasn't paying any attention to her when he should have been."

Cora fidgeted in her chair. She didn't know, for sure, how close her youngest daughter had actually come to drowning, but it must have been close enough to scare Josh. She massaged the back of her neck with her hand. She pursed her lips several times before speaking.

"Josh, have you ever been driving and because you were singing or daydreaming or just not paying attention, ran a stop sign or a red light and almost had a wreck?"

"No," Josh said totally straight-faced.

Cora shrugged, continued.

"Have you ever been with your friends and got to clowning around and barely missed having a mishap? Or maybe you were in a hurry and tried to pass somebody and almost got in an accident?"

Josh's mind jumped to last summer when he and a couple of friends decided to 'fly' on Roller Coaster Hills. Roller Coaster Hills was the nickname for West Forty-First Street. It was a hilly road, extremely steep in a couple of places that connected the communities of Berryhill and Prattville. Josh, who was driving, punched his car up to ninety miles an hour and literally left the pavement with all four tires when he crested the tops of the numerous hills. To make matters worse, he and his friends had turned around and did it again the very next night.

"No, I've never done anything that stupid," Josh replied to his mother.

"You will someday," she said. "Everybody who's ever lived, 'ceptin' Jesus, of course, messes up. Nobody's perfect. Not me. Not you. Not Bobby. Now, I'm not excusing the fact that Bobby should have been watching his sister better. He messed up. But, I think he knows that. I think he's outside right now beating himself up."

Josh pulled his bottom lip into his mouth and ran his tongue across it. Cora had seen her son do this many times. She couldn't remember him not doing it when he became edgy and a little nervous. He raised his hand and ran it through his thick, black hair. He had his father's hair. Josh was his father's son. The thought flushed Cora with melancholy; her exhaustion returned.

"Josh, if I haven't told you lately I want you to know how much I appreciate what you do for our family."

Josh looked at his mother quizzically.

"I know you're not happy here."

"That's not true. I . . ."

Cora waved at him to be quiet. "I know you wish you were off playing baseball somewhere, and I'm sorry that didn't work out. But, what I really regret is that you felt you had to quit school and get a job. I wish you hadn't done that."

Josh's jaw tightened. "Mom, we had to have some money. Dad was gone and you didn't have a job. We lost our nice house and would have lost the car if I hadn't gone to work."

"You're right, son," Cora lamented. "But I've got a job now, two in fact. Why don't you, at least, consider going to night school and finishing up?"

"Mother, we've talked about this, and I thought it was decided. I've got a good job with the railroad. A job I'd be crazy to give up. It doesn't pay much now, but in three or four years it will."

"I know, Son. You're right. I just so wanted all my kids to get an education."

"Mom, I just wish you'd let me help you out more with money. Do you realize I've got over two hundred dollars in the bank? Just think what we could do with that money? We could probably move out of this place."

"Josh, you do enough already. Like I've told you before, I'll not let you waste your future on my present."

"It's my present too," Josh grumbled. "We're all in this together. We're a family."

Cora reached across the table and gripped her eldest son's hand. It was rough and calloused from the hard work he did every day. It too reminded her of her husband. "Son, we don't have it so bad. We have food on the table and the rent's paid. Good grief, we've got two cars sitting in the driveway. How many people can say that?"

"Yeah, but one of 'em only runs when it wants to," Josh said in a lighter vein.

"How would you like to be Mr. Johnson next door? He's got a wife and four little girls under ten, all living in a little bitty shotgun house. And he couldn't make too much money working for that roofing outfit. If you ask me, the Lord has been good to us, Josh. We have everything we need."

Josh nodded his head unconvincingly. He got up from the table and headed towards the bathroom.

"One more thing, Son." Cora looked serenely at Josh. "Please remember that you're a man now, Bobby's not. He's on the verge and he may think he is, but he's not there yet. Be patient with him."

Josh looked back at his mother. Cora thought she saw a flicker of understanding in his dark eyes. He was a good boy. She was blessed to have him as a son. She took a deep breath. Boy was she tired.

Josh pulled open the bathroom door. Jonda looked up at him from the stool. "Momma, Josh is interfering with my privacy," she yelled.

He slammed the door shut. He turned to his mother, arms upraised in a pleading manner, "Why can't she learn to lock the door?"

Sarah, wiping off the kitchen counter, her back to her brother, giggled, then laughed outright.

\* \* \* \* \*

"I'm sorry. I screwed up."

Bobby stood at the far end of the low-cut hedge that bordered the front of their house, next to a blooming lilac bush growing by the Johnson's fence. He had his back to the front door. However, he knew it was his mother approaching by the sound of her light steps. Josh's would have been clompy, while Sarah had a hesitant way of walking. If it had been Jonda, he would have already heard something from her before she left the porch. Jonda's mouth, when she was awake, stayed closed only at brief intervals.

His mother laid her hand on his shoulder. She patted it twice. "The lilacs sure smell good tonight. I like spring. Everything smells so fresh and clean."

"I guess Josh told you about the fiasco at the swimmin' hole today? I feel really bad about it, Mom. I really do. It'll never happen again."

"I know it won't, Bobby. It sounds to me like you were the hero. If you hadn't done what you did, your sister might not be in there right now griping at your brother for, as she put it, 'interfering with her privacy.' Where does she learn such big words? She's too little to be talking like that."

Bobby chuckled. "Probably from Sarah. Sarah's always worried about her privacy and who's interfering or invading it."

Cora stepped up to the lilac bush and bent to sniff one of the blooms. "Goodness, these smell delicious. I think tomorrow I'll make a lilac bouquet and put them in the living room."

Bobby watched as his mother doodled with the flowers. She was a pretty woman; he knew that. His friends were always telling him that he had the prettiest mom of anyone at school. He didn't think she looked forty either, or was she forty-one? She still wore her blonde hair long and it had only a whisper of gray. Her nose turned up ever so slightly giving her face a forever girlish look and due to her demanding jobs, she'd kept her figure. Most women half her age were, no doubt, envious of her long legs and slim waistline. She even looked nice in her nondescript waitress uniform.

Cora picked a bloom and stuck it in her hair. She turned and smiled at her son.

*Why hadn't she remarried?* he wondered. Men were always asking her out, even the preacher seemed interested in her. But she always said, 'no'. *He didn't think she'd had a single date since Dad had died.* And even though he knew he was being selfish, he was glad.

"Bobby, have you thought about what you're going to do with your future?" Cora asked in a soft, non-threatening way.

Bobby looked down at his feet; he pawed at the grass like a hen scratching for grain. "I guess I'll work at the station. Big Jim told me I could eventually work up to be a mechanic."

"Have you thought about maybe going to college in the fall?"

"Mom, you know my grades aren't good enough. I barely made C's. There's no way I could get through a university." Bobby raised his head, stuck his hands in his pockets.

"You're plenty smart, young man. You didn't apply yourself in school."

"I think I'll stick to the gas station. Besides, what's wrong with pumpin' gas and cleanin' people's windshields? Lots of guys do it their whole lives."

"There's nothing wrong with any honorable employment. If that's what makes you happy, then I'm all for it. I just don't want you cutting yourself short, is all."

Bobby pulled his hands from his pockets, crossed his arms. "I'm not, Mom. I've even thought about someday opening up my own mechanic's shop. People will always need their cars fixed. I could have my own business."

"I like that idea, Son. Sounds like you really are thinking ahead. What about baseball? Your brother seems to think you're awfully good. Have you thought about giving it a try? The Oilers have a tryout every April, you know."

"Yeah, I know. But I don't think I'm really that good. Josh, as we all know, has got baseball on the brain. He's et up with it. I like it too, but not like him."

"He does love it. I'll agree with you there," Cora pushed to her tiptoes and kissed Bobby lightly on the cheek. "I'm proud of you, Son. Whatever you decide to do with your life I know you'll be successful at it. Just don't forget us little people when you're rich and famous," she joked.

"Now what was your name again, lady?" he said, grinning like a little boy.

# 4

Francine did not like Cameron's car. It was a convertible Buick Roadmaster with all the frills, a very popular car with college men and not cheap -- not cheap at all. She didn't care. Francine hated the giant albatross. She hated the white ragtop that Cameron constantly had to clean; and of course, was always trying to get her to help him. She didn't like the color of the car. It was a blue-black color that reminded her of a smelly, stagnant pond. But probably the single thing she hated most about Cameron's vehicle was the front, specifically the grill. It reminded her of an angry mouth. And not just someone who's emotionally upset over not getting a raise at work or throwing a gutter ball after getting two strikes in a row. No, the Buick had the face of a serial killer, a person who took people's lives without a second thought, a man who literally hated the world. Yes, that's what Cameron's car was; it was an evil machine, a criminal. Francine shuddered and scooted even closer to the driver. She reached for the radio and changed the channel from the tinny sounds of a Big-Band tune to a hipster station. The hard-driving sounds of Johnnie Ray singing his newest hit, "Cry," flooded over the open car and wafted upwards into the ether. *Well, at least this monster has a good radio,* she thought.

"Hey! Whydja change the channel? I happen to like that station." Cameron reached towards the radio to change it back. Francine swatted his hand down.

"If we have to go to Crystal City tonight, at least let me listen to some real music and not that out-of-date, old-fashioned junk."

"That old-fashioned junk as you call it was Tommy Dorsey, and he'll never go out of style."

"Oh, pish-posh on Tommy Dorsey. He's old hat. Rockabilly is what's hip now, old-timer. I'll take Carl Perkins, Johnny Burnette, and Ersel Hickey any time over that outa-date big band sound."

Cameron harrumphed loudly in derision of his date's views. He shook his head several times, decided to change the subject. "Now, tell me again why you don't want to go to Crystal City? I can't believe you've lived here ten years and have never been."

"I don't know why I've never been. Dad never took me, I guess."

"Oh come on, Francine. Everybody likes to ride roller coasters. Surely, you aren't afraid to ride Zingo? Are you?"

"No, I'm not afraid of a wimpy roller coaster." Francine fidgeted in her seat. Her peripheral vision caught a grin surfacing on her boyfriend's face. He looped his arm around her shoulders.

"That's not it at all. Dad just didn't want us going there."

Cameron's face registered surprise. He patted Francine's shoulder as if she were a deprived child. "Are you telling me you've never been to an amusement park in your whole life?"

"Of course I have," Francine answered, impatience showing in her voice. "That's not it at all. I've ridden dozens of roller coasters in my life, not to mention the Octopus, Loop-De-Loop, Tilt-A-Whirl, and so many others I can't remember."

"Then what's the problem? Why haven't you been to Crystal City? It's really a nice place."

Francine breathed deeply and blew the air out through pursed lips as if she were letting air out of an over-inflated balloon. Cameron lifted his right arm from her shoulders and gripped the steering wheel with both hands. He alternated glancing at her and the Eleventh Street bridge he was currently traversing.

"The bottom line is Dad doesn't like me going across the river. He doesn't want me hanging out on the Westside."

Cameron tilted his head quizzically. "And why is that, m'lady?"

"Oh, come on Cameron. You know good and well why."

"No, I don't." Cameron shook his head. "Honest Injun."

Francine squinted her eyes at the driver as if trying to see into his brain. Accepting his veracity, she answered, "Dad doesn't want me going on the Westside because of all the crime and filth."

Cameron remained silent. His eyes transfixed on the concrete lane of the bridge.

"Come on Cameron, you know as well as I do that most people who live on the Westside are thugs and hoodlums. I heard it has the highest crime rate in Oklahoma."

Cameron still said nothing.

"Plus that, everything's dirty over there because of the refineries and the railroad yard. Mom told me they can't keep anything clean, not even their underclothes."

A grin formed on Cameron's face, which blossomed into a smile. His mouth parted, a snicker escaped. "You mean to tell me that your dad, the man who acts like the perfect liberal gentleman, doesn't want his lovely, private-school educated daughter to fraternize with the low-lifes over on the Westside. That is precious. Unbelievably precious." Cameron smacked the steering wheel several times. His snicker morphed into outright, raucous laughter.

Francine slid to the other side of the seat. She crossed her arms and looked out the open window at the river below. She should have known he would react like a juvenile about the issue. Sometimes she hated him.

"Oh, come on Dumplin'," Cameron pleaded. "Come back over here. I'm sorry. I can't help it, but that was funny. You really mean to tell me you've never been to the Westside?"

"Of course, I've been *through* the Westside!" Francine almost screamed. "You have to when you're going to The City, you know."

After a few more light-hearted chuckles, Cameron quieted down. He patted the seat beside him motioning for Francine to return. She refused. "Really, I'm sorry. I just can't imagine that someone who's lived in Tulsa as long as you has never been to West Tulsa or Red Fork. Now, I can understand not going to Oakhurst. That place really is rough, but some of the best cafes around are west of the river."

"I bet they're not as good as Southern Hills Country Club or the Petroleum Club restaurants," Francine defended

"Probably not. You've got me there. But, they're good in a different kind of way. A homey, greasy kinda way. For example, if you like fried chicken you can't beat the Gingham Girl on Quanah. They have the best."

"I prefer my chicken baked, thank you."

"You would," Cameron said under his breath. "Okay, then. How 'bout chicken-fried steak? Ollie's is super!"

Francine shrugged. "I've never had chicken-fried steak. Is it good?"

"Oh, Francine, it's the best. I love it. I can't believe you live in Oklahoma and have never had it. You ought to get your "Italian" cook to fix you some."

"You think you are so funny, don't you. For your information, Mrs. Serio was born and raised in Tulsa. She's never even been to Italy."

"Okay, great, you're in luck because I guarantee you if she's from around here she knows how to make chicken-fried steak. The only thing I'd ask is when you get her to make some, invite me for dinner."

Francine smiled, her anger disappeared. She could never stay angry at Cameron for long. She returned to her place beside her obnoxious boyfriend.

Francine and Cameron drove the rest of the trip in relative silence. They zipped along Quanah Avenue through Red Fork, a small community west of West Tulsa, and passed several tidy motels complete with courtyards equipped with slides, merry-go-rounds, and swings for their young guests. Quanah Avenue doubled as Highway 66, which was the major east-west artery of the southwest. The same highway that so many "Okies" only a generation earlier had used to leave Oklahoma during the Dust Bowl Era for the chimeric riches of California.

Cameron pulled his shimmering convertible into the vast parking lot of the Crystal City Amusement Park and got lucky finding an open slot near the front. Francine didn't wait for her beau to come around and help her out. She sprang from the car, awe enveloping her face. The place was utterly magnificent.

Francine breathed in the amusement park smells. The aroma of hot, buttered popcorn and the sweet, sticky smell of cotton candy flooded her sinuses. Crowding the delicious scents rushing at her were the sounds of a hundred people laughing, ear-piercing shrieks of excitement, and the clank, clank, clank, of the packed roller coaster as it crept upwards along the wooden trestles to the pinnacle before plummeting its occupants downward. People were having fun. Their good-times filled the air.

The first thing that caught her eye was the massive wooden roller coaster called Zingo. She watched and listened as the jam-packed cars zoomed down the steep pitch of the ride and swooshed around tight curves almost sideways, while the screaming occupants held their arms in the air trying to convince onlookers of their bravery. Francine couldn't wait to ride Zingo. She loved roller coasters.

The next structure to capture her attention was a long rectangular building next to the park. Fancine quickly decided it was some type of dance pavilion as she could hear the distinct sounds of swing music cutting through the cacophony of the amusement park crowd

"Are you ready to go in?" Cameron asked. "It's really nicer on the inside than it appears from out here."

Francine looked at her boyfriend as if he was an idiot. He returned her acidic stare with a look of puzzlement. Her expression immediately softened.

"I want to ride the roller coaster first," she chirped. Francine grabbed Cameron's hand and pulled him towards the entrance.

*Philip D. Smith*

\* \* \* \* \*

Josh paid the concessionaire the fifty cents, grabbed the two drinks from the counter, and grumbled to himself all the way to the bench where Sarah and Jonda waited.

"What's got your panties all bunched up?" Sarah asked her brother.

"Panties bunched up. That's a good one, Sarah," Jonda laughed. "I'm gonna remember that one and use it on Bobby."

"No you're not, Munch. . . . young lady," Sarah reprimanded. "I shouldn't have said that. You'd better not repeat it, and if you do you'd best not tell where you heard it. I'll deny I ever said it."

Jonda feigned a hurt look. "I'm sorry, Sissy. I thought it was funny. You didn't say any cuss words or nuthin'. Panties ain't cussin' is it?"

"No, of course not, Jonda. There's just some things ladies shouldn't say in public and talking about underwear is one of 'em. You'll understand when you get older and start learning lady stuff."

"I'm ready, now."

"No you're not. You're still a little girl. There's a lot of things you wouldn't understand."

Jonda shrugged. "Okay, then I can say what's got your panties all bunched up in your hiney."

"Why don't you shut up and drink your limeade? Sometimes you are absolutely impossible. Now, scoot over so Josh can sit down." Sarah motioned for Jonda to sit closer to her so their brother could join them on the bench. She looked past her little sister to Josh, who seemed upset by something.

"What's bugging you, Josh? Why didn't you get a cherry-limeade?"

Josh sat down on the end of the bench next to Jonda, who immediately slid away from Sarah and moved close to her brother. He absently patted her on the head. "I'm not angry, I'm just . . . yeah, now that I think about it, I am mad! They're charging a quarter for a drink in this rip-off joint. Do you realize you can get a cherry-limeade at the Big Store for a nickel? It's highway robbery. They know you're gonna get thirsty when you're here so they overcharge you for a drink. They must think the people that come here are rich."

"I hate to tell you Josh, but look around. Most of these people walking around aren't Westsiders. They're from the other side of the river. They probably do have a lot of money."

"Then why don't they build their own stinkin' amusement park on their side of the river and leave us alone."

"Ahh! Did you hear what Josh said?" Jonda looked up at Sarah.

"Shut up!" Sarah and Josh demanded simultaneously.

Jonda hunkered down between her siblings.

"I hate to say it but if they ever do, this place will probably go out of business. People around here don't have enough money to come here much." Sarah took a long sip from her limeade.

"Where's Bobby?" Jonda asked out of the blue.

"I told you earlier," Josh sounded aggravated. "He came with Maundi. He's around here someplace."

"Maundi, Maundi," Jonda sang. "He's always hangin' around her. If you ask me, I think he likes her better than he does us."

"I think you're right," Sarah answered.

"I don't think there's any doubt," added Josh.

The sisters sat sipping their drink while Josh daydreamed and watched people as they passed by. Jonda offered her brother a drink four times but was rebuffed – each time more sternly.

After several minutes, Sarah turned to her brother, "Josh, why doesn't Momma get married again? Dad's been dead seven years now. Do you think she'll ever get remarried?"

"I don't know," Josh shrugged. "I guess she doesn't want to or maybe she hasn't found a man that can stack up to Dad. She seems okay to me, though. She's got us around so I doubt if she's lonely."

Sarah leaned back on the bench, pondering what her brother had said.

"When are we gonna ride the Ferris wheel like you promised," Jonda interrupted.

"Pretty quick Munchkin, as soon as you and Sarah finish your drinks."

Jonda slurped the last of her limeade through the straw, then began searching through the ice for something. "I can't believe this," she stammered. "I got cheated. I ain't got a cherry in my limeade. Josh, there's no cherry in my cherry-limeade!"

"What do you want me to do about it? I don't have one on me. They probably just forgot. It's no big deal."

"It is to me. That's why I get cherry-limeades so I can eat the cherry when I'm finished drinking."

"You can have mine, Jonda. I don't like maraschino cherries. They're too sweet."

"I don't want your cherry, Sarah. I want mine. I paid for it and I want it."

"Uh, I think Josh paid for your limeade, Munchkin."

Jonda didn't hear her sister because she'd already bolted from the bench and was headed, cup in hand, head held high, straight to the concession stand.

"I think you'd better stop her Josh before she makes a fool of herself."

"No, I don't think I will. I think I'll let mister twenty-five-cent drink man get a dose of the pink tornado."

Sarah giggled. She and Josh watched as their pig-tailed sister, clad in her usual attire of pink shorts and white top, stood patiently in line. When she, at last, reached the counter she stood up on her tip-toes, placed the empty cup on the counter and began jabbering. Although, because of the distance, Josh and Sarah could not hear a single word that was said, it was obvious to them that Jonda was getting the better of the contest. Her lips moved constantly while the concessionaire couldn't seem to get a word in edgewise. Finally, Jonda returned to the bench proudly holding two bright-red maraschino cherries by their stems.

"Are you satisfied? Can we ride the Ferris wheel now?" Josh playfully asked.

Smiling from ear to ear, Jonda answered by sticking both cherries into her mouth and chomping down on them. Cherry juice squirted from her mouth and splattered the front of her white top. "Oops," she gushed.

"I wish Mom could be here. She and Dad used to love to ride the Ferris wheel." Josh had taken off his baseball cap and placed it under his leg so it wouldn't blow off. He was glad he had. The wind rushed through his hair pushing the black locks off his forehead. He might very well have lost his cap if he'd kept it on.

"Me too," Sarah agreed.

Josh, Sarah, and Jonda rode the Ferris wheel together with Jonda sitting in the middle. Getting her to sit there had been a chore in itself. She'd finally agreed when Josh gave her the option of either sitting in the middle or watching her brother and sister as they rode it without her.

"Looky there," Jonda whispered.

"What?" Sarah mockingly whispered back.

"What's the big secret?" Josh joined Sarah in the mimic.

"Below us." Jonda continued whispering unaware that her siblings were making fun of her. She pointed downward. "There's black people in the car below us. Sshhh! Be quiet! They're above us now." Jonda tried to act normal. Josh and Sarah looked at each other and shook their heads in wonderment.

"Oh my goodness," Jonda shrieked. "Look what they're doin' now."

Josh peered below them. A smile crossed his face. Below their compartment was a Negro couple with a little boy riding the Ferris wheel. They were obviously having a good time. It appeared that every time they crested the pinnacle the father would kiss the mother. Not a lingering smoochy kiss, just a nice short peck on the lips. Although, Josh had never seen Negroes at the park, for some reason it did not bother him.

"It's no big deal, Munchkin," Josh patted his sister's knees. "It's just a mom and dad having fun. There's nothing wrong with what they're doing. I bet our mom and dad did it a hundred times when they were young."

"It's still yukky." Jonda let go of the safety bar and crossed her arms. "Plus that, I've never seen old people kiss before. It's kinda weird lookin'."

"What's gonna be weird is when you fall out of your seat and smash your face on the concrete. Now, grab that bar and don't let go of it till the ride is over." Sarah ordered.

Josh ignored his warring sisters. He had become mesmerized by the beauty that lay below him. And not just Crystal City. Although, it too had its appeal with the bright lights, colorful booths, and the hundreds of people scampering from ride to ride. No, what struck him as gorgeous was the distant city of Tulsa. The scores of tall buildings jutting majestically out of the flat plain and silhouetted against the heavens of indigo sent shivers of awe up and down his spine. How could man build such large structures? Why didn't the wind knock them down? Or a tornado? He knew there were bigger, taller buildings all over the country. In fact, Tulsa wouldn't even be considered a big city compared with New York, Chicago, or St. Louis. But Josh had never been to those far-away cities. To him, they were merely pictures you looked at in *Life* magazine or read about in a book. Tulsa was the only city he'd ever been to. He'd never even been to Oklahoma City, the state capital. Tulsa was his world and it was plenty big for him.

"Ughh," came a moan from beside him.

Jolted from his thoughts, Josh turned abruptly towards his little sister. "What's the matter, kiddo? Are you okay?"

Jonda looked up at her brother. "No," she groaned. "I think I'm gettin' sick. I might have to throw up."

"You better not vomit while we're on this ride. If you do, I'll kill you," an alarmed Sarah proclaimed.

"I can't help it, Sarah. If I'm sick, I'm sick," moaned Jonda.

*Then Sings My Soul*

"The ride's almost over, Little One. Try to hold it if you can," Josh said. He let go of the bar with his right hand and placed his arm around his sister, hugging her close to him. "At least if you get sick, let me have it and not Sarah. Okay?"

Jonda looked at her brother as if she were on her death bed. She nodded forlornly.

"Josh, if she throws up, I'm gonna be so embarrassed. I'll never come to this place again. What about the people below us? How're you gonna explain her throwing up on them?"

"Sarah, haven't you ever gotten sick in public? Don't say no because I remember you puking all over your first-grade teacher at the Christmas program. You ruined the poor lady's dress. I told Mom and Dad they oughta have you switch schools so you could make it into the second grade."

"That's different. I . . ."

"Eeeyuhh. . ."

Sarah pulled away from Jonda, practically climbing out of her seat in the moving ride. Josh hurriedly placed his hand under Jonda's mouth to try and catch as much of the puke as possible.

Instead, all that came out of Jonda's mouth was a huge, smelly belch – much too large for such a little girl.

Josh and Sarah looked at each other, stunned.

"Man, I feel a lot better now," Jonda joyously exclaimed. "I guess I only needed to burp."

\* \* \* \* \*

"Young man, remove your arm from that girl's shoulder. Please do it immediately."

Bobby Braun removed his hand and jerked around to face his verbal assailant, although he recognized the voice instantly. He held his hands up as if under arrest.

"Good one," laughed Jonda. "You got Bobby good, Josh."

"Oh, I think he knew we were behind him all along. What's up Brother?"

Bobby sidled up to Josh and clasped his bicep. In return, Josh patted his brother on the shoulder. The two stood facing each other a moment before speaking, the animosity of the previous night gone.

\* \* \* \* \*

Last night, Bobby had remained in the front yard until he thought everyone had gone to bed. When the lights went out he'd crept back in and silently made his way to the bedroom he shared with his older brother. Josh was in bed lying uncovered, totally still, and wearing nothing but briefs. At first, Bobby thought Josh was awake, but decided it was only the rustling of the wispy breeze coming through the open window. Bobby quickly undressed and slipped into his bed, which was separated from his brother's by no more than ten inches. He pulled the white, cotton sheet up to his chest and had already decided to dream about Maundi when Josh spoke: "I'm sorry I jumped on you like I did tonight. I don't know what got into me. You've always taken good care of little Miss Priss. I had no right to accuse you of almost killing our sister. If she ever gets killed it'll be of her own doing, I can tell you that for sure. Do you forgive me?"

Bobby rolled away from his brother. "Yeah, yeah, I forgive you. Can we go to sleep now?"

Bobby hated it when Josh got all noble on him. Not even twenty-one yet, Josh was only three years older than Bobby's seventeen, but sometimes, Josh acted like he was thirty.

"I'm just saying I'm sorry. We're brothers. We can't have anger between us. We just can't."

Bobby swabbed his lower lip with his tongue before answering. "I mean it, Josh. I really do forgive you."

Bobby pulled the covers up tighter around his neck hoping Josh would figure out that he didn't want to talk. The room became quiet.

Bobby tried to think about Maundi and her polka-dot swimsuit but Josh kept butting in. Josh was his big brother, and as such there was always going to be some tension and rivalry. But deep down, Bobby felt sorry for Josh, who had given up a lot for the family. He'd quit school after the tenth grade to go to work and help his mother. He'd turned down a baseball contract with the team of his dreams. He didn't even seem much interested in girls. He said he didn't have time what with working and running the railroad team. One thing you could definitely say about Josh; he wasn't selfish.

"Good night, Bobby."

"Good night to you, too."

\* \* \* \* \*

"Did you hear me, Bobby? I'm telling you, you need to be careful. Baseball season starts next week, and I can't have my number-one pitcher laid up because he's been out rough-housin'."

Josh's voice jarred Bobby back into the here and now. "What did you say? I'm sorry. I was thinkin' about something else."

"What I said," Josh narrowed his eyes at his brother. "Is that some of the Star bunch is roaming around the park. They're not wearing their jackets, which is a shock. I saw both Delaney brothers and Nick Lofton over by the Dodge-Em cars when I was riding the Ferris wheel."

"If George and Vernon are here, then Gibbo has to be someplace close," Bobby mumbled to himself. "Don't worry Josh, I'm not lookin' for trouble."

"I know you aren't, but they thrive on it. How much longer you gonna be here? I need to get Fizzle-Britches home and in bed. She's got church tomorrow."

"Hey, quit talking about me," Jonda yelped.

"Be quiet," Sarah demanded. She grabbed the back of Jonda's shirt and pulled her away from her brothers.

"I'm ready to go," Maundi spoke up.

"What do you mean? I thought you wanted to go through the funhouse? Maundi, we're not going to leave because we're afraid of a bunch of two-bit hoodlums. We came here to enjoy ourselves and, by Jove, we're going to enjoy ourselves! We're not going to let a bunch of punks ruin our Saturday night!" Bobby had worked himself into a tizzy by the time he finished his speech.

Maundi flicked Bobby an are-you-finished-showing-off-your-manhood-yet look. She ran her fingers through her short, reddish-brown hair, stuck her bottom lip out as if in a sulk and blew her immaculately straight bangs askew.

"Bobby, I'm ready to leave now. I don't want to go through the funhouse. Let's go and do something else." Maundi made this demand without rancor, without raising her voice. She stated it in a matter-of-fact, almost monotone voice. She ended with a devilish grin and wiggling her eyebrows several times for effect.

Bobby relaxed. Maundi had let him off the hook. He really didn't want to have an encounter with the Star gang tonight. He was with his girl. Bobby returned Maundi's grin.

\* \* \* \* \*

"Josh Braun? Josh Braun? Is that you?"

Josh turned from Bobby and Maundi as a young man towing a pretty girl approached. After a second, it clicked who he was.

"Hello Cameron. I didn't think I'd see you again until tomorrow at practice.

The two young men shook hands. Josh introduced Cameron to Bobby and Maundi, then to Sarah and Jonda. Cameron shook hands with all.

"Josh, Bobby, girls, I'd like you all to meet my girlfriend, Francine Fitzsimmons. She just graduated from Lansing Hall a few days ago."

Francine's body went rigid. *Why did he have to mention Lansing?* These people were obviously poor Westsiders who either didn't care that she went to a prestigious private high school or would be offended by it. Poor people were so class conscious it made her sick. She didn't understand it, but they were.

Francine dutifully shook hands with the cast of characters that looked like they were some kind of vaudeville act. She started with the youngest girl, a cute little urchin in an orphan kind of way and worked her way up. They seemed clean enough. The problem was their clothes. They were all dressed in out-of-fashion dungarees and washed-out cotton tops. For the life of her, she didn't understand why people like this didn't spend more money on clothes. Here they were, wasting their father's hard-earned cash on temporary thrills and over-priced popcorn when they could have, at the least, bought the two girls a blouse.

"It's nice to meet you, Miss Fitzsimmons," the last hand-shaker said in a too serious tone.

"Please call me Francine. I much prefer it."

"Then Francine it'll be," he said, releasing her hand.

In front of Francine stood a young man not much taller than she. He was obviously the older brother of the tall, muscular boy beside him. The shorter man was muscular too, but in a thicker, working-man sort of way, while his brother looked like an Olympic decathlete with a chance to win. Francine's attention was drawn to the stocky man's hair and eyes. She liked both. He had deep blue eyes that reminded her of a magazine photo she once saw of Gary Cooper in his Sgt. York uniform. Penetrating was probably the best word for both Cooper's and this man's eyes. She also liked his hair. It was thick and blue-black with a trace of a wave. He kept it cut short in a poor-man's Sam Spade style. He held a blue and red ball cap in his hands.

"What did you say your name was again? I'm sorry; I forgot."

"It's Joshua Braun. Call me Josh."

"Francine, these are two of the fellas I'll be playing ball with this summer. You'll be seeing a lot of them. Josh here's the catcher and his brother, Bobby, will be on the mound."

"Oh joy," Francine said, sounding as sarcastic as possible, "more baseball players."

"I take it you don't particularly like the game of baseball?" Josh asked in an overly polite way.

"Oh no, baseball is fine – if you're ten years old! I happen to be a firm believer in men acting like men. In other words, when we grow up we should lay aside our childish games and look to the future."

"So, you don't like the Major Leagues then?" Josh continued.

"Major League baseball is fine. If you can't do anything else. Most of those guys end up in the poorhouse when they can't play anymore. They're mainly losers who couldn't get into college."

Francine sensed she'd upset Mr. Braun. She could see his jaw clench and his right eye twitch. It dawned on her that he must be the head of the rinky-dink semi-pro team.

"I'm sorry you feel that way," Josh's voice quavered with anger. "I happen to disagree. I think baseball is a wonderful game and is an important part of our country."

Francine laughed out loud. "You've got to be kidding me, *Mister* Braun." She over-emphasized Mister derisively. "Now you're equating our national pastime with things like Wall Street, the defense department, and the White House. What a hoot!"

"I didn't say it was *that* important!" Josh's voice rose an octave. "But I'd hate to see our country without baseball. Boys grow up with it, and I know it's really helped me. It helped get me through the war."

Francine shook her head in disgust. The man in front of her was obviously a buffoon. "You've got to be kidding me. Baseball has only been around sixty or seventy years. How in the world did the country manage before Abner Doubleday? And if you relied on baseball to take your mind off the war while most of us were out picking up scrap metal and buying bonds, then you make me ill." Francine turned her back on Josh.

Josh stepped towards the young woman, but was restrained by

Bobby. "She's not worth it, Brother," he consoled. "She doesn't even know you."

"Nor do I want to know you," Francine added, her back still turned.

"Sorry guys," Cameron said. "I think we'd better be going. See you at practice tomorrow."

Josh, still held tightly by Bobby, watched as Cameron and the young woman walked away. Josh was positive she was shaking her rear end at him just to make him even madder.

# 5

Cora paused at the bedroom door, then grasped the ancient doorknob and slowly twisted it. She silently pushed it open as if she were a cat burglar creeping into the master bedroom of a great estate. This room, however, was tiny and contained only a small dresser, a single chest of drawers, and two twin-sized beds. On the far bed closest to the window rested her eldest: Josh. He lay on his side wrapped in a sheet, with his top leg propped on his extra pillow. It reminded her of the way another man liked to sleep, except that he used her hips to splay his legs across.

A look of reminiscence and sentimentality eased onto Cora's face. Her son was grown up. He was a man. And he reminded her so much of his father it was scary. He had the same thick bone structure, same dark coloring, same black hair and eyes as blue as the Mediterranean. Even his straight, too-long nose reminded her of John. He was practically a carbon-copy of her husband, her late husband. She wondered why none of her traits had seen fit to display themselves on her firstborn. But, she was glad they hadn't. Cora felt a solitary tear slide down her cheek. She absently wiped it away.

Cora clicked across the wooden floor in her Sunday pumps to her son's side. She sat on the edge of the bed and gently shook his shoulder.

He moaned a disagreement.

She shook him harder.

He moaned louder.

She shook him still harder.

He opened his eyes. "Mom, what are you doing? I'm tired and sleepy."

"I was hoping you'd come to church with the rest of us. You haven't been in over three months. I'm starting to worry about you, Son."

"I'm sorry, Mom, but Sundays are about the only time I get to sleep in. Church is just too early for a workin' man."

Cora flicked her bottom lip with her teeth. In the background, she could hear Sarah and Bobby arguing good-naturedly over whose turn it was to be at the bathroom sink and Jonda singing *When the Roll is Called Up Yonder* in her high-pitched soprano. Cora measured her response. She knew she couldn't make her grown son go to church with his family. She wanted him to *want* to go.

"I know you're tired, Son. I'm tired too. There's many a Sunday I'd as soon sleep in as hear a sermon on the evils of gambling or why we should be satisfied, indeed thankful, for what God has given us. But, we're church people. We go to church. I can't remember not going to church. My daddy took me when I was growing up, and after I married your father, we never missed a service. He was a deacon, you know."

Josh nodded, but made no move to get up. Cora continued, "I don't want to lay a guilt-trip on you, Son. I believe that would be the wrong reason for attending church. However, I think you know it was your father's desire that his kids attend church. He wanted his family to be people of faith. Your father loved the Lord with all his heart."

"I know Dad would want me in church, and I haven't quit. I'm going to start coming. Part of my problem is . . . I don't know. I'm just tired."

Cora looked quizzically at her son. He averted his eyes. She could tell he was looking past her, probably at the photo hanging on the wall of Dizzy Dean and Pepper Martin. He'd bought the picture and had it autographed by the two when Dean's traveling baseball team had come to Tulsa and played a team of blacks from the Negro League. Now, he was using it as a distraction, a way of not thinking about his mother and church.

What was really bothering him? Cora wondered. Was he ashamed of their plight? She decided to ask him.

"Josh, you're not ashamed because we're poor, are you?"

Josh raised up in bed. He rested his back on the headboard. "No, no, that's not it at all," he dismissively waved at his mother.

"Because you shouldn't be," she stated. "None of us should be. It's not our fault if we're poor. Things happen. Your dad died fighting for this country. If he were here, things would be different. We'd have a lot more like we did before he went away. He was a good man, and he provided for his family."

"I know he did," Josh said. "I wish you'd let me do more for us. It's not right, Mom. I make decent money."

Cora energetically shook her head. "No, Son. I'll not have you supporting us. You already help out a lot."

"Then why don't you go to the Federal Building and get on assistance? The government will help you out. The Donaldsons and the Ramseys are both on assistance."

Cora looked gravely at her son. She swallowed and ran her tongue across her lips before responding.

"Josh, I'm not going to say anything against the Donaldsons or Ramseys. What they do is their business, not mine. But, as long as I can work, this family won't be taking anything from the government. I won't be beholdin' to them for either my survival or my children's. I won't become their dependent."

Josh tilted his head. "I don't see anything wrong in it, Mom. The assistance program is set up to help widows like you. It's paid for out of taxpayer's money and the last time I checked you and I both pay taxes. So, it'd kinda be like gettin' some of your own money back? What's wrong with that?"

"Son, I hope someday you'll understand. My daddy and your father both believed that once you started accepting money or food or anything from the government because you're poor, then they've got you. They'll start trying to run your life and act like you owe them something. The only thing I want the government to do is balance the budget, protect us if we get attacked, and deliver the mail. Families should take care of themselves."

"What about the roads?" Josh laughed. "Can the government build the roads?"

Cora returned his laugh. "Yeah, I guess we'll let old Uncle Sam keep the roads up. Nevertheless, we need to be careful or they'll start stickin' their nose where it doesn't belong. I don't want any part of the government running my life. Who knows, they might want to start telling me what church I have to attend or worse, they won't let us go to church at all."

"Oh, Mom," Josh said. "I don't think getting a little help from the government is going to mean you can't go to Tabernacle Baptist. I don't think the government cares where you go to church."

"They do in Russia. Those communists don't like Christians. They don't even believe in God. Can you imagine that? People who don't believe in Providence? Brother Alex said that Christians in those communist countries have to meet in secret, and if they get caught with a Bible they're put in jail."

"To be honest, Mom," Josh decided to change the subject. "That's another thing I don't like about church. I don't much like Brother Alex. Don't get me wrong, he's an okay guy when he's not preaching. It's just that he's too hung up on sin and Hell. That's about the only thing he preaches about."

Cora couldn't believe her son. What was a minister supposed to be preaching about? He was trying to get people saved. Keep them from going to Hell. What did Josh want him to speak about -- the weather? Brother Alex did preach about loving your neighbor and being a good testimony to others, but he hadn't done so in a while. She might mention that to him. He seemed to value her opinion.

"Why don't you plan on coming next week, Son? Brother Alex might surprise you with his message. He's really a good man. I wish you'd get to know him better."

Cora rose from her son's bed and left the room.

Josh watched her as she left, wondering what she meant by her last statement.

\* \* \* \* \*

Josh fell into a deep slumber. He was in the middle of a glorious dream about a sandy-haired young woman hugging and kissing him after he'd hit the winning homerun in the seventh game of the World Series when he felt it.

The feeling assaulted his cheek with warm undulations. The warmth did not attack him with a steady onslaught, instead it smacked against his cheek over and over in short wispy waves. The essence of fried, crispy bacon accompanied the warmth and wafted into his nostrils. It smelled divine.

Josh fluttered his eyes, not really wanting to see what was there, yet knowing exactly what he would find.

"Good morning, sleepy-head," Jonda whispered as if afraid of waking him up. Too late. He was wide-eyed.

"Momma told me you wasn't goin' to church with us again. I wish you would, but I kinda don't blame you."

Josh rubbed sleep from his eyes and issued a long, loud yawn. He pulled his hands out from under the sheets and stretched mightily and noisily. Fascinated, Jonda stood back from the bed and watched her big brother.

"I know I should go with you, but I can't seem to get out of bed," Josh grinned.

"I don't got a choice," Jonda lamented. "If I don't get up, Sarah will throw a wet wash rag in my face. Plus that, I usually gotta pee."

"Church is good for you little sister. When I was your age, I never missed."

"Oh, I like goin' to church. I have fun in Sunday School. I just get awful scared when Brother Alex starts talkin' about what it's gonna be like in Hell if you ain't right with the Lord. I don't want to burn forever."

Josh reached for his sister; she bent towards him. He lightly pinched her nose and mussed her hair. "Don't worry about going to Hell, kiddo. Jesus isn't going to send little girls to the lake of fire. Especially, cute little girls like you."

Jonda actually blushed at her brother's compliment. For once she seemed speechless.

It didn't last long.

"I hope He won't send me to Hell 'cause once I burnt my finger tryin' to get some sausage out of the skillet, and boy did it burn. I ain't never hurt so bad, except for the time when Laci Matthews' stupid weiner dog bit me on the hiney at her birthday party, and even then I don't think it was as bad as the skillet burn, but it might have been. Momma had to put Oleo on my burned-up finger, and that didn't really stop the hurtin'. No, I'm gonna go to church and that's all there is to it." Jonda turned and marched towards Josh's door.

She stopped halfway out. "Josh, I know you're tired, but could you rest up real good and come to church with us in three weeks? I'm in the junior choir, and we're gonna sing in front of the big church. Please? We've been practicing forever so we could sing in front of the grownups." Jonda screwed her face up trying to look as pitiful as a rejected orphan."

Josh shook his head in amazement at his youngest sister.

"Jonda, you take the cake. If we lived in California they'd be beatin' our door down to get you to act in a movie. Or better yet, you should become a salesman someday. You'd be great at selling Kirbys. And yes,

I'll definitely come to church when you sing. I wouldn't miss it for the world."

Jonda grinned triumphantly at her brother. She left the room mumbling under her breath about how in the world could she be a salesman when she was a girl.

Josh vainly tried to go back to sleep. He attempted to remember his dream about the faceless blonde, but it was no use. The placid images refused to return.

He looked again at the only photograph on the plain white wall. The picture of Dizzy Dean and Pepper Martin. Two of the best to ever play the game. And he'd gotten to watch them play. The amazing thing was, as great as they were, the player he most remembered that day was the Negro pitcher, Satchel Paige. Paige had tossed a two-hit shutout against the Major Leaguers and had struck out both Martin and Dean twice each and made it look easy. There was no doubt in his mind that, black or white, Satchel Paige was the best pitcher he'd ever seen.

Why couldn't *he* be playing baseball right now? Why was he stuck working for the railroad? He knew most guys would die for his job, but it wasn't baseball. It wasn't what he'd dreamed of doing with his life. Why did he like baseball so much?

Josh silently cursed the war that had taken his dad. He cursed the Germans and Hitler. He despised the Japs and Hirohito. He blasphemed Musolini and smiled as he imagined the Italian hanging upside down from a rope. He even cursed the late president, the revered FDR, for sending his father to war.

He would be playing baseball right now, probably for the Cardinals, if the Japs had left Pearl Harbor alone, if Hitler hadn't been so greedy for power. Who knows? He might have played in an all-star game or two and maybe even a World Series. He definitely wouldn't be coaching a two-bit, semi-pro railroad team and still be living at home trying to help his mom out by taking his sisters to the amusement park.

*Then Sings My Soul*

And he wouldn't have ever met that snooty, rich girl who didn't like baseball and made fun of him for playing.

Josh felt his face grow hot. Just thinking about that terrible hoyden upset him. He ground his teeth. He had to admit she was a pretty girl in a snobby, fake way. The girl's name shot into his memory; Francine. Her name was Francine, and he didn't like her. He didn't like her at all. He wished he hadn't remembered her name. He didn't like her name either. It too, sounded uppity, like she was a lady in waiting at King Arthur's Court.

Josh turned onto his side, fluffed his pillow with his fist. He raised his head, pulled the pillow out, flipped it over, and replaced it under his head. He lay back down. He liked the coolness of a turned pillow against his head. Turning his pillow was normally the last thing he did before dropping off to sleep. He hoped the trick would work again.

"Hey Brother, not going to church again?"

Josh opened his eyes yet again and saw Bobby standing at the foot of the bed. He shook his head and closed his eyes.

"Suit yourself. I wanted to tell you that I'll meet you at Reed Park for practice. I'm not coming home with Mom after church. I'm going to eat out with Maundi's family at the Gingham Girl."

Josh, without opening his eyes, nodded his reception of the information. Bobby, apparently believing that his brother needed more explanation, continued, "Maundi's family eats out almost every Sunday after church. I think it has something to do with them being Methodist because I don't see how they can afford it. They're as poor as a sharecropper in Mississippi."

Josh, eyes still closed, nodded again.

Bobby turned to leave, then did an about-face and walked to the chest of drawers. He picked up his Timex and slid it onto his wrist. "This thing just keeps on a tickin'," he chuckled to himself. Bobby picked up Josh's ball cap, also on the chest, and turned towards his brother.

"Josh, you need a new cap. Why don't you buy one? This thing's gettin' awful cruddy lookin'."

"You know why I don't want another ball cap," Josh lashed out from the bed.

"I know, I know," Bobby held up his hands. "I know Dad bought you this right before he left for France. I didn't say you had to throw it away. If I were you, I'd buy another hat to wear and save this one for special occasions, so it will last longer. That's what I'd do."

Josh responded by turning onto his side, his back to his brother.

Bobby got the message and left the room.

Josh listened as the rest of the family loaded into Mom's old car and drove off to church. The house became totally quiet. Josh didn't even hear Sinbad whining because he'd been left alone. He's probably already gone back to sleep Josh figured, as he laid his arm across his forehead. He sighed deeply and wished he'd gotten out of bed and went to church with his family.

# 6

It took Josh two trips to haul the baseball equipment from his trunk to the field. "If Bobby was here instead of out eating with Maundi and her parents, I wouldn't have to make this second trip," he grouched to himself. "Oh well, I guess the extra walk won't hurt me."

Josh pulled the team's half-dozen bats from the army duffel and leaned them, knob up, along the fencing by the opening of the dugout. Leaving the bag on the ground, Josh examined each wooden bat for signs of cracks or splinters. All appeared to be okay except for a well-used big-barreled model. On it, he found the beginnings of a dangerous vein. "Dadgummit," he exclaimed. "Wouldn't you know it, my favorite bat, the bat that smacked eleven homers last year is busted. We'll definitely have to replace it, or I won't be able to hit worth nothin'." Josh walked back to the duffel bag and placed the damaged bat into the olive-green bag, clasping it shut. He didn't want anyone inadvertently using the broken bat during practice; it might splinter in their hands. He then hoisted the light bag to his shoulder and walked into the dugout, placing the duffel next to the bench.

Josh turned to leave the dugout then glanced at the old army duffel sitting on the concrete slab floor. He read the name 'Braun' stenciled near the top and misty memories of his father crept back to him. Josh stood frozen, his eyes locked on the stenciled name as he fought to remember his dad. He inhaled deeply and exhaled slowly, frustration showing on his brow. He rubbed his forehead squeezing the creases as if it would reinvigorate the memory part of his brain. Why did he have so much trouble remembering his father? He'd been fourteen when his dad died. He should be able to recall more. Of course, he remembered exactly *what* he looked like. Mom proudly displayed their wedding photo in the living room, as well as numerous framed pictures throughout their small house showing their dad in his railroad attire or leisure clothes. She kept a picture of him in his military uniform, the last photograph he'd ever taken, on her nightstand next to her bed. No, his likeness came easily. The things that seemed to be vanishing were the things that couldn't be captured by a lens.

Like the way he spoke.

Josh rubbed his forehead harder in his struggle to remember. It angered him that what only a year ago would have come so easily, so naturally, was now slipping from him like the grasp of the rope in a losing tug-of-war game. Josh knew that his dad had a deep, slow way of speaking, the way most Oklahomans spoke. It wasn't really a drawl like in the Deep South, nor was it Texan, but close, more like Texas-light. He remembered that his dad liked to tell jokes, but the only one Josh could think of was the one about what do you call a pretty girl in Kansas? -- a tourist.

However, Josh could vividly remember his father's smile. His dad had a large open-mouth smile, and he wasn't ashamed to laugh. He made no attempt to be sophisticated or urbane. If something struck him as funny, everyone in the room knew it. John Braun enjoyed life. He liked his job as an engineer for Frisco, and he loved his family. He was also a devout churchman and took his family three times a week to services. Josh remembered his dad getting in front of the congregation once, and giving a testimony about how God had blessed him.

Would he think himself blessed now? Now that he was dead and buried in a foreign country?

Josh sighed. Knowing his dad, he would say 'yes'. If John Braun could rise from the grave and give a speech, Josh had no doubt that his father would say he was proud to have given his life for his country. Glad that it had been him who'd gone to war instead of his children. Proud to be an American soldier standing up for what was right.

Josh left the dugout and reached for the small canvas bag holding the baseballs lying on the grass. He felt better. His anger drifted away. Because, even if such things as his father's voice and mannerisms were getting more difficult to recall, he still knew what kind of man his father had been. And even if he had been only a corporal, he had been a hero. His father had fought for his country, for his family.

Josh carefully examined each baseball and threw out a couple as being too worn and frayed to use. He mentally decided they'd need at least two-dozen new balls to get through the season. Last year, the team had gone through three-dozen, but Josh firmly believed they could get by with a dozen less this year. *Besides,* he ruminated, *if they ran out they could take up a collection and buy a few more.*

The distinct sound of a baseball smacking into a fence caught Josh's attention. He walked toward the sound and saw, through the trees of the adjacent park, a tall Negro man pitching to a backstop.

Josh watched for several minutes as the lanky black man zipped fastball after fastball into the square fencing. Josh was impressed. The man knew how to pitch. His windup was fluid and effortless. He had a high leg-kick and pushed off hard with his planted leg. Someone had taught this man the art of pitching, and he had mastered it well.

Josh watched a few more throws and estimated the Negro to be chunking the pill around eighty-five miles per hour, maybe a little faster.

An idea came to Josh.

He quickly made his way from the diamond, over the footbridge, and through the shade trees until he stood parallel to the pitcher. A pudgy woman in a red flowery dress lounged in front of him on a colorful quilt. A little boy stood beside her urging his father on with oohs and aahs at his daddy's skill.

Josh, not really knowing how to begin, decided to be bold. He strode forward and stood beside the young boy, who couldn't have been more than four or five.

* * * * *

The sun flitted through the leaves of the majestic elm trees creating a zig-zag pattern of light and dark on the prone man's white dress shirt. The relaxing man had discarded his lemon-colored tie practically as soon as he'd crossed the church threshold into the bright noon sunshine. The tie now lay stretched across the back of his car's front seat. Artemis Macintosh pulled his legs up into a V-position and rested his right ankle on his left knee. His bare foot looked odd sticking out from the cuffed brown, flannel slacks. He wiggled his toes and spread them to allow the fresh breeze to float more easily through the gaps.

"Shoo-wee! Them babies stink! I told you to put some powder in your shoes this morning."

Artemis tilted his head back and looked up at his wife, who cradled his head in her lap. Their son, lying on the quilt beside his father, also with his shoes and socks off, giggled like a teen-aged girl on her first date.

"I took a bath right before I got dressed. And you know I hate the way that powder smells. If I do say so myself, I think my stinky feet smell better than that foot powder. What do you think Satchy?"

Satchel Macintosh, who'd raised his legs mimicking his father, twisted his sockless foot towards his nose and inhaled as if smelling a prize-winning rose. "Smell's okay to me," he laughed.

Artemis patted his son's chest and laughed with him.

Claire shook her head at her husband and son as she ran her fingers through Artemis's curls. She recognized several maverick gray hairs but decided to say nothing. No sense in reminding her husband that in addition to having smelly feet, he was also getting old. She pinched one of the tell-tale locks and yanked it from his scalp.

"Ouch!" Artemis complained. "I'd kinda like to keep all my hair. It's thin enough without you harrowing it."

Claire patted her husband's head like a schoolmarm does an upset student. She ran her finger across the top of his ear and traced the outline of his smooth jaw. He grasped her finger and placed it against his mouth kissing it several times before releasing it. Claire bent down and lightly kissed Artemis's forehead.

"I'm glad we decided to have a picnic today. And, I hate to say it, I'm glad Mom and Dad went over to Aunt Rosie's for Sunday dinner. It's so nice out here. I wish we could stay here forever."

Artemis didn"t reply. He lay contentedly on his wife's lap, reveling in her attentions and dreaming of how lucky he was to be with her.

"Daddy, play ball with me."

Artemis's mind wandered to five years earlier and the night he and Claire had married. They'd been married in a small Kansas City church by a crusty, old AME preacher in an outdated 1920s pinstripe vest and suit. The miniscule, snorting reverend sported a bushy white mustache and white prickly hair that circled his black dome as if a horseshoe had been laid atop it. Artemis inwardly grinned, remembering that the old codger had demanded his five dollars before performing the wedding.

"Daddy, I want to play catch. Can we?"

Artemis also remembered Betty, the pastor's wife. She was a kindly, matronly lookin' lady who had stood for Claire during the ceremony. Of course, Satch stood in for him. Good old Satchel. Ornery, loveable Satchel. Despite pitching a full nine innings that day and because the fans insisted, pitching the last inning of the second game (Artemis's game), he'd taken the bride and groom out to eat at Louie's barbeque and given them twenty dollars for champagne and a nice motel. He'd even paid Reverend Jackson for the ceremony. "It was the least he could do," he'd said with a wink, "but to pay for the wedding of the second-best pitcher in the entire world." Artemis thought about his old friend, now playing up in St. Louis in the Majors; an aging man trying to strike out players half his age. He was but a shadow of his old self. There was no way he could play much longer. It was too bad America hadn't seen the great Leroy "Satchel" Paige in his prime. Too bad they'd denied him the opportunity to show the world he was the best. He would have rewritten the record books.

"Daddy . . . Come on, play with me."

Artemis's head bounced as Claire shook her legs. "Get up, lazy bones and play with your son. You're not supposed to sleep at a picnic; you're supposed to have fun."

"Sleeping is fun," Artemis mumbled, rising to his feet. He stretched as if he'd been asleep for several hours, then helped Satchy put on his mitt. Artemis picked up his glove and the bucket of balls he'd brought and father and son walked a few paces to a small chain-link backstop. Artemis placed little Satchel in front of the barrier and gave him a quick review on how to catch a thrown baseball. Placing himself only about a dozen feet from his son, Artemis put his mitt on his left hand and pounded the palm with his fist. It felt good. It felt as if it belonged, as natural as putting on your pants. Artemis reached into the bucket, grasped the top sphere, and tossed it over-handed to his son.

The ball flew past the reaching boy's mitt.

"That's okay, Son. You'll get the next one. Remember, let the ball come to you, don't jab at it."

A second ball whizzed past the open mitt.

"Artemis, why don't you pitch the ball underhanded? At least till he gets used to catching it?"

Artemis paused and looked at his wife. His first inclination was to reprove her for wanting him to pitch to his son like he was a sissy boy. However, looking at his beautiful wife sitting on the blue and gold quilt her mother had given them for Christmas, softened his initial response. He found it hard to snap at his wife and always had. "Honey, don't you understand if he's gonna be a player someday, he's got to learn to catch the ball properly."

"I know," she agreed. "You need to be careful, though."

Artemis tossed another ball to his son. He missed it, too.

The game of catch went on for several minutes and every now and then Satchel caught one in his mitt.

After a few more minutes, the boy began to nab most of the throws and appeared to be gaining confidence. Artemis believed his son was making great progress. It was the best game of catch the two had ever had.

"I'm tired. I'm gonna quit." With that, the boy trotted over to his mother and flopped down on the quilt. He removed his glove and handed it to his mom.

Artemis stood, arms akimbo, looking at his son. "Well, I'll be," he shook his head. "Just when we was makin' progress."

"Let's see if you've got anything left, old man," Claire challenged.

"Yeah, Daddy, pitch the ball," Satchel chimed in.

Artemis stood silent several moments. Slowly, the corners of his mouth began to turn upwards. He picked up the half-empty bucket and walked to the backstop where he began retrieving the baseballs. Satchel joined his father and the two of them quickly filled the bucket.

"Satchel, stand over to the side. Your mother would kill me if you got hit with a wild pitch." Artemis motioned his son away from the screen. The boy obeyed.

Artemis walked to where he guessed was the right distance from the backstop and placed his hand around the first baseball in the bucket, a dark, worn, tattered thing; a ball most players would have long ago tossed into the trash. Not him. Besides not being able to afford new ones, these balls and the bucket had been given to him by his pitching mate when he'd joined the Monarchs many years ago. Naturally, the giver had told him with a straight face, he needed to practice with them every day if he wanted to even approach the expertise of himself. The great Paige had then picked up one of the balls, perhaps this very one,

Artemis mused, and shown him how to throw his famous two-hump blooper. No, he would never throw any of *these* balls away.

The pitcher smacked the ball into the webbing of his glove three times and bent forward as if getting the sign from Josh Gibson. He went into his full-arm windup and let fly with a fastball. The ball clanged against the backstop. Satchel ran and retrieved the ball for his dad.

"Thanks, Satchy, but you don't need to do that. I've got a whole bucket of balls. You just stand over there and watch."

The boy eagerly nodded and returned to his place in front of the quilt and his mother. Artemis rotated his arm clockwise, then counter-clockwise checking for pain. There was none. His arm felt fine. This brought a smile to his lips. *I've still got it.* He twisted his head both directions and placed his fingers on the frayed seams of the ball.

Artemis let fly with ball after ball, he and Satchel picking them up only when he'd emptied the bucket. Although, there was little doubt in his mind, he'd lost a little zip on his fastball, his curve and change-up still looked good. He was quite pleased with himself and despite his arm muscles beginning to feel like warm jelly, there was no pain. Yes, he could still do it.

In his euphoria, Artemis did not notice the young white man watching him pitch from afar. Nor did he pay any attention to the stocky, dark-haired man when he approached for a closer look.

\* \* \* \* \*

"Are you sure you want me to play for you?" Artemis asked for the third time, disbelief still prominent on his face.

Josh sighed. He pushed his smile up even more. "Like I said, I need a pitcher and you more than fit the bill."

Artemis scratched his chin, reached down to Satchy and began playing with the boy's ear. Satchy pulled away. "It's just that I ain't never played with white boys before. Played against 'em many a time but never been with 'em. Are you sure?"

"I need a ballplayer and I'd really like you to join our team. By the way, where'd you learn to pitch like that?"

Artemis shrugged. "Nobody really taught me. I learned when I was little by watching the older boys play. Then when I started playing for a living, Satchel helped me out a lot."

Josh's face lit up. "You wouldn't be meaning Satchel Paige would you?"

"Nobody but," Artemis agreed. "He's my friend. My boy here's named after him."

Josh stood speechless. His mouth opened so wide a June bug family could have flown in and taken up residence. "Well, I'll be," he finally muttered. "You played for the Monarchs, unbelievable!"

"And my wife kept the books for the team." Artemis and Satchy turned towards Claire; he stuck out his hand, palm up, by way of introduction.

"Proud to meet you ma'am," Josh stuttered. "Is it okay with you if your husband plays ball with us?"

"I don't know. He's got a full-time job at the school; he's a janitor at Webster High School and there's a lot of work around the house."

"That's no problem," Josh interrupted. "We practice on Sundays and only play on Saturday afternoons. Uh . . . sometimes we play on Friday nights too, but not very often. In fact, today's our first practice of the season."

Claire Macintosh examined the young white man in front of her as if he were on auction. He seemed nice enough and he didn't appear to be a racist. She then looked at her husband and inwardly chuckled. He was chomping at the bit. He wanted to play ball with this team in the worst way. He still wasn't done with baseball.

"I guess it's okay with me as long as there's not any traveling involved. Artemis's got a family to take care of."

"Oh, no. No traveling at all, unless you count going to Broken Arrow and Coweta as traveling, and they're only a few miles away."

Claire laughed out loud. "Broken Arrow and Coweta will be okay."

Josh smiled at Artemis. Artemis grinned back. The two men and boy picked up the strewn baseballs and walked together through the elms to the practice field.

\* \* \* \* \*

Cameron parked the Buick on the far side of the parking lot under a leafy tree. He opened the trunk and lifted shiny metal cleats from a new Converse shoebox, and plopped down on the gravel surface to get ready for practice.

Francine briefly watched her boyfriend who was all decked out in a new pair of white baseball pants and blue Jayhawker T-shirt. He removed his pristine-white tennis shoes from his feet and deliberately placed them in the now-empty shoebox. She bored quickly and nonchalantly sauntered to the other side of the car.

The baseball field was located on the south side of the heavily treed park. A long rectangular red brick building, probably a school, could be seen through the leafy trees on the north end of the park. Between the baseball diamond and the school was a vast grove of large oak and elm trees that provided shade for scores of families eating their picnic lunch and enjoying the beautiful spring day.

Francine's eyes flitted to the entrance of the park and the old wooden sign tilted on a splintered post. Reed Park. She'd never been here before today. She'd never heard of Reed Park. The grounds of the park were rather shabby, but the trees were pretty. Directly behind the baseball field flowed a narrow, gurgling creek that looked as clean as the brook that ran by her house. A small wooded hill jutted south of the outfield fence giving the fans in the bleachers the sense of coziness and comfort. There was no denying the natural beauty of this Westside city park.

Francine walked to the creek and looked for any sign of fish in the clear water. She spied a couple of yellow perch darting in and out of the rocks that lined the creek bed. She strolled along the bank, stopping every few steps to look at the water below, and came to an ancient wooden footbridge. The simple structure spanned the ten or twelve-foot chasm with wide planks that looked like they'd been milled sometime prior to statehood. A flimsy handrail constructed of two-by-four pine lumber was the only protection from falling off the edge. The bridge didn't look safe, but no sooner had her brain warned caution than two racing kids barreled across the structure in a game of tag. Francine had to step back as first a young boy and then an older, bigger girl streaked by.

"Excuse me," yelled the girl as she zipped by a startled Francine.

"At least they've got a semblance of manners over here," Francine said to the bridge.

She turned away and headed for the diamond. In the distance, already on the outfield grass, Cameron sat stretching his legs for the initial workout. Francine scanned the ballpark and saw that it was in about the same shape as the sign and the bridge. Old. Worn-out. And not maintained very well.

Why don't these people take better care of their parks? She questioned. Their homes look okay. At least they keep their lawns mowed and houses painted. She didn't know what the insides of these cracker-box houses looked like and had no desire to find out. Francine snuffled. They were probably cluttered and the living-room walls plastered with dozens of photos of their uncountable children. No, she didn't care to visit any Westsiders.

Francine abruptly stopped at the entrance of the ballpark. It suddenly occurred to her that Reed Park was a city park -- a Tulsa city park. The City of Tulsa should be maintaining the park. Just like they maintained the parks on her side of town.

She trudged up the bleachers to the corner of the top riser. She wasn't tired. Not physically, anyway. She sat her purse beside her and with her hand clasped onto the side rail, gingerly leaning back against the top brace. Francine liked to sit at the top mainly for this reason, so she could lean back and relax.

The players slowly streamed into the park. Young men dressed in worn baseball togs, their bats slung over their shoulders, gloves stuffed into the back of their pants or hanging from their wooden bats. A few ballplayers wore khakis instead of woolens, and most of the men wore nothing more than a white cotton shirt for their top. The prevalent color of cap was blue although a couple, including Cameron, had on red. One player, the man Francine had met at the amusement park, wore a navy-blue cap with a red bill. The team even had a Negro player among them. Francine watched the black man a few moments and sensed that he felt uneasy around his teammates.

A short black woman with a youngster in tow sat down on the first riser, not noticing anyone sitting above her. Francine sat quietly and watched the little boy pretend he was a great baseball pitcher. He stood in front of his mother and wound up like he was Bob Feller or Hal Newhouser and let fly with an imaginary fastball. The boy even doubled as the umpire calling every pitch a 'strike!'

Francine decided to do it. She stood and made her way down the creaky planks of the bleacher. The woman heard her coming and craned her neck at the approaching visitor. The little pitcher stopped his motion in mid-windup and joined his mother in staring.

"Hi, you two. Care if I join you?"

"Oh no," the woman sounded perplexed. "By all means, have a seat." The mother scooted towards the end of the riser and patted the place she'd left. "My name's Claire and this here's my boy, Satchel." The black woman held out her hand.

Francine took the proffered hand and then shook the boy's hand as well.

"I'm Francine. My boyfriend plays on the team. That's him in the red cap out there in the outfield shagging flies." Francine pointed to a group of six or seven players catching fungos hit to them by the man she'd met the night before.

"My man's pitching over there," Claire pointed at Artemis, dropped her hand, and tittered. "I guess it's pretty obvious who my husband is."

With that remark, Francine immediately knew she liked this woman sitting beside her. It wasn't so much what the black woman had said, but how she'd said it. This was a woman at ease with herself and her race. She had joked about her husband's uniqueness without a hint of self-denigration or inferiority.

Francine sat beside Claire for the next thirty minutes as the team went through a snappy infield practice ran by the blue-capped man as if he were a Major League manager preparing his team for the World Series. He barked instructions at the players and constantly instructed them when they did something that didn't suit him. The amazing thing, to Francine at least, was that the other players listened and did not buck him. He was definitely their leader; they accepted it and did their best to please him.

Francine chatted with her new friend while they watched the team. Both she and Claire were surprised at how good the team was. Francine figured she was going to witness a bunch of has-beens trying to relive their high school glory, but nothing was further from the truth. These men could play. She wasn't so sure they weren't better than Cameron's college squad. In fact, she was pretty sure they were.

Batting practice started, and the pace of the workout slowed. Cameron batted first. Claire's husband pitched to him, throwing nothing but medium-speed fastballs down the center of the plate. Cameron stung the ball well, hitting several out of the park. The stocky player/coach appeared pleased. He spoke with Cameron after his turn, patting his back after the short conversation. Cameron retrieved his mitt from the bench, flashed Francine a wink, and loped to the outfield to shag balls.

The coach ambled to the dugout and shuffled through the row of bats looking for a suitable one. Francine watched him, wondering why he didn't already know which bat he would use. All the good players she'd ever known had a special bat they used each time they swung. *Maybe he left his bat at home,* Francine thought. *Or maybe he can coach but can't play. The latter was probably the case.*

"Hey man, did you lose your bat?" she quipped.

The man in the navy and red cap, Francine could now see that it was a St. Louis Cardinals cap, turned to her.

When the black-haired man glared at her, Francine immediately remembered his name. *'Josh.' Boy, did he look upset. He must still be angry with me for last night,* she thought. This did not deter her.

"Your team looks pretty good for a first practice. Your second baseman moves well and the third-sacker's got a good wing."

He grunted.

Francine continued, a plastic smile plastered on her face, "Yeah, you guys aren't nearly as bad as I expected. You might actually win a game or two."

She forced her mouth to stay upturned as the man's face and neck turned crimson. He swallowed twice, spit once, and inhaled as if he were about to blow up a giant balloon. He slowly calmed himself. She could tell he didn't want her to know how upset she'd made him. Too late.

"Thank you, Frannie," he stuttered. "I appreciate any and all input from *fans.*" He emphatically emphasized the last word and drew it out as if it were spelled with three vowels.

Josh grabbed the nearest bat and strode towards home plate.

"My goodness," Claire said. "I'd say that young man doesn't like you. Uh-uh, he doesn't like you at all. What'd you ever do to him?"

Francine heard Claire speaking to her. She didn't reply but kept her eyes and fake smile on the dark-headed man settling himself in the batter's box. If she'd known Claire better she would have quickly bet her a buck that the good-lookin' muscular guy about to take batting practice would glance back at her before the first pitch.

And she would have won that bet.

\* \* \* \* \*

"Can we count on you? I think you'd fit in well with the team, and I can guarantee you plenty of pitching time, although you have to understand that you'd be our number two. Bobby's our ace."

Bobby was glad to hear his brother tell the new pitcher he was still the ace. He plopped onto the grass in front of the dugout and tossed his cleats into the open gym bag. He picked up his right tennis shoe and tried to slide it onto his foot. There was a knot in the laces. Great. He pulled his legs up Indian-style and began fiddling with the knot. Boy was he tired. He'd thrown to the last six batters, and his arm felt it. Even though he was only chunking the biscuit half speed, he could tell he hadn't thrown as much as he should have the past couple of weeks. Ah well, it wouldn't take that much to get his arm in shape. He wasn't worried. He'd be ready by opening night.

Josh finished talking with the new player and joined Bobby on the ground.

"I think we've got ourselves another good pitcher, little brother. What do you think about that?"

Bobby tilted his head up at his brother, wiped sweat from his forehead, and returned his attention to the shoelace problem. "It's fine with me. I know I can't pitch every game and with Ray not playing this year, we had to get somebody. Do you think it'll be okay with the guys?"

Bobby again glanced at his brother. "You know, seeing as how our new pitcher is kinda dark and all?"

Josh looked genuinely hurt. He furrowed his brow as he wet his lips. "To be honest, I was a little concerned at first. But the guys all seemed to take to him pretty well. I saw Luke and Denver joking around with him during batting practice."

"Yeah, I guess he's okay with me too. I don't much care one way or the other. Right now, I'm just tired." Bobby succeeded in undoing the knot. He jammed his foot into the shoe and quickly tied the laces. "You do know who he is don't you?"

Josh nodded energetically. "His name's Artemis Macintosh and he played sixteen years in the Negro Leagues, the last seven with the Monarchs. He throws a pretty good fastball, a decent change-up, and one wicked twelve-to-six curve."

Bobby paused in midair, holding his left shoe inches from his toes. His mouth hung open like a baby waiting for his mother to spoon-feed him. He blinked. "Are you kidding me! That's amazing. All I was going to tell you is, he's also the janitor at Webster. They hired him after Christmas break when Roscoe Polite quit. Wow! He played for the Monarchs!"

"So, who cares about his day job," Josh chuckled. "I only care whether or not he can chunk the cowhide, and after watching him today I'd say he more than passes the test."

Bobby and Josh sprang from the grass, their exhaustion a thing of the past. Bobby picked up his gear and helped Josh bag up the bats. Together they headed out the gate.

"Hey, Josh? Got a second?" The steely voice came from behind. The brothers stopped and turned. Cameron, their other new player, caught up with them. His girlfriend, without so much as acknowledging they were alive, marched past them on her way to the parking lot.

"Hey Cameron," Bobby offered. "You looked good today. Glad to have you on the team."

Cameron acted as if he hadn't heard Bobby's compliments. He stood in front of Josh, catching and holding his eyes.

"I like the team, Josh. But, I'm not sure I want to play with somebody like *him*. You didn't tell me anything about darkies being on the team when we met."

Bobby could see his brother's jaw tighten. His eyes narrowed. "I didn't think it would matter to a ballplayer, especially a college man.

We needed another pitcher, and that's what Artemis is. Did you see him pitch? He's good. He's a former professional player."

"Yeah, I heard," snorted Cameron. "He played in the blackie leagues, which is about like playing high school ball all your life."

Josh sat his bags on the sidewalk and stepped towards Cameron. He had to look up into Cameron's eyes, but it was obvious he did not fear the taller man. The new player quickly stepped back. "Listen, Cameron. You're a good player and we need you to play shortstop for us, but you're not going to tell us who is and isn't gonna be on the team. Furthermore, I've seen several Negro League games and the brand of ball they play is about as close to the Majors as you can get."

Cameron stepped back another step. He held up his hands as if surrendering and snickered. "Hey man, I was just trying to warn you that the darkie's going to cause problems. That's all. I'll give it a try, but don't be surprised if you don't lose your team over that coon."

Cameron brushed past the brothers and strode to his car. His girlfriend leaned against the Buick, arms crossed.

Bobby chuckled at his seething brother. "You handled that well. I thought you were about to pop him."

"Believe me, I thought about it." Josh picked up the team's equipment. "Why can't we just have a team and play ball? I guess I don't understand this world."

Bobby laughed out loud. "Josh, that's because you only see things in terms of a bat and a ball. There's a whole lot more out there, you know."

Josh sighed. "Maybe you're right, Bobby. Oh, I know you're right. But, I think I'll keep living in my fantasy world as long as I can."

# 7

Cora checked her wristwatch hoping she wasn't too early. She hated waiting on the city bus, but it was far better than driving her worn-out car to work, especially when she had to go across the river. Her watch read 3:14. "Good grief," she muttered. "The darn thing's broken, again." Cora twisted the stem back and forth in a vain effort to revive the ancient Timex. She raised the timepiece to her ear, listened to the stillness, and then shook it, as if expecting the springs and rotors to magically burst into frenzied activity. Cora slid the watch from her wrist and placed the broken apparatus into her sweater pocket, changed her mind, and put the Timex back on her arm.

She glanced down Quanah Avenue searching for the big white bus. Nothing in sight. Not even a car. She pulled her sweater close around her, more for security than warmth. It wasn't cold. The morning was cool, but not exceptionally so. The sun had been up for over thirty minutes, and she could already tell that the late May day was going to be warm, the temperature probably in the mid-eighties. Cora leaned her shoulder against the bus stop pole and grumbled within herself about the lack of a bench for riders to sit on while waiting for the usually late city bus. All the bus stops on the other side of the river had benches, at least all the ones she'd waited at; so why didn't the Westside have any? She tossed the complaint from her mind. It wasn't worth thinking about. Instead, she straightened up and inhaled deeply. The crisp, sweet-smelling, fresh morning air rushed into her lungs and triggered a great big yawn, which

Cora executed with outstretched arms and a loud "ahh" as if she were in front of her bathroom mirror. In another hour this same air would smell like rubber, hot tar and exhaust fumes. However, this early in the morning it was almost like being in the middle of a meadow – almost.

"It's a nice morning, isn't it?" quipped an approaching man, a grin the size of Texas plastered across his not unhandsome face.

Cora, jolted from her pastoral dreaming, physically jumped from the sound of the man's voice.

"I'm sorry, Cora. I didn't mean to startle you," his smile growing exponentially.

"That's okay. I needed a good jolt to wake me up." Cora tried to remember the man's name, but couldn't. He obviously knew hers. She had seen him many times before, had spoken to him on several occasions. No name came to her.

The man, dressed in an off-the-rack J. C. Penney's gray wool suit with matching vest, checked his pocket watch. He pulled the golden orb from his vest pocket and held it so that the gold-plated back was exposed for Cora to see. She had seen the watch before, many times. It was a nice timepiece, no doubt expensive, but it also looked old, probably a family heirloom. She still could not remember his name.

"The bus should've been here two minutes ago. If it's running on schedule," he added.

"Then we've got, at least, another three or four minutes to wait," Cora complained. "In seven years of riding, I don't think it's been on schedule more than a handful of times."

The tall, gray-haired man sidled up next to her and leisurely reached above her and grasped the pole. The piquant scent of *Aqua Velva* attacked Cora's senses. She didn't necessarily find the aftershave disagreeable, but, nevertheless, she quietly slid to the other side of the pole, away from him.

The man inched closer, sliding his arm down the pole until it rested near Cora's shoulder.

"It's a beautiful morning, don't you think? And I hope you don't think I'm out of line, but I think you look quite fetching today." The man's mouth opened wide exposing a set of coffee and tobacco stained teeth in an effort at an all-out smile.

"Uh, thanks," Cora stammered. She instinctively glanced at the man's left hand and saw that it contained no wedding band. But, it didn't matter. She knew he was married. The white strip of flesh where the ring had been, probably less than ten minutes earlier, destroyed his ruse.

The next few minutes proved uneventful. The married man said little else to her. Upon entering the huge public vehicle, Cora worried that he might follow and attempt to sit beside her. But God was with her. She found an unoccupied aisle seat next to a crumpled, white-haired Hispanic woman, a woman Cora knew to be a domestic, like herself. The man, without even a glance, moved past her and sat far in the back.

Cora and the older woman exchanged perfunctory smiles, but said nothing. The woman pulled a skein of lemony yarn from a large vinyl bag snuggled on the floor in front of her and began knitting what looked to be an afghan in its primordial stage. Cora opened her small handbag and removed her paperback. She opened the worn book via the paper bookmark and began reading, but today the words were mere letters, the sentences meaningless and unmemorable. She replaced the bookmark and clamped the pages shut.

Cora ran her tongue over her lips, inhaled deeply and closed her eyes. She knew that men considered her pretty. She realized that some men were going to gape and ogle her. And she understood that once they found out she was a widow, they would attempt conversation, attempt to find out if she were interested in beginning anew after seven years of being alone.

She wasn't.

She still loved her husband. She still loved John Braun. Loved him as much today as when she last saw him that cold, dripping October evening of 1943 when he got on the airplane to fly to New York and the awaiting ship that would take him to Europe and his death.

Of course, she got lonely. Who didn't? Perhaps, some day she would find another husband, someone who would love her and her headstrong brood. A man interested not simply in money or carnal pleasures, but in church, in God. Churchmen, in these modern times, were difficult to find. Almost impossible. But, for now, she had her kids. Josh, her young man who'd given up so much for the family; Bobby, who was the first ever to graduate high school; Sarah, wanting desperately to be a woman and trying to help her mother with everything; and Jonda, little unruly Jonda, the baby of the family, not yet seven years old. Named after her father and born on the day of his death, the day he was struck down fighting Hitler's legions on the beaches of faraway France, although, Jonda did not know this terrible fact.

Cora had to walk the last five blocks to the Lamberson's house. She didn't mind. Walking to the Lamberson's was one of her favorite things to do. The hilly streets were lined with broad sidewalks and canopied by towering maples, elms and oaks that supplied the pedestrian not only shade, but a sense of protection, a sense of calm security. Cora enjoyed looking up at the leafy giants. She loved watching the feisty squirrels scamper from branch to branch, their tangy chatter filling the air.

She crossed the front yard and walked to the back. The Lambersons hid their extra key under a glazed swan. Cora entered the kitchen area and immediately smelled the lingering aroma of alcohol. "They must have entertained last night," she whispered to herself.

Cora shuffled into the living room and began picking up the empty bottles of wine and half-full goblets. She made three trips to the kitchen before she'd removed them all. She returned to the parlor and systematically straightened the cushions of the easy chairs and divan. She paused. She'd heard a noise. She stood still for several seconds until she heard it again. It came from upstairs. Someone was running water.

Cora continued straightening the living room. Mrs. Lamberson normally went to the beauty salon on Monday morning, but today she must have been too "under-the-weather" to go. The Lambersons were in their late fifties. He was an overweight, overpaid oil executive, while Mrs. Lamberson was a contented homemaker. Cora had seen Mr. Lamberson only a dozen or so times in the four years she'd been employed by the couple, which was fine with her. He was a leering old man with a dirty mouth, not the kind of person she liked to be around. Mrs. Lamberson, on the other hand, was pleasant, if not a little on the chatty side. She did a lot of charity work, which made her feel good about herself, and she loved telling Cora about the things she'd done for the less fortunate.

"I thought I heard someone down here."

For the second time that morning, Cora jumped. She whirled and faced the booming voice. Mr. Lamberson, dressed in a black and ivory, double-breasted pinstriped suit, stood at the top of the staircase, a mischievous look in his eyes.

The heavyset man tramped down the stairs like a Clydesdale pulling a beer wagon and strode across the parquet floor towards an obviously nervous Cora. Cora nearly shouted the first thing that entered her mind.

"How's Mrs. Lamberson, today? Will she be down soon? Would you two like something to eat?"

"No, no, I've got to get to work and Mrs. Lamberson is at the fix-her-up shop. Seems she got her hair a little disarrayed last night, you see." Mr. Lamberson winked at Cora, belly laughed, and patted her shoulder lightly.

Cora instinctively backed away from her boss, but did manage a forced laugh at his attempted joke. She reached down to the polished wood flooring and picked up an imaginary dust bunny. When she straightened, Mr. Lamberson was retrieving his briefcase from under the coat rack and headed for the front door.

"Have a nice day, Mr. Lamberson," Cora stuttered.

The big man waved his hand in an arc at his servant, grabbed the brass doorknob, and opened the door. He paused before exiting and despite not wanting to, Cora found herself looking at him. He opened his mouth; his lips curled. "You know, I bet it's been a long time since you've had your hair disarrayed, hasn't it?"

Cora's eyes bulged. She felt her face redden.

Mr. Lamberson chuckled at his bold wittiness and closed the door behind him on his way to work.

Cora, her heart beating like the Kentucky Derby winner, frantically cleaned the Lamberson's estate, praying for guidance the entire time.

\* \* \* \* \*

The traffic light seemed stuck on red. Francine had been standing, not so patiently, at the corner of Fifth and Boston Avenue for an hour. Or, at least, that's what it seemed like to her. She was on her way back to her dad's law office in the Mid-Continent building after delivering still another packet of who knows what to the courthouse. It was the first day of her summer job. It wasn't even noon yet and already she was bored working for her dad. She was ready for lunch.

She was a "runner." That was the job description. It was her job to take large manila envelopes bulging with papers and sometimes entire boxes, unbelievably heavy boxes, of contracts, depositions, lawyer briefs, requests for subpoenas, and who knew what else to the county courthouse or federal building over on Denver Avenue.

At least she was being well paid. She was earning seventy cents an hour, which was more than most of the full-time secretaries and definitely more than the other three runners, even the college guy who was on his third summer of employment with Bartley, Lancaster, Dubois, and Fitzsimmons.

Francine led a mob of coiffed professionals across the intersection and scurried into the Mid-Continent building. She rode the crowded elevator to the twenty-ninth floor, chatting with Sam, the operator, the entire trip. She'd known Sam her entire life, or at least it seemed that way. She couldn't remember when Sam had not been the operator of elevator number one.

Once off the elevator, Francine quickly surveyed the vast room like a solitary gazelle looking for tell-tale signs of a lion. Not seeing Mr. Levy, she speed-walked to the cloakroom and retrieved her purse. The instant before she re-entered elevator number one, she turned and informed Jan, the secretary, that she was going to lunch.

She was actually going to break up with her boyfriend.

She'd come to this decision the night before. As to why, she still wasn't totally sure. There was little doubt that a big part of it had to do with him playing baseball this summer and playing with a bunch of Westside losers. She really didn't want to spend every weekend and the fourth of July holiday sitting on splintery bleachers at various God-forsaken parks watching grown men throw and hit a ball like they were still twelve years old. She also didn't like the idea of Cameron giving up his goal of studying law for the chimera of a baseball career. It had hit her like a crowbar across the face that if Cameron were signed to a professional contract this summer, which was what he wanted, he would be giving up college. Instead of going to classes and studying for a lucrative career, he would spend the next several years tramping around the bush leagues making just enough money to keep from starving, hoping for that elusive chance of playing in the big leagues. No. That wasn't for her.

Francine stopped suddenly. She found herself at the entrance of Jim's Coney Island. She didn't even remember crossing Boston or Main Street. She steeled herself before entering, knowing she would have to be strong. Determined that she couldn't let him sweet-talk her out of what she'd come to do.

The scrumptious scent of chili and onions drifted into her nostrils. She inhaled deeply. She loved eating at Jim's Coney Island. They made the best chili dogs this side of the real Coney Island. She could eat three of the stubby hot dogs easily, and did when she was with her friends or dad. But anytime she was with Cameron, she always ordered only one. That was another thing. Today, in front of Cameron, she would order three coneys slathered with mustard and beef chili and topped with melted cheese and red onions -- and a big bag of potato chips, to boot.

Determined, she entered the small restaurant. Cameron, wearing khaki pants and a short-sleeved navy pullover that exposed his muscular biceps, was waiting for her at the counter. The young man casually turned to his girlfriend, tossed back his blue-black hair like an Arabian stallion, and, instantly and completely, captured her with his ultramarine eyes.

"I'm having three coneys, today," he said. "How many you want, Cutie Pie?"

Francine gazed longingly into her boyfriend's eyes, and the world around her disappeared. She could not hear the jostling of people getting up or sitting down or the clattering of the kitchen help as they busily cooked and cleaned. The buzz of lunchtime conversation diffused into nothing as if she'd suddenly gone deaf. The enticing smell of roasting wieners and simmering chili had no effect. As far as Francine was concerned, she was totally alone. Alone with only Cameron visible in front of her.

"Oh, me? I'll only have one. That's all I ever get."

\* \* \* \* \*

Josh audibly moaned as he pulled into the driveway and parked his Chrysler behind his mother's rusty Chevy because, parked next to her worn-out vehicle sat Pastor Alex's shiny, 1948 green Plymouth. Mom had obviously invited the preacher for supper.

Josh wearily climbed out of the Chrysler and slammed the car door hard, his way of expressing disapproval of the company. He jammed the keys into his pants pocket, turned and smacked into a rushing Jonda. She bounced backwards into the chain-link fence then sprang forwards into him. She dug her head into his stomach and wrapped her thin arms around his belt line.

"I'm so glad you're home, Josh. Sarah's tryin' to make me help her clean up the bedroom, and it's not my turn."

"Sometimes, little one, we have to do things we don't want to do or we think are unfair. I'm sorry, but that's just the way things are." Josh patted Jonda's head like she was a puppy dog excited to see him.

Jonda lifted her head upwards, her chin resting on Josh's abdomen. "But it's not fair. I dusted and swept the room last time."

Josh bent down and kissed the top of his sister's head. "I know. Try to help Sarah this time. I'm sure she's only doing what Mom told her to do. It looks like tonight's going to be a not-too-fun night," he added.

"Amen to that! I'm havin' to work when I'm not supposed to," Jonda emphatically stated. "Oh, I forgot to tell ya. Bro. Alex is eatin' with us tonight. We been waitin' to start till you got home."

"I know, Jonda. I know." Josh took his sister by the hand and together they walked into the house.

Little was said during the meal. The preacher had brought a ham, which Josh's mother cooked with fresh pineapples. They also had fried potatoes, sweet peas, and coconut pie for dessert. It was the best meal Josh, or any of them, had eaten since Christmas.

Sarah volunteered herself and Jonda to clear the dishes, so that the adults, as she put it, could visit in the living room. Josh was the first to leave the table, with Bobby hard on his heels. Josh hurried into the family room and plopped into the recliner before Bobby could claim it, even though it was Bobby's turn to sit in it. Instead of arguing, Bobby wordlessly breezed through the room and went out onto the porch letting the screen door slam. Josh opened his mouth to chide his brother for flinging the screen, but changed his mind. He decided not to risk a brouhaha.

Brother Alex ambled into the room, followed by Cora. The pastor sat at the end of the Braun's couch, while Cora detoured and went to the water cooler and turned it off before joining him on the divan. Josh wished she hadn't turned off the cooler. However, he understood why. It made too much noise for polite conversation, but the night was warm and the last thing he wanted to do was break a sweat in his own house.

Josh laced his fingers behind his head and leaned back in the overstuffed chair. He noticed his mother was sitting rather close to the preacher, too close if you asked him. Their legs were touching. There was plenty of room on the couch. Why *was* she sitting so close to him? Josh felt uneasy.

Jonda, squealing excitedly, and followed by a taciturn Sarah, raced into the room and leaped onto Josh's lap. Sarah, saying nothing, continued outside.

"Cora," Brother Alex spoke up. "That was as fine a meal as I've ever enjoyed. Thank you so much for cooking on your night off from the diner."

Instead of directly answering the pastor, Josh's mother looked at him. "Josh, Brother Alex bought the food for tonight's meal. Wasn't that nice of him?"

Josh fidgeted in his chair. Jonda reciprocated by wiggling her bottom. "Yeah, Pastor, that was nice. Thanks for the ham."

"He bought more than just the ham, Josh," Cora, with a hint of defensiveness in her voice, said. "He supplied everything: the potatoes, peas, and all the ingredients for the pie, including the flour for the crust."

"Uh, thanks again. That was sure nice of you."

The preacher waved his hand as if he did this sort of thing all the time, and to think nothing of it. Brother Alex had been their pastor for many years, even before their dad had died. In fact, John Braun and Pastor Alex Thomas had been close friends. Josh's dad had been one of the preacher's deacons. Before Mrs. Thomas had died of cancer the same year as their father's death, many a Sunday afternoon had been spent at the pastor's house eating fried chicken, mashed potatoes, and cole slaw, and playing outside with Jeff and Susan, the preacher's kids.

Jeff and Susan were both in Missouri going to college and, Josh guessed, Brother Alex was only missing a home-cooked meal. Josh concluded that that was all there was to this evening.

"Josh, how are things going at the railroad? Your mom tells me you're still coaching and playing baseball? How's the team going to be?"

"The railroad's fine Brother Alex and I think we've got a chance to have our best team ever. We've picked up a crackerjack shortstop, and I found another pitcher to help Bobby out. He's a little on the old side, but he's still got good stuff."

"Speaking of baseball, are you still dreaming of someday making it a career? The railroad's a mighty fine place to work, you know."

"Oh, I know," Josh calmly answered. "The railroad's a great place to work. But, I've always had my heart set on being a ballplayer."

Brother Alex turned to Cora, who smiled at him as if encouraging him to continue. He turned back to Josh. "Young man, I love baseball as much as the next person. It's our national pastime, but sometimes you have to face reality. Sometimes you have to ask God what His will is. Josh, how is your relationship with God? I haven't seen you at church much lately. Is there anything I can help you with?"

"Josh is coming in three weeks, when the junior choir sings," Jonda interrupted. "At least he promised me he would."

"I'll be there," Josh patted Jonda's leg.

"Great!" exclaimed Brother Alex. "It will be good to see you in church, Josh." He again glanced at Mrs. Braun before returning his attention to Josh. "Have you ever thought about going to night school and finishing up your education and maybe even getting into management with the railroad?"

Josh eyed the preacher intently then looked over at his mom. She sat with her hands clasped smiling at him. He looked back at the preacher. "I can't do that right now. I'm committed to the baseball team."

"And I understand that. But, next year you might seriously think about your future. Someday you'll want to get married and have a home.

A railroad manager makes a considerable bigger income than a common brakeman. Plus, it's mainly indoor work and not so hard on the body. It's a sad part of life, but no less a true part, Josh, that we must all eventually put things like baseball behind us and go on with our lives."

Josh rose from the chair. Jonda slid down his leg and scrambled into the recliner. Josh's eyes locked onto the pastor. He said in even, unhurried tones, "Brother Alex, I know you mean well, and you may even be right. But, right now I'm not ready to give up baseball. Right now, baseball *is* my life. I don't expect you to understand this, or you either Mother," Josh glanced at his mom, then refocused on the pastor. "It's the one thing I look forward to every day. It's the main thing that keeps me going. I know it sounds silly, but when I'm listening to KMOX and the Cardinals are playing the Cubs or the Dodgers, it's as if I'm there. It's like I'm actually at Sportsman's Park crouched behind home plate or really at Wrigley Field, or looking at the red brick of Ebbets Field while I swing a bat in the on-deck circle."

"Oh, I know it's a dream and a dream that may never come true. But, it's my dream and right now I've got to do everything in my power to fulfill it. If I don't, I won't be able to live with myself. That's why I have to keep playing baseball. That's why I have to keep trying. It's who I am. I'm a baseball player."

Josh inhaled slowly waiting for the pastor or his mother to respond. They did not. Brother Alex slid back on the couch and rubbed his chin with his index and middle fingers. Josh's mom looked away towards the kitchen.

Jonda bolted upright in her chair. "I think you're a good baseball player, Josh. I know 'cause I've seen you play a buncha times. You're the best hind catcher on the team."

Josh pivoted towards his little sister. She sat in the recliner, her small limbs draped over the cushioned arms like a grownup sitting in a giant's chair. She looked up at him as if he were a god and she, a supplicant. Josh relaxed.

"Thanks Sissy, that means a lot to me." He mussed her hair, which she obviously disliked, and walked out of the house onto the porch.

\* \* \* \* \*

The breeze had picked up considerably since Bobby had come outside. The May air, quite warm during sunlight hours, cooled rapidly once the sun dipped over the horizon. Bobby wished he was wearing a jacket, but he definitely did not want to go inside and fetch one. Sarah had joined him on the porch swing and, of course, she'd been smart enough to bring a sweater. She sat quietly next to him with her turquoise sweater draped over her shoulders examining the myriad stars of the eastern sky.

"Boy, Brother Alex sure is giving Josh a lecture and a half, isn't he?"

Sarah answered her brother without taking her eyes off the twinkling constellations. "Yeah, I wish he'd leave Josh alone. Josh is doing fine. I think Mom put him up to it."

Bobby tilted his head quizzically. "Ya think so? Why would she do that? Josh never misses work, and he'd give her more money than he already does if she'd let him. Josh is weird, but he does the best he can."

Sarah giggled. "Josh is not weird. You just say that because you don't love baseball the way he does. And I think Mom wanted Brother Alex to talk with him because she's worried."

"Worried?" Bobby gasped. "About what? Is she afraid he's going to die and go to Hell?"

Sarah batted Bobby on the arm. "No silly, that's not it. Josh is a Christian. He's a little backslidden right now, is all. What Mom's worried about is that if he doesn't get another chance at playing baseball, he's going to go nuts."

Bobby nodded. "Josh is definitely crazy about baseball. That's for sure. I like it too; it's a fun game, but not like him. That's all he ever talks about. We had an argument the other day about who was better, Joe DiMaggio or Ted Williams. When I said Williams was the best player in the game I thought he was going to lose it. He told me I didn't know a whit about baseball if I thought Ted Williams was better than Joe DiMaggio. Williams was the better hitter, he conceded, but DiMaggio was the better all-around player. He was about to go haywire over the whole thing.

"Then I made the ultimate mistake."

"Uh, Oh! What'd you say?" Sarah turned towards her brother.

"I told him I didn't care who was better. I told him, if the truth be known, Duke Snider was better than either of them. That really set him off."

"What'd he do then? He didn't hit you, did he?"

"No, nothin' like that. He merely shook his head and beat his chest with his fist and told me that was what was wrong with me -- I didn't have any heart for the game."

"He said all that simply because you disagreed with him on who was a better player, Williams or DiMaggio?"

"Yep. Now do you think he's not crazy?"

"I guess I'm glad Brother Alex is trying to talk some sense into him, then," Sarah said.

Bobby agreed. "Josh had his chance. It wasn't his fault Dad got killed in the war. Baseball just wasn't in the cards for him. He's got to move on with his life. Heck, he doesn't even have a girlfriend and isn't smart enough to see it when one's attracted to him."

"What do you mean, Bobby?" Sarah asked.

The screen door flew open and out walked Josh.

Bobby and Sarah watched their older brother pace the length of the porch several times. Neither said a word. Bobby reached into his shirt pocket and removed a solitary cigarette and a book of matches. He placed the cigarette in the corner of his mouth and lit up. Josh stopped directly in front of him.

"What in the world are you doing?" Josh whined at his brother as if he were taking arsenic. "We're depending on you to be our main pitcher, and you're out here destroying what little stamina you have." Josh snapped the lighted cigarette from Bobby's mouth, threw it onto the porch, and squished it with the sole of his shoe like it was a venomous black widow spider. "Real ballplayers don't smoke. That's what gangsters and hoodlums do. Ballplayers chew."

Bobby jumped to his feet, his face the color of a racing fire truck. "Maybe I'm not a *real* ballplayer, whatever that is. Maybe, like most people, I play the game for fun, something to do instead of going bowling or a movie on Saturday nights."

Josh looked totally nonplussed. His mouth hung open and his pupils dilated into blackened orbs as if he'd just walked out of a haunted house on Halloween night.

Bobby silently watched as his brother tried to collect himself. Josh blinked several times, closed his mouth, and breathed heavily through his nose. He pulled his lips inwards until a slight smacking noise escaped. He jammed his hands into his front pockets. Thinking himself composed, he responded in a shaky, breaking voice. "Bobby, you don't know what you're saying. You're one of the best pitching prospects in Oklahoma. If you don't get signed by a scout this summer, I'll be shocked."

Josh stepped back from his brother, glanced at the concrete porch before resuming, "You're a lot better than me, Bobby. You're the kind of player I've only dreamed about being. You've got the gift. All you need is to work at it. Bobby, don't throw away your gift. Most guys would do anything to have your talent." Josh looked down again at the porch and whispered, "I know I would . . ."

Bobby gaped at his brother. Sometimes, he forgot how much taller he was than his older sibling. The two stood silent for several seconds, neither blinking. Bobby did not like how Josh had softened the disagreement.

"Josh," Bobby began. "You know I like baseball. It's the greatest game ever invented. But, to be honest with you, I'm more interested in life. I'm trying to think about my future, what I'll be doing in ten, fifteen years. Good grief, Josh, you're so narrow minded about a silly game that you can't even see when a girl's sweet on you."

Josh blinked as he adjusted his weight from his right to his left foot.

"I'm talking about Francine, you big goof. She's got a crush on you. Haven't you noticed?"

Bobby could see his brother's jaw tighten. Josh shouted a string of uncharacteristic curse words, twirled and stomped towards the screen door past his mother and the preacher, who'd come onto the porch for some fresh air. Cora and Brother Alex stood silently, stunned looks on both their faces.

\* \* \* \* \*

Evenings were never completely quiet. At least, not the way people who live in the country claim. In the city, there was always noise coming from somewhere. It might be a lone car sputtering down the street, clanking and rattling as if it were falling apart every time a wheel crunched into a neglected pothole. It might be a faraway whistle announcing lunchtime for the night shift at one of the refineries. Or, if it was an especially calm night, it might be the sound of boxcars coupling and uncoupling in the distant rail yard. If these mechanical disturbances were absent, there would still be something breaking the solitude. The noise might be as simple as a solitary tree branch rustled by a light breeze slapping against the siding of the house.

Cora lay in bed on the screened-in back porch that doubled as her bedroom; the covers pulled up to her chin. She wanted desperately to sleep. She had a full day of work ahead of her tomorrow, but her mind refused to rest.

Just thinking of Josh on the front porch blowing up at Bobby over nothing more than an innocent observation thrust itself again to the forefront of her thoughts. The funny thing was she really wasn't all that upset over the crude language Josh hurled at Bobby in front of Sarah.

Yes, she was embarrassed at his loss of control, especially since Brother Alex was present when it happened, and she was concerned about Josh's loss of interest in attending church. Nevertheless, Josh was a Christian. He would get back in church. She felt sure of that. He would not reject his upbringing. All her children were good kids. She was proud of each of them. The more she thought about her children the less concerned she was. They were going to be all right.

She closed her eyes expecting instant sleep. When it did not immediately come she opened her eyes and gazed into the darkness. Thoughts of her children did not return. Nor, she finally realized, were they the true cause of her sleeplessness. The image of her husband returned once again. He stood before her, young and smiling, in his khaki uniform showing her the new corporal stripes on his sleeves. It was the day of his departure to Europe, the last time she would ever see him alive or dead. He looked so handsome in his uniform and so proud.

There was a widow, two blocks over on Olympia, who was bitter to the point of anger over her husband's death. She claimed America had no right to attack Germany because it was the Japanese who'd attacked Pearl Harbor, not the Germans. In her opinion, America should have minded its own business when it came to the war in Europe and instead, should have focused all its energies on defeating Japan, then her husband would still be alive.

Cora didn't know much about politics, but she did know that the war against the Nazis was right. If America had not gotten involved, Hitler might still be alive and killing even millions more. It had crushed her when the soldiers arrived at her front door with the telegram informing her of John's death, but she truly believed, as did her husband, that what he was doing was right. America simply *had* to stop Hitler.

A tear swept down her cheek. Cora thought about her husband's grave. A grave she'd never visited. John Braun was buried alongside many other soldiers in faraway France. The army had given her a photo of his tombstone and a gold star to hang in the parlor window, which she did until 1946. And all this was nice of them, but she yearned to go there herself. She silently prayed that someday she would have enough money to make the trip. She wanted nothing more than to walk where her husband had walked, breathe the air that he'd breathed, to be able to put flowers on his grave.

Cora turned onto her side. The photo of her husband still sat on the edge of the nightstand as it had for almost seven years. She looked at it for the ten-thousandth time. She missed him so. The pain of losing him still had not lessened after so many years. Instead, her sorrow was joined by yet another pain; loneliness. This, too, bothered Cora. Because, despite her undying love for her husband, she realized that she missed the company of a man. And it wasn't so much a romantic or carnal sensation. It was much more pedantic. She missed having someone to talk with at night, someone to share her problems with. Someone to laugh with. Someone to come home to her.

Cora slid her hand from the comfort of the sheet and reached toward the nightstand. She removed the framed photo of her husband and, in the dark, held it close to her eyes. She rolled onto her back and embraced the photo to her breast as if it were a soft, cuddly teddy bear. She closed her eyes and quickly fell asleep.

# 8

Francine had never before had to wait outside her father's office with the secretary. She'd always walked right in. But this time, when she announced to Meg, her dad's long-time private secretary, that she was heading into his office, the stylishly dressed, fortyish woman motioned for her to stop. It seemed her dad was in the middle of an important meeting with a prospective hire and couldn't be disturbed.

So Francine plopped into the leather upright across from Meg Stanley and waited. The first five minutes she leafed through various law journals and political magazines lying on the oblong table beside her. Then she spent several minutes trying to get Meg to converse about her husband, her kids, the weather, President Truman, Clark Gable, Randolph Scott, Gary Cooper, the new Fords, the new Chevys, indoor plants, outdoor flowers, the paint on the walls, you name it. No luck. Meg Stanley wanted to work, not talk. Giving up, Francine sat quietly and tried to think about what she would say to her father.

She hoped she wasn't overstepping her boundaries, but she simply couldn't keep quiet. Her dad was a good man. He was a boss, a partner. Surely, he could do something. Surely, he would understand how wrong it was.

Francine was upset about Claire. Claire, the receptionist. Claire, the wife of the tall pitcher. Claire, the Negress with the small son. She wasn't upset with Claire, she was upset *about* Claire. Her job, to be more succinct.

Francine had seen the receptionist as soon as she reported for work. She immediately recognized the black lady from the baseball practice. She went right up to the woman and reintroduced herself and the two took up right where they'd left off, only this time they seemed even more at ease with each other.

About halfway through their initial conversation, Francine remembered that yesterday Claire had told her she had a college degree in accounting from some school in Kansas City. Naturally, Francine, who'd never been known for her subtlety, wanted to know why Claire was working as a receptionist instead of in her field?

After Claire told her that this was the only job she'd been able to land thus far, Francine found herself getting angry. She left Claire and tried to do her job as a runner, but the idea of a college grad sitting behind a receptionist's desk grated on her sense of justice the entire day. She got to wondering if her father knew what was happening in his own law firm?

A skinny man in a dark blue suit slinked from her dad's office. Francine pegged him for a recent graduate, probably from one of the public law schools. He didn't have that look-at-me-I'm-a-stallion-attitude. So, when he passed her, still not looking up, she figured he didn't get the position.

"Hi Dad," Francine plopped into the over-stuffed leather chair in front of her father's expansive antique desk.

"Hi Baby," Mr. Fitzsimmons responded, sitting down in his black leather chair. "Hang on just a sec." He swiveled around in the chair, pulled open a drawer to a filing cabinet, and stuck a manila folder into it. He clanked it shut, spun back around, and folded his hands in front of him as if he were about to recite the rosary. He smiled at his daughter. "What's up, Francine? How's the summer job going?"

"Fine, Daddy. And by the look on that young fella's face that just left, I'd say a whole lot better than his."

Mr. Fitzsimmons nodded understanding. "I hate dashing a young man's hopes, but he wasn't right for the position."

"What was up? Did he make bad grades in Contracts and Torts or what?"

Mr. Fitzsimmons took a deep breath. It was almost as if he were exhausted over the ordeal. He sat there for over a minute in deep thought like he was Siddhartha Gautama meditating under the Bo tree. He unclasped and clasped his hands several times. His eyes seemed to be examining the grain of his desk. Francine, more than a little surprised at her father's reticence, sat quietly not moving a muscle, not even when her nose started itching. Finally, he raised his head and tried to act as if nothing was bothering him. Francine quickly scratched her nose.

"No Francine, that wasn't the problem. The boy was highly qualified. In fact, he finished number two in his class. He came across as competent and very capable."

"Then why didn't you hire him? You've been saying for months that the firm needed a couple more attorneys to handle the Warren contract. Was he a communist? A fellow traveler?"

Mr. Fitzsimmons chuckled. "No Francine, nothing like that. He wasn't a communist or a supporter of Marx. The problem was his background. Where he was from."

Francine squinched her brows at her father, but he was pretty sure she knew what he was getting at. Just in case, he decided to explain:

"You see, Honey, this firm represents some of the wealthiest and most influential citizens of Tulsa. We also have as our clients many of the top-echelon companies and businesses in the region. It takes a special attorney to not only guide them legally, but to mesh with them socially. You know how many cocktail parties and get-togethers your mother and I attend on a regular basis. We do this as much for business as for pleasure, although your mother does enjoy them immensely."

"The young man who just left was from Sapulpa. His father runs a shoe repair shop and his mother works at the ceramic factory, probably making dinner plates and ashtrays. There is no way a boy from that background could fit in with our clientele. He would not be accepted. Ergo, it would make us look bad for hiring him. I'm sorry, but things are starting to pick up since the war, and I can't afford to take a chance on an over-achieving local. Do you understand? I'd like to hire him, I simply can't."

Francine remained quiet a few moments. She wanted badly to speak with him about Claire. But was Claire any different than the skinny guy? She too didn't fit the mold of Bartley, Lancaster, Dubois, and Fitzsimmons. But, then again, an accountant wouldn't be dealing with clients the way a lawyer did. Most of the time, they would be conversing with clients through the mail or, every now and then, on the phone. There would be no need for an accountant to attend dinner parties with clients. That was the attorney's job. She really felt bad for the skinny guy, but she completely understood. Her dad's firm was high-profile and it couldn't afford to take a chance on a Westside wannabe. However, she felt Claire's case was completely different. She understood that now was probably the worst time or the best time to talk with her Dad about Claire. Like she'd planned while waiting with Meg, she plunged her fork into the center of the meat.

"Dad, I don't know if you're aware of this, but you've got a college graduate working the welcome desk. And her degree's in accounting. I've heard you say many times that good accountants are hard to come by. Why isn't Claire Macintosh in accounting where she belongs?"

Mr. Fitzsimmons was taken aback. His jaw slid downward until he sat there like an infant waiting for the airplane of oatmeal to land in his mouth.

Francine, not liking the silent pause, continued: "You probably didn't know anything about it. I can tell you didn't. Knowing you Dad," Francine faked a laugh, "you probably haven't even noticed the new receptionist. Anyway, she's the real pretty black lady; the one who carries herself like she was of royal African blood or the daughter of the Liberian ambassador." Francine had no earthly idea why she'd made this last comment other than that she wanted her father to realize Claire was something special. She knew she had to sell Claire to her Dad. She had to make him like her and want to promote her into the accounting department.

Mr. Fitzsimmons leaned back in his chair, lacing his fingers behind his head. A softness emerged on his face. "Francine, I'm sure your new friend is a competent bookkeeper. And I'm sure she's a nice lady. But again, we are running a very visible firm here, and we must be extremely cautious how the public perceives us. If we were to place a Negress in an important position, what would our clients think? And believe me, they would find out. It's not like we're an Eastern law firm that glories in its liberalism. This is Oklahoma. We have to be more circumspect."

Francine interrupted. "Dad, I understand that. But sometimes you have to do what's right and forget about what a bunch of Neanderthals think."

"Uh, those Neanderthals pay our salary. Besides, Claire is black. Blacks don't expect to hold the same positions as whites, especially in an all-white law firm. Listen Honey, I personally like Negroes, but we can't change society. We can't change Oklahoma. Things are the way they are. Have been for a hundred years and will be for the next hundred. Heck, most people around here are still grousing about the riot of '21 and that was thirty years ago. Perhaps in a year or so when people accept Miss Claire, we might give her a go in accounting. How's that sound?" Mr. Fitzsimmons sounded excited and flashed a daddy-knows-best look at his daughter.

Francine was stunned. She'd never heard her father speak this way; never heard him talk about Negroes as if they were second-class people, as if they were less human than whites. Anger gushed through her. She felt her cheeks grow hot. She stood and faced her Father.

Upon standing, Francine suddenly felt her anger dissipate. In its place sadness entered and seeped through her, coursing down her chest and out to her arms and legs until she felt utterly tired, totally defeated. Her father rose from his chair and silently faced his daughter for several seconds. Mr. Fitzsimmons could tell his little girl was not happy. The smile faded from his lips.

"Daddy, I've always been proud of you and everything you've done. I love that you're an attorney, and I know Mom does too. I've always looked at you as the greatest father a girl could ever have. But after today, I'll be looking at you through different eyes. Daddy, I think I just grew up. I don't think I'm a kid anymore and I'm pretty sad about it too."

Francine turned from her Father and walked to the door, the image of his crestfallen face vivid in her mind. He seemed to have aged right before her. She reached for the doorknob of antique brass.

"Francine, Francine," her father practically shouted, consternation evident in his voice.

She stopped and pivoted towards her father.

He pulled his bottom lip inwards and clamped it with his teeth. His eyes narrowed. They narrowed, but not in anger. This was the way her dad concentrated when he was trying to come to a tough decision.

Mr. Fitzsimmons rubbed his mouth with his hand, scratched the back of his head with the same hand. He nodded at his daughter giving her, not an actual smile, but a look of genuine approval and agreement. "Young lady, I think you may be right. I'm going to take a look at Claire Macintosh's credentials and see if we need her in the accounting department." He paused. "Kiddo, you *have* grown up, and I think I like what I see." Now, he really did smile.

Francine's eyes filled with tears of joy. She wanted to pump her fist in the air. She'd won! She'd actually convinced her father to change his mind. She nodded at her dad and left the room. It took every bit of will power she had not to shout hallelujah in front of Meg Stanley, who was busy typing away.

# 9

When you maneuver up the gravel drive to Howard Park, the first thing you notice is not the baseball field. Your eyes are not swept to the coziness of a small city park with the customary wooden bleachers surrounding the chain-link fencing of the playing surface. Nor do you pay much attention to the brilliant green Bermuda outfield inundated with clumps of seedling dandelions swaying in the spring breeze ready to spread their golden flowers wherever the wind wills. No, the first thing you notice is the shady pecan orchard stretching between the park and Quanah Avenue. There were around thirty trees on the small plot and they formed an umbrella for summer picnickers, church fellowships, and later for the scores of harvesters, who seemed to know the exact day the first pecan would let go and plop to the ground.

Josh parked his car on the back row of the parking lot adjacent to the right field foul pole. He parked far away from the entrance for one simple reason -- foul balls. He'd seen too many windows shattered and hoods dented to take a chance with his car. Not that his vehicle was anything special, it wasn't. However, he didn't want to be out thirty or forty bucks for a new windshield and he definitely couldn't afford a new fender or hood. He grabbed his cleats and catcher's mitt from the back seat, tossed his keys onto the front floorboard, and headed towards the third base dugout. They were the home team tonight and the home team always sat in the third base dugout. Coming to an abrupt halt, Josh let out a disgusted blast of air, turned, and tromped back to his car. He retrieved his keys from the front floorboard and stomped to the trunk. He opened it and tossed his glove and cleats beside the equipment bags. Mumbling, he lifted the heavy bat bag from the trunk and slung it across his right shoulder. Next, he placed his catcher's bag over his left shoulder. He opened the canvas ball bag lying next to the spare tire and tried to cram his mitt into it. With the glove refusing to go all the way inside, Josh couldn't get the bag closed. In disgust, he grabbed the bag as if it was his hated enemy. The glove stuck out of the bag like a leather ice cream cone, but luckily nothing spilled out. With equipment bags across both shoulders and holding the ball bag and mitt in his left hand, Josh bent down, being careful not to let the bats slip off his shoulder, and using the fingertips of his thumb and first two digits lifted his baseball spikes from the trunk. He shut the trunk with his forehead and again started across the parking lot to the faraway dugout looking like a loaded-down camel clomping along the Silk Road. "Why can't anyone ever get here when I tell them and help me with this stuff!" he muttered, irritation evident in his voice. Josh knew he was suffering from pre-game/pre-season jitters, but he couldn't help it. It seemed like he did *everything* for the Frisco Westsiders.

"Need some help?"

"That's an understatement," Josh answered without looking, knowing who it was by the voice. Josh felt the weight of the bat bag removed from his shoulder. He stuck his arm out sideways and allowed the canvas straps to slide down. He pulled his cleats through the gap, thus freeing himself completely.

"Thanks Artemis. How long you been here? I'm usually the first to show up at the field."

"I'm used to getting to the park early. The Monarchs always had a full batting practice before every game. I pretty much lived at the ballpark back then. Where's your brother? Is he playing tonight or did he have to work?"

"Naw, he'll be here. My mom took off tonight to see the first game of the season, so he's bringing her and my two little sisters. Mom's car ain't too good and you never know when it's gonna break down. Where's your wife and boy?"

"They're coming. Actually, they've already been here. They dropped me off and went to get a sundae at the drug store over in South Haven. My son loves ice cream. I think he could eat it three times a day if we'd let him."

Josh nodded, his mind registering the fact that mother and son had to drive clear to the South Haven drugstore located in "colored" town rather than motoring a few blocks to Crown Drugstore. "Yeah, I've got a sister just like him."

The two men chuckled their agreement.

Josh and Artemis arranged the bats near the opening of the fenced dugout. Josh placed the ball bag outside on the dirt, so the players could grab a ball and play catch. Josh removed the new game ball and tossed it to Artemis.

Artemis caught the white ball barehanded and began vigorously rubbing it with his hands as if he were on the mound preparing to pitch to Joe DiMaggio.

"Bobby's gonna start tonight. But I'll try to get you a couple of innings. Bobby probably can't go the full nine so early in the season. Plus that, you need to throw some to get back into the groove."

Artemis flashed Josh a toothy grin. "You're the coach. Whatever you say is fine with me." He underhanded the ball to Josh, picked up his glove from the bench, and slid the brown, weathered mitt onto his left hand. He smacked the palm several times with his fisted hand making a thudding noise so common and so enjoyable to players across the land. Artemis checked the laces of the glove, tightening a couple with his free hand and teeth.

Enthralled by the ritual going on before him, Josh watched in fascination bordering on amazement as the black man examined every eye and lace, every crease and fold of the ancient mitt. It was a ceremony the pitcher obviously had performed hundreds, if not thousands, of times. A rite Artemis took seriously: the preparation of the glove.

The rest of the team and their opponent slowly trooped in. Bobby was one of the last to arrive, which bothered Josh until he saw the exasperation in his brother's blues. He chose to say nothing. He was pretty sure he knew what had happened: Sarah and her pre-going-out ablutions had once again nearly caused the family to be late. She was fourteen, almost a woman.

Josh played three-way catch with his brother and Artemis. After a short while, both were popping his mitt with each throw. Artemis had good velocity, especially for a pitcher in his late thirties, but Bobby could really bring it. Bobby's throws zinged into his glove, exploding into the leather like a howitzer hitting its target. *Unbelievable*, Josh shook his head. *How can he throw so hard. What a lucky dog!*

The pre-game infield was snappy, and everyone exuded an abundance of early season brio. Artemis took grounders at first base and appeared to be more than adequate for the position. Bobby shagged a few flies in right field, his position when not chunking the cowhide.

Once the game started, Josh finally relaxed. He took his position behind home plate and began flashing signs to his brother as if winter had never occurred. As if they'd played only yesterday.

Bobby mowed down the Liners of Sand Springs like they were Pee-Wee players just learning the game. He struck out the first seven before anyone even got any lumber on his blazing fastball and then it was only a broken-bat roller to the mound. The umpire, a retired mailman who'd once played as high as Double-A ball for the Red Sox, marveled to Josh that Bobby had to be throwing ninety-five, maybe ninety-six or seven. Josh did not disagree.

The Westsiders, beginning in the first inning, worked over the Liner hurler. They scored four runs on a three-run blast by their new shortstop and a solo shot by Josh. They added two more in the third and a single tally in the fifth. Going into the seventh, they were cruising with a 7 to 0 lead. The only bad thing was Artemis. And it wasn't his fault. In three at bats, he'd singled and then been hit with a pitch and walked on four straight inside offerings. Josh was starting to get concerned. He commented to the Sand Springs coach about throwing too close to his first sacker, but the man had replied by snarling and grunting like an angry razorback.

Josh noticed Bobby was tiring as early as the fifth inning. He seemed to have lost a wrinkle on the heater. Josh began signaling for more curves, but Bobby didn't like to throw off-speed. Nor could he throw a curveball well. And he had no change-up whatsoever. Bobby was strictly a here-it-comes-see-if-you-can-hit-it pitcher.

The Liners scored two runs in the seventh inning and with two outs, had runners on second and third. Another hit and they'd be back in the game. The mailman/former bush leaguer/umpire remarked that Bobby's heat was probably down to around eighty-nine or ninety. Josh agreed. He glanced towards the mound. His brother's jersey was soaked. Bobby stood behind the rubber, cap in hand, swabbing his dripping brow with his sleeve. He looked pooped.

Josh called time and trudged to the hill. Halfway there he motioned for Artemis to join them. The rest of the infield, thinking they too were invited, jogged to the mound.

"Good job, Hoss. You looked great tonight. Let's let Artemis finish for you."

A closed-lip Bobby said nothing. He inhaled through his nose as if smelling an especially pungent rose. He exhaled with equal force. Nodding to his brother, Bobby underhanded the ball to Artemis, ambled off the mound and with head down, trudged towards the dugout and the water jug. Several people in the bleachers applauded his performance. Bobby raised his head, smiled at his mother, then winked at his girlfriend.

\* \* \* \* \*

*Maybe I shouldn't have told Josh I'd play with 'em. I really don't belong here. I should've just hung 'em up like I said I was going to. I can't afford to get hurt. I've got a family to feed.* These thoughts and more bombarded Artemis's mind as he toed the rubber for his first warm-up pitch. He raised his hands above his head, brought them together, and lowered them to his chest. He zipped a fastball towards the plate. Josh returned the pitch and signaled for Artemis to practice his curve. He snapped off two pretty good ones then lobbed his change-up toward home plate. He finished his practice tosses with a four-seam fastball, which he liked to use against strong righties. The pitch had a tendency to ride up and in, jamming the batter.

Artemis stood behind the plate rubbing the ball one last time and resining his pitching hand. He surveyed the field making sure his fielders were in place. Next, he glanced at the runners. Both were standing leisurely on their base and would until he touched the pitching rubber.

When he glanced at the third-base runner, he noticed it was the opposing pitcher. He rubbed the ball with more gusto. Boy, how he wished that was the guy at the plate. He'd like to give him some of his own medicine. There was little doubt in his mind that the Liner hurler had been throwing at him -- and throwing at his head. It was one thing to nudge a batter who was crowding the plate, but Artemis never crowded the plate. He liked to stand away from the dish more than most. It allowed him to extend his long arms and get more whip action into his swing.

Artemis turned his attention to the chore at hand. Of course, it was the biggest player on the opposing team, a huge man twirling his bat as if it were a toothpick. His thinking was that the behemoth would take the first pitch so he could get a look at what Artemis had. Josh was thinking the same and Artemis was glad when his catcher signaled for an inside fastball. Artemis went into his stretch and let fly with all his might.

He was right.

The giant let the pitch alone. Strike one.

Next, Artemis wanted to really mess up the batter with his

dipsy-doozy slow ball. He bent down to take the sign. The briefest smile flickered across his face as Josh flashed the signal for the change-up. "Atta boy", mumbled the old pitcher. "Good thinkin'. Let's trick this ogre."

Artemis caught a glimpse of Bobby sitting on the Frisco bench with his black warm-up draped across his shoulders, drinking water from a paper cup. *You need to watch this, young man, because if you had any junk at all, you'd still be out here on this mound.* During the game, Artemis had watched Bobby from first base and been amazed at how hard the boy threw. He didn't throw as fast as ole Satch in his prime, but pretty darn close. And Satchel Paige was the fastest pitcher he'd ever seen, *'ceptn maybe Bobby Feller and even then he wadn't so sure that Satch wadn't a hair faster.* The problem was -- that was all Bobby Braun was. A hard thrower. He wasn't a pitcher. He didn't work the batters. In the third inning, Artemis hinted to the boy that it was just as much fun sneaking a curve or floater past a hitter as it was blowing it by 'em and, plus that, it would save wear and tear on the chicken wing. But the young'en, like most flamethrowers, didn't want to hear it. He was too busy struttin' his stuff.

The burly batter missed Artemis's blooper by a foot. He was so far out in front of it, he could have swung twice.

Artemis threw a fastball next, but chunked it about a foot outside. It was a waste pitch to mess up the hitter's timing and set up the final offering.

Artemis couldn't believe how knowledgeable his catcher was. He wanted to throw his slow curve to finish off the man, and that was exactly what Josh signaled. Artemis decided to throw it from two o'clock instead of high noon and aimed the pitch right at the batter's belt line. Artemis snapped off the pitch, then stood back and watched as the hitter bailed out of the box. The slow-moving twister, headed right for the hitter's pudgy belly, broke perfectly and caught the inside

*Then Sings My Soul*

corner for strike three. The big man pounded his bat into the ground and slinked to the dugout.

Artemis smacked his mitt in satisfaction and loped off the field.

Josh met him on the other side of the chalked line, a huge grin plastered across his face. "That was fun! Let's do it again next inning."

"That's a date," Artemis bubbled, "but first I've got to loosen the lumber. I'm leading off this inning."

\* \* \* \* \*

Bobby sat at the end of the bench and sipped water from a paper cup. Despite knowing in his mind that Josh had done the right thing taking him out, he was nonetheless groused. He didn't like coming out of a game. He was the starter and he should have finished the game. It wasn't like he was behind or anything. Heck, he had a five-run lead. He could have held that lead even if his arm was dead, which it was. He swigged the last of the water and crumpled the waxy paper in his hand. He tossed it at the wide-mouthed trash can at the other end of the bench and missed. Alvin Sedderston, the back-up shortstop, picked up the wadded cup and finished the job. Bobby also didn't like the new guy, the new pitcher, trying to give him lessons on how to pitch. *Who did he think he was, joining the team on Sunday and then trying to coach everybody on Saturday?* Besides, he didn't need a bunch of junk pitches. *Curves and slow stuff were for old guys, pitchers who couldn't bring it anymore.* Bobby scuffed the packed dirt in front of him with his spikes. He grunted. He didn't need some washed-up Negro Leaguer teaching him how to throw a baseball.

"Hey Bobby, did you and Josh have an argument? Is that why he took you out? Are you mad at him? I would be if he took me out. You guys aren't gonna have a fight are you? Momma's here and I don't think she'd like that. She took off work to watch you play, not to watch you and Josh fight."

Bobby turned his head towards his little sister. She stood behind him with her nose sticking through the chain-link dugout and her fingers clutching the metal links. With him sitting and her standing, she was still not at eye-level. He couldn't help but smile. She looked as serious as a lawyer whose client might very well get the electric chair.

"Jonda, you're not supposed to be over here. You know that. You can't bother the players during the game. That's a rule. Now, get back in the stands."

Anyone watching the exchange might have thought the little girl in the pink shorts was deaf. She didn't so much as flinch.

"Momma said you were doing good till you got tired. Are you tired, Bobby? Sarah said you were, but I told her you was just sweatin' cause it's so hot. Are you hot? Hey, I've got a little Dr. Pepper left. You want me to go get my pop? I left it in the bleachers by Sarah and she'd better not drink any. I told her not to."

"For heavens sake, Jonda, get out of here. I'm gonna tan your hide if you don't leave," Bobby exclaimed along with a few choice words he immediately regretted saying.

Jonda gasped. She stepped back from the dugout fence and held her hands over her mouth. Her eyes swelled like she'd seen a haint. "You cussed, Bobby," she muffled. "You took the Lord's name in vain and I'm tellin'." She lowered her hands and pointed at her brother. "It's a good thing Brother Alex didn't hear you say that, or he'd say you're goin' to Hell." Jonda stuck out her lower lip and blew a puff of air into her golden bangs. She turned from her brother and marched righteously to her mother. Bobby shook his head at the antics of his youngest sister. She never ceased to amaze him. She was one of a kind.

He turned his attention to the game and watched as Artemis easily disposed of Sand Springs' top home run hitter. He had to admit that Artemis' trick pitches were effective and fun to watch. But, he's old. That's the only way he can get people out.

Josh was to bat third that inning. Bobby slipped his jacket on and ambled into the third-base coaching box. He'd help his brother out. He didn't mind coaching a base, especially third. He liked flashing the batter the bunt, take, or hit-and-run signal. Mostly, he just stood there and clapped after every pitch.

Artemis stepped to the plate. Bobby urged him to lead things off with a hit. Artemis wagged his bat over the plate and readied himself. The pitcher went into his exaggerated windup and plunked Artemis on the shoulder with the first offering. The lanky man went down.

Bobby took a few steps towards home plate and asked Artemis if he was okay. The Frisco bleachers bellowed their disapproval at the Sand Springs team. Bobby could hear several wives and girlfriends yell that the pitcher had done it on purpose. A cluster of railroad workers yelled for the umpire to kick the pitcher out of the game after that beanball. They also iterated a few things they shouldn't have about the pitcher and his mother.

Rising, Artemis dusted the seat of his pants with his hands and glared at the man on the mound. He nodded to Bobby that he was fine.

Even though the Sand Springs pitcher had plopped Artemis on the shoulder, nothing more would have happened. At least, Bobby didn't think so, if it hadn't been for the catcher. He's the one that really started it.

The stumpy receiver jerked his mask off and tossed it behind him. The wire cage rolled to the foot of the backstop. It leaned on the screening and faced the diamond as if anticipating a raucous melee and wanted a front-row seat. It would not be disappointed.

The stocky catcher jumped in front of Artemis, shielding his pitcher. He eyeballed the tall man and grunted twice before speaking: "Blacky, don't even think about doing anything or you'll be sorry. Take your base and keep your mouth shut."

Bobby, less than ten feet from home plate, yelled at the umpire to take charge of the game. The mailman/former minor league player/now part-time umpire stood there unmoving as if he were paralyzed by a massive stroke or held fast in the grasp of a giant wraith. He would be no help, whatsoever.

Artemis grinned at the shorter man. He had been in situations like this many times before. He'd been nose-to-nose with far bigger, far tougher catchers than the stumpy flattop in front of him. Unlike his nemesis, there was no fear in his eyes. His voice did not quaver. It was strong and had a frolicsome lilt to it as if he were on a weekend lark in the woods with his wife and son. The catcher recognized the fearlessness and it make him angrier and, although he'd never admit it, somewhat afraid.

"Will do," Artemis complied, his grin widening, his eyes boring into the catcher. "It's okay. I do believe yon pitcher bats next inning." Without taking his gaze from the shorter man, he nodded in the direction of the mound. "I'm gonna give him my barber pitch. You think he'll like it?"

Stumpy hissed like an enraged snake. He actually pawed the dirt with his cleated foot in front of Artemis as if he were a desperate bull readying himself for the final charge at the mocking matador. Bobby could tell that the catcher was getting ready to attack. He didn't think Artemis realized how upset the squatty backstop really was. Bobby knew he had to move quickly.

Bobby was only half right. Artemis knew he'd infuriated the opposing team's catcher. He was also pretty sure there was going to be a fight. What he wasn't ready for was the head-down, battering-ram charge of mister flattop. Artemis figured the guy would launch a wild haymaker at him, which he could easily avoid and retaliate with a couple of quick punches to the jaw of the off-balance pugilist. The brawl would be over before it was actually a brawl.

Instead, the rampaging lunatic head-butted Artemis in the solar plexus. With the catcher's square head mashing into his stomach, Artemis shot backwards through the air, his legs and arms splayed in front of his body as if he were some kind of mutant octopus with only four tentacles. Wind whooshed from his diaphragm. He tried to gulp air, but nothing was there. He grabbed the head of the battering ram hoping to stymie the force. He could not. With Stubby-Head still encased in his gut, Artemis crash-landed on home plate. He plopped directly in the center of the white rubber base and scooted across it as if he were purposely cleaning it with his pants. Flattop now began driving him into the ground, his short powerful legs pumping like Detroit pistons specially designed for an expensive sports car.

Bobby joined the fray. He grabbed the catcher's arm and twisted it behind his back flipping the man over and off of Artemis. The short man yelped in pain. With his free hand, he tried to poke Bobby in the eye. Bobby kept twisting until he had Stubby on his back. He then straddled the thick catcher and delivered a short chopping punch to his jaw. Amazingly, the catcher's eyes rolled back in his head and he stopped resisting. Bobby couldn't believe it. He'd knocked the catcher out with one punch! Maybe he should take up boxing. Beside him, Artemis gasped for breath.

Bobby rose to help his pitching partner, but was knocked to the ground. This time by two Sand Springs players. He quickly managed to get one attacker in a headlock. It was their skinny shortstop. Unfortunately, his other opponent, -- he had no idea who it was, but he was ridiculously strong -- had him in a bear hug. The three rolled around on the dirt behind home plate like a sandwich cookie with Bobby acting as the filling. Despite the pleas from the shortstop that his head was about to explode, Bobby refused to let go, mainly because the guy who had a hold of him from behind was about to shatter his ribs. Bobby estimated the three held on to each other in their fanatical death lock for at least thirty minutes. Later he admitted it might have been only a minute or so -- at the most.

# 10

Encircled with an elliptical brand, the intaglio in the center of the bat read "Louisville Slugger." And the thick barrel of the yellowy ash wood read "model P72". The bat was less than a year old and it was cracked. Although the crack was miniscule, it ran from the tip of the club almost to the twin l's of Louisville, which made it worthless. In fact, if you were to try and hit with it, even if you sanded the crack until you could barely see it, the bat would probably break in half or worse, shatter into shards and fly pell-mell into the air like a World War II land mine.

The bat was Josh's and why he hadn't thrown it in the trash was a question he didn't know the answer to. Perhaps it was because he'd gotten the game-winning hit with it against the Lion's Club in last year's playoffs. Or maybe it was because he'd never batted so well until he'd bought the club at Buck's Sporting Goods during their mid-season sale. He no longer used the bat in games. He had a new stick. But for some reason, he'd grabbed it when the brouhaha with the Liners started.

He had absolutely no intention of using it. In fact, he had tossed it aside when he entered the fray and began separating combatants and yelling for everyone to please calm down. It took him, a few ballplayers on both sides, and the two umpires over five minutes to accomplish this task.

Now he stood, leaning on the bat like it was a walking cane, talking with the umpires about their decision regarding the game. The Liner coach glared at him from across the field, arms crossed like a genii and snarling like a wolverine. Neither manager had been allowed to give their two cents. The umpires stated matter of factly that they'd seen the whole thing, discussed it, and were now simply informing the teams of their ruling. Josh wanted to say that if they'd done a little more to stop the "whole thing" rather than watch the "whole thing" there wouldn't have been a fight and thus no need for this meeting. But he didn't.

The umpire's decided that, due to the brawl, the game was over. And since it had gone at least five innings, it would not be replayed. Frisco was awarded a 7 to 2 win. Furthermore, both umpires would be filing a report over the incident with the commissioner. The Liner coach started to protest but was cut off by the home plate umpire. "And," he looked straight at the Sands Springs manager, "we both agree that it was *your* catcher that started the whole thing."

Josh couldn't help it; a smile crept onto his face. He put his hand over his mouth and pretended to cough.

"That's it, boys," the former minor league player/now semi-pro umpire announced. "I'd like to see you two shake, but that's up to you."

Josh lowered his hand to his side and waited to see what his opposite would do.

The man turned and walked away.

Josh shrugged at the umpires. They both shook their heads; the base umpire rolled his eyes. He thought about saying something profound like "you guys made the right decision," but thought better of it. He silently shook their hands and returned to his team who had finished sacking up the equipment and were outside the dugout awaiting the news. As Josh strode to his team, he quickly looked them over and decided they were in pretty good shape, considering. Alvin Seddersten looked the worst. His lower lip was busted and trickling bright-red blood and his left eye was nearly swollen shut. Leon Fetterly had a yellowish knot right in the center of his forehead that reminded Josh of a unicorn trying to sprout a new horn and Bobby's cheek shined red as if he'd been burned. The rest of the boys looked okay. Even Artemis showed no visible signs of the tussle, although his stomach had to be sore after the head-butting he took from the catcher.

The team huddled around Josh as he informed them of the umpire's decision. Several of them let out whoops of delight, but most took the news stoically. Less than thirty seconds later the players were picking up their equipment and joining their wives and girlfriends on the way out of the park.

"Hey, Cameron. Got a sec? We need to talk."

Cameron picked up the blue tote with KU stenciled on the side and slowly, somewhat hesitantly, ambled towards Josh.

Josh nodded at Bobby beside him and the latter instinctively knew his brother wished to talk to Cameron alone. Bobby returned the nod and sauntered towards the dugout and the team's equipment bags. Still within hearing, but far enough away for propriety's sake, he picked up the bat bag, opened the neck, and pretended to count the bats inside.

"What's up, Josh?" the shortstop asked, trying to sound like he had no idea why his coach wanted to see him, examining Josh with a surely-you're-not-going-to-say-something-to-me look.

Josh curled his bottom lip inside and pulled a heavy draught of air through his nose. He crossed his arms.

"We did pretty well tonight; I thought." Cameron spouted. "I was three for three and that home run I walloped would have gone out of any park. I think we can have a real good team."

Josh nodded his head, still thinking. He wanted to say what he had to say exactly right. He wanted whatever came out of his mouth to be perfect. He didn't want his emotions, his anger, to control the output and he didn't want to get into a yelling match with the man before him. However, he wasn't very good at confrontations like this, and he knew it. So, he decided to just say what was on his mind and let, as his dad used to say, "the poop hit the carpet".

"We're a team," he began.

"And, if you ask me, a good one," Cameron interrupted.

Josh waved him off. "Let me say what I've got to say then you can talk." He looked down to regain his thoughts, kicked a loose pebble towards third base. He straightened. "Our *TEAM* was in a fight tonight. Now, I don't condone trying to punch out the competition, but you saw what happened and things got out of control, and *WE* got into a fight."

Cameron nodded, shrugged.

"What I'm saying is that when *WE* got in a fight. *YOU* stayed on the bench. You never came off the bench to either help your teammates or to help me stop the fight. I wanna know why?"

There was a pause.

Josh hoped Cameron was trying to formulate an ideological answer as to his pacifist leanings. Josh hoped that maybe the man before him was a Quaker or a total opponent to war and violence no matter what the situation. He hoped that Cameron had done what he did – or didn't do – because it was contrary to some ethereal principle and he'd promised a dying mother, father, best friend, that he'd never break his vow. That no matter what happened, he would stay true to his word.

It was nothing of the sort.

"As far as I'm concerned, the darkie got what he had comin'. To tell you the truth, I wish they'd hurt him a lot worse. I don't like the black boy and can't stand playing with him. I wouldn't help him if we were in the World Series, and he was pitching a no-hitter against the Yankees." Cameron wrapped his arms across his chest like an angry Buddha, turned his head and spat on the dirt.

Josh could feel his face heating up. He uncrossed his arms and placed them on his hips. He stepped closer to the shortstop and lowered his voice to just above a whisper.

"Artemis is not a darkie or a black boy. He's a teammate. What you're telling me is that you wouldn't help a teammate."

Cameron answered in the same conspiratorial tone. "Call him

whatever you want to, Mr. Frisco Brakeman, but I'm not going to help no darkie ever. As far as I'm concerned, he's not *my* teammate."

Josh beamed at the shortstop. A sharp snicker broke in his throat. "You are absolutely right, Mr. VanDeaver. He's *not* your teammate because you are no longer a part of this team."

Cameron's eyes narrowed. He ran his tongue across his top lip. An impish smirk emerged on his face. "You guys are such losers, such low-class losers!" Cameron shook his head feigning disgust, turned and walked to the gate.

"It's a good thing you're leaving because I'd have no compunction kicking your butt," Josh calmly stated. "Seeing as how you are no longer my teammate."

Cameron hesitated at the gate. He muttered something under his breath and shook his head again. He swung the gate open and walked out. He never looked back.

Bobby walked over to Josh, squeezed his shoulder. "You did the right thing, Brother. We're better off without him. He's not our kind."

Josh nodded. "I hope you're right. He's definitely a jerk. But a jerk who could sure play ball."

\* \* \* \* \*

Francine watched from the passenger seat of the giant Buick as her boyfriend banged on the steering wheel with his forehead and uttered expletives under his breath. She'd never seen his face so red. Not even the time he'd slipped and fallen on the cafeteria tile while approaching the improvised stage and the end of his triumphant stroll in front of two hundred people to accept the "Athlete of the Year" award at Lansing Hall's all-sports banquet. He looked beside himself. In a rage was probably a more apt way to put it. And in a perverse way, Francine was glad. She was glad because his outburst was making it a whole lot easier to finally say what she needed to say. His anger and foul mouth gave her courage.

*Then Sings My Soul*

"Cameron, I need to talk to you."

The handsome ballplayer, his head still resting on the cloth-covered steering wheel, turned towards his girlfriend. Deep crimson pulsated across his cheeks. His nostrils flared. His hands squeezed the wheel as if he wanted to rip it from the dashboard and jam it through the windshield.

"Can you tell that I'd rather *not talk* right now? Because I'm really not in the mood. Can it wait?"

Francine squirmed in her seat. She glanced out of the convertible at the ball field surrounded by the darkening woods. Several people stood around in concentric circles, visiting, leisurely leaving. Her courage waned. She gulped a wad of saliva and air and steadied herself. Her courage seeped back. "I can't help it, Cameron. We've got to talk. I don't think I want to go with you anymore," she blurted.

"What do you mean you don't want to go with me anymore? Are you talking about the ball games? Because we won't be coming back here. In case you haven't figured it out, I quit that stinkin' team."

"No, no. That's not what I mean. What I'm trying to say is that I think you and I should cool it for a while. I think we should see other people."

"Hey!" Cameron yelled. Francine jumped. But he was not looking at her. He was looking past her at an elm tree about ten feet away. "Get away from here, you little pint-sized snoop." Cameron pointed at the shape hovering beyond the tree.

The little girl poked her blonde head from behind the trunk. She stepped away from her protection and pointed at her chest as if to ask "who, me?" She was wearing a white dashiki and straggly pink shorts. Her sneakers looked way too big for her and both they and her ankle socks were covered in a patina of dust as if she'd been running on the infield dirt pretending to be a ball player, which she had. She flashed them several grins. She didn't look, in the least, afraid.

"Whoever you are, go back to whomever you belong. This is a

private conversation. No Munchkins allowed." Francine could tell that Cameron was trying to be civil to the little girl. He was failing badly.

The pig-tailed ragamuffin shrugged her shoulders and held out her arms as if she didn't understand English.

"You heard me. Now, go away." Cameron shooed the girl towards the ball field.

"Mister, I ain't no Munchkin. Munchkins are those short people in the *Wizard of Oz*. They were grown-ups who were little because God made 'em that way. I'm just a girl like Dorothy."

Cameron expelled a whoosh of exasperation. He shooed her with his hands again. "I don't care if you're Dorothy in the flesh, get out of here. We're having a private conversation."

The little girl laughed. "I ain't Dorothy. I got blonde hair and she has dark hair. Besides, I've never even seen a real Munchkin in person. Just at the Cameo Theater. My brother, Bobby, takes me there when he's not with Maundi. That's his girlfriend. Sometimes Josh does too when he's got time."

"Good grief," Cameron exclaimed. "The whole family's after me." He pulled the ballcap from his head and tossed it in the backseat. He wet his fingers and smoothed down an inchoate cowlick on the crown of his head.

Francine had enjoyed the entire exchange. Cameron didn't have a little sister. Let alone an ornery little sister. He couldn't handle it. She decided to defuse the situation.

"Aren't you Jonda?" she asked.

"Yep, that's me," the girl answered, a perkiness exuding from her voice.

"Listen, Jonda. We're trying to have a serious conversation here. Would you mind too terribly if we had it without you listening."

Jonda looked upset. "I wasn't listenin' lady. I was mindin' my own business and lookin' for horny toads. I can't help it if your boyfriend talks so loud. What's that one word he keeps using mean? I ain't never heard it before."

Francine was caught off guard. She had to think for a moment. "Oh . . ." it dawned on her what *that word* was that Jonda was referring to. But before Jonda could clarify what word she was asking about, Francine blurted, "It's no big deal, Jonda. It just means a female dog, that's all. It's nothing bad."

Jonda screwed her face up like she didn't believe it. "That's okay. I'll ask Josh or my momma what it means." Without another word, the little girl turned and skipped away.

Francine turned back to Cameron. "How'd you like to live with that live wire?"

"I wouldn't," Cameron grumbled. "I'd shoot her."

The two sat quietly for several moments. Francine kept her eyes on the dash while Cameron sat watching her. He was the first to break the silence. The anger and rancor had left his voice.

"I thought something was up. I could tell there was something wrong at the hot dog place."

Francine forced herself to look at him. Sadness swept through her. She still didn't understand why she was breaking up, but she was at ease with it. It just seemed right. Only a few days ago she'd been contemplating spending the rest of her life with this man. Now, she was telling him it was over. And she felt good about her decision.

"I'm sorry, Cameron. I wish it didn't have to be this way. I really do."

Cameron's visage abruptly changed. Anger returned. His cheeks flushed red; his eyes boiled. "What do you mean by, 'it didn't have to be this way'?" he hissed. "It's this way because you're breaking up with me. You! Not me!" His voice rose until he was on the verge of screaming.

Francine, not knowing what to do, got out of the car. She didn't think he would have hit her, but she was taking no chances. She closed the door and backed up three steps.

"You need to get hold of yourself," she pleaded. "What's gotten into you?"

"Nothing's wrong with me," he snarled. "I finally see what a witch you really are! He reached for the ignition and started the engine. The big Buick roared as he mashed the accelerator.

"You're not leaving me here, are you?" a wide-eyed Francine shrieked.

"You betcha, Honey. You can hitch a ride home with those river rats over there." He jerked his head in the direction of Josh and his family. "I'm sure they've got room for a Lansing girl in their jalopy." Cameron rammed the gear stick into first, popped the clutch, and peeled out of the gravel parking lot.

Francine watched her former boyfriend's car squall towards the main road, hoping he'd come back and get her, happy when he didn't. After his lights were nothing more than a mirage, she turned towards the diamond. A tall, slender woman approached her.

\* \* \* \* \*

She figured she liked baseball because her husband had loved it so much. It was the first thing he looked for in the morning paper and at night, he was always trying to find a game on the old Victrola. Not any game, mind you. A Cardinals game. The St. Louis Cardinals, that is. Her husband's, and pretty much everybody around Tulsa's favorite team. There were a few locals who liked the Reds, and a few more that favored the Yankees, mainly because they won so much and had Joe DiMaggio, the world's best player, on the team. Even so, if a vote were taken, she knew the result would be overwhelming for the Redbirds.

Cora's husband played semi-pro ball until he was thirty. He would have played longer if his knees would have allowed it. And, with three kids to feed, he didn't want to lose his job with the railroad to play a game.

Now, she wished he'd continued playing, continued squatting behind home plate, continued blocking the precious scuffed white base when a pounding runner lowered his shoulder and barreled into him. Maybe he would have destroyed his knees. Maybe he would have torn them so badly that the army would have rejected him. Maybe they would have said, "thanks, but no thanks," when they examined him for military service. And then, just maybe he would have been with her tonight watching their boys, their young men, play the game of baseball.

"I hate baseball. Why did I have to come tonight? Besides, they didn't finish the game. They were too busy fighting."

"Sarah, I told you this was a family outing. Your brothers like to play ball, and we should support them when we can. I took off work to be with my family tonight. Heaven knows we don't spend enough time together." Cora Braun placed her arm across her daughter's shoulders and pulled her tight. Sarah did not respond. "By the way, where'd Jonda spirit off to?"

Sarah nodded towards the parking lot. "She's out there looking for horny toads. You'd think she was a boy the way she's always huntin' critters."

"I remember a time when you liked turtles and crawdads. I'll never forget when you brought that snapping turtle home you found at the creek. How it didn't bite one of your fingers off is still a mystery to me. It sure was snapping at me when I took it from you." Cora squeezed her daughter again. This time Sarah nudged her mom's shoulder with her head.

"I guess you're right. At least I grew out of it. I don't think Ornery Britches ever will. She looks up to Josh and Bobby too much."

"Oh, I don't know," Cora, said. "She loves pink and you wouldn't catch a boy wearing that color. So there's hope."

Cora turned her attention to Josh. He was talking with the new guy on the team -- the new white guy. She couldn't hear anything that was being said, but she could tell by her son's crossed arms and steeled eyes that it wasn't a friendly chat. The team's other new player, the black man, had exited the gate and was hugging his wife.

Cora had gone out of her way to meet the Negro woman. Her name was Claire. They'd sat together the first four innings. Jonda and her son played leapfrog and a short game of stickball beside the bleachers before Jonda lost interest and slipped under the stands looking for coins. Another woman, a girl actually, also sat with them. Cora couldn't remember her name, but she was the girlfriend of the man her son was presently having a heart-to-heart with. It seemed she already knew Claire. Cora hadn't said much to the young lady. But she and Sarah had conversed freely for several minutes. About what, only they and the Lord knew.

Cora noticed Bobby keeping a close watch on Josh and was thankful. And proud. So, when the meeting was over, and it was apparent the two were not going to exchange blows, Cora, with Sarah beside her, walked to the gate. The black family was leaving. She spoke to them first, "Mr. Macintosh, I'm Cora Braun, Josh's mother. I really appreciate you playing ball with my boys. You're an awfully good pitcher, and you're going to be a great help to the team."

"Call me Artemis, Mrs. Braun. You've got a couple of fine sons." The tall man stuck out his hand and Cora took it. The man's grip was firm, but he did not try to squeeze too hard the way many men did to women.

"Please call me Cora, Artemis. I hate to tell you this, but your boy favors your wife a lot more than he does you." A wisp of a smile crossed her lips.

Artemis nodded, a big grin wafting across his face. "I know he does and I'm mighty proud of the fact. I shore wouldn't want him stuck with a mug like this." He stuck out his chin and wiggled his brows.

Claire Macintosh punched her husband's bicep. "Come on. Get your son. We've got to get home. We haven't eaten supper yet."

The new pitcher and his family headed out the main gate to the parking lot. A little splotch of pink skipped by them, then, as if in a panic, sprinted to her mother. Cora caught the pink blur with both hands and held her at arm's length.

"Stop right there, young lady. The time for running's over. Go help your brothers with the equipment. You can carry the ball bag."

"Momma, Momma, you're not gonna believe what happened," Jonda exclaimed.

"What? Did a horny toad pee on you?" Sarah interrupted.

"No Smarty Pants, that's not what happened." Jonda stuck her tongue out at her sister.

"Would you two stop it," Cora pleaded. "Put your tongue back where it belongs and tell me what happened."

Jonda complied, but not before tossing Sarah an exaggerated squint-eyed stare that was supposed to scare her older sister. She returned her attention to her mother, her eyes wide as chocolate cookies. "There's a mean man out there. He was cussin' and beatin' on his car. He was saying all sorts of bad things. Hey Mom, I know what you call a girl dog now. It's too bad Sinbad's a boy. Momma, is that really what you call a girl dog?"

Cora ran her fingers through her daughter's soft, fine hair. She pursed her lips then ran her tongue over them. "Jonda honey, you don't worry about those words. Jesus doesn't like them so you need to forget you heard them. Okay? Will you do that for me?"

Jonda, obviously still curious, looked down at the ground. "But Momma, I wanna know what it means then I'll forget it. That man called Josh all sorts of cuss words and then that girl got mad and got out of his car, and then he left her standing there." She looked up at her mother. "I don't think he's comin' back, either. He told that girl to get a ride with a bunch of rats."

Cora couldn't help herself. She laughed out loud. Sarah joined her.

"Jonda, you stay here with your sister, and I'll go find out if that young lady needs any help." Cora started for the parking lot. She skidded to a stop, turned, and shook her head at Sarah when she faintly heard Jonda whispering to her sister asking if that's really what you call a girl dog.

She turned back to the lady in distress and headed towards her. However, try as she might, she couldn't stop the smile that kept invading her face.

* * * * *

"Artemis, I really think you should quit."

Artemis looked over at his wife. He did not answer her immediately. For him, this was normal, and she did not press the issue. He would reply in his own time. He smiled ever so slightly hoping she would realize he wasn't angry or put off by her statement. He loved his wife more than anything in the world. The last thing he wished to do was disappoint her. She sat on the opposite side of their old '41 Ford, a car he'd bought with his winnings when the Monarchs defeated the Homestead Grays and won the Negro League World Series in 1942. Little Satchel lay between them; his head rested on his mother's lap. He'd been so proud of the car when he bought it and still felt a strong sentimental attachment. Through the years, it had hauled him and five or six other players all over the country and patiently waited in hundreds of parking lots while he, and his mates played the game of baseball. The once pristine vehicle had a lot of wear and tear. The shiny ebony finish had turned a dull black with several nicks and creases in both doors caused by recklessly opened car doors and flying debris from the myriad dirt and gravel roads the Ford had been down. On the inside, there was no headliner, just the metal roof. And the soft, cushiony seats were worn down to nothing more than cloth-covered springs. It was impossible to sit in the backseat driver's side for any length of time without getting pinched on your bottom by a naked metal coil that randomly sprang through a hole in the cushion. Artemis laughingly had named it "the cobra" because you never knew when it was going to strike. Nevertheless, it bothered him when it got someone.

"Honey, I don't think I should. Not after tonight."

Claire shifted in her seat from her husband's response. Satchel murmured something in his sleep. His mother stroked his cheek and whispered, "there, there. Go back to sleep," until she was satisfied that he had.

"What do you mean not after tonight? That other team was trying to kill you. Don't you realize that?"

"That's one way of looking at it," he quietly answered.

"That's the way I'm looking at it," Claire quickly retorted. "Artemis, you've got a wife and son to think about. We can't have you lying in a hospital bed because some white boy chunked one in your ear."

Artemis grinned at his clearly upset wife. "Claire, I think you underestimate my reflexes and overestimate the opposition."

"This is NOT funny, Mr. Macintosh. You're thirty-eight years old. Don't you think it's time to get on with your life? We're your life now, aren't we? Not baseball. That's your past."

This hit the mark. Artemis's visage drooped. He took his eyes from his wife and studied the road as if he were a novice driver practicing for the licensing exam. Claire knew she'd hurt him.

"I'm sorry, Honey. I just don't want to see you get hurt." She paused. "Artemis, you were one of the best. I love to watch you play ball. That's what attracted me to you. The first game I ever attended, you were pitching. Did I ever tell you that?"

Artemis nodded. He bit his bottom lip as if trying to stay depressed.

"You were so handsome in your red and white uniform. I knew the first time I saw you I could love you."

Artemis glanced at his wife. He winked. "I understand. Who could blame you?"

Claire reached across the seat and swatted her husband on the arm.

"You sound like Satchel, now. I always worried that his vain posturing would rub off on you."

Artemis chuckled. "There's only one Satchel Paige. He was the best. And not only at baseball. I guess that's why he's in the Bigs."

Neither said anything for over a minute. A red light at Quanah and Twenty-Eighth Street caught them where Crown Drug was located. The two watched as a young night clerk turned out the lights and locked the wide front doors. He saw them watching him and nodded. Claire turned to her husband and quietly said, "You were good enough, too. It just wasn't our time."

"I know," Artemis said, sadness permeated his voice.

The light flashed green. The old black car heaved through the intersection.

"Did I ever tell you about the time in Atlanta when I struck out six Major Leaguers in a row?"

He had. Claire pretended she'd never heard the story as her husband reminisced about the past.

"A bunch of us Monarchs and a few players we picked up, like Josh Gibson and Lou Dials, was barnstormin' through the south, and we hooked up with Dizzy Dean's team for a double-header. Naturally, Satch pitched the first game, and we won easily, but Satchel said he was feelin' a might weary and asked me if I'd throw the second game. Course I agreed, and if I do say so myself, threw a gem. We beat them Majors 2 to 1, and I finished the game by striking out six batters in a row including Hank Greenburg and ole Dean hisself."

"Wasn't Dizzy Dean a pitcher?" Claire mischievously asked. "I thought pitchers were weak hitters?"

Artemis nodded, smiled. "That's true and Dean didn't carry much of a stick, but he's about the only white man I've ever knowed that could match Satch word-for-word, brag-for-brag. So, just shuttin' him up was a big deal."

"How'd the white men take you beating them?" Claire genuinely asked. "Were they upset?"

"Sure, they were down cause they lost and some of 'em wouldn't shake our hands afterwards. But Claire, you'd be surprised at how many of them whites are just like us. All they want to do is play the game. And when it was over they shook our hands, slapped our backs, and loaded up to go play the next game. Dean was one of the best of 'em. Even though we whipped 'em two straight, he was jokin' and visitin' with us like we was cousins or something. You know Dizzy Dean's a Arkansas boy, don't you?"

"I thought he was from Oklahoma. Seems like I read that somewhere."

"Naw, he's from Arkansas. He tells people he's from Oklahoma or Kansas or Louisiana just to mess with 'em. He's an Arkie through and through."

"Sounds like he was quite a guy," Claire said.

"He was. Dizzy Dean was definitely one of a kind."

The two drove silently through Red Fork. They passed the Crystal City Amusement Park and were glad Satchel remained asleep. Claire continued thinking about what Artemis had said about wanting to play *because* of tonight. She wasn't sure what he meant. She decided to ask him. "Honey, a while back you said you didn't want to quit the team because of what happened tonight? What exactly did you mean? Do you want to get hurt?"

Artemis shook his head in exasperation, "of course not. Only a crazy man goes lookin' for trouble. What I meant was, I don't see how I can quit after the way my teammates took up for me. Do you realize they were fightin' to protect me? How often do you see white men defending a black man? How can I walk away after tonight? On top of that, Josh kicked that rich boy off the team because he wouldn't take up for me. What kind of man would I be to walk out on a bunch of guys like that?"

Claire now understood. This had become about so much more than baseball. It was about acceptance. Her husband, in a small way, was replicating what Jackie Robinson had done four years earlier. She hoped he didn't have to go through all the trials and tribulations that young man had weathered, and didn't think he would because Jackie Robinson had blazed the trail. But, he might have to get knocked down a few more times and maybe even punched once or twice before the league accepted him.

She studied her husband as he drove through the neighborhoods of South Haven. It dawned on her that he really had been good enough to play in the Major Leagues. He had been voted onto the Negro League All-Star team four times and could have made it more, except he pitched behind the great Satchel Paige, his life-long friend and mentor. He was a good player in his own right. All the men in the Negro Leagues were superior ballplayers. She hoped future generations of black kids, and white kids too, realized how good these players were and what they'd gone through so that Jackie Robinson could even have a chance to play with the white men. If it hadn't been for men like her husband, there would have been no Jackie Robinson. If her husband and hundreds of other nameless ballplayers had not persevered in the Negro Leagues, had not spent their off-time barnstorming through the countryside playing anyone and everyone, then Jackie Robinson would not have been possible. Jackie Robinson was a hero. Definitely. He was the one that made the leap; the one that suffered ridicule and abuse to pave the way for others. But, he wasn't the only hero. She watched her husband as he drove. Sadness edged through her body; a tear slipped from her eye. In fifty years, who would remember Artemis Macintosh? Who would remember the players who never got the chance to play in front of white folks? Who would remember Lou Dials? Who would remember Buck O'Neill or Turkey Stearnes, or Newt Allen? For that matter, would people forget the indomitable Josh Gibson? Or Cool Papa Bell, the fastest man ever to steal a base? Or the great Newark Eagles pitcher, Leon Day? And what about John Henry Lloyd and Bullet Joe Rogan? It wasn't fair. She looked at her husband through a different set of eyes.

Artemis loved playing baseball simply because he loved the game. But, it was much more. It made him feel like a man. It made him feel equal. No matter how many times he was derided while walking down a public street. No matter how many times he was turned down for a job because of his color. When he stepped on the field with these white players, when he walked to the mound to pitch, he was one of them. There was no difference. They were all ballplayers.

"Artemis, I was wrong. I'm glad you're going to continue playing. I think it's a good thing."

Artemis looked at his wife and smiled. "I think it's a good thing, too. Baseball is a good thing."

# 11

Josh's Chrysler was dark green, the color of oak leaves in the midst of the gloaming. The heavy car was not sporty, nor was it especially popular with the younger set. It was advertised in the papers and on the radio as a roomy, dependable family car. The vehicle's interior listed towards a dark chestnut, almost cinnamon. An abundance of chrome on the dashboard and side panels brightened the sulky interior and symbiotically formed a leavening effect, which resulted in a quiet, comfortable feeling for the passenger.

The car easily held five. His mother sat directly behind him with Sarah occupying the opposite side of the backseat. Jonda perched in the middle between her mother and sister. However, most of the time, with her chin resting on the front seat and her arms draped over, she seemed on the verge of climbing over the top to join her big brother. And would have if her mother had allowed it. Josh, of course, drove and their guest leaned against the passenger door. They were driving down Quanah Avenue headed towards Garden City.

Jonda was the first to notice the young woman edged against the window. "I hope that door dudn't open or you're gonna bounce on the concrete like a pumpkin."

Sarah expelled a gust of exasperated breath and from her corner of the backseat intoned, "silly, pumpkins don't bounce."

Jonda flipped her head and grinned at her sister, then at the rider. "I know."

"Why don't you scoot over a tetch before my little sister has a conniption." Josh motioned for the girl to move towards him.

She complied.

They drove in silence a few blocks before Jonda started up again. "Hey, Francine. What's your last name?"

"Fitzsimmons," the young lady replied.

"What kinda name is that? It don't sound American to me."

"It's Irish," Francine patiently answered the little girl. "My great-great-grandfather came to America in 1860, just in time for the Civil War. He fought with Grant against Lee. He was wounded at Petersburg."

Josh laughed.

"What's so funny?" Francine mischievously narrowed her eyes at the driver.

"Oh nuthin', really."

"Come on. Out with it," she pushed.

"Yeah Josh, what's so funny?" Jonda slid further over the front seat. She seemed determined to join her brother and the young woman in the front. Her mother grabbed her blouse and pulled her back.

"Mom, you wanta tell 'em?" Josh looked in the rearview mirror for his mother's visage but couldn't see her. She was directly behind him.

"No, Honey, you go ahead. You're the one who's got them curious."

Josh ran his tongue across his top lip then quickly over the bottom as if getting ready to taste the first barbequed rib of a steaming, sweet-smelling full rack. He glanced again at the mirror in hopes of catching his mother's eye. She remained hidden.

An unexpected chuckle escaped his throat. He tried to cover it up by coughing like he was coming down with a head cold. He even pretend sniffled for effect. "It's actually quite simple and not really that humorous."

"Then why'd you laugh a while ago?" Jonda questioned.

"Because Frannie said her great-great-great grandfather was wounded at Petersburg . . ."

"I think she said it was her great-great grandfather," Sarah joined the conversation.

"I did," Francine agreed. "And the name is Francine."

Ignoring the name correction, Josh continued. "It doesn't matter if he was your great-great, or your great-great-great grandpa. What's interesting or funny or whatever-you-want-to-call-it is that our great-great grandfather, Grandpa Tilden, was also at Petersburg. Only on the other side. He fought with General Lee and, if I remember the story right, he was given a medal during the battle for shooting several Yankees and capturing a bunch more. Who knows? He might've been the Confederate who wounded your great-great grandpa."

Francine Fitzsimmons turned her head towards Josh and again narrowed her eyes. Only this time it was more of an I-don't-think-so or a that-would-be-impossible look.

"Who's Grandpa Tilden?" Jonda asked. "I thought our name was Braun?"

Sarah tapped the back of her sister's head like she was trying to jar her memory. "It is, goofy. Grandpa Tilden was Momma's grandpa. Momma's maiden name is Tilden. Remember?"

Jonda slapped her forehead with the palm of her hand like she'd just remembered something simple and obvious. "Oh, yeah, I knew that." Then she jerked towards her older sister. "Keep your hands off me, Sarah. I don't appreciate you hitting me."

Sarah looked at her mother and raised her arms, palms up, in a what-did-I-do gesture. Cora Braun slowly shook her head and rolled her eyes at her daughter, telling her nonverbally to forget it.

Josh turned towards Francine, then quickly back to the road. "Hey, it coulda happened. Who's to say it didn't?"

"My grandfather was never captured. He was shot in the oblique, but it was only a flesh wound. He returned to duty the very next day. He was also at Appomattox when the South surrendered to the North. His unit oversaw the disarming and paroling of the Rebels."

"Uh . . . You don't say," Josh stumbled. He paused a few seconds before continuing, like he was trying to think of something to say. Which he was. "Grandpa Tilden didn't surrender. He and several of his men escaped into the Shenandoah Valley and continued fighting for three or four more months. They finally got tired of killing Yanks and went home to Texas. That's where the Tilden's hail from, in case you didn't know. Where's the Fitzsimmons from?"

"Ireland," Francine curtly replied. "I thought I told you that already Do you have an ear problem?"

Josh turned his head to the lowered window and muttered under his breath to the rushing air, "I know I'd sure like to box yours."

"Pardon? I didn't catch that."

Josh flashed her a big fake smile, teeth included. "Nothing. I meant to ask what state your family settled in."

"The Fitzsimmons, like many Irish immigrants, migrated to the Bay State. I still have relatives there."

Josh stared at Francine. He had no idea which state was called the Bay State. Francine's face took on the form of a Miss America contestant standing in front of the audience waiting for the World Peace question. She knew he didn't know which state was known as the Bay State. She cocked her eyebrows. Josh watched as her incisors appeared to lengthen a quarter of an inch. He knew that she knew he didn't know. He did know that a lot of Irish lived in New York and New Jersey. New York was bigger and probably a better guess. He decided to go for it and see if he was right.

He was saved from embarrassment by his little sister once again interrupting.

"What's a oblique?" Jonda asked, seriousness evident in her voice.

Josh grasped at the chance to change the subject. "It's the muscles on the side of your stomach, Jonda." He reached over the seat and lightly pinched his sister in the side. "Right there. That's your oblique muscles."

Josh turned his attention to the road ahead. He could feel his passenger's disdainful glare and ridiculing grin.

"Well, looky here. Home already. That was fast." Josh turned into the driveway on Maybelle Street. He guided the big Chrysler to the side gate, slid the transmission into neutral, and applied the emergency brake.

The backseat passengers disembarked. Cora Braun opened the swinging gate for her daughters then slid the horseshoe latch in place.

"I still don't see why I can't go with Josh to take Frannie home," Jonda whined.

Cora looked sternly at her daughter. "It's real simple, young lady. I said you can't and that's the end of it. Now, pick up your feet, you know scooting across the sidewalk like you're a figure skater is bad for the soles of your shoes, and get in the house." She tossed Josh a quick wave, turned and shouted at Sarah. "Sarah, make sure Sinbad's feet are dry before you let him in. I don't want to have to mop muddy paw prints off the linoleum."

Josh backed out of the driveway and headed east. The night was dark, almost pitch black. The moon, a narrow crescent shape, barely flickered through the canopy of stretching oaks that encased the neighborhood street in a blackness reminiscent of a Transylvania carriage path leading to Dracula's castle. However, this road led to the oil refinery, the belching, smoking, sizzling, oil refinery. Josh skirted alongside a row of white and gray oil tanks sitting serenely in the tall waving grass looking like giant canisters filled with flour, sugar, or corn meal. Of course, these canisters contained something more valuable than cake ingredients or cornbread mix. They contained oil. Black gold. The primary source of wealth for Oklahoma and the vital blood that pumped through America's economic arteries. Josh said nothing as they drove past the tank farm, nor did Francine. Both stared straight ahead as if mesmerized by the dark road before them.

They turned right on well-lit Quanah Avenue and resumed their eastward movement. Josh broke the silence. "The other night when you were at Crystal City did you and Cameron go to Casa Loma?"

Francine slowly turned her head towards Josh. "No. Is that a ride or something?"

Josh chuckled. "No Frannie, it's a ballroom. They have live music and a huge dance floor. I'm surprised you didn't go. You look like a dancer."

"And what does that mean?" Francine petulantly asked. "Are you saying I look like a floozy?"

"Heavens to Betsy, no," Josh replied, exasperated. "I was paying you a compliment. You've got the body of a dancer. And that's good."

"Oh . . . thanks. No, we didn't go." She turned her head back to the front.

They drove in silence for several seconds.

Francine, still looking straight ahead, asked: "What kind of music do they play at this Casa Loma?"

Josh kept his eyes on the road. "Pretty much any kind. It depends on who they've got booked. They have a lot of western swing and country. That's what's popular around here, but sometimes they'll have a famous singer or a jazz band. Patti Page and Vivian Vance have sung there several times."

"That's nice." Francine answered in a tone that implied she was tired of talking about Casa Loma.

Josh glanced at his passenger and wondered how such a pretty girl could be such a snot. Must be her upbringing, he decided.

They drove past the feed store in complete silence and were approaching the Cameo Theater when Josh blurted, without thinking and without knowing why, that he thought since it was early, they should go check out Casa Loma. He was equally mystified when Francine answered, still without looking at him, "okay."

Josh turned his vehicle around in the Cameo parking lot and headed back the way they'd come on Quanah. He drove a little faster this time.

"Well? What do you think?"

Francine surveyed the vast dance hall before answering. Dozens of couples, the girls dressed in bright-colored flowing skirts, the boys in rolled-up khakis and button-up shirts, juked and jived to an Ersel Hickey tune. It was *Lollipop on the Boardwalk*. Francine found herself tapping her left foot with the tune. From her vantage point, she couldn't see clearly to decide if it was, indeed, Ersel Hickey. The band was playing on the far side of the ballroom and there were too many bodies and too much smoke between her and the crooner.

"Is that Ersel Hickey singing? I can't tell from here."

Josh grinned at Francine. "I'm sure it is. He's been here before. I know one sure way to find out." He offered Francine his hand and she took it. They walked onto the dance floor and weaved in and out of the dancing couples. About three quarters across they could get no closer due to the swell of gyrating bodies. But they were close enough. They could plainly see that the singer was definitely Ersel Hickey.

"Well, I'll be," Francine exclaimed above the din.

"Since we're here, we might as well boogie a little." Josh spun around for effect. He was feeling the music.

Francine giggled like a junior high school girl and flashed her palms at her partner in a let's-get-with-it movement. Josh grabbed her hand and spun her around in a perfect pirouette. The two began to dance to the fast-paced music, laughing and smiling as they worked their way through the crowd and closer to the stage.

After three jiving songs, Hickey and his band let loose with a slow, mellow ballad. The tune was new to Francine, but she immediately liked it. It was about puppy love turning into true and everlasting love. Josh slipped his hand around her waist and nudged her close. She complied willingly. She allowed her partner to pull her even closer until they were practically cheek-to-cheek. Despite having played a baseball game less than an hour earlier, Josh smelled remarkably good. His body emitted a musky, masculine scent and his warm, sweet breath made her want to inhale deeply rather than turn away. She also liked the way he held his hand in the small of her back. He was gentle yet firm. He didn't let his hand wander south nor did he lightly massage her flesh the way so many boys did when slow-dancing. Whoever had taught Josh Braun to dance had also taught him to be a gentleman. This surprised her and brought the slightest hint of a smile to her lips.

"You're a good dancer, Frannie Fitzsimmons. Who taught you to dance?"

Francine laid her head on Josh's shoulder. "Fred Astaire Dance Studios," she mumbled.

"Fred did a good job. You dance a lot better than my usual partner."

"And who would that be? Your girlfriend?"

Josh chuckled. "No. I don't have a girlfriend. Sometimes we dance at home to the phonograph. I usually get stuck with Jonda. At least you're taller and don't ask as many questions."

Francine laughed. She believed she could have danced all night like this and would have loved to have tried. She was startled when Josh broke their embrace.

He turned from her.

"What's the matter? Did I do something?"

Josh twisted his head towards her. "I'm sorry. No, you didn't do anything. I think Bobby's in trouble."

Josh strode away from her into the crowd, roughly pushing people out of his way. Francine followed in his wake.

* * * * *

"Bobby, I don't think you should drink anymore. Three is enough."

"One more won't hurt me. This stuff's like drinking flavored water. I thought beer was supposed to give you a buzz. I don't feel anything." He bent over the open trunk of the old Chevy and lifted another bottle from the six-pack. "Besides, you've only had one. Somebody's got to drink 'em. We paid for 'em.

Maundi snapped her boyfriend a disgusted look and grabbed the last Budweiser. She turned from Bobby and pretending great effort, popped the cap with her key-chain opener and poured the amber liquid onto the blacktop. It cascaded from the bottle onto the asphalt like a remote Peruvian waterfall and splattered on the dark surface immediately reforming into several minute rivulets that zigzagged away from the couple to disappear into a wide black crack. Bobby didn't seem to notice what Maundi had done with the last beer. He was still struggling with the obstinate cap on his own bottle.

"How's your ribs? Do you think any are busted?"

Bobby raised his head. He still hadn't wrested the cap from the bottle. Maundi nonchalantly took the bottle from him. She hugged the beer close to her and slowly, quietly removed the cap. She held the bottle at her side and tilted it until there was a silent stream of beer purling next to her hand-me-down Oxfords.

"They're okay. Sore, but okay." Bobby rubbed his side with his left hand. He winced slightly, hopefully imperceptibly. His ribs were tender, but otherwise fine. He'd been hurt worse, many times. By game time next week, he'd be strong as a stallion. Ready to go the full nine. There was no way he was going to let somebody from Sand Springs keep him out of a ball game. No. It wasn't going to happen. He picked up the three empty bottles from the parking lot and returned them to the carton in the trunk of his car -- his mother's car actually -- and sat on the lip waiting for Maundi to finish her drink. After a few moments he realized he did have a buzz and wished he'd only drunk one bottle instead of three. He really shouldn't be drinking at all. It had been a stupid idea. Bobby tried to think of why he'd been so adamant about buying some booze. He guessed it was because of the fight. You were supposed to get smashed after something like that. John Wayne and Lee Marvin always did.

Bobby's thoughts returned to the game. Before the fight. His mind flitted to the inning when Artemis was on the mound. The inning the Negro had taken over for him and retired the best Liner hitter like it was child's play. He'd done it without throwing a pitch above ninety. Probably not above eighty-five. Bobby had struggled against the same batter. He'd given up a clean hit and several long foul balls to the slugger. Maybe there was something to this junk pitching? Maybe, like the Negro told him, it could supplement his heater and make him that much more dangerous. It was definitely something to think about.

"Are we going to go inside and dance or just stand here by the car and gawk at each other?"

Maundi stood before him with her arms crossed and tapped her shoes against the asphalt in a steady rhythm that reminded Bobby of the ticking of a clock. Or, on second thought, more like the ticking of a bomb.

"Well?" Maundi raised her voice. "What's it gonna be? Dancing or standing? If it's the latter you can take me home and stand by your car all night if you want to." Jolted back into the present, Bobby sprang from his perch. He swayed for a sliver of a second before regaining his equilibrium. He wrapped his arm around his girl and smacked her cheek with a loud kiss. "I'm sorry. I was daydreaming. I was dreaming that we were walking along a beach . . . it was sunset . . . we were picking up seashells . . . uh . . . the kind you can hear the ocean in . . ."

"Was this beach in California or Florida?" Maundi asked, a sparkle in her eyes.

"California, of course. Everybody knows they've got the best sand. I've even heard that Hawaii buys sand from California when they run low. Anyway, we were walking along the boardwalk trying to decide whether to go snorkeling or surfing . . ."

"I thought we were on the beach picking up shells? Now you've got us on a boardwalk? Which is it?" Maundi drew closer to Bobby. She bumped his nose with hers. "Are you drunk, Bobby Braun? Or are you suffering from a brain disorder?"

Bobby looked into his girlfriend's pale green eyes. He backed up half a step. Now, he could also see the field of freckles dotting her cheeks. He liked her freckles. They made her cute face that much cuter.

Maundi edged closer, yet again.

Now Bobby focused on her nose. Her narrow, upturned nose that he'd always thought was so adorable. It too had freckles. Tiny, reddish-brown flecks that looked like she'd been sprinkled with fairy dust.

Despite still feeling the effects of Mr. Busch's brew, he contorted his face into its best I-love-you-pose. He tilted his head slightly, hoping the artificial rays of the pole light would capture the twinkle Maundi once lovingly purred was in his eyes. "I give up," he said. "I do have a brain disorder. I'm crazy about you. You drive me absolutely bonkers. Maundi Cordray, I think I love you." He stuck his puckered face towards her and lightly brushed her lips.

"Come on, you big goofball. Let's go inside and dance that alcohol out of your system." Maundi grabbed her boyfriend's hand and pulled him towards the entrance.

The third time they bumped into him, Bobby realized it was no accident.

He maneuvered Maundi towards the edge of the bouncing crowd and scanned the mass of weaving, twirling bodies. At first, he saw nothing. He didn't recognize anyone who would do him intentional harm. He saw Boyd Richardson and Della Lane; they were his friends. He'd hugged Della only a few days ago at the graduation ceremony and shook Buck-Toothed Boyd's hand moments later. Towards the middle of the floor, he spied Eddie Butler dancing with a girl he didn't know. He and Eddie worked together at the filling station. Mark him off.

Bobby searched the crowd one last time before leading his girl back into the gyrating thicket. He immediately realized his error. To his left, not five-feet away, partnered with a skanky-looking redhead, was a member of the Star gang sans jacket. Actually, it was the leader of the gang. It was Gibbo Ross. *So this is how he can move around the Westside without fighting constantly. He dresses like a civilian.* Bobby tried to find the Delaney brothers. He didn't see them, but he knew with total certainty they were somewhere close.

Bobby, with Maundi following his lead, purposely veered towards the gangster. There was no way he was going to let some hoodlum dictate where he danced!

He didn't have to wait long for a reaction. Except, this time Gibbo Ross did the unexpected. With no warning, Gibbo pushed his partner into Maundi. Hard. Maundi and the red-headed moll sprawled towards the floor, the hood yelling expletives on her way down. Bobby reached for his girlfriend, but missed her flailing arms. Maundi crashed onto the parquet with a loud thud, luckily taking the force of the fall directly on her rump. The hood was not so fortunate. She smacked her right shoulder against the inflexible wood planks followed by her skull clunking on the solid floor like a ten-pound bag of potatoes.

Bobby rushed to Maundi. He bent over his girlfriend offering her his arms for support, both physical and emotional. She looked at him with the terrified eyes of a wild animal seeing a human for the first time. She opened her mouth to speak. Bobby didn't hear her. Not because she was voiceless. But because someone or several someones jerked him away from the girl in need.

They pinned both of his arms behind him and before Bobby ever saw their ugly mugs or smelled their whiskey breath, he knew who held him. The Delaney brothers had come out of their hidey-hole to help their master.

Gibbo Ross strode confidently and triumphantly to him. He seemed to have forgotten the girl he'd brought to the dance, the girl who now lay writhing, groaning on the hard, wooden floor.

"You don't belong here, Braun. This place is for respectable people. I don't remember giving you or your little girlie permission to leave your filthy neighborhood." Gibbo reared back to throw a one-punch knockout blow. He arced his haymaker intending for it to blast Bobby's jaw and shatter it into a hundred pieces so that Bobby wouldn't be able to eat any solid food for a month. Bobby felt George and Vernon tighten their grip on his arms. He ducked.

The powerful hook missed Bobby's head by less than an inch. Instead, the punch landed squarely on George's forehead and sent the surprised, dazed hoodlum tumbling towards the two girls and the crowd encircling them. Or it might have been Vernon who went tumbling. After all these years, Bobby still had trouble telling the two apart.

Bobby jerked free from the clutches of the other hyena. Vernon Delaney offered no resistance. He was too busy gawking at the splayed, unmoving form of his brother lying face down on the dance floor. Instinctively, Bobby shielded his face from the next Gibbo Ross punch he knew was coming. It didn't come. Bobby peeked over his forearm and saw why. A chortle arose in his throat and pushed its way out of his clenched teeth. Before him, Gibbo Ross lay flat on his back, his arms wrapped around his head like he was afraid of the dark. Bobby's brother straddled the wiry thug, pounding the man's arms trying to get a clean punch to the head through the gangster's shield of flesh.

Bobby turned to Vernon and knocked him down with a straight, crisp right to the nose. Blood spewed from the downed man's busted nozzle and quickly formed a crimson pool on the glossy hardwood. Bobby wanted to administer more damage to his attackers, but was unable to do so. A burly bouncer with a head the size of a giant melon and just as bald grabbed him in a bear hug and squeezed. "Not again! Not my ribs! Come on. Give me a break!" He winced. Terrific pain shot through his midsection making him grimace. He expelled a gush of air and with it a groan so loud several bystanders backed away. Bobby closed his eyes trying to fight back tears of pain. When he opened them again, he felt relief. Not because Mr. Clean had loosened his grip. He hadn't. But by what he saw. A few feet away, pulling Josh off a battered Gibbo Ross, was Pauley DelGiorno, one of Josh's long-time buddies.

Pauley, a former linebacker at Webster and Oklahoma State, was the head bouncer at Casa Loma. He rushed Bobby, Josh, and their dates into his office where he asked a few perfunctory questions. Unfortunately, Francine didn't understand that Pauley was on their side and wanted to give him a blow-by-blow account. Nonetheless, after about fifteen minutes they were allowed to leave with the simple warning not to come back for a few weeks until everyone had forgotten the incident and their faces. He escorted them to the back door and told them not to worry. He'd take care of the police who were presently questioning their adversaries.

Bobby and Josh didn't hang around the parking lot. Bobby thanked Josh for helping him and with Maundi in tow, headed for his car. Maundi had not uttered a single word during the entire episode. She remained quiet, a steamy quiet; kind of like the slow heating of water in a teakettle before it begins screaming. Francine, on the other hand, hadn't stopped talking since the fight. She'd been the one explaining in detail what had gone on immediately before and during the fight, even though it was apparent that Pauley had no interest in the details. Pauley interrupted her once, then saw it was useless, and let her run down. As Bobby closed the door for Maundi, he couldn't help but shake his head and chuckle. A few rows over, his brother was desperately trying to get Francine into the car, but she wouldn't get in. She stood outside the opened vehicle, arms crossed, demanding to know if Westsiders did anything for recreation besides engage in fisticuffs?

# 12

The room she sat in was cold. Even though the morning temperature outside hovered around eighty, none of the sun's warmth penetrated the substantial brick and mortar walls. She pulled her nylon breaker tighter. Francine had been on the clock for nearly two hours and had yet to leave the break-room where the runners lounged until called to hand-carry information to the county courthouse or a fellow (sometimes rival) attorney's office.

Francine relaxed on the upholstered couch, resting her head and neck on the soft cushiony fabric. She crossed her legs like a boy does, not caring that she was wearing a dress. She and Penelope were the only two in the room and Penny had her nose buried in a *Life* magazine.

"Hey Penny, shouldn't Cheryl be back by now? She only went to the courthouse didn't she? She left over an hour ago."

Penelope Andrews, her face looking like she'd eaten a persimmon, lowered the magazine to her lap. She examined her wristwatch several seconds as if she were the captain of a World War II platoon marking zero hour for a surprise attack on a secret Nazi ammunition depot. She raised her head and made eye contact with Francine before answering. "Cheryl's only been gone forty-seven minutes," she marmishly intoned. "That's not time enough for her to go to the federal courthouse and also to the Hoiberg law offices."

"Oh. I didn't know she was going to the federal building or Hoiberg's. I thought she had a straight shot to state and back."

"No." Penelope shook her head. She glanced at Francine's crossed legs, picked up her *Life,* and resumed reading.

Francine re-crossed her legs in the proper way, held up her hands, and examined her painted fingernails. She hoped she didn't become snooty when she started college.

Francine wanted to tell Penny all about her Saturday night: the baseball game, the brawl, dancing at Casa Loma, the fight, the ride home with Josh listening to his dream of becoming a big-league player and the reality of his father's death and the responsibilities that followed.

Sitting on the couch in the quiet of the morning it was easy for her to admit she found the Westsider interesting if not exciting. Moreover, she had to admit to herself that she even liked his calling her "Frannie". It was also obvious to her that nothing could ever come from their unspoken attraction. In spite of the fighting, she'd had a good time with Josh. Nevertheless, that was the end of it. Nothing further could come of it. He was from a different station. He was poor. He didn't even have a high school diploma. Her parents would never approve.

Nor would she. Francine liked Josh Braun. She could admit that much. Then again, he also infuriated her. His carefree attitude about fighting was so low-class and his incessant and chimerical rambling about playing a boy's game the rest of his life laughable. And his constant worrying about his family, although noble, struck her as, well, middle-aged. She left for college in the fall. A new and exciting adventure chocked with parties, football games, and study groups awaited her. While, on the other hand, Josh would be a Frisco brakeman and in twenty years, he'd still be a common laborer with calloused hands and a weathered face.

Depressed over her ruminations, Francine rose from the couch and headed for the door. Over her shoulder she informed Penelope she was headed to the restroom in case anyone came looking for her.

Francine shuffled down the carpeted hallway, her hands jammed into the pockets of her jacket. The restroom was on the opposite end of the floor and she had to pass several closed doors, including her father's, on her trek to freshen up. A young man emerged from one of the associate's offices. He glanced her way, flicked her a salutatory smile, and rustled away towards the elevator and his next court appearance or important deposition. The man's blue-black hair and long, masculine gait reminded Francine of Cameron and it occurred to her that she'd not once thought about her boyfriend since their break-up. This increased her already profound melancholy, and she jolted to a stop. Francine looked straight ahead at nothing. She thought she might cry, but her eyes remained dry. The thought of Cameron saddened her. However, the truly sad thing, and the thing that depressed her more than anything was that she'd totally forgotten about the argument with her long-time beau and the consequent break-up until now. Until she'd seen the young man who'd reminded her of him.

Had her relationship with Cameron been that shallow? Had the last three years meant so little that a single blow-up signaled the irrevocable end? Had she ever really loved Cameron? Standing alone in the hall she realized she had not. Maybe that was why she'd subconsciously wanted to end it at the hotdog place. She never dreamed about him. Her heart knew he was not there. But it had taken a smack to the brain to wake it up.

Francine no sooner began walking again when she was nearly conked on the head with a swooshing door. She jumped back. Claire Macintosh sashayed from the open entry, smiling like a happy bride.

"Hi, Francine," Claire boomed, with no hint she'd almost knocked out her friend.

"Hi, Claire. How're you doing?" Francine couldn't help it. She returned the woman's smile.

Francine and Claire walked together down the hall, their shoes sinking into the deep-blue carpet like cruise ships on still waters.

"Well, Francine, I'm doing great, and it's in large part due to you. Thank you so much."

*Then Sings My Soul*

Francine glanced at the shorter woman, incomprehension evident on her face.

"Come on, don't act coy, your father told me you spoke with him about me. And I really, really appreciate it. He's moving me to billing and giving me a dollar raise. I can't wait to get home and tell Artemis."

"It's true I talked to my father about you, Claire. But you're not getting anything you don't deserve. You're the one who earned the college degree. You're the one who studied her tail off night after night."

"That may be true," Claire piped as she darted into the closing elevator. She turned to Francine. "But I'd still be behind the front desk if you hadn't said anything. You stood up for me and I won't forget it."

Francine paused in front of the closed elevator door. The metal door muffled the last thing Claire said. It didn't matter. She'd heard it clearly enough. And it made her feel good all inside. Once again, she completely forgot about Cameron.

\* \* \* \* \*

Cora arrived at the Lamberson's thirty minutes late. On purpose. It had been a week since her vulgar confrontation with Mr. Lamberson and she didn't want a repeat. She busied herself in the kitchen, washing the Sunday dinnerware, wiping the table, and bagging up the leftover meatloaf and sweet peas. The Lambersons didn't eat leftovers. Everything not eaten went into the trash. Cora poured herself a cup of coffee and spooned a teaspoon of Pream into it. She loved Pream, but it was much too expensive for her to buy. At home, she used milk to soften her coffee. The Lamberson's kitchen was practically brand new. Cora remembered how amazed she was the first time she'd entered the sparkling kitchen. Instead of a square cook stove, Mrs. Lamberson owned a brand-new O'Keefe & Merritt gas stove with a shiny white enamel finish and gleaming stainless steel handles. The oven lighted up at the flick of a switch so you could check on the progress of your entrée without even opening the door and the rounded shape of the appliance looked like something in a sci-fi movie. Cora cleaned the counter and emptied the toaster of its crumbs. She did this by turning the heavy toaster upside down and shaking the tiny morsels into the sink. As she worked, she began humming an old war tune about not sitting under an apple tree with anyone else but me. She did this absently, reflexively. Her mind wasn't on the bygone war or even her lost husband. It was centered on her eldest, Josh. And also on Alex. Cora paused in her domestic duties and thought about what her mind had just whispered. She'd called Brother Alex, Alex. She'd left off his Christian appellation. He'd been trying to get her, in private, to drop the "brother" and simply refer to him as Alex. He no longer, except in church, called her Sister Cora. He was such a good man, Cora reflected. John had been his deacon and close friend for well over ten years. And his wife, Betty, had been a good woman. The whole time she fought the cancer, she continued coming to church. Even after they took her breasts and her long golden hair began to fall away, there she was every Sunday sitting on the front pew singing praises and holding her hands toward heaven.

Why didn't Josh like Alex? Cora didn't understand, but she knew it was true. Josh was polite to the minister and he never so much as gave the older man a disdainful glance. But it was there. She knew her son. For whatever reason, Josh did not like his own minister. Maybe that's why he had stopped attending church? Perhaps that was the reason for his unhappiness. She always thought it had to do with baseball and his missed chance with the Cardinals. It'd never occurred to her that he had developed anger, ill feelings toward another human being, especially someone so nice and meek as Pastor Alex Thomas. He'd have to get over it; she quickly and sternly decided. She didn't pick Josh's friends, and he wasn't going to pick hers. Nor would he choose her next husband.

Cora slammed to a complete standstill. She stopped wiping the sides of the metallic toaster, nearly dropping it on the Formica counter. "Her next husband," she whispered to herself. In the six plus years of widowhood, today, this morning, was the first time she'd ever so much as thought about marrying again, let alone zeroing in on a particular man. She didn't even know if Brother Alex thought of her in that way. He was probably just lonely. She also didn't know if she thought of him like that. They were two lonely people who'd found solace in each other's company. They were friends. Could long-time friends -- friends whose spouses had also been part of their fellowship -- find happiness in a marriage to each other? Could they be intimate? Could they be lovers? Cora stared at her arm as goose bumps bubbled to the surface. A chill rifled through her body. She was afraid.

"You seem to be in deep contemplation this morning."

A scream raced through Cora's throat. She managed to stifle it after a few shrill vowels of" EEE!" escaped as she whirled around to face the voice. Her brain identified the owner, but not before she embarrassed herself with the muffled shriek.

"I'm sorry," Mr. Lamberson laughed. "I didn't mean to startle you."

Cora expelled a puff of nervous breath, stepped back against the kitchen counter. Lamberson edged closer. "It's okay. I thought everyone was gone. I guess I was daydreaming ."

"You have a remarkable mouth, Cora. Has anyone ever told you that?" He nudged even closer.

Cora could smell his Colgate breath and too-sweet cologne. Maintaining eye contact, she slid along the counter away from him and towards the back door. She tried to control her respiration, but could not. Her breathing turned into a gasping pant much like a scared monkey hovering in the back of its cage as it's taken from its jungle home. Lamberson noticed. He appeared amused.

"I've never been to your house, Cora. Do you have a kitchen like this?" He arced his hands like a tour guide showcasing a room full of Renaissance art. "Of course you don't. You live in West Tulsa if memory serves me right. Probably in one of those squalid shotgun houses."

*Actually, Garden City*, Cora thought. *And we own a two-bedroom bungalow, thank you very much.* She slid closer to the door.

"Have you ever dreamed of living, of owning, a house like this? With your looks there's no telling what kind of man a widow like you could catch. There's no telling what lies in your future. Heck, someday you might live here." He extended his arms again and waved them in an exaggerated motion.

*Not unless you die and will me this monster. And even then I might sell it and buy something cozier.* Cora was now at the end of the counter. She felt confident she could beat him to the screen door, but getting it open before he grabbed her might be a little more difficult.

"Cora," his voice softened to almost a whisper, "I want to apologize to you. I told a little fib last time we talked. I want to be honest with you because I respect you and care for you more than you realize. I intimated that my wife and I, well, that we have a thriving marriage. That's not true."

Cora's eyes bulged. She gulped a swatch of air.

Lamberson held his hand out like a stop sign. "Hear me out, Cora. I need to say this."

Cora crossed her arms over her breasts.

"Since my wife's gotten older, she's lost all desire for a physical relationship. In fact, she and I have grown rather distant. We seldom touch, let alone become intimate. I've tried to explain to her that a love life is important to me, but she doesn't seem to care. It wouldn't surprise me if one day she up and left. She's quite wealthy in her own regard. Her father was one of the founders of Tulsa, you see."

Cora realized that her mouth was now gaped open from the unbelievable private utterances of Mr. Lamberson. She snapped it shut. He didn't seem to notice; it was as if he had to tell someone his problems. He had to get it out. Cora no longer felt afraid. Her fear turned to pity, tempered with disgust. Here was this fabulously rich man standing in front of her spilling his guts about his unhappy marriage and making a play for her at the same time. Wow!

"Anyway," he continued, still in his wimpy,

don't-you-feel-sorry-for-me-wouldn't-you-like-to-get-to-know-me voice. "Cora, I really like you. Could you ever see yourself as the lady of this house?"

Mr. Lamberson stepped away from Cora. It was as if he was a salesman and had made his best pitch and now it was time for the customer to decide. He attempted a happy face; it fell flat. He looked like a little boy who'd picked the neighbor's tulips and was trying to get out of trouble by giving them to his mom.

For some reason, Cora didn't want to destroy the man before her. She did not like him. He was a despicable, sickening human being, contemptuous beyond any doubt. However, he was also sad and unhappy. She'd never noticed this before. Even with all his money, he was miserable. Despite all her trouble and sorrow, she wouldn't trade places with him for one minute. Knowing this made her feel good about herself, her family, about where she lived. Garden City wasn't such a bad place to live after all. A person could be happy on the other side of the river. Contentment didn't only reside in the big houses on the east side of the Arkansas River.

"I'm sorry Mr. Lamberson; I still love my husband. Many people think a widow should remarry quickly for the sake of her children. But we are doing fine. We are happy living on the Westside. We have a small house and few amenities, but we have each other and God is the center of our home."

Mr. Lamberson dipped his head and nodded in a show of defeat and resignation. He silently turned and shuffled from the room.

Cora watched him leave somehow knowing he would never bother her again. She was pretty sure they might even become friends. She decided to get to know better the frivolous and fluffy Mrs. Lamberson and drop a few hints her way about paying more attention to her husband.

\* \* \* \* \*

By three o'clock, Josh decided he'd had way too much on his mind for a Monday. Mondays were supposed to be a day to rest up from the weekend, a day to get back into the hang of work. Instead, Josh had spent the entire day rehashing the baseball game, the brouhaha with the Liners, his brother's knack for getting into fistfights with every thug on the Westside, dancing at Casa Loma with Francine-I'm-better-than-you, still another fight, and finally, the weekly battle with his mother over church.

No, he hadn't gone to church yesterday. Yes, it visibly bothered his mother to the point of tears. Yes, he still believed in God; but no, he wasn't going to be cajoled into going. He would attend church when he was good and ready. He didn't feel anyone should be made to go to church; that is except Jonda, who would be running around the neighborhood like a heathen if it weren't for her fear of eternal damnation.

What's more, he would be there in a few weeks. He'd promised Jonda he'd come and hear her sing in the junior choir and the only thing that would stop him would be death or something awfully close to it. That should make his mother and Brother Alex happy. Maybe, they'd both stay off his back for a while.

Thinking about Brother Alex reminded him of the conversation he and his mother had had less than a week earlier. He told her he didn't especially care for Rev. Alex's sermons; and he didn't. He flat didn't like hellfire and brimstone preachers, even if they were speaking the truth. He didn't believe in scaring people into Heaven. It didn't seem right. Besides, he'd read the Bible, and he couldn't remember any place where Jesus had yelled and screamed at sinners for being little more than human. Didn't the Bible say that everyone sinned? What was the big deal?

Josh motioned for the engineer to stop the train. He stepped over the iron railing and approached the switch. The conductor and train crew had detrained less than a minute earlier and were ambling down the barren hill towards the locker room and a hot shower.

The switch felt jammed, and Josh could not shift it into place. "Come on, rascal, get moving or you'll have me sinning." He laughed at his own joke. Brother Alex would not have laughed; he was sure of that. Still another thing he didn't like about the preacher. The man had no sense of humor -- too serious.

"Oh, come on, Josh," he mumbled to himself and the birds. "Admit it. The reason you don't like Brother Alex is because you think he's sweet on your mom. Isn't that the real story?"

"Shut up!" He demanded. However, it was too late. He wouldn't listen to himself. He had to get it out.

"Okay, that's a big part of it. I don't want a preacher as a stepfather. Then I'd really get the heat to go to church."

Josh continued struggling with the switch. It'd been a long time since he'd fought one this stubborn. *At least it wasn't January*, he thought.

He stopped momentarily to regain his strength. He believed with one more yank he'd pry it loose. Josh wiped the sweat from his brow onto the sleeve of his dirty work shirt. He looked to the sky. "I give up. You're right," he proclaimed. "It's not so much that Brother Alex is a man of God. It's that he's a man, period. I admit it. I don't want my mother marrying again. I don't want another father. I loved the one I had and You took him. Why did You do that?"

Josh again wiped his face with his shirt. This time it wasn't all perspiration. He bent down to the rusty switch and pulled as hard as he could. It flipped into place as if it'd been greased. Josh stumbled backwards and tripped over the railing. He plopped onto the ground landing on his rump and sliding several feet in the loose gravel. Like an angry boxer who's been stunned by a lucky punch, Josh sprang to his feet and glared into the heavens. "Thanks a lot God. I know you're still the boss. You don't have to remind me."

# 13

The long black nose of the Chevy snaked in and out of the rushing traffic. The fifteen-year-old vehicle sped past bigger and newer automobiles like a fire truck racing to a three-alarm fire.

"Hey, Bub! What's the hurry?" yelled a gray-suited man in a brand-new Cadillac.

The blond driver ignored him. He cut in front of the Caddy as soon as his rear bumper had clearance.

"Slow down!" a disheveled and tired mailman barked as the young man passed him. "What do you think this is, the Indianapolis 500?"

Bobby again chose not to reply. He mashed the gas pedal until it touched the floorboard gaining ever more speed. He whizzed by three more dawdling vehicles before sliding back into the line of cars heading for home after a full day on the job. Bobby slowed his vehicle and remained in the informal parade for two blocks before stretching his arm out the window and turning left onto Thirty-Fifth Street. In less than three minutes, he was gliding down Maybelle Street and into the narrow driveway of his home.

Bobby checked the mail before going into the house; nothing except a couple of utility bills. The screen door was unlatched and the front door wide open. When he entered, he immediately sensed that nobody was home. It was too quiet. This puzzled him because normally Sarah and Jonda would be around. They were probably down the street at the Probis's. Mrs. Probis was a quilter and Sarah had gotten it into her head a few weeks back that quilting would be a great hobby. Sinbad ambled onto the front porch and nosed the screen door checking to make sure it was a family member who'd snuck in under his watch and not a burglar. Satisfied, he turned and trotted to his guard post under the cottonwood and quickly resumed his prone telepathic position.

Bobby stretched and yawned in the middle of the living room like he'd just gotten out of bed. He unbuttoned his damp work shirt and tossed it on the back of the recliner. Realizing what he'd done, he picked up the shirt and placed it on the chair, front side down, so that the sweaty back wouldn't leach onto the cloth. "There. That's better," he said proudly and walked into the kitchen. Bobby poured himself a glass of tap water and stood in front of the small, rectangular window above the sink and looked out. He couldn't see much due to his own reflection bouncing back at him. He quickly swigged the cool water, laid the glass on the counter, and headed to his bedroom. The telephone rang.

After a conversation of less than a minute, a conversation in which he said little other than "yes" and "I understand," Bobby grabbed a clean shirt from the closet and ran out the door to the car, buttoning the shirt as he went. He backed the Chevy onto the street without so much as a glance and sped down the treed lane like he was headed to the hospital.

J. C. Penney's was located on Main Street between Third and Fourth. As usual, there were no parking slots available. Bobby spent over five minutes patrolling Main until giving up and driving a block over to Boston Avenue where he easily found a space on the east side near Fifth Street.

He jammed a nickel into the meter and sprinted two blocks to the department store. Flying through the double doors, he accosted the first saleslady he saw. After hearing the young man's near hysteria, she pointed to the elevator and held up two fingers.

Bobby found his sisters in a small windowless room behind Customer Service; they were seated on straight-backed chairs. A dark-haired man not much older than Bobby sat in front of them behind a square wooden desk where a single bright purple blouse lay draped over the edge like a decorative curtain. The man wore a black pinstriped suit and orangey-red tie. He twirled a ballpoint pen in his fingers as if he were a baton twirler performing in the Rose Bowl parade. He was not smiling.

Sarah and Jonda yanked their heads upwards when Bobby entered the silent room. Sarah at once dropped her head back towards her lap. Jonda, on the other hand, beamed at her brother and waved. "Hi Bobby," she chirped. "Whatcha doin'? Me and Sarah's in trouble, but I didn't do anything. Sarah tried to steal a blouse, but she got caught."

Sarah raised her head slightly and hissed at her sister, "shut up you little moron. You're not helping a bit."

"I'm only telling the truth," Jonda pleaded. "Momma always said to never lie and you did try to steal that purple shirt." She looked at her brother. "And if it hadn't a been for that mean man over there," she pointed at the man behind the desk as if he were Frankenstein's monster, "Sarah would have made a clean getaway."

The young man rose and turned to Bobby. He did not offer his hand. "My name is Lawrence Bolton. I'm assuming these are your sisters?" he asked.

Bobby nodded.

Lawrence Bolton sighed, louder than was called for. "I guess you've figured out our situation here," he motioned with an open hand towards the two girls. "We caught the older one purloining an expensive top. She also attempted to avoid arrest by ignoring my commands to stop and running through the lingerie department. Those hoydens knocked over two mannequins before we finally corralled them."

"He's not telling the truth, Bobby," Jonda shouted. She sprang from her seat and jumped up and down like she was riding a pogo stick. "Sarah didn't purloin nuthin'. All she did was try to steal that stupid blouse. I think it's ugly anyway, and I told her it was before she even did it. Plus that, we only knocked down one of those dummies. He knocked down the other one trying to catch me."

Bobby looked at the perturbed security man, then at his sisters. Jonda stopped bouncing and stood with her arms crossed in her mad position. Sarah remained seated, head down. "How'd you girls get downtown, anyway?" Bobby asked, incredulity etched on his face.

Jonda answered, "We rode the bus. How'd you think we got down here? I sure wadn't gonna walk."

Bobby said nothing. He looked again at Sarah, then back to Jonda. He scratched his head and puffed his cheeks like he was a novice trumpet player.

"In case you're wondering," Jonda continued. "We got the money for the bus fare out of that cigar box in your drawer. Don't worry though, Sarah said she'd pay you back as soon as she gets her allowance for keepin' the house clean."

"It appears that J.C. Penney is not the only party to be offended financially. These two young ladies have been on quite the crime spree." Bolton stated, contempt and arrogance evident in his voice.

Bobby stared at the man behind the desk for several seconds. He glanced back at his sisters. He motioned for Jonda to sit down; which, to his amazement, she did without saying a word. He stepped to the table. The young man also returned to his seat.

"Mr. Bolton, I'm sorry this happened, and you can rest assured it will never happen again. We are not a family of thieves." Bobby glanced at Sarah. She did not raise her head. "I have a full-time job at Jim Taylor's filling station on the Westside and my brother works for the railroad. We are not poor people. If you want, I will gladly pay for the blouse when I get my next paycheck, but I would really appreciate it if you didn't call the police. My sister's only fourteen. She's never been in trouble before today."

Lawrence Bolton tapped his fingers on the desk. He seemed to be weighing the options, deciding what to do. He examined Sarah, head still obsequiously lowered; at Jonda, who actually did not stick her tongue out at the man, although you could tell she wanted to; and at Bobby, who was trying to look stoic and pulling it off remarkably well. "I don't want to call the police. I don't want to cause your family more hardship than you already have. However, . . ." He pulled a single sheet of paper from the desk drawer and slid it and the ballpoint towards Bobby. "I will require that you and your sister sign this affidavit swearing that you will not enter the J.C. Penney premises for one year."

Bobby picked up the pen, laid it back down. He looked at the seated man for several seconds until Bolton looked up and made eye contact. "I don't think you want us doing that. I've given you my word this will never happen again. That should be good enough. Besides, we buy all our clothes at this store and there are five of us. We have a charge account here. Would the store manager like it that you are sending us to Froug's or Kress's because a young girl made an impulsive mistake?"

Bolton rubbed his mouth with his hand and mumbled something about the word of a Westsider. Sarah and Jonda could not have heard him. Bobby did. Bobby stiffened but said nothing.

"Okay. I'm going to be Mr. Nice Guy today. I'm going to believe that you are good people. However, I know what you look like, and I will be watching you any time you frequent our store. Do you understand, young lady?" He glared at Sarah.

Sarah raised her head and nodded at Lawrence Bolton. "Yes, sir," she mumbled.

"You may all leave." He turned to Bobby. "Please do no further 'shopping' today."

Quietly, Bobby, Sarah, and Jonda filed out of the room. Mr. Bolton did not rise from his chair as they left.

Once out of the room, Bobby told Sarah and Jonda to wait for him by the Customer Service counter. He needed to go back. He'd forgotten to tell Mr. Lawrence Bolton something.

He returned to his sisters in under a minute.

The three of them said nothing to each other until they'd left the store and were standing on Main Street in front of the entrance.

"Hey Bobby, can we get some ice cream? I'm hungry."

"Jonda, you simply amaze me," Bobby nervously laughed. "You almost got arrested back there. Don't you realize that?

"I didn't do anything wrong. Sarah's the thief, not me."

"Would you please shut up before I kill you!" Sarah shrieked, bursting into a loud sobbing cry. She buried her head in Bobby's chest, and he had no choice but to hold his sister the way a father would hold his daughter.

\* \* \* \* \*

When Cora walked into her house at a quarter past four, no one was home. This surprised her somewhat because usually her entire brood would be waiting for her. She laid her purse on the coffee table and slipped her shoes from her feet. The brown and red fibers of their frayed area rug squished between her toes massaging and tickling her tired feet at the same time. Cora raised her right foot and swished it back and forth across the carpet enjoying the prickly sensation on the sole of her foot. She switched feet and repeated the ritual with her left foot and thought about giving her right a double dose until she spied the filthy blue shirt splayed across Josh's favorite chair. She grabbed it and held it in front of her and read "Jim's Auto" embroidered over the left pocket. Cora shook her head and trudged to the back porch. On the way, she tossed Bobby's work shirt into the dirty-clothes hamper.

Cora sat on the side of the bed in her little alcove and gazed out the window. She silently watched as a half-dozen robins bounced around the yard pausing every few hops to explore the spring grass and moist ground beneath. Cora mouthed a prayer for God to watch over her children, a prayer she repeated a hundred times a day, but never in rote. She picked up her Bible from the nightstand and turned to Psalms and took up reading in chapter twenty-two. She loved reading the Psalms. They gave her peace. She didn't know how people in other countries, places where they'd never heard of Jesus and the Bible, made it through rough times. She truly didn't.

After reading two chapters, her daily goal, Cora returned the sacred book to its place next to her husband's photo and lied down on top of the quilt she used as a bedspread. It was a double wedding ring quilt with blue and mauve fabric on a white background. Her mother had made the quilt for her and John as a wedding present. It still looked nice. Her mother had died less than three months after the wedding. It was the last quilt she'd ever made.

Unable to sleep, Cora rose and walked through the house. She stood at the screen door and stared at the pock-marked street expecting to see her children come zooming up – if Bobby were driving – any second. Instead, she found herself watching Sinbad roll around in the clover like someone with a bad case of poison ivy all over his back. Cora smiled at the antics of the family pet and returned to her back porch/ bedroom. She again sat on the side of the bed and picked up the telephone. She dialed Brother Alex's number.

In less than ten minutes, Rev. Alex Thomas stood on the Braun's front porch knocking. Cora showed her pastor into the house and fixed iced tea while he relaxed on the sofa.

"You do know how to make tea, Cora. Is it the same recipe they use at the diner?"

"Pretty much," she nodded. "I don't brew mine quite as long. Theirs is a little strong for me."

"Well, this is perfect. Where are the kids? It's unusual to be in this house and not hear little Miss Jonda a jammerin'."

Cora glanced out the screen door then at Brother Alex. "I have no idea. They were gone when I got home."

Brother Alex finished his glass of tea, waved off Cora who rose to get him a refill, and set the empty container on the coffee table. He twisted around on the couch so that he was facing his again-seated host. Cora tried to muster a smile, sipped her tea.

"Cora, what's bothering you? You seem sad today. Are you okay?"

"I'm fine," she answered. "I've been going through a few trials lately; that's all."

The preacher turned yet again on the couch to his original position. He stared straight ahead at the far wall and the family photo taken before the war. Jonda was not in the picture. Cora's late husband, John, was. He slowly, methodically rose from the sofa, like a man getting ready to take the long walk to his own hanging. Out of the corner of his eye, he peeked at his parishioner. Averting his eyes from the goal, the minister inched closer to the woman and sat beside her. She did not seem to mind.

Cora was not upset and, deep down, was glad when Brother Alex moved close to her. His nearness relaxed her. She was not afraid. She knew she could trust her own pastor. When he coyly glanced at her, she flashed him a close-mouthed smile hoping to reassure his decision.

"Cora . . ." he stammered.

She did not reply, preferring to allow him all the latitude he needed to say what he obviously wanted to say. She sipped the last of her tea and reached across him to lay it on the table. His scent filled her nostrils. It was a good scent, the smell of soap and after shave. What kind she didn't know. It had a good, strong aroma. Not sweet. But manly and virile. Brother Alex smelled like a man should.

"Cora," he began again.

"Yes, Pastor?"

"Call me Alex. I know I'm a preacher, and I understand that's hard to get over or around, but I'm also a man. A man just like any other. I'm no different than anybody except God has called me to lead people to Him and to help my flock with their spiritual life."

"I know, Alex. I know you're a man. And a fine man, if you'll allow me to say so."

"I not only allow it, Cora, I am flattered by it." He edged closer. "Surely you realize how much you mean to me? How much I care for you?"

"Of course I do, Alex. You love everyone in your congregation. That's why I feel so proud to be a member of Tabernacle Church."

Brother Alex flinched. He opened his mouth to answer, closed it again and wet his lips. He tried a different approach. "Cora Braun, do you think you could ever see me in any way other than as a preacher? Could you see me as a man? A man who cares deeply for you in . . . other ways than just as a member of my church? . . . Oh Lord! Help me through this." Brother Alex flopped back against the sofa and covered his face with both hands. He spread two of his fingers and peered out at Cora to see her reaction to his bold statement. It reminded her of an infant playing peek-a-boo with his momma. She thought it was adorable.

The first thing Cora did was look at her hands; her fingers actually; her ring finger to be exact. She'd not worn her wedding ring in over five years. There was no longer any trace of it. The once pale circle had darkened and was indistinguishable from her other digits. She gazed at the wall, at the same photograph Brother Alex had examined only moments earlier. Her beloved John looked down from the frame; his blue eyes filled the room. To his left was his wife; in front of him, grinning like they'd spent the day at the fair, stood his three young children: Joshua, Robert, and Sarah.

Cora swallowed and pulled her bottom lip into her teeth. She scraped her lip with her front teeth and thought about how her family had changed, how it had moved on. John was gone. He was in Heaven. And Jonda had never known her father. Nor would she ever know him, at least not on this earth. Jonda knew she was named after her father, and someday Cora would tell her that coincidentally -- no, that wasn't right, -- *miraculously* she'd been born on the same day her father had died. But that would hold until she was older, much older. Jonda didn't need to know something like that at such a young age. Cora thought again about how things had changed, about how Josh and Bobby and Sarah had helped her so much the past seven years. How the four of them had raised Jonda since she didn't have a father.

Cora looked again at Alex, who'd finally and bravely lowered his hands to his lap. He tried to wrinkle a smile, but his nervousness caused his lips to shudder. She'd never seen him so scared. Alex was normally a bastion of strength, a pillar to rest on. He was used to dealing with death, with consoling grieving parents and spouses, with trying to piece broken marriages back together, with rebellious sons and wayward daughters. Sitting in front of her, he looked timid and boyish. He was out of his element.

"I do like you, Alex. You are kind, considerate, a gentleman. And a little bashful, as I just found out."

Alex's face flushed the color of a ripe beet, but he refused to take his eyes from Cora's. "Cora, I hope I'm not being too bold or forward." He paused. "I'd like to ask your permission to kiss you. However, if you think we should wait until a more proper time or maybe until you . . ."

"I think I'd like that," Cora interrupted her new beau. "Yes Alex, you may kiss me now."

Clumsily, but no longer shyly, Brother Alex placed his hands on Cora's shoulders and pulled her close. He kissed her softly and tenderly on the lips lingering just long enough for a first kiss.

"Thank you, Cora. You are a wonderful lady."

Cora grinned at Alex. "Okay preacher, you've had your kiss. When are you taking me out on the town?"

\* \* \* \* \*

Jonda skipped ahead of Bobby and Sarah as if they were on a spring shopping excursion. She paused briefly at the department store windows looking at the colorful mannequins draped in light, summer attire. Or longer when she saw the long row of red bicycles through the Otasco windowpane, many with deep white baskets and silver horns on the handlebars.

Sarah walked the two blocks to the car in total silence. Rarely, except at intersections, raising her head from its entranced study of the various cracks and imperfections of the concrete sidewalk. Bobby tried to keep his eyes straight ahead, but found them, like magnets, flitting towards his sister. She appeared devastated, totally humiliated. He felt sorry for Sarah. He was no longer angry with her, not in the least.

When he first learned on the telephone about her being held by security for trying to steal a blouse, he'd been furious, enraged, livid. His anger only increased on the drive to the department store and he'd become beside himself when he couldn't find a parking space close to Penney's. However, something changed him, calmed him, almost the moment he'd entered the plush, air-conditioned surroundings of the downtown department store. Talking to the perfumed, well-dressed saleslady, although she was extremely polite, was his first modification. By the time Bobby swished through the racks of enticing dresses and slacks, ridden up the elevator with two chattering women, their arms laden with purchases, and entered the room where the smug, aristocratic Lawrence Bolton sat holding court for his oldest sister, the transformation was complete. Bobby was no longer upset with Sarah. He was not in the least angry with her for trying to steal a silly blouse. He knew what she had done was wrong. There was no getting around that. He also felt sure she'd never do it again. Standing in the second-story windowless room behind the Customer Service counter listening to the swooshing cold air travel through the miles of ducts and looking at his little sisters dressed in clean, but out-of-fashion, out-of-date clothes, engulfed him in a melancholy that almost drowned him in sadness and pity. He felt sorry for Sarah and Jonda, but especially Sarah. Sorry they didn't have the things a lot of girls took for granted. Little things like a new hairbrush or barrettes. Big things like a fancy Easter dress or new shoes to wear to the spring dance. Sarah was on the verge of being a young woman and she needed nice clothes; she needed to feel good about herself.

And when the anger returned, it wasn't because of his sisters. Mr. Lawrence Bolton disgusted Bobby. Couldn't he tell that the girls he'd strong-armed were good kids? That they'd simply made a mistake. He didn't have to humiliate them the way he did. Oh sure, it was his job. A job he'd most likely gone to college to study for. They probably taught him that this was the way to treat undesirables, people who tried to take something that didn't belong to them, thieves. Sarah wasn't a thief. She wasn't a criminal.

Bobby opened the door for Jonda, who popped into the back seat without complaining and held it open for Sarah. She climbed into the front seat, uttered a sincere "thank you" when Bobby closed the door for her like they were steadies on a Friday night date.

"I'm sorry, Bobby. I don't know what got into me. One minute I was admiring the top, the next it was stuffed into my purse. Jonda had nothing to do with it. . . other than being the reason I got caught."

"What do you mean?" Bobby asked, more amused than upset.

"Yeah, I didn't do nuthin," Jonda defended, hanging over the front seat.

"Other than alert everyone within hearing that I'd just crammed a purple blouse into my purse, you're right; you didn't do anything. But I'm glad you did little sister. I'm glad I got caught. I couldn't have slept with myself if I'd made it home with that blouse."

"I'm proud of you, Sarah. You took responsibility for what you did. You didn't try to weasel out of it like a lot of people do."

"Thanks, Bobby. I'm glad you're not mad at me. I screwed up and that's all there is to it. It's just that . . . well . . . it's just that I want to wear what everyone else is wearing. That's all."

"I know," Bobby sighed. "I know."

"Besides," Sarah giggled. "I don't know why I took the darn thing anyway. It was a size too small."

They both laughed at this.

"Hey Bobby," Jonda broke the laughter.

"Hey what?" Bobby answered

"I sure am hungry. Me and Sarah didn't get nuthin' to eat for lunch today. We was too busy lookin' at purple shirts. Do you got any money?"

Bobby twisted his head towards his sister. She was not looking at him. She was gazing past him at the diner across the street.

Bobby knew what was there without looking. It was Nelson's Buffeteria, one of the best eating establishments in Tulsa. Their specialty was chicken-fried steak and coconut pie, two of his favorites. It'd been a long time since he'd had the money to eat there.

He fished into his pocket and withdrew his wallet. He opened it and saw that he had four dollars, the last of his money until payday – over a week away. He sighed and hesitated as if in a deep struggle over what to do. It wasn't really a tough decision. He'd known what he was going to do as soon as he saw the folded greens tucked in his billfold. "Let's go get some chow," he declared flashing Jonda and then Sarah a great, big smile.

"Are you sure?" Sarah questioned. "I don't want you spending your money on us. We can eat at home. I was going to fix ham and macaroni tonight."

"Yippee," squealed Jonda as she barreled over the front seat and reached across her sister for the door handle.

Bobby nodded at Sarah and widened his smile. "You bet I'm sure. I've got plenty of money."

For the next forty-five minutes Bobby, Sarah, and Jonda enjoyed one of the best meals they'd ever had. The flour-coated steak was tender and the cream gravy thick and delicious. The mashed potatoes were homemade, the dinner rolls fluffy and hot. Bobby, who didn't normally like green beans, ate his entire helping like they were apple cobbler. And speaking of dessert, the coconut pie was simply out of this world. It was every bit as good as any pie at the annual dinner-on-the-grounds service at Tabernacle Baptist. The bill rang up at $2.71. After paying, Bobby gave a quarter to Jonda to put on the table for a tip. Jonda obeyed her big brother – reluctantly.

Emerging from the café, Bobby swigged a huge expanse of cool, spring air. It tasted good. Warmer times were directly ahead, and something told him it was going to be a great summer for the Brauns. He just knew it.

"Bobby, I've been dying to ask you this since we left Penney's but I've been too afraid," Sarah said.

"Go ahead, Sis. Ask away. I've got a full belly and two of my favorite people beside me. Go for it."

"Okay." She hesitated several seconds.

Bobby decided not to rush her. He and his dark-headed sister stood a few paces in front of the door to Nelson's watching the cars ramble by. Jonda was a few feet away piddling with a parking meter trying to figure out a way to get it to spit out a few coins. Who knows? Maybe there would be a criminal in the family.

"When you went back and talked to Mr. Bolton, what did you say? Did you pay him for the blouse or what?"

Bobby couldn't help himself; he chuckled. "No. I wouldn't give that little tyrant the time of day."

"What did you say, then?"

Bobby studied his much shorter sibling, decided to tell her. "I told him I'd better never, ever catch him on the Westside."

Sarah gulped.

Bobby patted her on the shoulder.

Jonda, giving up on extracting any money from the metal sentries, bounced to her waiting brother and sister. "I got an idea," she pronounced. "Why don't we go see a movie? That sounds like fun, don't it?"

"It does, Jonda," Sarah calmly answered. "But I've got to get home. It's after five."

"After five!" Bobby exclaimed. "Oh, no. I forgot all about Artemis.

# 14

The ride to Oiler Park was tranquil and uneventful. If anything, too quiet. Josh had been hesitant about calling the rich girl to see if she wanted to catch a ball game with him, and surprised when, after a short pause, she said "yes." Of course, shortly after setting up the date – *was it an actual date? He wasn't sure* – his foreman "asked" if he could work a couple of overtime hours. He considered saying no to his boss, but how do you say no to a guy who's letting you off every weekend so you can play baseball? Josh agreed, called his mother to let her know his plans and went back to work for two more hours. After showering at the yard and grabbing a hamburger at Mac's Drive-in, Josh drove across the river to pick up Frannie.

Saturday, when he'd taken Francine home, it had been dark and he hadn't gotten a good look at her house. Now Josh could see the Fitzsimmons estate clearly. His first reaction was, "Wow, you could fit four or five houses like ours inside this place!" Of course after looking at the mansion closer he adjusted his opinion upwards to eight or nine.

Surprisingly, Francine answered the door chime. Josh figured he would be greeted by a maid in a black dress, white apron, and starched linen cap. So, when Francine pulled back the wide, heavy door and flashed him a demure smile, Josh was momentarily taken aback.

"What?" Francine asked. "You look like you're shocked to see me."

"I'm sorry. It's nothing. I was . . .a . . . I'm just surprised that you're wearing shorts to the game." Josh pointed to her white, cuffed shorts and immediately felt foolish, embarrassed.

Francine shook her head. "I'm not wearing these, silly. I was headed to my room to change when I heard the doorbell. You *are* a little early, you know."

Josh reflexively looked at the watch on his wrist. It was 6:30. He was fifteen minutes ahead of schedule. "Oh," was all he could think of in reply.

She waved him inside. "It's no big deal, Josh. You'll simply have to wait in the parlor while I get dressed." She led him through a wide hall papered in mauve and turquoise and complete with hanging chandelier and several framed oil paintings. He followed, feeling like a hungry puppy trailing its mistress. They turned left in front of a polished wood staircase. Josh thought about Jonda and how long it would take her before she snuck to the top and slid down the banister – about thirty seconds, he decided. Then they entered a high-ceilinged room with long, rectangular, wrap-around windows, and multi-colored Persian rugs splashed across the glistening parquet floor. Francine led him to a plain brown sofa which, to Josh, looked out of place in the big, fancy room. It appeared old and out of fashion. In fact, when Josh examined the room, all the furniture looked ancient. It was as if he were sitting in a nineteenth-century hotel lobby. Good grief, he thought. You'd think with all their money, they could afford new furniture.

"I won't be long," Francine smiled.

And she wasn't.

Within ten minutes Josh and Francine were in his Chrysler headed to the ballpark.

Josh purchased general admission seats, then right before he and Francine spun through the turnstiles, stopped and headed back to the ticket booth.

"Hey," Francine hollered. "Where are you going? The ball game's starting in a minute." She looked at her bare arm as if she were wearing a watch.

"I got the wrong tickets. I meant to buy box seats. It'll just take me a sec to exchange these."

"Nonsense, Josh. Don't buy box seats. I like sitting in the bleachers. They're the best seats in the house. It's where my dad and I always sat when I used to come with him."

Josh knew she was lying. He could see it in her face. She'd never sat in the cheap seats in her life. It made him that much more excited about her.

With the money he saved, Josh bought himself and Francine a hotdog and a large Coke. For a Monday night, the stands were unusually full. The couple made their way down the third base side of the stadium and found two empty spaces past the Oilers' dugout.

They sat behind a married couple with three kids, none over seven. As soon as they were seated, Josh immediately figured out why there were so many fans to see a Monday night game against El Paso. It was Oiler balloon night. Every child under the age of twelve, and many who looked a lot older, received a red or white balloon as they passed through the turnstiles. Naturally, the three kids directly in front of them were waving theirs like it was game one of the World Series. Josh found himself weaving and bobbing like Joe Louis so he could see past the helium obstacles. Francine sat quietly beside him, an amused smirk littering her face.

"We still have time to exchange our tickets and sit closer, if you want. It's no big deal. It only costs a dollar more."

"I don't want. Besides, the game's starting. There go our boys onto the field."

The crowd stood for the National Anthem and at . . . *by the dawns early light*, the youngest, a girl no older than two, relaxed her grip on her red balloon and off it went into the wild blue yonder. Somewhere around *the rocket red glare* a second balloon escaped and drifted towards the

*Then Sings My Soul*

ether and a meeting in the sky with its brother. This left only a solitary balloon – white – to hamper Josh's vision of the game.

When they were reseated, the umpire hollered "play ball' and the real noise commenced. Josh asked Francine if she wanted a refill on her drink, but gave up when she couldn't hear him no matter how loudly he yelled. First, the announcer, who had a voice as strong as any opera tenor shouted into the public address system "Let's gooooooooooooo Tulsa!" Then, the organist took over and began pounding "charge" on the keyboard while everyone in the wooden stadium stomped their feet to the rhythm of the staccato sounds. Francine looked startled at first, caught the fever and clomped her feet on the planks helping to create a noise that sounded like the cadent booms of a battleship's guns. She handed the last third of her hotdog to Josh, who downed it in one bite. Francine grinned. Josh thought she was having fun. He sure hoped so.

"Josh?" Francine asked after the noise subsided, somewhat. "Why didn't you get a beer at the concession? They asked if you wanted one. Don't you drink?"

Josh didn't know how to take this. Nor did he know what answer she was looking for. Would she think he was some kind of dweeb if he didn't drink? A religious nut? Most guys his age drank. He didn't. And he didn't plan on ever starting. His father was a teetotaler, his mother hated it, and he, personally, didn't see any value in drinking alcohol. He decided to be honest.

"I don't drink, Frannie. Besides being five months too young, my mom would kill me if she ever found out. Worse, she'd be disappointed in me. It would break her heart."

"Your mom means a lot to you doesn't she?"

Josh nodded.

"Don't get me wrong," Francine added as if embarrassed. "I love my mom, too. It's just that your family seems much closer than mine. I don't know. Maybe it's because I'm an only child."

"I'm sure you love your mom," Josh said. "Everybody loves their mom. I think we're so close because my dad's gone." He paused. Froze is probably the better word. It was as if he wanted to continue but simply couldn't. His mind was locked, his eyes distant.

Francine could tell the man next to her was far away, probably on the battlefields of Europe or even a time much, much earlier. "I'm sorry about your dad, Josh. A lot of men died in that terrible war. A lot of good men. I was lucky. My father didn't have to go overseas. He was stationed in North Carolina during the war."

Josh returned to the present. "I'm glad you were lucky. I wouldn't want anyone to experience what we've been through the past seven years. My mom's changed so much since then it's scary. No, change that. It's sad."

"I know what you mean, and I don't see how she does it, working two jobs and trying to raise a family. You've been a big help to her. Surely, you see that?"

He dipped his chin in a half nod, half droop. "I wish she didn't have to wait tables and clean houses for rich people – nothing personal," he added. Francine blinked that she understood. "But it's more than that. It's like she's lost her joy, her happiness. That's it." Josh straightened his head, looked directly at Francine. "Yes, that's it. My mother is still grieving and I don't know what to do about it. She may never be happy again."

"She will," Francine said matter-of-factly. "She'll get her act together. I've only met her once, but I can tell she's a strong woman. Someday she'll meet someone who will dampen the heartache. Who knows? She may have already met him. Is she seeing anyone? Anyone at all?"

Josh shook his head. "No. No one." Even as he answered, Rev. Alex's face flashed before him. His mom liked the preacher. There was no doubt about it. But who didn't like their pastor? He inwardly laughed. There was no way his mom would ever date, let alone marry, a preacher.

"Josh? Could I ask you something and you not get angry? I'm not going to ask it unless I know you won't blow your top."

"No, I don't fight every night. And I'm not planning on fighting tonight unless you get lippy."

"Ha, ha, Mr. Smartypants. I'll have you know I took Judo at Lansing. I'm pretty good too, if I do say so myself. That's not what I was going to ask. I already know how much you Westsiders like to roughhouse."

"Well... ask." Josh shrugged.

Francine stared deep into Josh's eyes as if she were an ophthalmologist looking for cataracts. She swallowed. "Josh, why *are* you obsessed with the *game* of baseball? Why do you and half the men in America spend every waking minute talking about, reading, or -- in your case -- playing baseball? Why don't you go to school and make something of yourself instead of wasting your time on a silly *game*?"

Both times, Josh noticed, she'd emphasized the word "game." Of course, that's all it was to her, a game played by boys or by men acting like boys. He'd heard it before. Many times. Even his mother was starting to adopt this line of reasoning.

If Frannie had said to him what she'd just said last Friday night, he'd have exploded. He would have told her not to worry about what he did or didn't do. He would have explained to her that she could never understand, being a girl. He would have put her in her place.

Now, he found himself wanting to answer her. Wanting to explain to her why baseball was so important to him and other men (and a lot of women, too) and to America. Didn't she understand that baseball was our nation's sport? Our national pastime? That our culture, our history, our very existence as a people was all wrapped up inside a round, leather ball and a wooden ash bat? Surely, she'd read about the Civil War and how Yankee prisoners taught the game to the southerners? About how baseball helped unite and heal the nation after four years of horrific bloodshed? Didn't they teach that at Lansing Hall?

Josh's mind settled on the Negro Leagues. On the great black ballplayers who'd been denied their rights as Americans to play a game, *yes a game,* they loved. He thought about how they'd formed their own league, so they too could participate in American culture. About how they'd persisted despite being denied the opportunity to compete at the highest level. Finally, America had seen the light, and players like Jackie Robinson, Larry Doby, and the great Satchel Paige were stealing bases and hitting home runs and striking out batters in places like New York's Yankee Stadium, Boston's Fenway Park, Chicago's Wrigley Field, and the Cardinals home, Sportsman's Park in St. Louis. Josh had never been to an actual big league game played in a big league park, let alone a game in which one of the Negro ballplayers played. He wondered what it was like to hear white folks holler for a black player? Did they? If he knew baseball fans, as long as a player wore the home team's uniform, they would get cheers. Just like an opposing player, no matter his skin color, would be booed and jeered. Who knows, Josh thought. Maybe baseball would bring the races together? If blacks and whites could play on the same field why couldn't they sit in the same stands? Buy a Coke from the same concessionaire? Or heck, live in the same neighborhood? Maybe that was asking too much from *a game*?

Josh wanted to say these things, and more, to Frannie. He wanted to tell her everything. Instead, when he opened his mouth, all that came out was: "I just love the game. I don't know what I'd do if I couldn't play."

\* \* \* \* \*

Francine half expected Josh to be offended at her question. So, when he answered with such a simple reason and in such a quiet, unassuming voice, she'd been disarmed. She sat quietly for several seconds not sure how to continue the conversation.

"I guess that's as good a reason as any," she finally mustered. "If it means that much to you, then go for it."

She couldn't believe she'd just said that. She couldn't believe she'd told him to keep playing a silly game no matter how much it retarded his future. Here he was, a high school dropout with a decent job, but nothing that would make him wealthy, and she was advising him to keep playing a little boy's sport rather than trying to optimize his potential.

The Oilers apparently had a good team, or El Paso had a weak one. After four innings, Tulsa was ahead of the visitors 6 to 0, and they'd hit three out of the park onto Fifteenth Street where a group of adolescent boys scrambled after the white sphere like it was a bouncing gem of great worth.

In the top of the fifth, Francine excused herself to go to the restroom. Josh asked if she wanted him to escort her; she laughed and told him she could find her way just fine. Later, she realized he was only trying to be a gentleman.

She barely made it down the ramp before being confronted by an irate Cameron. He grabbed her shoulder from behind and twirled her around like she was a human top; then he backed her against the wall. Cameron opened his mouth in an ugly snarl. He hissed, "I see why you dumped me the other night. You wanted to be with that river rat all along. Didn't you? Go on admit it. You like that white trash from the Westside."

"Hi, Cameron. It's nice to see you, too," she smiled. "Are you enjoying the ball game? The Oilers sure have a nifty team. They're pounding those Texans." Francine forced her face to widen its pseudo grin. She stared into the angry face of her former boyfriend and refused to blink. He edged closer until their noses actually bumped. He smelled of beer and peanuts. A prickly stubble covered his normally smooth face.

Cameron backed up a step. He crossed his arms over his chest. "Come on, Francine," he whined. "What are you doing here with a guy like that?" He bobbed his head at the ramp. "You've got no business with a guy like that."

"A guy like what?" Francine felt her hackles rising. Now that Cameron's anger had subsided somewhat, she felt herself becoming irritated.

"You know. A guy like Braun. He's nothing but a loser. Good grief, Francine. He's a novice brakeman for the railroad, for crying out loud!"

A calmness pervaded her. She was no longer upset. She was no longer angry. She didn't care what Cameron said or thought; he did not matter. He was out of her life. She was through with him. And she was glad. What she'd ever seen in him was beyond her. She guessed it had been because he was the high school stud, the big man on campus. A lot of girls went crazy over guys simply because they were athletically gifted or extremely good-looking. Or, in Cameron's case, both. These were the popular guys in high school; they ran the school. All the guys wanted to be like them; all the girls wanted to be with them. Francine had been no different. She realized this; she also realized the guy in front of her turned her stomach. He was a little man who staked his worth and importance on the fact that his family had money. Cameron was despicable. She wanted nothing but to get away from him. She brushed past him; again felt him reach out and grab her by the shoulder.

"Francine, Honey, are you all right? I saw you in the stands and when you got up to come to the concession area, I followed so I could say "hi." Is everything okay?"

At the recognition of the voice, Cameron dropped his hand from Francine's shoulder.

Francine turned to her father. She wanted to kiss him for interrupting, and later wished she had. "Hi, Dad. No, everything's fine. Cameron and I were visiting, but we're through now." She turned towards the silent young man. "I'll see ya around, Cameron." She flicked a fake smile at him. He got the message and shuffled off towards the ramp. She turned again to her father. "Daddy, I didn't know you still came to baseball games. Do you come a lot?"

"Not a lot, but I enjoy a game here and there. Once it's in your blood, it's hard to get it out." He lowered his head as if he'd been caught doing something wrong.

"Well, I'm enjoying the game, too. The Oilers are pretty good. I don't guess I've seen them play since I was a little girl – since you took me."

Mr. Fitzsimmons' eyes lit up like a Christmas tree. He bobbed his head up and down excitedly. "They are good this year. I think they've got a chance to win the pennant. That is if the parent club doesn't call up a bunch of their players. That's a big problem with minor league clubs. If they're good, the players who make them good usually don't hang around. They get promoted to the big time. At least we get to watch them for a while. That's part of the fun, too; trying to pick out the players who will make it to the Majors."

Francine and her Father talked for another five minutes. Or rather he talked – about the Oilers and baseball in general – while she listened. It became quickly apparent that her Dad still loved the game. Francine did not know this and she didn't think her mother did either. She thought he'd gotten over it as he became older and more involved in the firm.

"Who's the young man you're with?" her Dad asked. "A new boy in town? Does he belong to the country club?"

"No, he doesn't. He's just a baseball fan, like you," she said.

Her father nodded, his eyes and entire face shimmering in the fluorescent lights of Oiler Park.

"And I'd better get back up there or he'll think I've abandoned him."

"Or Francine, he might think you don't like baseball," her dad winked.

\* \* \* \* \*

The drive to South Haven went without incident. Bobby had been to colored town several times, however, never at night. In any case, he didn't have to go through Oakhurst, he thought. That's where the Star bunch hung out. Oakhurst was farther west and north than where the blacks lived.

Bobby had never been to Artemis's house. He found the pitcher's address in Josh's steno book. Josh kept the address and phone number of every player, in case he needed to call them when a game was canceled due to bad weather. Artemis lived on Fifty-Fifth Street. That should be easy to find, Bobby thought. South Haven wasn't that big.

When Bobby arrived home with his sisters, he got out for a few minutes to find the pitcher's address and to smooth things over with his mom. He'd driven home with the idea of telling her everything that'd happened, but when he saw the preacher's car in the driveway, changed his plans. He walked into the house behind Sarah and Jonda, and immediately began extolling the deliciousness of Nelson's Buffeteria and how he and the girls had, on a whim, hopped into the car and went to eat out. Rev. Alex chimed in, agreeing that Nelson's was one of the best, if not *the* best place to eat in Tulsa. Amazingly, Jonda said nothing about the purple-blouse episode. After their pastor finished describing how good Nelson's strawberry shortcake was, Jonda jumped in and as she rubbed her belly, bragged that their coconut pie was the best in the world. The only thing their mom asked concerning the excursion to the other side of the river was that if they'd wanted to eat out so badly why didn't they come to the diner where they could have gotten a discount. Rev. Alex answered her before Bobby had a chance – and Bobby was glad he did. The preacher told their mother that Nelson's was better than the diner even with the discount. He promised to take her there sometime. Bobby had been more than a little surprised when his mother responded that anytime he had the money, she had the time.

Artemis's home was actually quite nice. It was a white clapboard house with yellow shutters and a fenced backyard. Bobby thought about his mom when he saw the big covered concrete porch. It was almost an exact replica of the kind they'd had on their old house. A lot of Westside houses had those big porches. He hadn't known they built them in South Haven, too. Bobby parked in front by the curb. It was after eight and other than a small area illuminated by a solitary streetlight, dark as a Halloween night.

Artemis's wife answered the door. To say she looked surprised would be a vast understatement. "You're Bobby, aren't you?" she stammered.

Bobby nodded. "Yes ma'am. Is Artemis here?"

Claire turned sideways and ushered the young man into her home.

Artemis sat in a high-backed upholstered chair, his son asleep in his arms. The lanky man dipped his head in greeting. He did not smile.

Claire motioned for Bobby to sit on a short green couch. He accepted the invitation. The short, pudgy woman went to her husband who gently handed her their son. She left the room, presumably to put the boy to bed.

Artemis's living room consisted of two stuffed chairs, a small couch, and a wide, oval coffee table. Pictures of their son smothered the walls and as Bobby's eyes scanned the first four years of a little boy's life, they landed on a framed photo of two ballplayers. The men stood side-by-side in their Monarchs uniforms; their arms draped over the other's shoulder, grinning like they'd won the New York lottery. It was Artemis and Satchel Paige. Bobby was sure of it. He'd seen the great pitcher play once when the Monarchs came to Tulsa. He was taller than Artemis, but not by much, and he was even skinnier than the thin man now sitting across from him. Artemis watched as the young man admired the photo and couldn't keep a sparkle from his face. Bobby saw it too, and it emboldened him to say why he'd come. First, he decided he needed to apologize.

"Artemis, I'm sorry about standin' you up. I didn't mean to, honest. I know I was supposed to meet you at the high school practice field. Something came up and I plumb forgot. I hope you didn't wait for me long."

"Why are you here now? Surely not to say 'you're sorry.' You could have done that this weekend before the game."

Bobby lowered his eyes to the hardwood floor. They were so shiny he could see his visage bounce back to him. He steeled himself and raised his head. "No, and this may sound crazy, but I was hopin' you might have a little time before you went to bed to work with me. I'd sure like you to show me how to throw a curveball and that nasty change-up you've got."

Bobby didn't know how the man sitting in front of him would react. He was ready to be escorted from the house for interrupting a man when he's spending time with his family. And he wouldn't have blamed Artemis if he did just that. It'd been him, after all, who'd forgotten about their appointment. He was the one who'd messed up.

Artemis rose from his chair. He said nothing. He left the room and returned in less than a minute with a cap on his graying head and a ball and glove in his hand. He went to the door and pulled it open, then turned to the still-seated Bobby. "Well, come on young man. It's getting later by the minute. I'm assuming you brought your mitt with you or am I gonna have to supply that, too?"

Bobby hopped up from the sofa and swished by the man holding the door. He hurried to his car to fetch his ball glove before the old pitcher changed his mind.

Under the streetlight, Bobby and Artemis worked on pitching for over two hours. Artemis showed the youngster how to throw a proper curve and talked to him about when to throw it. He said it wasn't enough to know a bunch of different pitches; you had to know *when* to throw them. Satchel always told him the most important part of a pitcher wasn't his arm, it was his brain. A pitcher had to be smarter than the batter. Which wasn't hard, he always added with a wink, because batters are notoriously dumb as Missouri mules.

At first, Artemis didn't want to show Bobby the change-up, or the Two-Hump Blooper as Satchel called it. It was Satchel's special pitch and it'd been a long time before the great one showed it to Artemis. Finally, right before they were going to call it quits for the night, Artemis decided that Satchel wouldn't mind if a white boy learned the magic of the Blooper. Almost reverently, the older man taught Bobby how to hold and throw the most famous pitch in Satchel Paige's repertoire.

Claire, from her bedroom window, watched her husband tutor the white kid. She was glad he was doing it. She was proud of him. As the two worked long after Artemis's bedtime, she thought about calling him in, decided against it. The grin on his face told her he was having too much fun to be bothered with sleep. She shook her head in bewilderment. "Why does he love the game so much?"

# 15

Sarah and Jonda's bedroom was smaller than their brothers' and opened to the kitchen. The lack of a door proved a constant source of complaint, primarily from Sarah. Last fall in an attempt to buoy her older daughter's feelings, Cora bought two gallons of Columbia-blue paint for the girls to brighten their room. After helping her girls tape over the molding and spread newspaper on the floor, Cora stood back as her two youngest delved into the messy job. Of course, Sarah did most of the work and did it well. She was a meticulous painter, careful not to slosh the floor or splotch the woodwork. Jonda, on the other hand, saw the endeavor as playtime. By the end of the day, her shirt and shorts looked like they'd been dipped in blue sludge and her face resembled that of a Celtic warrior. After supper and a backyard scrubbing and hosing down of Jonda that would have made even the biggest dog yelp, Cora managed to find a dollar in change from her grocery-depleted tip can and slipped it to Sarah for working so hard and putting up with her sister with nary a word.

Cora stood in the bedroom doorway as Sarah and Jonda got ready for bed. Both had metal-framed beds with no headboard, and neither had a bedspread. Everyone in the Braun family used cotton sheets and hand-me-down quilts for covering except Sarah, who preferred fuzzy blankets.

"Jonda, did you brush your teeth?" Cora asked, knowing the answer. The blonde girl froze in mid-climb into her bed. "No Momma, I forgot." She backed out of her bed and moped past her mother to the bathroom as if she'd been asked to drink a tablespoonful of castor oil.

"How do you seem to forget every night?" Cora good-naturedly chided her youngest.

Jonda shrugged. "I dunno. It's probably because Sarah takes so long in the bathroom pulling hairs out of her eyebrows and checking to see if her boobies are growing that makes me not remember."

"Oh, shut up Jonda. That's not true and you know it," Sarah, already in bed, yelled.

"It is too!" Jonda marched to the threshold of the door and glared at her horizontal sister. "You do too check out your boobies. I seen you do it. Last Saturday. You was standin' in front of the mirror pushing and shoving on them things for at least thirty minutes. I don't know, maybe an hour. You was, too."

Sarah jerked upright. "For your information, little Miss Liar, last Saturday, I stayed the night with Helen Baker. I wasn't even home. Maybe you were looking at yourself in the mirror and thought it was me." She plopped back onto her pillow and slammed her eyes shut.

"Oh," Jonda looked stunned. She stood beside her mother, quietly, for several moments.

"Jonda, go brush your teeth, now. You've bothered your sister enough for one night."

She dropped her head and slinked towards the bathroom, toothbrush in hand. "Well, maybe it wadn't Saturday night," she mumbled to herself. "But I seen her do it or my name ain't Jonda Lynn Braun."

Cora watched the tiny girl slink into the bathroom. She wanted to scold Jonda over her poor grammar, decided not to. Her fireball had calmed and was finally brushing her teeth. The last thing she wanted to do was get her youngest riled again. Instead, she sauntered over to Sarah and sat on the side of the bed.

"Sarah, Honey."

Sarah looked up at her mother. She pulled the covers under her chin.

Cora stroked her daughter's thick black locks. "I love your hair, Sarah. I've always liked black hair. It's what first attracted me to your dad. He had the most gorgeous black hair I've ever seen. You've got your father's hair."

"I know," Sarah softly spoke. "I've also got his short, thick body."

"And don't forget his blue eyes and solid personality. You are definitely your father's daughter. And Josh is his father's son. You should be proud of that."

"I know," Sarah pulled her arms from the covers and held her mother's hands. "I'm glad I'm like Daddy in a lot of ways. I wish I looked a little bit like you though. Why couldn't I be tall, like you, and have blonde hair? Look at Jonda. She looks almost exactly like you did when you were her age."

"Oh, Honey. You have beautiful hair and a beautiful face. I'm so jealous of your thick hair; I sometimes have to pray extra hard for forgiveness. Someday, Jonda's gonna feel the same way. She and I have fine, stringy hair that's hard to manage and a constant battle with split ends."

"I know, but everybody thinks blonde girls are prettier."

"They do?" Cora exclaimed. "I bet that's news to Elizabeth Taylor and Jane Russell and Jane Wyman. Somebody needs to tell them they're not pretty. And while they're at it, they need to tell Wyman and Taylor they're too short."

"Okay, okay, I give," Sarah held up her hands in surrender. She laughed. "If black hair is good enough for Elizabeth Taylor, then it's good enough for me."

"Atta girl. Be proud of who you are! Because I sure am." Cora patted her daughter's head, reached down and kissed her cheek. "Sarah, one last thing and I'll let you go to sleep. I hope you know how much I appreciate all the things you do around the house. If you didn't help me so much with the housework, cooking, and minding your sister, I don't know how we'd make it. God will bless you for it. I have absolutely no doubt."

"Thanks, Mom." Sarah said, wetness seeping into her eyes. "I'm sorry you have to work so much."

*Me too*, Cora thought. *Me too.*

Cora tucked Jonda into bed with minimal resistance, went into the kitchen, and warmed up the last of the coffee. Padding softly across the linoleum floor, she dispatched a mug from the cabinet and poured herself the remaining java from the percolator. Entering the front room, she slipped off her shoes and pulled her legs under her body while she relaxed on the end of the sofa. She thought about turning on the radio, but decided it might keep the girls awake; and the last thing she wanted was for Jonda to have trouble falling asleep.

She had drunk half her coffee when Josh, grinning like he'd been eating stolen apples, strode through the door and plopped into the recliner. His smile widened when he saw his mom.

"I guess you had a good time tonight?" Cora questioned, unable to keep from smiling even though she had no idea why she should be happy. "The Oilers win?"

"Yes they did," he pronounced emphatically. "They beat El Paso nine to one. It was pretty much over by the fifth inning."

"That's good. Is that why you're so excited? The Oilers have a good team?"

Josh hesitated. Cora could tell he was arguing within himself over whether or not to tell her the truth. It didn't matter. Cora already knew Josh had gone out with the rich girl from the other side of the river, the girl whose father was some high-powered lawyer. Part of her found this exciting. Her son was dating a girl from one of the most respected and wealthiest families in Tulsa. A bigger part of her worried, worried that her son would have his heart broken if he seriously tried to court the girl. There was no way the girl's family would allow her to consider marrying a Westside man, especially one who worked for the railroad. It wouldn't happen.

"Partly," he stammered. "That and I . . . uh . . . I sure had a good time with Frannie. You remember Frannie, don't you? She was the girl whose boyfriend played shortstop the first game. Remember? We took her home after they got in a fight?"

Cora nodded that she remembered the girl.

"Anyway, she went with me to the game, and she's actually a nice girl. She's different than I originally thought. And Mom, you oughta see their house. It's huge! I bet our whole house would fit in their living room, or as they call it, *the parlor.*"

"I know the house, son. It's very nice. Her father must make a nice living."

"He does. He's an attorney. He used to be a ballplayer. He actually played in the Majors once. Can you imagine that? I'd like to talk to him about what it was like. Maybe I will someday."

"I hope you can, Josh. I hope you can."

Josh opened his mouth to gush forth more exciting news, but was cut short when something crashed against the screen door. Cora and Josh simultaneously jumped from their seats. Cora spilled the last of her coffee on the hardwood floor.

"What was that?" Josh, his eyes wide, his mouth agape, asked.

"I have no idea unless it was Sinbad. The last I looked Sinbad was asleep in his doghouse. Plus that, it sounded too large to be him."

Cora, with Josh leading, slinked to the door. Cora peeked over her son's shoulder as he quietly cracked open the door. As soon as he saw what lay on the porch, he jerked it open the rest of the way.

"Bobby!" Cora screamed. "Oh, Lord, help us!"

Bobby lay crumpled on the concrete porch. His body arranged in a fetal position except for one bloody arm that splayed from the torso like a melting cherry Popsicle. Josh tried to open the screen door, found he couldn't due to his brother's weight. He turned and sprinted through the house and out the back door. Josh was at his brother's side in less than ten seconds. He cradled his brother's head and staunched the stream of blood oozing from Bobby's nose and lips with a dishtowel he'd grabbed on his dash through the kitchen. Sarah and Jonda, wakened by their mother's scream, ran into the front room. Cora grabbed her daughters and held them close to her as Josh examined and questioned their brother about what happened.

Several minutes later, Bobby, half-carried by Josh, limped into the living room. Cora motioned for Josh to put him on the sofa where she knelt before her son and began cleaning his wounds with the warm wash rags Sarah procured from the bathroom.

Both eyes were swelled and turning purple; blood seeped from the corners. Bobby's nose bled, but it did not appear broken. He had four or five slash wounds on his forearms probably caused by a knife. Cora was sure at least two of them would need stitches. The last thing she noticed was Bobby's knuckles. They were scraped and swollen. By looking at his hands, Cora knew her son had put up a tremendous fight. This did not surprise her and, in an odd way, made her proud.

Josh stood behind her; his arms wrapped around Jonda, while she and Sarah ministered to Bobby. When they'd cleaned up most of the blood, he spoke: "I think he's going to be okay. Bobby, are you all right? They didn't cut out your tongue, did they?"

"Yeah, I'm fine." As if knowing what Josh intended, he added, "Give me a few minutes and I'll go with you."

"What do you mean go with him?" Cora said. "Nobody's going anywhere except to the hospital. You need stitches, young man."

"No I don't, Mom. I'm as good as new. I just need a couple of minutes to get my strength back."

"Mom's right," Josh stated to his brother, determination manifest in his eyes. "You need those cuts on your arms sewn up. I'll get Lonnie and Frank to help me. You know they always help me with my light work." He mustered a laugh from his throat, but everyone in the room could tell it was forced. "Mom, Bobby'll be able to walk in a few minutes. You don't need me to go to the hospital. Sarah will help. The Star gang did this and they're going to pay for it –tonight."

"Please don't go, Josh," Cora pleaded. "You'll end up like your brother or worse."

Josh looked at his mother, confusion evident on his face. "I have to go, Mother. Don't you understand? I can't let them get away with this or none of us will be safe." Josh grabbed his keys from the coffee table and strode from the house. They listened as he fired up the engine and drove away. He did not speed.

\* \* \* \* \*

Bobby, despite the battering he'd taken, felt much better after his wounds were cleaned. He was having trouble seeing out of both eyes, his head throbbed like someone was whacking him with a ball-peen hammer, and the gashes on his arms wouldn't stop leaking. Other than that he was doing pretty well. He would be fine in a few days. He guessed he would have to appease his mother and go to the hospital. He would rather have gone with his brother because, despite what he'd said, he knew Josh was going alone. His brother had no intention of taking anyone with him. Not for this fight.

\* \* \* \* \*

Gibbo Ross and the Delaney brothers weren't hard to find. They had not moved from their perch atop Gibbo's Chevy parked in front of the Cove Theater. Why they were hanging out in Red Fork and not their usual haunt in Oakhurst was beyond Josh. Nor did he give it much thought. At this point, he didn't care.

Josh drove under the speed limit so he wouldn't attract any unwanted guests, like cops. He drove west on Forty-First Street into the community of Red Fork. The dividing line was Union Avenue where the big Baptist church stood like a welcoming pillar. He slowed dramatically as soon as he passed South Twenty-Third; the theater lay in darkness a mere half block away.

Josh parked directly across from the theater. He spied Gibbo and the Delaneys lounging on the hood of the black car. When Josh turned off the engine and swung open the door, none of the three moved. It was like they were slouching hood ornaments permanently attached to the paint. The theater, with its darkened marquee, towered behind the trio. Josh could only make out the words on the marquee closest to him: *Quiet Man* and below that, *John Wayne*. Directly behind the three men the moon-drenched ticket booth and empty glass foyer danced with swirling shadows caused by leafy tree limbs jostling in the night breeze. Josh's hands began shaking. He jammed them into his pants pockets so his nemeses would not see his nervousness. He swigged a mouthful of clean air and blew it out his nose. It steadied him.

Josh crossed the street and approached the three hoodlums in a steady, determined pace. He realized that if he'd come only an hour earlier, the theater would have been lit up; the streets and sidewalks crowded with moviegoers. A thought occurred to Josh: *The theater would definitely have been open when the thugs attacked Bobby. Why hadn't anyone helped him? Why weren't the police called?* Josh's face streamed red with anger. He couldn't decide whom he wanted to hit first.

The three gangsters, as if in practiced unison, hopped off the hood. The Delaney brothers took the vanguard, while Gibbo slouched behind. Josh could see his opponents more clearly now. The Delaneys looked solemn, their mouths a thin straight line, their eyes dull and tired-looking. Both stood taller than Josh. Nevertheless, Josh, thick and sturdy due to tough, demanding railroad work, definitely had the muscle advantage. Josh noticed Vernon sported a shiner and a nasty little slice on his left cheek that trickled a trace of blood, which the big man (as if realizing that Josh had noticed his wound) pushed from his face with the back of his hand. The other Delaney appeared unmarked. However, as Josh closed with the brothers, he discerned a puffy purplish knot above George's right eye. Bobby had obviously gotten in some good licks before being overwhelmed. A satisfied smile slipped onto Josh's face; he snickered loud enough that the brothers hesitated their advance. They glanced at each other, then back at Gibbo. Gibbo nodded and grinned like a possum who's found a trash can full of half-eaten jelly sandwiches.

Vernon, who seemed to be the braver of the two, strode to Josh and raised his fist above his head to deliver a haymaker to Josh's chin. Josh promptly punched him squarely in the nose, knocking him to the ground. The thug's nose burst forth with crimson like an Independence Day fireworks fountain. The downed man groaned and cursed, infuriated and surprised.

No sooner did Vernon go down, then George charged. Josh dispatched him to his brother's side on the pavement with a well-placed kick in the groin and a short left hook to the temple.

Josh was expecting Gibbo to attack, but he held back. Instead, the Delaneys bounced from their prone position on the concrete with renewed determination. George reached into his pocket and withdrew a narrow knife which he flicked open by pressing a switch. The long, thin silver blade glowed under the moonlit sky. Vernon mimicked his brother and now the two crept towards Josh, switchblades in their hands, a look of confidence on their faces. Josh instinctively backed up, keeping his eyes glued to the pointed metal waving menacingly before him. As he cautiously retreated towards his car, he noticed that Vernon's sticker was covered in a dark reddish substance. *It had to be Bobby's. It had to be his brother's blood!* A boiling rage washed through Josh's body and erupted from his throat and flooded through clenched teeth in a ghoulish scream of anger and pain that sounded like a Medieval Huguenot on the rack during the Inquisition. Luckily, Josh's macabre shriek worked in his favor. The blade-wielding goons halted their charge; George actually lowered his knife to his waist. Josh, snarling like a rabid dog, his eyes flitting back and forth from one Delaney to the other as if on the verge of striking, found a brief moment of respite. His body needed no rest. It ached to attack. It begged to rejoin the fray without consideration of tactics or outcome and with haste. Josh literally forced his limbs and muscles to refrain. Somewhere in the back of his mind, he realized his animal instincts, the overwhelming desire for battle, for revenge, had gained control. He also understood that if he was going to be successful, he had to come up with a different plan of attack. Facing three men with pulled knives, three men who weren't afraid or ashamed to use them on an unarmed adversary, he realized he couldn't just charge head down like a ram battling for territory during mating season. No, he had to think of something else.

Josh, still snarling, filched another step back. The movement was not lost on the Delaneys or Gibbo Ross. From the rear, Gibbo chuckled like a vampire who realizes his victim has lost his faith. "Well boys, it looks like Mr. Tough-Guy ain't so tough after all. It wouldn't surprise me if he doesn't wet his drawers in a minute or two."

Vernon and George laughed at Gibbo's humor as if he was Bob Hope come to West Tulsa. Both stood less than five feet from Josh, their bodies no longer in a defensive posture, their arms hanging loosely at their sides.

Josh grabbed the opportunity offered by the pause in hostilities to execute his new and improved plan of action. He turned his back on the Delaneys and strode to his car. He reached the driver's door after five quick steps.

"Looky there," George snickered. "Sissy boy's had enough. He wants to go home to his mommy."

"Yeah," Vernon agreed. "All them Brauns are nuthin'. What would you expect? They're Germans. Look how we whipped 'em in the war."

None of the Delaneys' diatribes affected Josh. His mind was set. He had a plan.

Josh, during the lull in the confrontation, decided he really did need some help. Why he'd thought he could take Gibbo and the Delaneys without any assistance escaped him now. Luckily, between rushes of rage, he'd thought of who could help him. Josh reached through the open window of the backseat and pulled Mr. Rawlings through it. He turned and faced the Star Gang with his new helper. Despite trying hard, he couldn't help grinning.

"That stick of wood ain't gonna help you any," Gibbo confidently predicted. "Boys, spread out and let's end this thing."

The Delaneys resumed their fighting stance. Taking their leader's advice, George, jabbing his knife into the night air like he was harpooning a killer whale, shuffled towards Josh's left while Vernon eased to the right. Immediately, Josh decided he couldn't allow them to form a semicircle around him and pinch him against his own vehicle. He needed room to swing his newfound friend.

He attacked.

Josh, mainly because the knife theatrics irritated him, chose George first and walloped him in the stomach with his thirty-six-ounce bat. Ribs cracked; air whooshed from the falling man. George dropped his switchblade and rolled into the fetal position groaning and gasping for a breath of precious air. He made no attempt to retrieve his knife. Josh kicked it under the car.

Josh about-faced and went into his home run swing. The bat cut through the air menacingly close to Vernon's dodging face. The Delaney twin jolted backwards leaving his feet as if he were a flying crawdad. Vernon, eyes wide-open and his face suddenly drenched pale, audibly gulped, then turned and ran away down the dark, empty street.

"I guess it's just you and me, big boy," Gibbo Ross stated from the shadows of the theater. The leader of the Star Gang had moved to the far side of the street; he didn't appear ready to give up the struggle. "Come on over here and I'll show you how a real man fights. But, I want to warn you. It'll be the last fight you're ever in."

Josh turned towards the voice. In the shadows, he spied Gibbo perched atop the hood of a car. He was fairly certain Gibbo was trying to put his bluff in, otherwise, why had he backed away from the fight? The truth be told, he didn't care. He was going to end this tonight, one way or the other. Josh marched to the other side of the street, bat lying across his shoulder like he was Babe Ruth advancing to the plate.

Gibbo sprang from the hood of the car. He glided through the air, knife extended, like an avenging daemon sweeping through an unsuspecting village from the clouds above. Except Josh proved quicker. He flicked Mr. Rawlings at the shadowy shape and felt the bat connect solidly with the long, steel blade and the knuckles surrounding it. The battered hand released its weapon, and the knife flew into the darkness and bounced harmlessly into the sewer drain. Gibbo landed at his enemy's feet and swiftly rolled away.

The leader of the Star Gang leapt to his feet and frantically searched the ground for his lost knife. Josh watched him, delight dancing in his eyes. The fruitless search continued for another twenty seconds before Gibbo realized it was in vain. Josh thought his enemy might turn and run and was somewhat surprised when, instead, the gangster challenged him. "Why don't you drop the bat and fight like a man, Braun," Gibbo said. "Or are you yella?"

Josh thought about reminding his adversary that less than five minutes earlier, he and two of his thugs had seen no problem in attacking him with knives, while he had only his fists. But testosterone got in his way. He wanted to show Mr. Ross, Mr. Tough-Stuff Gangster that he wasn't nearly as mean as he thought he was.

Josh dropped his bat.

Gibbo immediately charged.

The hoodlum came at Josh like a windmill in a hurricane. Josh found himself backing away from the onslaught, blocking as many roundhouses as he could. However, a few slipped past his defenses. He was hit with a grazing blow across the forehead and absorbed a solid wallop flush on the ear that made him cringe in pain but also filled him with renewed rage. Josh counterattacked. He dipped his head to avoid a fight-ending hook aimed at his jaw and rocked the younger man with an uppercut to his gut. Gibbo grimaced and dropped his hands. Josh powered another punch to the man's midsection more to ensure that his opponent's hands remained lowered than to inflict further damage, then moved upstairs. Josh connected with a devastating right cross to Gibbo's eye and through his knuckles felt the man's eyebrow rip apart. Blood spurted from the gaping trench and splattered the front of Josh's shirt. Josh didn't let up. He forced the gangster to pedal backwards with a flurry of punches to the mouth and nose. Blood spurted from tears in both lips and from his nostrils. Josh paused his onslaught to survey the damage. Gibbo teetered on wobbly legs, his arms at his sides, remaining vertical through willpower alone.

Josh took his time and administered the coup de grace, a chopping right to the jaw. Gibbo crumbled onto the street; the back of his head thudding on the concrete with a sickening crunch. Josh felt absolutely no pity for his fallen foe. He strode to the moaning, injured man and glared down at him, utter disdain and contempt evident on his sneering mouth. He knelt beside him and gripping his bloody maw, forced the hoodlum to look at him. Gibbo complied and reached to his blood-engorged eye socket with his hand to clear his vision. Josh knocked away his hand.

"Listen, you scumbag," Josh snarled. "And listen good. If you ever, ever bother anyone in my family again, I will hunt you down and make sure you never hurt anyone again. That's a promise. Do you understand?"

Gibbo Ross, through immense pain, nodded that he understood.

Josh rose and walked calmly to his car leaving Gibbo Ross, far closer to death than life, and a still-moaning George Delaney on the dark street. Vernon Delaney was nowhere to be seen.

Josh Braun got into his car and started the engine. He killed it and got out. He walked back to the unmoving, but alive Gibbo Ross, bent down beside him and picked up Mr. Rawlings. He returned to his car, tossed the life-saving baseball bat into the backseat and drove off. He did not go over the speed limit the entire trip home.

# 16

"Dang it!" the tall, skinny man exclaimed. "I hate when it gets hot."

Josh looked at his fellow brakeman and chuckled. 'Dang it' was Lonnie Corlett's favorite expression anytime he was dissatisfied with something. "What's the problem over there?" Josh asked. "The itty, bitty switch too tough for ya? You want me to come over there and help ya?"

"No, it's got nuthin' ta do with the lousy switch; it's stuck, but nuthin' I can't handle. The problem is I'm sweatin' so bad it's makin' my glasses slide down my nose. I'm sick and tired of having to constantly push 'em back up. It's a royal pain in the patooter."

"Why don't you just take 'em off and put 'em in your pocket till you're finished?" Josh asked, trying his best to look serious.

Lonnie rose from the switch handle, shook his head at his friend. "Cause if I did that, you big goofball, I wouldn't be able to see what I was doin'. I'd have cars loaded with lumber headin' to Oregon and cars with steel headin' to Pittsburgh! Then me and you both would get fired and probably have to start workin' for the city or some other awful company."

"Ya got me there. The last thing I want to do the rest of my life is flip burgers at Macs. I'd weigh three hundred pounds in no time."

Josh, after he maneuvered his own switch in place, went to Lonnie's track and helped him pull his. It proved stubborn. It took both men to pull the switch so they could hump the cars onto the correct tracks.

Josh and Lonnie stood to the side as the next car, loaded with Oregon pine, slid down the tracks from the humping hill onto the correct terminus where it coupled onto the other loaded cars waiting in the hot sun for the final leg of the journey -- Dallas. Lonnie lifted a pack of Camels from his shirt pocket and jammed one into his mouth. He offered a cigarette to his friend knowing full well he would be rebuffed. The lean young man lit the Camel and inhaled the acrid smoke. He loved to smoke and didn't understand at all why Josh didn't. Everybody smoked. He wasn't sure you were really an American if you didn't like a cig now and then.

"Well, looky there," Lonnie said in between puffs. "Old man Thompkins decided to get out of his nice, cool office and check on the hired help. Sure hope he doesn't break a sweat."

Josh turned towards the terminal and saw the ancient yard chief heading their way. Josh liked Harry Thompkins. He'd always treated him well. After the war, it'd been Mr. Thompkins who placed Josh's name at the top of the list for hiring. It was also Mr. Thompkins who pushed for Frisco to sponsor the baseball team and work around the schedules of the ballplayers. Even though Mr. Thompkins was a Cub's fan, Josh still liked him. The chief couldn't help it if he'd spent his early childhood in the windy city and become attached to St. Louis's biggest rival.

The big boss, who was big only because of his position with the railroad, crept along the steep stairway as if he were climbing Mount Everest. Josh and Lonnie watched the tiny, gray-haired man struggle up the steps.

"Whatever it is, it must be important for him not to wait an hour till we clocked out," Lonnie observed.

"Must be," Josh mumbled in agreement.

Mr. Thompkins, after cresting the stairs, paused, then ambled towards the two standing brakemen.

"Hello, Mr. Thompkins," Lonnie said. "What's got you out on such a hot day?"

Harry Thompkins looked at Lonnie, said nothing; he turned to Josh. Josh had no idea why the yard chief had trekked up the hill, but after examining his boss's face he felt confident it wasn't to bring bad news. Despite trying to look solemn and businesslike, Josh could see the wrinkles at the tips of Thompkins' lips. He was desperately fighting a grin.

"Josh," he began, looking directly into the young man's eyes. "I just got off the phone with a Mr. Runt Marr. Ever heard of him?"

Now it was Josh's lips' turn to curl. He definitely had heard of Runt Marr; he had even met him once. "Yes, sir. I know who he is."

"Well, he's gonna be in town this weekend and wanted to know what time you fellas played on Saturday. So I told him. I hope that was alright?"

Josh knew that Mr. Thompkins knew it was perfectly okay to tell Mr. Marr when they played, but he played along.

"Yes sir, that was fine. I appreciate you talking to him."

Mr. Thompkins nodded. Saying nothing more, the little boss turned from the brakemen and shuffled back to the staircase. This time he didn't have as much trouble navigating the stairs. He seemed able to descend better than climb.

"What in tarnation was that all about?" Lonnie asked. "Who's Runt Marr? Is he a baseball fan who useta work for Frisco or what? And where in heavens did he get a name like Runt?"

Josh backed away from the track as another car headed for Dallas rolled down the slope, passed them, and coupled with the line of cars forming a train. His mind flitted from Marr to Bobby to the game on Saturday to Frannie and what she'd think, back to Marr. Finally, it registered in his racing brain what Lonnie had asked. "I'm sure he is a baseball fan, Lonnie. He'd 'bout have to be as many games as he sees every year. He works for the St. Louis Cardinals. He's a scout. As far as his name goes, you'd know why they call him that if you ever saw him."

"Well, I'll be," Lonnie exclaimed. "You mean a real scout who can offer you money and sign you to a contract."

"Nuthin' but. He'll even buy you a train ticket to whatever city they send you. Heck, if you're good enough he can give you a bonus to get you started."

"Dang it!" Lonnie yelped.

"What's the matter now?"

"It's just that it looks like Saturday might be the biggest game of the year and I gotta work," he groused. Lonnie Corlett walked to the switch and checked that it was still in the right position. He turned towards Josh, a mischievous look splashed over his face. "Hey buddy, why don't you swap shifts with me, so I can go to the game and see a real, live Big League scout?"

"Okay Lonnie, I'll switch. But you'll have to catch for me. You don't mind catching Bobby do you? You can use my gear. The mask might be a tad big for you, but I doubt if it will slip, too much. And looking at your legs, there's no way my shin guards are gonna cover all the way to your knees. Oh well, Bobby usually doesn't throw too many in the dirt. You'll be fine."

"I was only kidding, my friend. I really have no desire to see a Major League scout up close. You go ahead and go to your game. I'll stay here and make sure America's heart keeps beating."

Josh practically dove into his car when he got off work. Normally, he was one of the last to leave. He didn't like creeping along in the protracted parade of vehicles waiting impatiently at the yard entrance for a clearing in the going-home traffic. This time, however, he was first to clock out, first to his car, and first to dart onto the busy street that ran parallel to the Frisco yard. Josh snaked in and out of the traffic, zigzagging through the meandering procession like he was a stock-car driver zooming around the Creek County Fairgrounds track. Not used to such heroic driving, he gripped the steering wheel tightly, several times having to flex his sore hands to regain circulation. His right hand was especially tender; it'd been the one he'd delivered most of the blows to Gibbo Ross's face. He'd taken two aspirins that morning before work, and they helped ease the pain for most of the day. Now, the aching returned with a vengeance. "Oh well," he said looking at his scraped, swollen knuckles. "I don't think Gibbo and his Star bunch are gonna bother the Brauns anymore."

Josh streaked into Big Jim's Texaco Station and whisked past the pumps like they were traffic signals glowing green. Big Jim Taylor, all two hundred and seventy pounds of him, straightened from cleaning the windshield of a '47 Caddy and glowered at the Chrysler slashing through his station. Josh didn't notice the former football star's impatient frown. His eyes were locked on his brother fixing a flat on a bicycle tube. A chubby redheaded boy stood beside him. Josh pulled up directly in front of the pair and threw the door open. Bobby and the flat-topped kid looked up from the bubbling inner tube.

"Hey little brother, whatcha doin?" Josh gushed.

"What's it look like I'm doing? I'm trying to fix this kid's bicycle tube. I think he must have ridden through a thumbtack garden, there're so many holes in it."

"Did not," the boy sounded hurt. "I told you, Bobby, I went around the corner over on South Twenty-Seventh and accidentally rode through a bunch of glass in the street. I think somebody threw a Coke bottle out their window."

"Loosen up, kid," Bobby gently scolded. "I'm just messin' with ya. It ain't no big deal how it happened. I'll get it fixed, but it might cost ya a cold Pepsi in addition to the quarter Big Jim charges for flats."

"All I gots is the quarter for the flat. That's all my mom gave me. I could owe ya. I come here all the time; you know that. I'll buy ya one later."

Bobby reached down and tousled the kid's hair. The boy looked at Bobby and finally realized he was kidding. They exchanged chuckles.

"How 'bouts I buy you one, William, for being one of Big Jim's best customers?" Bobby scrounged in his pocket and came out with a nickel. He flipped it to the boy who caught it in mid-stride on his way to the pop machine. Bobby watched the boy scamper around the corner.

"Is this what you do all day? Give away your wages? Funny, you never buy me a Pepsi when I gas up."

Bobby glanced again at the boy's path. "It's a wonder he's got a quarter to fix this old tube. His dad's dead and his step-dad's little more than a drunk. William's got four sisters, all younger, and his mom's got a nuthin' job over at B & B Grocery. I know for a fact William spends most of his paper-route money on food for his family cuz I've seen him do it. That's why I don't mind fixin' this old shredded tube any day of the week." Bobby dipped the tube into the water again. Several air bubbles from three or four holes plinked to the surface.

Josh dropped his head. He'd known William Lassiter's father. His name also had been William, but everybody called him Bill. He too was lost in the war; killed fighting the Japanese on some God-forsaken place called Wake Island. Suddenly, Josh didn't feel quite so excited about Mr. Runt Marr.

"Well? Are you gonna tell me why you zoomed in here so fast it about gave Big Jim a heart attack or are you gonna stand there and look at the beautiful blacktop?"

Josh peeked over his shoulder towards Big Jim. The owner of the filling station was pumping gas into a black 1950 Ford. Bobby's favorite car! A sign from Heaven? He hoped so. The bursting grin returned to his face. He turned back to Bobby, who was scraping the damaged tube in preparation for the patch. "Runt Marr is coming to West Tulsa Saturday to watch us play."

"So?" Bobby said without looking up from the tube. "Who's Runt

Marr? Is he the head umpire or a league official wondering why we fight more than we play ball?"

"Not hardly. Runt Marr is the head scout for the St. Louis Cardinals baseball team and he's coming to watch us play."

Neither said anything for several seconds. It was as if the news was so shocking to the brain that it was bouncing off instead of being absorbed into the memory circuits. Slowly, Bobby hoisted his head. He looked at his grinning brother as if they'd just robbed the First National Bank and gotten away with it.

"You're joshing me, aren't you?"

Josh smiled at his younger brother. "Josh doesn't josh about baseball. You know that. This is our big chance, kiddo. And we aren't gonna mess it up!"

\* \* \* \* \*

Artemis again tried to show Bobby that he needed to flip his wrist more when throwing the curve. Bobby wanted to release the ball like he was pointing at home plate rather than snapping it out of his fingers. Therefore, he wasn't getting enough spin, which meant less break. Artemis opened his protégé's hand and correctly manipulated the ball into the fingers.

He stepped back and had Bobby flip the ball to him, so he could check the rotation. It wasn't bad this time. He returned the ball to his student and challenged him to do it again.

Artemis held up his hand, looked around. He didn't see Satchy. Where had he gone?

"Bobby? Did you happen to see where Satchy went? He was sitting on the curb fiddlin' with that old mitt of mine a second ago."

Bobby shook his head. Both began searching for the misplaced boy.

Artemis walked along the street until he could see around the side of the house. He noticed Bobby doing the same. Artemis wished he hadn't agreed to help Bobby today. He'd forgotten that Claire and her mother were going shopping, and he had to watch Satchel. Besides, Bobby was in no mood to practice; he was too excited.

"I see him," yelled Bobby. "It looks like he's found a kitty."

"Oh great," Artemis mumbled. "He'll probably want to keep it." He strode towards the far end of his house behind Bobby. When Artemis turned the corner, Bobby was reaching for the cat. It darted out of his reach and scampered over the fence into the neighbor's yard.

"There goes my new friend," Satchy complained. "His name was Rascal."

*Thank the Lord,* Artemis thought.

"How do you know his name's Rascal?" Bobby asked Satchy.

"Cause he told me that was his name," Satchy proudly answered.

Artemis slipped his mitt back onto his hand and flipped the ball to Bobby. "Now, where were we?"

Bobby looked at the solemn man before him then back at the little boy sitting, head bowed, on the curb. "Why don't we call it a day," he said. "Satchy needs someone to play with, and you've been in the dumps ever since I told you about the scout."

Artemis agreed. He pulled his glove from his hand and tossed it to the grass. He stretched out on the concrete and leaned on the heels of his hands. Satchy looked forlornly at his father.

"Now, Mr. Gloomy Gus. What's bothering you? Why aren't you excited about Saturday?"

Artemis tilted his head back and stared at the pale sky. After thirty seconds or so of quiet, somber contemplation, he turned and searched Bobby's face. "I'm happy for you. I really am. Bobby you've got a good chance of catching his attention. Other than ole Satchel and Feller, you throw as hard as anyone I've ever seen. Those Big League scouts like hard throwers; yes they do."

"But you oughta be excited, Artemis. You never know; you might get signed, too."

Artemis couldn't help himself. He guffawed derisively. He quickly halted when he saw that Bobby was offended. "Sorry man, but I'd be the last one Mr. Marr, head Cardinal scout, would sign."

"Hey, you never know. They're signing black players all the time now. I've already told Josh to let you pitch a couple of innings, so the scout can watch you."

Artemis looked at the young man before him with fresh appreciation. "Bobby, that's one of the nicest things anyone's ever said to me. To think that a young stallion like you would give up pitching time so an old cuss like me could maybe impress a scout is downright amazin'. Truly amazin' when you consider you're white and I'm black. Unfortunately, my time has passed. I was born too early."

Bobby sat down beside his mentor. "You'd do the same for me. I know you would. Besides, you're not too old. Look at your friend, Satchel Paige. He's still pitching and he's way older than you are."

Artemis chuckled. "I ain't no Satchel Paige. Nowhere close. I'm smart enough to know that. There's only one Satchel . . ." his voice trailed off.

"You could lie about your age," Bobby protested. "People do it all the time. I knew a guy who told the army he was eighteen when he was only fifteen so he could join. Just borrow a birth certificate from somebody you know and doctor the name."

Artemis leaned forward and stuck out his arm. "Here's the problem, young man. The chicken wing don't lie. It's old and pretty much used up. Any scout worth his salt will be able to see that. Baseball's a young man's game, and my youth was yesterday."

Bobby bowed his head. "I'm sorry, Artemis. You should have been allowed to play in the Majors. It wasn't right."

Artemis patted his friend on the shoulder. "Hey! Pep up. I had a great time playing for the Monarchs. Why, if I'd played in the Big Leagues, I doubt if I'd ever met Claire and that means I wouldn't have Satchy. Both of them are more important than wearin' some silly uniform that says Dodgers or Yankees across the front. Nosiree, I've had a great life with no regrets."

Bobby rose from the cool concrete. He told Artemis goodbye and headed to his car. As he drove off Artemis flashed him a smile and a nod. Bobby returned it, thinking no matter what Artemis said, no matter how he glossed over it; it still wasn't right.

\* \* \* \* \*

They were lucky. They found an empty slot at Pennington's Drive-In on the first loop through the lot. Every space contained a car and about a dozen waiting customers cruised the popular restaurant's parking lot looking for back-up lights, returned trays, or other telltale signs a vehicle was about to vacate a slot. Carhops, carrying trays loaded with drinks and burgers, glided from the restaurant to their customers' cars on shiny roller skates, their white leather boots decorated with tassels of pink, orange, red, and aqua. The pony-tailed girls, dressed in white monogrammed blouses and tight black pants, swayed and bopped to the lively music blaring from the restaurant speakers. Frannie and Josh ordered Black Bottom Pie and vanilla Cokes. Josh had never eaten Black Bottom Pie, Pennington's specialty, which was why they were there. When Josh came by Frannie's house to tell her something 'really, really important', she suggested they zip over to Pennington's and eat dessert while he laid it on her. Now, halfway through the rich chocolate pie, he still hadn't told her what was so pressing.

"Is this really the first time you've eaten at Pennington's?" Frannie asked.

Josh bobbed his head up and down as he finished the last of his pie. After the final bite, he stuck the empty fork in his mouth and pulled it out slowly between pressed lips to get the last bit of chocolate flavor from the tines.

"It's pretty good, isn't it?"

Josh looked at her like she was the dumbest person in the world.

"I do believe it's the best chocolate pie I've ever eaten," he stated with certainty.

"I still can't believe you've never been to Pennington's. This is my dad's favorite place to get a hamburger. Well, this place and Weber's Root Beer Stand. Please don't tell me you haven't been there either."

Josh examined his fork as if looking for traces of chocolate. "Okay, I won't tell you."

Frannie tilted her head quizzically, opened her mouth . . . closed it. She shook her head at Josh like an exasperated mother whose son has just told her the biggest whopper she's ever heard.

"Hey, Josh?"

"Hey, what?"

"Are you ever going to tell me the big news that you were practically bursting to tell me before you discovered Black Bottom pie?"

Josh looked up from his fork. He smiled. "I did forget to tell you, didn't I? For some reason, now it almost seems anticlimactic."

"Please tell me anyway," Frannie insisted, her voice sounding almost irritated.

"Sure. It's real simple. There's a Major League scout coming to watch us play this weekend. The rumor is he's got contracts in his pocket and bonus checks already signed."

Frannie studied the man behind the wheel. His voice may have told her the news in a matter-of-fact voice, but the rest of him shouted excitement. His eyes gleamed; he kept wetting his lips, and a redness seeped into his still-puffy cheeks that made him look like an adolescent girl experimenting with rouge for the first time. "So, you think you've got a shot at getting signed?"

"I'd better. My whole future depends on it."

Frannie didn't say anything for a few seconds. She wanted him to go on, to examine the profound statement he'd uttered. He didn't. She realized she could simply smile and wish him luck, and everything would be fine; that is unless he didn't get signed. Or, she could try to get him to see how foolish he was to risk his entire future on a game, on the chance that a stranger happens to like the way you throw a ball or swing a bat. She struggled with what to do, but not for very long. She knew what she had to do; she couldn't play the Pollyanna part. She had to say something. "Josh. You know I want nothing more than for you to realize your dream. I hope this scout thinks you're the greatest ballplayer since Babe Ruth. But what are you going to do if you aren't offered a contract? Have you thought about that?"

Josh chuckled at her question. "Listen Frannie, what you don't realize is this same scout offered me a baseball contract two years ago, and I'm a lot better player now than I was then. I'm stronger, leaner, and faster. There's no way I won't get signed. I've worked too hard. I'm a baseball player and if I do say so myself, a darn good one!"

"I know you are," Frannie agreed. "But what if, for whatever reason, you don't get signed? Perhaps they don't need any catchers this year or maybe since you turned them down once they won't give you another chance? If that happens, what's your plan B? What will you do then?"

Josh dipped his head then looked again at the girl across from him. He didn't appear upset or nervous or irritated. He looked confident and determined. "Frannie, there is no plan B. Since I was a little boy, I've wanted nothing else but to be a ballplayer. Baseball is my life and always will be. It's what I dream about. It's what I think about. It's what keeps me going. I'm not sure I'd want to be alive if I couldn't play baseball."

By the time he finished his short soliloquy, his voice had dropped to a whisper. Frannie nodded and bit off the part she was going to say about him being innately intelligent and a natural-born leader and how well he could do in the business world. He didn't care about those things.

She didn't understand why she was drawn to this boy. Because, despite his many responsibilities and a man's job, that's what he was, a boy trying desperately to carve his niche in a rugged world. He had little education. His family was poor. He obsessed about a game she didn't care for, yet there was something about him she liked; there was something in his eyes and in his walk and, yes, in his cocky manner that thrilled her. She scooted close to him. She immediately recognized fear in his eyes; it excited her even more. She looked directly into his ocean blue eyes. He did not turn away. "I hope, more than anything in the world, that your dreams come true." She crossed the neutral zone and lightly kissed his cheek. He sat there, bewilderment mixing with the fear in his eyes. This time when she kissed him, it was firmly on the mouth. He responded with an eagerness and roughness that was . . . well . . . that was boyish. Even with his obvious lack of experience, he kissed far better than suave, conceited Cameron ever could.

Frannie leaned against the front seat when they finished their fourth, and most passionate kiss. She sighed.

"Say, I've got a great idea!" Josh exclaimed. He lowered his head to hers as if to tell her a great secret.

Many things flashed through Frannie's mind in that instant. What he suggested was definitely not one of them.

"Why don't we get another piece of pie?" He whispered.

# 17

Cora filled the men's cups for the fourth time. They'd finished eating over half an hour earlier and sat relaxing, smoking, and visiting before they headed home. She didn't mind. She had less than ten minutes on her shift, and they were her only customers. They'd already given her a good tip, and she didn't care if the four men were still puffing when she left. It'd happened many times before.

She swigged the last of her lukewarm coffee from the mug she kept on the counter and gathered her things. Before leaving, she checked the schedule (as if it had magically changed so she could be off tomorrow for prayer meeting) and stuffed the envelope containing her night's tips into her purse.

A ripple of cool night air tousled her hair, and swept over her face like a springtime breeze. For almost a minute, Cora stood near the entrance with her eyes closed, and breathed in the gentle wind. After being shut inside the smoky, grease-infested diner, the refreshing night air washed over her, revitalizing her tired body.

"Hello Cora, how are you this evening? Just get off work?"

Cora tensed. The man who'd spoken to her leaned against the driver's door of a blue Chevrolet. Cora nodded at the familiar voice.

"Hello, Mr. Cornwell. It sure is a pleasant night."

Cora had seen Robert Cornwell many times since their first disgusting meeting. Anytime he came to the diner, which was practically every night, he sat in her section and always acted the gentleman. Twice he'd offered apologies, which she waved off saying it was all in the past. She did this mainly because she didn't want to discuss his impropriety or actually to discuss anything with him. Robert Cornwell quickly became her biggest tipper, several times leaving a silver dollar, and once two crisp greenbacks beside his plate. Cora read nothing into this, other than the man's desire to flash his affluence and power. Never again had he touched her or said anything slightly untoward or flirtatious.

"I told you not to call me mister anymore. I don't know what got into me when we first met. Like I told you, I think I was stressed over my new job and wanted to make sure my subordinates saw me as their superior." Cornwell lowered his head and dabbed at the gravel with his foot as if he was looking for a dropped coin. His actions reminded Cora of a little boy enduring a scolding by his disappointed mother.

"I'm sorry, Mr. Cornwell. I don't feel at ease calling you by your first name." She flicked a quick smile at the big tipper who raised his eyes in time to catch the evaporating gesture.

He leaped at Cora's sign of cordiality and returned her friendliness with a wide, gleaming grin.

"I understand. You're a fine, forgiving Christian woman just to be civil with me. It's too bad there's not a time machine. I'd go back and relive that awful night when I acted so caddy. I know I've said it a dozen times before, but I'm going to say it again. Cora, I'm terribly sorry about how I acted the first time we met." Cornwell crossed his arms. He stood before the offended woman, eyes searching hers, hoping she truly was forgiving.

Cora opened her mouth, closed it

Cornwell's lips curled, creating boyish dimples that Cora, in all the times she'd waited on the man, had never noticed. Perhaps she'd been wrong about him. Maybe what he'd done to her really was an aberration. Or maybe she was a prude. It'd been so long since she'd been around a man perhaps she'd forgotten how they acted. John had never acted that way. He'd never been crude to her or around her. However, he was different. He was a churchman, a deacon, a husband and father who read his Bible every night before turning out the light and cuddling with her.

Cora checked her wristwatch. Bobby was fifteen minutes late. He must have fallen asleep on the couch, or simply forgotten to pick her up – again. She drew in a deep swatch of air and expelled it as if she were blowing out a hundred birthday candles.

"Did your ride forget you?" Cornwell asked, concern evident in his eyes.

"It's nothing new. My youngest son has a tendency to doze off anytime he's still for more than five minutes. It's no big deal. Something will wake him up, and he'll remember his old mother."

Cornwell chuckled. "You're not old, Cora," he said with a straight face. "Far from it."

Cora looked away. She searched the parking lot and the street beyond as if looking for her late son, but in reality, she was trying to hiding her discomfort.

"Listen, Cora," Cornwell practically whispered. "I know you're leery about me. And you have every right to be. But I'd sure like to drive you home. It would be an honor."

Cora shook her head. "Oh, no. That won't be necessary. Bobby will be here shortly."

"Are you sure?" his voice sounded sad, wounded. "It's really no trouble. None at all."

"No, I can't let you do it. You live on the other side of the river, and Garden City is the opposite way."

Cornwell nodded, turned and opened his car door. He looked back at Cora. "Really, Cora, I don't mind at all. It bothers me to see you standing out here like this. Taking you home would really help me, too. It would help me make it up to you for, you know, for what I did."

A flash of embarrassment zoomed through Cora. She pulled in her bottom lip and scraped her teeth across it. The well-dressed man half-in, half-out of his shiny car looked at her with innocent blue eyes. She felt herself relax. Maybe she'd misread Mr. Cornwell. Perhaps it was time to forgive him and become friends. Everyone deserved a second chance.

She nodded. "Alright, Mr. Cornwell, you may take me home." She trooped down the steps of the Frisco Diner and walked around the black Ford to the passenger side. Cornwell followed the woman and opened the door for her.

Cora thanked him, but bristled when she saw him looking at her legs as she stretched her white skirt over her knees. She was tempted to get out right then, but not wanting to hurt the Good Samaritan's feelings; she didn't. This critical moment would haunt and torture her in both her waking hours and in her sleep, and she would replay her decision to stay in the car for the rest of her life.

They zipped out of the parking lot, turned onto poorly-lit Quanah Avenue and headed towards Garden City. Cornwell drove along the main thoroughfare flicking glances at Cora, saying nothing. Cora looked straight ahead and, for the first time, noticed that over half the streetlights were burned out.

They passed the feed store and Community Bank in silence. When they went by the ghostly Howard Park and still her driver had said nothing, Cora decided to attempt conversation. "Mr. Cornwell, how do you like Tulsa?" She turned and forced a smile onto her face.

Robert Cornwell continued staring ahead, both hands on the steering wheel. He gripped the circular guide like a race car driver about to be passed. Cora didn't think she could have peeled his hands from the wheel with a crowbar. They were now beside the giant Texaco tank farm.

"It's okay," he mumbled.

Cora could barely understand him.

"I liked California better, but for a quaint, superstitious state, Oklahoma's fine. I don't plan on staying that long anyway. I figure a year or two, and then I'll be outta here."

"Really," Cora wanted to keep him talking. Why, she didn't know.

It seemed that Robert Cornwell had undergone a metamorphosis since entering his dark automobile, and she felt it prudent to keep him talking. "Where do you think you'll go next? Back to California?"

"Not hardly," Cornwell, for the first time since leaving the diner, looked at his passenger. "I'll end up in Houston. Houston's where the people who run the company work. Someday the entire oil industry will move there. The era of Tulsa as the Oil Capital of the World is about to be over. This place will probably end up withering away like the old gold-rush towns of the last century."

Cora didn't know what Cornwell was talking about. Oil is what had made Tulsa the second biggest city in Oklahoma. Who knows, someday they might even surpass Oklahoma City as the largest. Every few years at the fairgrounds, the city of Tulsa hosted the Petroleum Exposition where oilmen from all over the world came to see the latest inventions and improvements in the industry. Tulsa had erected a giant oilman outside the exposition doors to welcome the wealthy oil barons to the big show. There was no way oil companies would move to Houston. Robert Cornwell was dreaming.

They turned onto Thirty-Fifth Street and headed into Garden City.

Cornwell glanced at Cora making her feel that much more uneasy. She was certain he'd leered at her, a disgusting, despicable leer; one that brought goose bumps to her arms. One that made her want to leap from the moving car. Hopefully, she was wrong. Maybe he'd only smiled, and the darkness had turned his gracious act into something sinister, something evil.

They were on Rosedale Avenue, less than six blocks from her home and only two blocks from the first house in the Garden City community. To their left rose the giant belching spires of the refinery, to their right a flat, sparsely treed expanse with railroad tracks running through the middle. Cornwell suddenly, and without braking, turned off the paved road and onto the waving grass of the bleak, empty field. He sped up and raced towards a clump of leafy elms growing serenely alongside the railroad tracks. Cora, because of the sudden turn, was thrown against the door. She let out a yelp, then a gasp.

Cornwell, moments before ramming into a majestic elm, slammed the brakes. This time Cora pitched forward, bumping her head on the windshield. Pain rifled above her eyes. She reached to her head to see if she were cut. Before she could touch her throbbing brow, Cornwell grabbed her wrist and pulled her across the seat.

"Listen, you big tease!" he threatened through clenched teeth. "If you so much as whimper, I'll kill you. Do you understand?"

Cora gazed into the demon's eyes, only inches from her own. She nodded once and shut her eyes.

A malevolent snigger erupted from Cornwell's mouth. He sounded like a mad hobgoblin who'd found a helpless child wandering alone through the forest.

A tear escaped from Cora's closed lids and hurtled down her cheek. Others soon followed. Still, Cora refused to cry out. She silently prayed to God for strength.

\* \* \* \* \*

*Oh no, I've done it again!* Bobby thought as he jumped off the porch and dived into the car. *Mom is going to be so mad at me I'll probably never get to drive the car again.*

By the time Bobby pulled in front of the Frisco Diner, he was thirty minutes late. His mother was nowhere in sight. Usually, she waited serenely by the entrance, but not tonight. The stoop was empty. Bobby turned into the first parking space he found, and bounded towards the brightly-lit restaurant. He leaped onto the porch, his feet never touching the steps.

After talking with Mr. Porter a few minutes, they both agreed that Bobby's mom had hitched a ride with Susan or Abby, waitresses who got off work the same time as Cora. As he drove home, Bobby felt better about the situation. However, he knew he was in for a scolding when he got home.

For some unknown whim, Bobby suddenly turned into the parking lot of Howard Park. He drove past the pecan orchard and along the right-field fence to the visitor's dugout. He idled the engine while looking at the grassy field. Baseball diamonds were pretty; he had to admit that much. And he really did enjoy playing the game. He liked to pitch. He loved throwing the ball past a batter and hearing the futile whooshing of the bat through the air; the look on a hitter's face when he'd swung for the third time at the same pitch and come up empty. He got a kick out of it. That's why he'd never cared much for junk pitches like the curve and change-up. It seemed like you were almost cheating when you tricked a batter rather than challenging him with the hard stuff. But maybe Artemis was right. A truly good pitcher, one who wanted to get the top hitters out, needed to be able to throw more than a fastball. There was no maybe to it. Artemis was right.

Bobby turned off the engine and got out of the car. He walked to the front of the vehicle and sat on the warm hood. A night bird squawked as it flew past him towards the inviting pecan trees. He leaned back on the hood holding himself up with his palms and thought about the next game he'd be playing and the professional scout who'd be watching. When Josh told him about Mr. Marr coming to the game, he'd been excited. Then after practicing with Artemis, his exhilaration had dissipated into apathy. In reality, what chance did he have of getting signed? Sure he could throw the ball hard; but his curve was mediocre at best, and he was getting nowhere with the blooper. Why couldn't he have met Artemis earlier? Why had he been so hardheaded?

Another black swoop headed towards the trees behind him, no doubt to join his friend. Bobby plopped from the hood and returned to the driver's seat. He fired up the engine and crunched through the gravel parking lot back to the main road.

As if impelled by an unseen force, Bobby twisted in the seat and looked again at the community baseball field. He wet his lips. Why couldn't he be a Major League ballplayer? Why couldn't he get Big Leaguers out? Well, maybe not Williams or DiMaggio, but surely he could compete with the average player. Bobby felt his pulse quicken, his heart thumping in his chest. Why couldn't he be a Major League pitcher? Josh and Artemis seemed to think he could.

He turned back onto the paved road, a grin firmly etched on his face. He wished tomorrow was Saturday; he was ready to pitch. Suddenly, it occurred to him that he hadn't told Maundi. She would want to know, would be angry with him for not telling her sooner. He checked his watch. It was late, however, he doubted she was in bed. He nodded his head in agreement with his decision and mashed the foot pedal to the floor.

\* \* \* \* \*

Josh immediately noticed that his mother wasn't her usual self. She appeared listless, distant. She entered the house, said nothing to him or the girls, who were lounging on their stomachs in front of the radio listening to *The Shadow*, and trudged to the privacy of her bedroom/porch. Josh followed her with his eyes until she turned into the kitchen. He didn't return to the radio and his sisters until he heard the gentle closing of her door.

"Gee, what's up with Mom? Who's she mad at? And where's Bobby?" Sarah sat up and twisted towards her brother.

"I don't know, but shut up cause I'm trying to listen to the show," Jonda demanded.

"Oh, pish posh on the show. You know The Shadow's gonna win. He always does," Sarah retorted.

"Josh, tell Sarah to be quiet. I'm trying to listen and she's ruinin' it for me."

Josh ignored his youngest sibling. He looked at Sarah, concern chiseled on his face. He shrugged. "She probably just had a bad night at work. You know how those oilmen are. Sometimes they can be pretty mean and grouchy when it comes to their food. Plus that, it looks like Bobby forgot to pick her up again."

Sarah nodded, still not satisfied with what he was saying. Everything Josh said could be true and probably was, nevertheless, she felt certain there was more to it than just an obnoxious customer or being stranded. Earlier, when her mother raced through the living room, Sarah noticed something her brother and sister had not. Two buttons were missing from her shift, and the material on her left shoulder was torn as if it had gotten caught on a thorn bush.

* * * * *

After closing the door and slipping the hook into the ring, Cora shuffled to the screen door and stood before it letting the night air dance on her uniform. She wiped a tardy tear from her cheek. She thought she'd closed that spigot before entering her home, nonetheless, one seeped through.

Cora stepped back and sat on the edge of her narrow bed. She slipped her shoes from her feet and absently massaged her toes. As if in a trance, she stood and unfastened the remaining buttons of her white dress and let it fall to the floor. She wrapped her housecoat around herself and trudged through the kitchen, stopping briefly at the cabinets to retrieve a bottle of vinegar, which she hid under her robe as if it were expensive champagne. She continued her long, short trip into the bathroom looking like a Haitian zombie recently resurrected from the dead.

Cora spent the next ten minutes cleaning herself with the vinegar. She was fairly certain the vinegar would do the job. However, to make sure, she completed the job with warm soapy water, which burnt her insides as if there was an open wound.

Lastly, Cora filled the tub with steaming water and took a bath. She always bathed after her shift at the diner, so she didn't have to worry about the kids becoming suspicious. She couldn't let her children know what had happened to her, especially Josh and Bobby.

That meant she could not go to the law. Not that she would have, anyway. What good was her word against the word of a rich oilman like Robert Cornwell? They would laugh her out of court. He would hire some fancy lawyer and by the time the trial was over, all of Tulsa and the world would believe it was her fault she'd been raped.

Had it been her fault? Cora forced herself into the scalding water until the only part of her not submerged was her face. Was she a tease? Had she worn too much make-up? Had her speech in any way egged him on?

Of course not!

The only mistake she had made was getting into the car with him. She should have known better. That's where she'd messed up.

Cora quickly toweled off and tiptoed to her bedroom. She put on a pair of John's flannel pajamas. They were much too big for her, but she didn't care. They were warm and felt perfect to her. Josh and Bobby wore most of their dad's old clothes. For some reason, she'd kept one pair for herself. She was glad she had.

Cora again sat on the side of her bed, not yet ready to lie down. She took a deep breath and held it several seconds before expelling it with a mighty gust. What would she do now? She couldn't go back to the diner. There was no way she could ever again face Mr. Cornwell. If he walked through the door of the café, she would either go completely to pieces or pick up one of the steak knives and stab him through his black heart. She honestly wasn't sure which it would be.

But she had to work. She had to provide for her family, at least for the girls. She couldn't make Josh and Bobby become responsible for her children. She didn't want them to feel as if they had to help her. It wasn't fair to them. Cora gritted her teeth. She wasn't helpless. God would see her through this terrible ordeal. It would be with God's strength she would get through this. She lowered her head and silently prayed that God would help her and her family. Fresh tears splashed into her lap.

"Are you okay, Momma?" Sarah stood, with Jonda peeking from behind her, in the doorway.

Cora jerked up. "Of course I'm fine. I'm just really tired. You know how sometimes you get a little weepy when you're totally pooped. Shouldn't you two be in bed?"

Jonda stepped from behind her sister. "I don't cry when I'm tired, Momma. I only cry when Sarah hits me."

Sarah glared at her sister. Jonda ignored her.

"Come here you two," Cora said, rising from the bed.

The sisters hurried to their mother's open arms and hugged her like they hadn't seen her in a month.

"See? I'm fine. Everything's gonna be okay; you'll see. We oughta go to the zoo sometime. Would you like that?"

Jonda looked at her watery-eyed mother and didn't notice anything amiss. "Yeah! That sounds neat. I heard they got a whole island full of monkeys."

Sarah said nothing. She didn't know what, but there was something dreadfully wrong with her mother.

# 18

"I'm glad you don't have to clean that stupid house today, Mom. You need a day off." Josh finished his toast and downed the last of his orange juice, then reached across the table and tasted Sarah's. She did not protest. She didn't seem to notice. He was running late for work, but he wouldn't get in trouble. He couldn't remember the last time he'd been tardy. He was deeply worried about his mother.

His mother stopped washing the breakfast cups and plates to scold Bobby and Jonda. They were horsing around, playing cowboys and Indians. Jonda had stuck a feather in her hair and was chasing Bobby around the table trying to scalp him with a plastic knife. Bobby pretended to be wounded in the leg and limped through the kitchen barely keeping ahead of his yelping sister.

Her harshness towards Bobby and Jonda seemed totally out of character for his mother. Normally, in the mornings, she was a smiling ball of happiness encouraging everyone to have a good day.

Today she was different. He couldn't put his finger on it, but she was. Maybe she hadn't slept well. Or maybe she was worried about the wages she wouldn't be getting because the Lambersons suddenly decided to go to Florida on a second honeymoon. Who knew? She might even be upset with Pastor Alex. Maybe he had hit on her and she didn't like it.

This last thought disturbed Josh. A deep-set frown settled on his face. If Brother Alex had been bothering his mother, he'd put a stop to it. He didn't care if he was a preacher. He wasn't going to let him upset his mom.

Josh abruptly rose, left the kitchen, and retrieved his lunch pail and cap from the living room coffee table. He had to hurry or he'd be really late.

"Have a good day, Josh. I love you."

Cora stood in the doorway to the kitchen, dishtowel in her hand. A smile that looked forced formed on her face. It widened until it looked genuine.

"You too, Mom. You know I love you, too."

Josh flipped open the screen and bounded from the porch. It was not in eagerness to get to work that made him hurry to his car. It was more like he was fleeing from a place he didn't want to be; a place that was no longer as comfortable as a thick, woolen robe and as happy as a birthday party.

Josh jammed the keys into the ignition and backed the car from the driveway. He sped away down the pitted street desperately trying to rid himself of the memory of his mother standing before him wishing him a good day as tears streamed unabated down her cheeks.

\* \* \* \* \*

The amazing thing was that Artemis was not furious. He had been, but a night's sleep calmed him. When a tearful Claire informed him she had been demoted to the switchboard, she'd made him promise not to confront the accounting department manager, Mr. Sanderson. Artemis agreed to this emotional demand but during a restless night realized he had not promised his wife he would not speak with Mr. Fitzsimmons, a partner in the firm and the one who'd promoted Claire in the first place.

Artemis did not have an appointment with Mr. Fitzsimmons, so when he entered the expansive outer office of the important man, he'd expected to be rebuffed by the stern-looking woman guarding the door or, at least, to be kept waiting an interminable time. Neither happened.

When Artemis stepped into the plush office, the lady behind the desk politely asked his name and if he had an appointment. When Artemis answered negatively to the second part, the woman picked up the phone and called her boss. After a quick conversation, she returned the phone to the cradle, and told Artemis that Mr. Fitzsimmons would see him shortly.

Artemis made himself comfortable in a high-backed chair, picked up a newspaper he'd never read before, *The Wall Street Journal*, from a long, oblong table in front of him and sat back expecting a lengthy stay. He didn't even have time to look for the funny pages before the secretary spoke to him.

"Mr. Fitzsimmons can see you now," she announced in a flat, unemotional voice.

Artemis laid the newspaper back on the weird-shaped table and trooped past the typing secretary.

Mr. Fitzsimmons' inner office was not what Artemis expected. It was far, far better. As soon as he swished through the doorway his shoes sank into a thick, plush carpet. For some quirky reason the carpet made him think of his childhood when he would get up early in the morning and tromp through the wet, thick grass on his way to the outhouse. Artemis crossed the dark blue rug, and passed under an enormous light fixture of brass that doubled as a slow-moving fan. He figured the wide blades were more for show than comfort. However, when he sat down in front of the lawyer's intimidating desk, he found the gentle breeze cascading down his face and neck both refreshing and relaxing.

The desk and furniture were huge and looked like they cost a fortune. Mr. Fitzsimmons, dressed in a charcoal suit, sat behind a magnificent shimmering desk of cherry in a black, leather, high-backed chair that probably cost more than Artemis' house. When Artemis neared the expansive desk, the silver-haired man rose and grasped his visitor's hand like they were fast friends. He introduced himself as Patrick Fitzsimmons. Artemis had never before met an attorney, and he completely forgot to tell him his name. He nodded several times and sat down in a chair similar to the one in the outer office.

Artemis refused an offer of coffee and crème-filled chocolates. He twisted in his seat several times seemingly trying to get comfortable, in reality, trying to fight off a case of nerves. While he forced himself to breathe through his nose, he glanced at the paneled walls, and saw a picture hanging next to Mr. Fitzsimmons' law degree that heartened him and caused his jitteriness to evaporate.

"Are you a baseball fan?" Artemis asked pointing at the black-and-white photo matted and encased in a sparkling golden frame.

Mr. Fitzsimmons reflexively turned his head towards the picture in question, although he knew exactly what the man before him was referring to. "Yes, I am. Isn't everyone?"

Artemis continued examining the photo from afar. Recognition came to him and caused him to open his mouth in a wide smile. "If I'm not mistaken, that's you holding the bat, next to the catcher. And If I'm not mistaken, you're wearing a Wichita Wrangler uniform?"

"Correct on both assumptions. I'm surprised you recognized the old Wrangler togs. I tried making it as a ballplayer, but I couldn't hit a curveball so here I am stuck in an office building instead of breaking DiMaggio's hit-streak record." He laughed when he said the last item. "Really, how did you recognize those old uniforms? They don't wear them anymore. Are you from Kansas?"

"Not really. Well, kinda. I used to play ball up in Kansas City, and we played the Wranglers a few times. You know, just for practice."

Patrick Fitzsimmons leaned forward in his chair. He stared at Artemis for several seconds, making his guest somewhat uneasy.

"You're a pitcher, aren't you?" Mr. Fitzsimmons asked.

Artemis nodded. "Used to be." He paused. "I guess I still am. I'm playing ball for a semi-pro team over on the Westside."

"Is your name Macintosh, by any chance?"

Artemis again nodded. "Yes sir, it is. I'm Artemis Macintosh and my wife's name is Claire."

Patrick Fitzsimmons seemed not to have heard the name, Claire, because he continued staring at his guest with an amusing grin plastered on his face. "Did you happen to play in an exhibition game in Lawrence back in '34 against a bunch of white Minor Leaguers?" As soon as he said this, Mr. Fitzsimmons sat back in his chair and waved off what he'd just asked. "Of course you wouldn't remember something so trivial. That was such a long time ago, and you would have been so young then."

"I do remember," Artemis stated. "We played a Saturday night double-header at the high school field. I remember because we lost the first game on a home run that must have gone over four hundred feet. We came back and won the second game on a two-hit shutout."

Mr. Fitzsimmons beamed. He coughed several times as if he were nervous. "I don't want to brag, but I was the one who hit the home run, and I hit it off Satchel Paige. Other than my brief stint in the big leagues, it's my favorite memory."

Now it was Artemis' turn to grin. "I don't want to brag, either, but I pitched the second game and if memory serves, I struck out the guy who beat us with a home run three times in a row."

Patrick Fitzsimmons laughed like he hadn't laughed in a long time. Artemis joined him.

"You kept getting me with that wicked curve of yours. No offence to Mr. Paige, but I do believe it's the best curveball I ever saw. You were really good, Mr. Macintosh."

"So were you, Mr. Fitzsimmons," answered Artemis.

Patrick Fitzsimmons waved his hands as if surrendering. "I was good as long as the pitchers threw me fastballs. When they figured out I couldn't hit curves, I quickly became mediocre."

Artemis thought there wouldn't be a better time in the conversation to broach why he'd come, so he dived in: "Mr. Fitzsimmons, the reason I came is because of my wife, Claire."

The attorney and former ballplayer sat back in his chair as if trying to remember something.

Artemis thought he'd help his new friend.

"Claire was the receptionist and then you moved her to accounting, and now she's the switchboard operator. She needs to be put back into accounting."

"Yes, yes. I know who Claire Macintosh is," he stated firmly.

Now he was the attorney. Artemis immediately noticed the change. His jocular tone and friendly smile vanished, replaced with a serious visage and business-like demeanor.

The two men sat silently a few moments. Artemis wanted to argue his case before his wife's boss, decided to wait and see what Mr. Fitzsimmons would say first. He figured he could counter whatever lame excuse the executive offered and hopefully get him to see how qualified Claire was.

"You say she's working on the switchboard?" he began.

Artemis almost spoke, but realized Mr. Fitzsimmons was thinking aloud.

"I would have sworn I moved her to the accounting department. I guess my orders got crossed up or something." He looked across at his visitor. "I'll straighten things out, Mr. Macintosh. It's probably a simple gaff."

"Please call me Artemis, sir. And I don't think it was a simple mistake. Claire was in accounting for a day until she was transferred out."

"Sanderson, that curmudgeon!" Mr. Fitzsimmons blurted. "He had no authority to countermand my instructions."

Patrick Fitzsimmons was visibly angry. He rose from his desk, slapped the top like he was squashing a spider. "I'm sorry, Artemis. This shouldn't have happened. Sanderson is a good man, but he's a throwback." He chuckled, which eased the sudden tension. "Much like I was until a few days ago when I got a much-needed lesson in progress from my daughter. A lesson I should have learned many years ago -- like when I was swinging futilely at the Macintosh curveball." Patrick Fitzsimmons sat back down. He appeared relaxed, back in control.

He looked across his desk at the black man; the man who'd once struck him out three times in one game. "Again, I'm sorry. This shouldn't have happened. I'll rectify it immediately. I guess you know why it happened."

"Yes, sir, I do," said Artemis.

"Barney Sanderson is a good guy. I know you probably don't believe that after what he's done to your wife. But believe me. He is. What's wrong with Barney is what's wrong with America. We still see things in black and white. I know it's not right, and it's probably not going to change. At least not right away. I hate to say it, but it's probably going to take a major shock before America wakes up. I am convinced that someday we will. I didn't always believe that. I'll be honest with you, Artemis, when I grew up, I was no different than the Barney Sandersons of the world. I liked blacks personally, but not as a people. I loved playing ball against you because you were so good, and it tested us, made us better. However, I was as much against Jackie Robinson as the next guy. And I was wrong. I admit that now; getting my fellow racists to admit it is going to take some doing."

Mr. Fitzsimmons laughed again. Artemis remained silent, hardly believing that a rich white guy was using him as a therapist, using him to unload his feelings about race relations.

He continued: "Sorry. I'm laughing because it occurred to me that it's too bad everyone's not a baseball fan. It's too bad, because if everyone could see what's happening in baseball: how whites and blacks are working in concert, how they are striving to get along so they can have a good team and compete for the World Series, then maybe everyone could see the benefits of working together for a common goal."

"And what goal is that?" Artemis interrupted.

"Peace," Mr. Fitzsimmons answered stoically. His voice softened, sounded almost sad. "Our country's filling up. Cities are getting crowded. If white people don't start treating black Americans better, there's going to be trouble, trouble like we've never seen before."

"Are you talking about a race war, Mr. Fitzsimmons? Hopefully, that won't happen. Surely, people will learn to get along."

"I hope so. It's white Americans who have to step up to the plate. After all, we're the ones in the wrong. We're the ones who've mistreated our fellow Americans for over two hundred years. We're the ones who enslaved your ancestors."

Artemis dropped his head and looked at his hands. He did not like to talk about the past, about slavery and how his ancestors had come to America. He especially didn't want to discuss it with a white man.

Artemis lifted his head. He looked squarely at Mr. Fitzsimmons. "America's a good country. She'll make things right. You'll see."

Patrick Fitzsimmons rose from his chair. He reached across the desk and offered Artemis his hand. Artemis stood, and the two men shook.

"Don't you worry about a thing, Mr. Macintosh. I'll straighten things out. Your wife will be in accounting by lunchtime.

Artemis nodded, turned and left the room. Mr. Fitzsimmons walked with his guest to the door where the two shook hands again.

\* \* \* \* \*

"Darn it," Frannie proclaimed to no one. She whisked through the circular doors and into the Mid-Continent building and headed for the elevator. She was ten minutes late for work, but that was not why she'd uttered the mild expletive. Her problem was one she'd struggled with the night before and all morning. She couldn't get Josh Braun out of her head. Despite not wanting to, she had to admit she liked the guy. Why? Who knew? He was totally opposite what she wanted, what she needed in a man. He was poor. He had no education. He had a no-future job. He wasn't particularly tall or handsome in the Clark Gable or Cary Grant mold. And he was obsessed with a stupid game.

On the other hand, he was kind and responsible and possessed strong convictions. He'd shown her that, when he stood up for the black man against her former beau. He did have a propensity for getting into fights, but when she thought about it, he'd started none of the scuffles. Frannie realized she was smitten by the rowdy Westsider, and this rankled her even more. She wanted to be in control of any relationship. She wanted to set the boundaries. "Good grief," she mumbled. "I actually kissed him first. He probably thinks I'm a strumpet!"

Frannie breezed by the receptionist, a woman she didn't know, and started for the elevator. She skidded to a stop and turned back to the information desk. Behind the receptionist, sitting in front of the switchboard, was Claire.

A bewildered expression formed on Frannie's face. Anger quickly replaced the look of puzzlement. She strode past the receptionist to the switchboard.

She stood quietly, simmering, as Claire finished with a call. Finally, her friend turned to her. "Hi, Frannie."

"Hi, Claire," she answered by rote. "What are you doing here?"

"This is my new job. I guess they didn't like me in accounting. I'm doing fine, though."

Frannie could tell Claire was not doing fine. She could see it in her eyes. Once again, her father let her down. He'd not done what he said he would. Or worse, he had played a game of Let's-Shuffle-Claire-From-Department-to-Department-So-Frannie-Won't-Get-Mad. Well, it wasn't going to work. She wheeled towards the elevators. Claire grabbed her arm and pulled her around.

"Listen, Frannie. You've been awfully nice to me, and I really appreciate it. However, I don't want you causing any trouble. I know you mean well, but it will be me who gets labeled a troublemaker, and that's the last thing I want. I need this job, and I want to get along with the people I work with and for. You'll be gone after the summer, while I'll still be here. I have to work with these people, hopefully for a long time."

Frannie could see that Claire was serious. Claire didn't want her to do anything. She bit down on her bottom lip and said, "okay. I see what you mean. The last thing I want is to cause trouble for you."

"Thanks." Claire sat down at the switchboard and resumed answering calls.

Frannie stood watching her friend a few moments, then, completely discouraged, shuffled away down the hall.

She couldn't help herself. Despite what she'd promised Claire, Frannie headed straight to her father's office. She rationalized it by thinking that if she didn't stand up for Claire, who would? She marched into her father's office and up to Meg Stanley, who promptly told her he was with someone and couldn't be disturbed.

Frannie left the office and paced up and down the hallway. She knew she needed to report for work, but couldn't bring herself to leave the vicinity of her dad's office. On each trip past his office, she glanced into the window to see if his door was still closed. She made several more trips up and down the hall and was again becoming discouraged. Who knows, she thought? Her dad might be talking with one of his golfing buddies, which could last for hours. She was about to give up and come back later when she saw his big, heavy door swing open. She skidded to a stop and looked through the window.

A black man Frannie immediately recognized as Claire's husband, stepped through the door. Her father followed him. The two men exchanged smiles and gripped each other's hand as if sealing a deal.

Relief washed over her. She instinctively knew what they'd been talking about. She knew she would not have to speak with her father.

Frannie took off down the hall; the briskness returned to her step. She felt good about the world again. One problem was solved, but the other again flashed to the fore. A grin emerged on her face as she admitted to herself that she actually enjoyed ruminating on her newest problem.

# 19

Bobby watched his brother crunch through the gravel of the Frisco parking lot. He was walking with Lonnie Corlett, and they didn't seem to be in any hurry whatsoever. This irritated Bobby because he'd been waiting for his brother to get off work for almost fifteen minutes. Fifteen minutes he could have spent at home or, better yet, over at Maundi's sitting with her in the porch swing.

Josh had called him soon after he got to work at Big Jim's and told him his car almost quit on him before he made it to the yard. Bobby and Jim spent their lunch hour driving to the railroad yard, checking out Josh's car, then after deciding it needed some carburetor work, babying it back to Big Jim's. Jim would have it up and running by the end of the workday tomorrow, in the meantime Bobby would have to taxi his brother around.

"Thanks for taking your time, Brother. It's not like I have anything else to do besides haul you around."

Josh plopped into the front seat, breathed deeply, exhaled, and removed his cap. He pointed towards the exit and said in an overly haughty tone, "Drive, Robert. I must be home by 4:15. Please do not exceed the speed limit, though. I become perplexed when my driver goes too fast. Oh, by the way," his voice returned to normal. "What's up with my car? And how much is it gonna cost me?"

Bobby shifted the Chevy into second and eased into the going-home traffic. "The carburetor's bad and I don't know how much it's gonna cost, probably ten bucks or so."

"Ten bucks for a carburetor? That's highway robbery. What's he puttin' in it, a Cadillac carburetor?"

"I've been doin' a lot of thinkin' lately," Josh continued, not expecting a reply. "I think, if for some unseen reason, I don't get signed by the Cardinals, I'm gonna go back to school and get my diploma. Then I'm going to one of those business schools downtown and learn how to make some real money."

"Huh?" Bobby looked incredulous. "You've got a good job already. Why do you want to quit and go back to school?"

"I'm not gonna quit. I'll go to night school. They've got classes at Webster on Tuesdays and Thursdays. I can do it in a year; year and half tops."

"I don't understand. The railroad's a great place to work. Pop worked there most of his life. Heck, I was seriously considering trying to get on. I'm getting' kinda tired of pumping gas, cleaning windshields, and checking people's oil. I think it would be neat to be an engineer and drive my own train."

"If you drove a train the way you drive a car, you'd wreck it in a week. What you oughta do is be a race car driver. That's probably your true calling."

Bobby seemed to sit up straighter in his seat. He obviously liked the idea of racing cars. He hadn't thought of it before. It was a good idea.

\* \* \* \* \*

The car hadn't even stopped before Josh swung open the door and bounded onto the porch. He was trying to beat Bobby inside so that he, for once, could get a swig of water from the icebox before his brother downed it. He entered the front room and was halfway through when he abruptly stopped. Sarah and Jonda sat listlessly on the couch. The radio was off.

"What are you two sulking about?" Josh asked.

"We ain't sulking. We're sad cuz Momma's sick and actin' like she don't like us anymore."

Josh looked at Sarah. "What's really wrong, Sarah?"

Sarah nodded towards her sister. "That's about it. Josh, there's something bad wrong with Momma. I noticed it last night when she came home from work, and she's even worse today."

"I did too, Sis. When I left this morning, she was crying. I guess I was a coward because I just watched her cry and didn't even ask why. I bet it's that sorry preacher. I think he's been chasing her."

Sarah shook her head. "I don't think so. I think something happened to her at work. I should have told you this last night, but I'm pretty sure her dress was torn when she came home."

"It was! It was!" Jonda shouted. "When she tucked me in bed I asked her if she'd got in a fight, and she said she hadn't, but I think she was lyin'. I think somebody beat her up."

"What's up?" Bobby asked coming through the screen door. "Why's everybody so glum?"

"We're worried about Momma. We think she got in a fight."

"Oh, we don't either, Jonda. Knock it off! Momma did not get in a fight. She's probably just sad because she can't get anyone to take you off her hands."

Jonda crossed her arms and gritted her teeth.

"Now's not the time to be kidding, Sarah," Josh scolded. He walked to Jonda and pulled her close to him. Unexpectedly, she turned and burying her head in his stomach, hugged him around the waist.

"I don't think it's Brother Alex," Bobby exclaimed. "I heard Momma praying the other night, and she confessed to God that she thought she loved Brother Alex, and she was asking forgiveness for wanting to marry another man."

Josh and Sarah looked dumbfounded. Jonda peeked from her brother's stomach.

"Well, I don't know what's the matter with her," Sarah said. "But I do know it's serious. She spent almost the entire morning in the bathroom crying and throwing up."

"I guess she went to work?" Josh asked, sadness evident in his voice.

"She did, but I don't know how," Sarah answered.

"How'd she get to work?" Bobby asked. "I had her car. She was supposed to call the station if she got to feeling better."

"Abby came by and picked her up. She was still crying when she left."

"What are we going to do?" Bobby absently asked.

"We're going to call Brother Alex and get him to go with us to the diner. We're going to find out what's wrong with our mother." Josh picked Jonda up and carried her to the magazine rack where they kept their phone.

Mr. Porter appeared relieved when the Braun family and their pastor walked into the diner. He pointed towards a table at the far end of the restaurant, where their mother sat facing the wall. As Josh and the others passed by the diner manager, he shook his head and said there was something terribly wrong with Cora; he just didn't know what.

Josh strode to his mother, who appeared to be in a stupor, and kissed her on the cheek. His brother and sisters followed their brother's example, with Jonda going last and adding a hug for good measure. Brother Alex stood a respectful distance from the table, and might have remained there except Bobby and Sarah motioned for him to come forward. When their mother realized he was with her children, she rose and hugged the preacher. Josh felt a little embarrassed, but he noticed the others were smiling.

They pulled up chairs and sat around the table, except Jonda, who sat on Bobby's lap. Josh sat to the left of his mother, while Brother Alex was on her right. Bobby, Jonda, and Sarah occupied the far side of the table.

Josh and Bobby and finally Sarah tried to get their mother to tell them what was wrong. She refused. She kept insisting nothing was amiss.

In the end, it was Brother Alex who got their mother to divulge what had happened. He did it by praying for her health and asking God to heal her of any disease she might have in her body. Josh noticed that this made her cry even more.

Next, the pastor took her hand, kissed it, and softly told her that he and her family could not help her if they didn't know what was wrong. He covertly motioned to Josh with his head for him to take her other hand, which Josh eagerly did. He kissed his mother's wet hand and wiped fresh tears from her face with his free hand. Several seconds of silence ensued in which nobody, not even Jonda, uttered a sound. Then, out of the blue, Cora Braun turned to Brother Alex and in a voice barely above a whisper said: "I've been raped."

\* \* \* \* \*

The police arrived at the hospital not long after Cora and her family. Frannie pulled up right behind them.

Frannie passed the slow-walking officers and burst into the emergency room waiting area and immediately spied Josh and Bobby and their two sisters. She hurried to them and hugged Josh unashamedly. He had told her on the phone what had happened to his mother. Frannie and her parents were sitting down to dinner when the call came. Frannie quickly swallowed a few bites of salad and lasagna. In between bites, she told her father the situation and he somewhat surprised her when he told her to let him know if there was anything he or the firm could do to help.

"How is she?" Frannie asked.

Josh, his eyes red from wiping away tears, looked at Frannie and attempted a smile. "I guess she's doing about as well as can be expected. She's in there," he pointed at a cubicle with the curtain drawn, "waiting for the police to come."

"They're here. That's them over at the information desk, probably finding out where your mother is."

"Good. I think Mom's ready to let them know who did this to her."

"You mean she hasn't said yet?" Frannie looked startled.

"No, she won't tell us. Seems she's afraid Bobby and I might hunt her attacker down and beat him to death," Josh said between clenched teeth.

"Imagine that!" Frannie tried to make light of it. "Who would have ever thought the Braun boys might get violent? She's a pretty smart woman, isn't she?"

At first, anger flashed through Josh. It was quickly replaced by a sense of relief. He chuckled. Frannie's lame attempt at humor had taken the bite off his rage, off his frustration at being unable to help his mother. He hugged her again, this time longer and more affectionately. He kissed her forehead and mouthed the words, "thank you."

"Where are your sisters?" Frannie asked. "They were here a minute ago. How's Bobby? Is he still blaming himself for what happened?"

"The preacher gave the girls a dollar so they could get some supper. I guess they slipped off to the snack bar to get a hamburger. They'll be all right, Sarah's used to handling Jonda. Bobby, I'm not so sure about. He's been beating himself up ever since he found out what happened."

"Has your mom talked to him?" Frannie asked.

"Yeah, but I'm not sure it helped any. He knows if he hadn't been late picking her up, this would not have happened."

"Maybe not when it did, but if the man who did this was stalking your mom, he was going to attack her sooner or later. Bobby's got to understand that. Would it do any good if I talked to him?"

"Be my guest," Josh sighed. "He's sitting over there by himself."

Frannie turned and headed for the distraught young man.

A few minutes later, the two police officers walked past Josh to Cora's cubicle and, without so much as announcing their intentions, pulled the curtains open. A startled Brother Alex jumped from his chair,

"Oh, it's the police," he said in a relieved voice. He motioned for Josh to join him next to Cora. Frannie and a solemn Bobby followed Josh into the provisional hospital room.

The police stood at the end of the bed. The shorter of the two, a stocky young man with a recently-cut flattop, removed a small notepad and pen from his front pocket and flipped it open. He clicked the pen preparing to take notes.

The taller of the two stood next to his partner, scratching his chin as if not knowing where to begin. He looked at Cora, then at Brother Alex standing to the right of her bed and lastly, at Josh, Frannie, and Bobby. "Are you sure you want all these people in here while we talk about this? It could get kinda, well you know, graphic."

Cora opened her mouth to reply; Brother Alex answered instead. "I think the officer's right, Cora. Perhaps the men should leave. Frannie could stay with you and when Sarah gets back we'll send her in."

Josh bucked at this. "I think we should all stay. She's our mother. You shouldn't be making decisions for her or us." Josh glared defiantly at the preacher.

"Josh, Josh," Cora quietly said. She placed her hand on his wrist and patted it softly. "Alex is right. I wouldn't be able to say what I need to say if men are present. Please don't read anything into this. Frannie and Sarah will be here with me. But I don't need Jonda. She's yours for the night." Cora tried her best to laugh.

"I'll do what you want me to, Momma. But I'm a man and the head of this house. I think I should be here." Josh turned towards Brother Alex when he spoke of being 'the head of the house.'

Cora's pastor dipped his head and left the cubicle.

Reluctantly Josh left his mother's side.

Bobby started out with his brother, but was pulled to the bed by his mother. She wrapped her arms around him and covered his face with kisses. "Listen here, young man. Quit blaming yourself for your silly mother getting into that car. Everything is going to be fine; you'll see."

Bobby, with quivering lips and tear-filled eyes, nodded. He was still nodding when he left her presence.

"Now then, Mrs. Braun, give us your full name."

The police officer spent the next five minutes asking Cora administrative questions about her age, birth date, address, phone number, occupation, employer, and so on. Sarah arrived about halfway through the mundane questioning and took the place vacated by Brother Alex. Frannie, feeling a little uncomfortable since she really didn't know Josh's mother well, edged away from the bed. Mrs. Braun noticed it and grasped the young woman's hand in hers and held it tight. Frannie could feel the fear racing through Cora's body. Her hand trembled. Frannie squeezed it, imagining what it would be like if someone had violated her in the same manner. Tears welled in her eyes.

The questioning officer paused and looked at his partner to make sure he was caught up with his notes. He scratched his not small belly and said, "Now, Mrs. Braun, to the nitty-gritty. From the beginning, tell us what happened. And leave nothing out, not even the smallest of details."

Fifteen minutes and a thousand tears later, shed mainly by Frannie and Sarah, Cora Braun finished her nightmare. The two officers, looking as if they'd just heard a boring lecture on photosynthesis rather than a heartbreaking story about a woman being brutally ravished, nodded at the victim as if they were desperately trying to fight off sleep. Mrs. Braun informed them that the man who had violated her was named Robert Cornwell. The name meant nothing to Frannie and after looking at Sarah, it was obvious she didn't know him either.

The taller officer again glanced at his partner to check his note progress. He turned back to Mrs. Braun. "You say you were raped last night by this Mr. Cornwell. Is that right? And that he's the assistant manager at the refinery?"

Cora nodded.

*Then Sings My Soul*

"Then why did you wait until now to come to the hospital and report the crime?"

Frannie didn't think it was a fair question, nor did she like the accusing tone the policeman had suddenly taken. Frannie started to say something. The officer stopped her.

"Let her answer, Missy. You weren't there, and I have to ask the question."

"It's okay," Cora squeezed her hand. "The officer has to do his job."

Frannie glanced over at Sarah. The girl seemed petrified. You could barely tell she was breathing.

"Officer, I didn't come to the hospital or report it because I wasn't going to tell anyone. I was going to keep it a secret."

"And why is that? Could it be because, in fact, you and Mr. Cornwell were actually on a date, and things merely got a little rough?"

"Absolutely not! I would never go out with someone like Robert Cornwell. Never! You can ask anyone."

"Calm down, Mrs. Braun. It will be easier if you simply answer the questions. By the way, we will ask everyone about your relationship with Mr. Cornwell. You can count on it."

The police officer said the last part rather hatefully, Frannie thought. Apparently, his partner thought so too because he looked up from his pad and frowned.

"What were you wearing last night?" The policeman asked.

"My waitress uniform. It's white."

"Is it low cut? Does it show any cleavage?"

"Of course not! It's what I work in."

"How did you have your hair? Did you fix up special last night? Did you wear your hair down?"

"I wore my hair the way I always wear my hair when I'm working. Nothing was special last night."

The officer continued; he edged closer to the bed. "What about your make-up? Do you wear a lot of rouge? Do you wear red lipstick?"

"Huh? What kind of question is that? Sure I wear make-up. I wear base and a little rouge. I'm forty-one years old and starting to show it," she declared.

"Mrs. Braun, you are an extremely nice-looking woman. If I didn't know, I would have guessed you to be in your early thirties." Without a pause, he went on: "Mrs. Braun do you like to flirt with your customers? You know, maybe smile at them a lot in order to get bigger tips? And what kind of a tipper was Mr. Cornwell?"

Frannie had had enough. The policemen acted as if Mrs. Braun was the criminal and the rapist the victim. He was bullying her, pure and simple. When a nurse peeked around the curtain and asked Josh's mother if she needed anything, Frannie pounced.

"Excuse me, is there a telephone I could use?"

"Yes, Miss. There's one out here at the nurse's desk. You're welcome to use it?"

"Will it stretch in here? I really hate to leave Mrs. Braun."

The nurse stood silent for a moment, pondering if the cord would reach. "I think it will." She disappeared for the briefest of moments and came back carrying a phone.

The commotion stopped the questioning and seemed to irritate the tall policeman. He gave Frannie a what-do-you-think-you're-doing stare. She smiled at him.

Frannie quickly dialed her home and when her father answered, she launched into a loud summary of how the officers were treating Mrs. Braun. On purpose, she twice mentioned the mayor and what he would think about policemen like these. From the corner of her eye, she saw officer flat-top gulp and wipe his brow.

"Excuse me, sir," she said to the bully. "My father, Patrick Fitzsimmons, attorney at law, would like to speak with you." She handed him the phone.

Five minutes later and after many 'yes sirs,' and 'we'll take care of it, sir,' the officer handed the phone back to Frannie. She thanked her dad, who seemed genuinely pleased he could help Mrs. Braun.

"Mrs. Braun, I wish you had told us you had a lawyer. He should have been present when we questioned you. I'm terribly sorry if we caused you any inconvenience. Rest assured, we will apprehend Mr. Cornwell within the hour and put him in a place where he will never hurt anyone again."

Cora Braun looked absolutely bewildered. Luckily, she didn't say anything; like, for example, that she'd never even met Mr. Patrick Fitzsimmons, attorney at law, and golfing buddy of Mayor George Stoner. Frannie was thankful for that.

The police officers doffed their caps and quickly left the hospital.

Josh, Bobby, Jonda, and Brother Alex flooded into the room. They took turns hugging Cora, and telling her everything was going to be all right. Frannie couldn't help but notice that after their hug, Cora gave the preacher a quick peck on his cheek. She glanced at Josh and saw that he'd noticed it too.

# 20

Frannie didn't like cheeseburgers. However, she'd quickly learned that Josh loved them. His favorite, other than homemade, were Sandy burgers. Frannie stopped at the drive-up restaurant on Harvard Avenue and ordered a Big Sandy, which was three pieces of bread, two pieces of meat, double cheese, with lots of lettuce and pickles. She got a side order of fries to go with the mammoth burger and a vanilla milkshake to wash it down.

Frannie drove into the dusty yard, just as a large group of workers were tramping down the hill on their way to the locker room to fetch their lunch pails. Josh was not expecting her to bring him his lunch, and he might not approve; men were funny that way. Regardless, she had to see him. She wanted to tell him the good news about her dad, and also let him in on some not-so-good information. She parked next to the locker-room door and hopped out hoping Josh was somewhere in the crowd. He was not. Instead, several hot, dirty men ogled her as they passed close enough for her to smell the unpleasant odor of cigarettes and sweat.

Three more men sidled down the hill -- no one seemed to bother with the steps -- but again, Josh was not among them. As the second group passed, they glanced at her, smiled and resumed their conversation, which sounded more like an argument than amiable banter. The tallest and loudest of the three, a man wearing the striped cap of an engineer, insisted to his co-workers that Jersey Joe Walcott, the world boxing champion, would beat the newest challenger to come along, a young fighter named Rocky Marciano, to a pulp any day of the week. His two colleagues strongly shook their heads and tried to offer an explanation as to why Marciano was the better fighter but were shouted down by the beefy engineer.

Two more groups of men crested the hill and made their way down. Still no Josh.

In a show of exasperated futility, Frannie blew a gust of air into her bangs. She was upset at herself for trying to surprise Josh. And despite knowing she shouldn't be, a little peeved at him for not coming down the hill to eat lunch like every other Frisco employee. The sack in her hand was slowly absorbing grease from the burger and the once creamy milkshake would have to be drunk like a glass of water rather than eaten with a spoon.

"Oh well, it sounded like a good idea at the time," she muttered. She pushed off the trunk and trudged to the car door trying to decide whether to trash the burger and fries or offer them to one of the boxing fans.

"Hey? What's up? If you're looking for Josh, he isn't inside. He was, but he's not anymore."

Frannie's hand flew from the car door, and at the sound of the voice behind her, jumped into the air like a crazed kangaroo. She dropped the white Sandy's sack on the sidewalk, a half dozen French fries tumbled out of the overturned bag. She jerked towards the familiar voice. "Good gracious, Josh. You scared the dickens out of me. Where have you been? I've been waiting for over ten minutes."

Josh smiled at the distraught woman, grinned, and pointed to the ground. "Is that for me?"

Frannie bent down and picked up the soggy sack. She handed it and the melting shake to him as if the burger and drink were radioactive. She angrily marched to the back of her car where she assumed her previous position with her back to the locker room. Behind her, she could hear Josh alternating between slurping the vanilla shake and melodramatizing an overly loud "Ahh" after every swallow.

"Now that's what I call a cheeseburger," he proclaimed. "Ain't nobody can make a burger as good as this. Nosiree, Bob. Nobody."

Frannie shook her head as if she couldn't believe what she was hearing.

Josh crunched through the gravel until he was face-to-face with his girlfriend. He flashed her a mischievous mayonnaise-streaked grin, raised his cheeseburger, and, still grinning, chomped another huge bite. "I . . . o . . . cha . . . ain . . . mad . . . eben . . . doe . . . ya . . . got . . . cha arms crossed . . . ya . . . eyes are . . . smilin'."

"Huh?" Frannie stuck her chin towards Josh. She frowned. "Please, swallow so I can understand you."

Josh chewed a few more seconds then audibly gulped the last of his burger. "I said, I can tell you aren't mad even though your arms are crossed because inside you're smiling." He nodded his head like he'd made a profound philosophical statement that was the final word on the existence of mankind and the universe. Despite not wanting to, Frannie tittered at the sweaty man before her.

"Thanks for the cheeseburger. It hit the spot." He patted his flat stomach.

"You're welcome. I guess you're wondering why I came to see you?"

Josh suddenly looked downcast. "You mean it wasn't to bring me a scrumptious meal from Sandy's? And here I thought I was special."

Frannie playfully punched him on the shoulder. "Of course, silly, that was part of it. I also wanted to tell you something, and I couldn't wait till tonight."

Josh reached into the bag, came out with a French fry, and tossed it into his mouth. He sucked the last of the milkshake through the straw, dropped the paper container into the empty sack. He winked and nodded at Frannie in thanks, and took up a position next to her on the trunk.

"Okay, what's up? It'd better be good news. I've had enough bad to last me a lifetime."

"Most of it is," she stammered. "At least the most important part is."

She sighed deeply and looked into his eyes. Despite the jocularity of the past five minutes, Frannie could see the concern in Josh's eyes. Worry and anxiety were etched in his face. There was no doubt in her mind that Josh was acting goofy in order to hide his emotions, to mask his fear. He looked like he hadn't slept in days. She hoped what she had to say would buoy him. "Do you remember when we talked last night, and I told you my dad was really upset about what happened to your mother?"

Josh nodded silently.

"Well, this morning at a meeting with his partners he told them what happened . . ."

Josh interrupted. "Thanks, Frannie, that's just what my family needs is for everyone in Tulsa to know my mom was raped!" His voice was scratchy, angry, hurt.

Once she got over the initial shock of Josh's outburst, Frannie realized he was speaking out of emotion, not malice. She continued. "I'm sorry Josh, you told me your mom needed help. I'm just trying to help; that's all." She grasped the top of his hand. He turned his hand palm up and held hers tightly. She could feel a slight trembling in his grip. "Josh, Dad's partners are all good men. They're used to keeping secrets. It's called client confidentiality. Attorneys don't go around blabbing about people's private lives. But they have to know what happened if they're going to help."

"But these lawyers you're talking about don't represent my mom. They don't even know her."

"That's what I came to tell you, Josh," Frannie beamed. "Dad's law firm wants to help the D.A. with the case. They're going to ensure that that scumbag gets put behind bars for a long, long time. And they're willing to do it pro bono."

Josh furrowed his brow, deep in thought. He dropped his head and pursed his lips. He remained quiet a long time.

Frannie didn't get it. She thought Josh would be excited. She thought he'd be thrilled. One of the top law firms in Tulsa was going to help his mother get justice, and they were going to do it for free. What was his problem?

Josh quietly raised his head. He looked at her like a little boy who is stumped at the school spelling bee. His anger was gone, evaporated like the morning dew.

She understood. She grinned. "Pro bono means they'll do it for free."

He returned her grin and wiped his brow as if he were rolling in sweat. "Great! Now, what's the bad news?"

"Uh, well, it has to do with your sister. With Sarah."

Frannie spent the next ten minutes telling Josh what she'd overheard while eating lunch at Jim's Coney Island. She tried to get him to understand the young men at the table next to hers might not have been talking about his sister, but unless there was another Sarah, who was fourteen years old and lived in Garden City, then she was not mistaken. As she told him about this older boy named Benny Matthews, who was hitting on Sarah, Frannie could see the information visibly upset Josh. He stood, biting his lower lip while she informed him that his kid sister might be surreptitiously dating an older boy. Her secret beau was employed at the Mayo Hotel, and Frannie was pretty sure they didn't hire high school kids to valet or man the front desk.

"Sorry, Josh. I wish all I had to tell you was the good news about your mother's case. I shouldn't have said anything or, at least, reversed the stories. That way you wouldn't be so down right now."

Josh leaned towards Frannie and kissed her lightly on the cheek. "It's okay. I'd rather you have told me about Sarah than for me to find out from one of these clowns I work with."

Frannie returned Josh's kiss, only she refused the offer of his cheek, instead, going straight to his mouth. It was bad timing because no sooner had she reached to kiss him when four men burst from the locker room. She froze in mid-pucker.

"Hey Josh," yelled the burly man in the striped cap. "Where'd you order that hamburger from? I want service like that!"

Josh turned to the laughing men and their leader. "Harold, you wouldn't know what to do with a girl like this. You'd probably take her to a fight or worse, to your momma's house where you could all sit on the porch and watch the morning glories close for the night." Josh turned to Frannie and kissed her boldly on the lips.

\* \* \* \* \*

The long, rectangular dining hall felt colder than usual. The overhead fans appeared to be rotating a smidgen faster. The evening breeze rushed through the door every time someone went in or out sending goose bumps scampering across Cora's arms. Cora stood behind the counter and rubbed her arms with her hands trying to will the blood to flow faster and bring warmth to her limbs. She twisted and glanced at the clock behind her. Ten minutes to go. Normally at the end of her shift, she was blotting beads of perspiration from her forehead. Not tonight. Tonight, her first night back on the job after being attacked, she was cold. No, she was freezing. She strode to the small closet by the public restrooms and pulled her sweater from the hanger. She draped the cotton jacket over her shoulders and returned to her station at the end of the counter.

She looked around to see if Mr. Porter was watching. He was nowhere in sight. He wouldn't mind, though. It was the end of her shift, and she had no customers. Don Porter said little to Cora the entire evening. The normally chatty manager seemed reluctant to talk to her. When she'd first shown up for work, he told her how sorry he was for what had happened to her. Of course, he'd been careful not to mention the terrible crime and offered his help with anything she might need.

However, after their initial conversation, he'd been mum most of the night. Cora understood. Don Porter was a good man. He simply didn't know what to say to her. He was a man and couldn't possibly understand the range of emotions she was experiencing.

The door swung open.

Cora instinctively slipped the sweater from her shoulders.

A man walked into the diner. It was Alex Thomas.

He immediately spied her and waved a half-full bottle of Chocolate Soldier. In his other hand was a Mallo Cup, which he tossed into his smiling mouth and began to chew. The preacher washed the candy down with a huge swig of the chocolate drink and sauntered to the counter. Cora pulled the sweater back onto her shoulders and waited for her last customer to take a seat.

He did not sit down. Instead, Reverend Alex Thomas confidently walked behind the counter, sat his drink down, and hugged Cora. He hugged her as if he hadn't seen her in ages, as if they were long-lost lovers meeting by chance on a moonlit beach or in the crowded lobby of a far-away hotel. At first, his embrace startled Cora. As the heat of his body rifled through hers, she relaxed and wrapped her arms around his neck and pulled him close. She was surprised at his actions, but she didn't mind. She needed someone to hug her; someone to let her know everything was going to be all right. She was especially glad that someone was Alex.

"Cora, I hope you don't mind; I called Bobby and told him I'd pick you up." He separated himself from her and returned to the customer side of the counter.

She nodded her head that she didn't mind.

"Would it be okay if we stop at the church for a sec? I need to check on something."

"No, I don't mind. The kids will be fine a few minutes longer without me."

Rev. Alex turned on Seventeenth Street and drove the short distance to Phoenix Avenue where his church, Tabernacle Baptist, was located. He parked in the pastor's slot and quickly rushed around the car, so he could open the door for Cora. He didn't quite make it. She'd already opened the door and was halfway out before he arrived. He took her hand and helped her the rest of the way.

"Why, thank you, Alex. I'm not used to such gentlemanly ways. Perhaps, you could give my two sons a lesson in courtesy?" She said half-laughing.

The church was a long narrow building made of red brick. In order to enter the sanctuary a parishioner had to walk up a flight of steep concrete steps to an equally narrow porch where a set of double doors led to the sanctuary. The church was old, but well maintained. Reverend Thomas counted among his flock of over two hundred members of whom several were carpenters, plumbers, and electricians. It was a workingman's church, and the good condition of the building proved it.

Alex took Cora by the hand, and the two strolled around the building. Cora had no idea why they were walking around the church in the dark, but said nothing. She actually kind of liked it. Her attack of the shivers was over and the cool breeze felt refreshing gliding across her exposed cheek. A night bird whistled at them from the leafy midst of an ancient oak and the smell of nature, of God, entered her body with every breath. Cora loved the outdoors. She wished she had more time to spend outside.

After a single trip, Alex stopped. He turned to Cora, took a deep, nervous gulp of air and began: "Cora, I realize you've just gone through the most harrowing experience of your life. I know that now, tonight, may not be the best time to approach this subject, and I apologize in advance for my boldness. However, despite what happened, actually because of what happened, I've come to realize how much you mean to me. Cora, I love you."

Cora felt her eyeballs grow three inches. She gulped in the night air. Alex knelt before her. He took her hands in his.

"Cora, I love you more than life itself. You are the most wonderful woman on the face of the earth. There's nothing I wouldn't do for you. I love everything about you: the way you walk on your toes, the way you drawl your r's and l's, and how you bat your eyelids when you're angry. I think you've done an unbelievable job raising four kids, and I love every one of them. Heck, I even love Jonda's old yellow dog." He laughed. Then his voice softened. "Cora, I want you to marry me and become my wife. I'll take good care of you and your children. You'll never want for anything again."

Cora looked down at the man kneeling in front of her. Her eyes bulged like she'd seen a ghost. This was the absolute last thing she could have imagined would happen tonight. Alex Thomas, her pastor, was proposing marriage to her.

He sat on his knees, waiting for a reply. Hope emanated from his eyes. She stammered. "I ... uh... Alex ... I do care for you." Once she got this much out, the rest came easier. She relaxed. Her voice, although gentle and quiet, did not quaver. "I don't think I can marry you." She dropped her head. She could not look at him. "I'm unclean," she stated. Now, she couldn't help herself; she began to weep. Huge warm tears fell from her eyes and splattered in the dark grass below.

Alex stood and embraced the shattered woman. He held her close and silently prayed that God would give her strength to get through this terrible ordeal. Maybe he shouldn't have asked her so soon after her attack? Maybe he'd misread her? When he decided to ask for her hand, it seemed like a great idea, like the perfect thing to get her mind off the ravaging. Perhaps he'd been wrong, especially about her feelings towards him. But, regardless of whether or not she loved him, she was not unclean! There was nothing wrong with her! He had to make her understand that!

He pulled back from their embrace and placed his hands on her shoulders. Cora, tears continuing to streak down her face, raised her head.

"Whether you marry me or not, Cora Braun, I don't ever want to hear you say you are unclean. You did absolutely nothing wrong. You're the victim. You're the one who was wronged. In God's eyes and in mine, you are nothing less than perfect." He pulled her close to him and softly touched her wet cheek with his lips, lingering on her flesh as her salty tears seeped into his mouth.

"Do you really mean it?" she questioned. "Do you honestly still love me and aren't just asking me out of pity?"

"Oh, my Cora." He hugged her tightly. "I love you so much. The only person I'll pity will be myself if you say no."

Cora lightly pushed away. She wiped her tears with the back of her hand; a smile slowly grew on her face. "Alex Thomas, I'd be honored to be your wife. I accept your proposal of marriage."

Alex kissed his betrothed. "There's one more thing, though, and I hope it's not going to be a problem."

Cora's brow furrowed. Curiosity spread across her face.

"As a minister's wife, you're going to be extremely busy. To start with, I'll want you to attend the weekly ladies Bible study, be in charge of Vacation Bible School, oversee the food and clothing charities, and go with me when I visit hospitals. It really takes two to pastor a church. What I'm saying is you're going to be too busy with church duties to hold an outside job. I hope you won't mind giving up your position at the diner and your other job, cleaning that couple's house?"

The creases in her brow vanished, replaced by a huge grin that covered her entire face. She sighed in mock exasperation. "I guess I could do that for you. Of course, I'll expect to proofread and offer suggestions on your sermons."

"I welcome any help I can get in that regard, my dear lady. Yes, indeed."

This time it was Cora who initiated the hugging and kissing. As she held her future husband in her arms, her mind began racing to what she would wear on her wedding day.

Philip D. Smith

\* \* \* \* \*

They drove to the hotel in relative silence. When Josh told Bobby about the older boy hitting on Sarah, he'd taken it rather calmly, too calmly as far as Josh was concerned. He didn't even ask the boy's name or where he lived or anything. When Josh suggested they pay Sarah's admirer a visit, Bobby had been against it, saying they should wait and see if Sarah continued the uneven relationship. However, once Josh told Bobby he was going to see who Benny Matthews was for himself, Bobby agreed to go with him.

The Mayo Hotel was downtown and Josh hoped he'd find a parking space in front of the hotel or across the street. He was wrong on both accounts. Apparently, someone was throwing a big shindig because the place teemed with people and cars. There was no place to park; that is unless you were willing to pay a dollar for valet parking.

Josh puttered past the hotel, closely looking at each attendant's nametag in case one of them might say 'Benny', which would make the night's enterprise a lot easier. No such luck.

He continued past the hotel, his eyes flitting back and forth in search of an empty slot. Bobby seemed bored. He was stretched out on the seat with his eyes closed, periodically smacking his lips as if he were eating soft gooey taffy. At least Bobby finally seemed to be coming out of his depression over their mother. Josh ignored him and kept looking for a place to park.

He finally found a space two blocks away near Main. He parked behind a yellow Cadillac and shook his brother awake. Josh took off walking at a brisk pace towards the hotel. Bobby trailed behind stretching and yawning as if he'd been asleep for two days.

The Mayo soared majestically above the brothers like the crimson face of a steep cliff. Josh tilted his head until it seemingly pressed against his back in order to see the top. He guessed it was eighteen or nineteen stories, maybe even twenty. For a hotel, it was gigantic. The third and top two stories were ringed in white stone with the middle floors decorated in glistening red brick. Thick, rounded columns that looked like they belonged in Athens ringed the bottom floor.

"I think these are Doric columns," Bobby offered, seeing his brother mesmerized by the giants. "We learned about them in World History."

"I never got to take that class," Josh said with a hint of sadness in his voice. "What's that layer above the columns called? The stone area with the fancy scrollwork?"

"I'm not sure, but I think it's called the entablature. Keep in mind I made a 'C' in history."

"A 'C's better than not ever taking the class."

Bobby stepped to his brother and gripped his shoulder. "It wasn't your fault, Josh. Besides," he added with a mischievous grin, "that's why I'm here, to be the brains of the operation."

"Well, that makes me feel a lot better." Josh chuckled and shook his head as he headed toward the entrance.

The entryway proved equally impressive. Josh and Bobby walked between four sets of double columns and under a black canopy to enter the hotel. Amazingly, they were not stopped by any of the valets or the doorman, who smiled graciously and opened the middle of three glass doors. Josh and Bobby strode into the lobby as if they were oil tycoons. They screeched to a halt, before them lay the Great Hall of the Mayo Hotel. It was breathtaking. Their eyes widened and seemed to glaze over as they took in the extravagance of the high-ceilinged room. Golden tiles, outlined with small black squares, covered the floor. Square white columns extending upwards into the mezzanine level surrounded the rectangular hall. Wait staff, dressed in black and white scurried across the golden floor carrying pillows, blankets, or silver trays with containers of ice and drinks.

"Wow, look at that," Bobby pointed upwards.

Josh followed his finger and gulped. Above them, suspended from a broad, wide beam, was an enormous round chandelier with dozens of thick glass rods hanging down reminding Josh of giant icicles. Circling the top of the chandelier was a row of lights that looked like flameless candles. "I wonder who changes those light bulbs?" Josh absently commented. His eyes reached beyond the chandelier to a ceiling of glass, not just ordinary glass -- stained glass. If the panels had contained religious themes like the Ascension or the Last Supper rather than the striking geometric designs, the panels of the Mayo Hotel would have made any European cathedral proud.

"Can you believe this place?" Bobby gushed.

"I've never seen anything like it. I didn't know Tulsa had such a fancy place."

"Excuse me, gentlemen, may I help you?"

Josh and Bobby took their eyes from the ceiling. In front of them stood a skeletal man in a black suit and black bow tie. His deep-set, gray eyes darted from brother to brother; his pencil-thin mustache twitched as he looked with disapproving eyes at their wrinkled cotton shirts and faded blue jeans.

"We're looking for a friend of ours. We've got something important to tell him. His name's Benny Matthews. Do you know him?"

"Know him?" the man replied, his eyebrows rising. "I hired him. He works in the kitchen. I believe he's a dishwasher."

"You don't say," Josh nodded. "Which way to the kitchen?"

Josh could faintly hear Bobby chuckling and mumbling something. He decided not to ask what his brother was saying for fear they might get tossed out on their ears.

"The dining area is through there." Mr. Boss of the Mayo Hotel nodded towards a wide opening across the hall. Josh and Bobby stepped towards it. "However, gentlemen, I would prefer you use the back entrance to gain access to the kitchen. You will have to exit the building in order to do so." He smiled at them as if his lips had been glued together and he liked them that way.

"Uh, that's okay," Josh returned the smug smile. "It'll be faster if we take the shortcut." The brothers strode away from the befuddled manager, his finger pointing at them as if he wanted to demand they leave the premises at once.

People crowded the dining room eating colorful food from gleaming china that rested on tables of ironed, white tablecloths. Stiff waiters stood close by the round tables with bottles of wine or grinders of pepper ready to leap into action at the slightest indication their services were needed. Conversation at the tables was barely above a whisper, almost to the point of library quiet.

"I think that's where we need to go," Bobby said. "He headed towards some metal swinging doors. Josh followed.

The brothers shouldered through the doors and emerged into a bustling kitchen jammed with people fixing salads, cutting pieces of cheesecake, or arranging grilled chicken or prime rib on sparkling plates so that they lay contentedly next to the green and orange vegetables.

Bobby was the first to see him. Behind the hectic workstations of the cooks and bakers was a long metal table stacked with cups, saucers, plates, and silverware. Standing with his back to them, hunched over a steaming sink full of dirty dishes, was a lanky boy dressed in white. Josh took off. Bobby followed.

"Hey," Josh yelled, without even a hint of goodwill. "Are you Benny Matthews?"

The boy turned around. Josh jammed on the breaks, took a step back. Bobby skidded beside him.

Benny Matthews looked from one brother to the next. He had a blank stare on his face as if he had no idea who the two men were, which he didn't. He wiped his soapy hands on his white apron then used the apron to swab beads of perspiration from his forehead. On top of his head of short reddish hair, he wore a paper cone hat that was soggy from the steam of the hot dishwater. He took it off and rubbed his apron across it as if that would help the soaked fibers. His long, thin face was covered with tiny red pimples and splotches of uneven freckles. He looked about twelve. He definitely wasn't nineteen.

Bobby took the initiative. He stretched out his hand and said in a polite voice: "Hi, I'm Bobby Braun. This is Josh." He bobbed his head at his brother. "We're Sarah's brothers."

Benny Matthew's eyes bulged as if he were being charged by an angry lion. He cautiously shook hands with Bobby then offered his hand to Josh. Josh shook it. Surprisingly, Benny had a firm grip. He'd obviously worked most of his life.

With the pleasantries out of the way, Josh asked the young man how old he was.

Benny glanced around the room before answering. "I'll be sixteen in September. Everybody here thinks I'm already sixteen. You're not going to tell anybody, are you?" he added a few seconds later.

Josh looked at his brother. Bobby grinned. He turned back to Sarah's boyfriend. "No, of course not. We came here for something else. There's a rumor going around town that you kinda like our sister? Sarah? Is that true?"

The dishwasher admitted he did, nervousness in his eyes from not knowing what was coming next. "I like her a lot. She's funny."

Josh again glanced at Bobby. "Sarah funny?" He laughed. "That's a new one."

Bobby decided it was time for him to speak to the kid. "Listen, Benny. I hope you understand why we're here? When we heard Sarah had a new boyfriend, we felt it our duty as her big brothers to check the guy out."

Benny dropped his head and nodded.

Bobby continued, "Anyway, after meeting you, we've decided you're okay. We're not thrilled about having red-headed nephews and nieces, but you seem like a nice enough guy."

Benny raised his head, terror in his eyes. "Oh, we're not gonna get married or anything. We just like hanging around each other. We're too young to get married. I'll only be a sophomore next year."

"That's even better," Bobby said trying to sound serious. "I think I'm gonna like you. Where do you live, Benny?"

"I live in Red Fork on the south side of the tracks by the Methodist church."

"We *really* like you now," Josh said. "You're a Westsider, like us. Why don't you come over some time, so we can really get to know you? Sarah's a good cook. Tell her you want to eat supper with us some time."

"Really? You want me to come over?"

"You betcha, Benny Matthews. You come visit us anytime you like."

Despite seeing the back door that the manager wanted them to use, Josh and Bobby excited through the main lobby. They didn't see Mr. Prim-and-Proper on their way out.

"Just when did Sarah have another boyfriend?" Josh asked as they jauntily walked to their car.

"She hasn't. I just wanted to make her sound a little more exotic."

"Exotic? Huh?" How does having a prior boyfriend make Sarah more exotic?"

"Oh, shut up, Josh. Let's go home and get some rest. We've got a big game tomorrow."

# 21

For ballplayers, the most anxious and nerve-racking time is immediately before a game. A ballplayer has a routine he religiously follows and when it's done, it's time to play. If you don't play right then, that's when the nerves set in. That's when you start thinking too much, start fidgeting, start double guessing yourself. Josh had finished playing catch; he'd taken a few swings in the batting cage; he'd warmed up Bobby; he'd hit grounders to the infield. He was ready to play. The umpires weren't. They were still in the umpire's room dressing and probably chit-chatting about the weather, their families, their jobs or where's the best place to get some good barbeque after the game.

Josh sat on the end of the wooden bench; his back leaned against the chain-link fence. Everyone else was still going through their pre-game routines or just standing around shooting the breeze. Josh had sat in this dugout, on this very bench, hundreds of times. How many games had he played at Howard Park? He had no idea. He hadn't kept track. Around forty or fifty a year for the last seven years was about as close as he could figure.

Josh twisted around and surveyed the bleachers. He didn't see the stubby form of Runt Marr anywhere. The Cardinal scout had yet to arrive. That surprised him a little. Most scouts came early so they could watch batting practice and the fielders work. It was an excellent way to evaluate a player's fundamentals; see if the mechanics of their swing was good or if an infielder executed the crossover technique correctly.

Josh decided Marr's tardiness was no big thing. The scout had seen him play before and was coming to watch him play again. In fact, Marr once offered him a contract. Josh just hoped Mr. Marr also liked Bobby. Bobby definitely threw hard enough, and everybody was always looking for the next Carl Hubbell or Dizzy Dean. Wouldn't it be fantastic if both of them signed with the Cardinals?

A warm gust of air pelted Josh's face. It felt good. Josh liked playing when the temperature rose; his body felt better. He didn't like playing when it was cool; he had trouble getting his muscles loosened, and his limbs stretched properly. He smiled. That was another reason to play for the Cardinals. It was a lot warmer in St. Louis than in Boston or New York.

A group of people entering the gate caught Josh's attention. It was his mother and sisters – and Reverend Thomas. How had his Mom gotten off work again? That was strange. In the past, she'd been able to see only a few games because she was always working. Josh was glad to see her, excited actually. However, he worried about her job situation *and* her mental well being. His mother noticed him looking their way and waved. Reverend Thomas, walking next to his mother, also waved. Josh smiled at his mom and waved to her. He ignored the preacher.

\* \* \* \* \*

"Hey, hot-shot! What are you dreaming about? You look kinda sad and moony-eyed sitting all by yourself, while the rest of your little friends are out there having fun."

Josh glanced at the girl on the other side of the dugout fence. The blazing sun swooshed across her shoulder and blasted his eyes. He shielded them, trying to see the blur before him by putting the side of his hand across his brow like a Plains Indian scout looking for paleface soldiers who've invaded his ancestral lands. Even then he couldn't discern her features. The glowing indistinct body before him looked like an ethereal being encased in a golden, heavenly aura. Like an angel.

An angel standing with her hands on her hips being sarcastic. It didn't matter. He knew who she was. He'd grown accustomed to her voice. He liked her voice, even when she waxed cynical. She had a smooth, flirtatious voice, deeper and lower than most girls.

"Hi, Frannie. Thanks for coming. You look bright today."

"Oh." She turned and looked at the sun as if verifying what he'd said was true. She scooted several feet away, shading Josh from the sun's glare.

"Thanks," Josh nodded, lowering his hand. "And I meant it when I said I appreciate you coming. I know how busy you are with your tea parties and debutante balls."

Now it was Frannie's turn to squint at Josh. Only she didn't do it because of the sun. "You're quite the comedian, aren't you?" she grinned.

"I learned from the best," he nodded at her.

Frannie looked from Josh towards the opposing team's dugout. "I guess you know who's on the Eastside team?"

"Yeah. I saw him when he walked in. He's where he belongs. Those are his kind of guys."

"Hey," Frannie piped. "I know most of those 'guys.' They're not so bad."

"I'm sorry. I'm sure they're all good fellas. Even Cameron was okay most of the time. He just doesn't like black people, which is too bad because you can't find a better guy than Artemis."

Frannie's gaze settled on her former boyfriend. He was standing in the dirt on the outfield side of second base taking grounders from a puffy coach. Cameron's slender, athletic body glided rhythmically to the scooting ball and squeezed the white sphere with his mitt as if cuddling a newborn. Cameron straightened and zipped the ball to a freckled catcher, already accoutered in shin guards standing next to the uniformed coach. Frannie noticed that Cameron's silky black tresses jutted from his cap and touched the top of his ears. That was unusual, she thought. It wasn't like him to let his personal hygiene slip. He probably hadn't had a haircut in three or four weeks. She'd never seen him like this.

Cameron fielded two more ground balls, then trotted to the dugout. He looked Frannie's way, and saw her watching him. He raised his hand like a school crossing guard and accompanied the stiff gesture with a smarmy grin. Without thinking, Frannie returned the wave – but not the smile. As if coming out of a hypnotic trance, she vigorously shook her head. She turned away from her ex and found Josh looking at her like she'd stolen his lunch money.

"Which side are you sitting on tonight?" he asked in a sonorous, overly solemn voice.

"Very funny." She screwed her face at him in mock anger. "Why, of course, I'm sitting on the other side – with *my* people." Frannie left the dugout and headed in the direction of the Eastsiders' bleachers. About halfway there she veered away and found a place next to Sarah among the Frisco supporters.

\* \* \* \* \*

When she walked through the gate, her first urge was to run to the dugout where Josh sat, gather her children together, and tell them the wonderful news. On second thought, she decided not to. Josh and Bobby were getting ready to play a game and, according to Josh, a very important game. The news of her engagement would have to wait until it was over.

Cora led Alex, Sarah, and Jonda to the bleachers where they took their place on the second row. Jonda immediately ran off to play stickball with little Satchel. This was perfectly fine with Cora. Jonda had way too much energy to sit and watch a baseball game. Cora sat between Sarah and Alex, and it was hard not to grasp her fiancés' hand. She satisfied herself, and him, by swapping winks and hints of kisses from afar. After Cora accepted her pastor's proposal, they talked and decided to act like nothing had happened until Cora could tell her children. They both felt that Josh, Bobby, Sarah, and Jonda should be the first to know. She'd wanted to tell them last night as soon as she got home, but strange as it seemed, and it was unusual; everyone was asleep. Then when she awoke this morning, Josh had already gone to work. So, she'd had to keep the fantastic news to herself all day long.

That afternoon brought more good news. A man from the district attorney's office paid her a visit. He told her that after some serious coaxing, splashed with a few threats about his cell and throwing away the key, Robert Cornwell had confessed to molesting her. He signed a confession, and it was already on a judge's desk waiting for him to read and decide what to do with the scoundrel. Before leaving, the young prosecutor, still seeing Cora's anxiety had patted her arm and told her she had nothing more to worry about. She'd never, ever have to see Mr. Robert Cornwell again. He was now the ward of the state of Oklahoma, and they would make sure he wore stripes for a long, long time.

\* \* \* \* \*

"Whatcha doin'? Is Bobby gonna pitch the baseball?"

"Yep. He's tonight's pitcher." Artemis, who was sitting on a bucket turned upside down, rainbowed the ball back to Bobby. Bobby was finished with his pre-game routine and was whiling away the time by working on the blooper and his curveball. Bobby stood less than thirty feet from Artemis and flipped the ball to him without bothering to go into his windup. He was still trying to get the spin right on the difficult pitches.

"Don't get so close, kids," Artemis said to Jonda and Satchel. The children had crept closer and closer to Satchel's dad by pretending to smash invisible June bugs with the toes of their shoes. Satchel jumped backwards like he'd stepped in dog poo. Jonda eased back a half step.

"Did you know that someday Bobby's gonna pitch baseballs for the St. Louis Cardinals? They play in St. Louis. That's a long way away.

And my other brother, Josh, he's gonna be the catcher for the Cardinals. He told me he was." Jonda crossed her arms and stuck her chin out towards the seated Artemis like he was the cool kid at school, and she wanted nothing more than to impress him. "And Bobby told me he'd teach me how to pitch when I get older and who knows, I might pitch for the St. Louis Cardinals, too. I might be the best pitcher in the whole world someday."

"Wouldn't you rather play for the Yankees?" Artemis asked the future Hall-of-Famer. "They're awfully good."

Jonda shook her head like a dog trying to shake water from its fur and stamped her foot on the ground. "Nope. I ain't playin' for the Yankees. I'm gonna play for the St. Louis Cardinals." She turned to her friend who, imitating the older girl, also stood with his arms folded over his chest. "Who's the Yankees, Satchy? Is that who your daddy played for?"

Satchel shook his head and shrugged his shoulders.

Jonda turned back to the grown-up on the bucket. She looked at her brother who stood a few feet away staring at the white ball in his hand. "Hey, why idn't Bobby pitchin' like he usually does?" Jonda asked the seated catcher. "He usually stands way back there and waves his arms over his head before he throws." Jonda, with exaggerated movements, pantomimed her brother's pitching motion. Satchel, standing beside her, did the same.

With his peripheral vision, Artemis watched the antics of his son and the little girl and couldn't keep a smile from forming on his face. Bobby didn't seem to notice. He was engrossed in how he was holding the baseball, determined to figure out Satchel Paige's famous pitch.

Artemis turned his head slightly towards the youngsters. "Next time your brother comes to my house to practice why don't you come with him? You can play with Satchy while we play catch. I'll get my wife to bake a chocolate cake. Do you like chocolate cake?"

Jonda smacked her lips together several times saying, "um, um, do

I ever." Little Satchel copied his older friend and rubbed his belly for good measure.

Artemis laughed out loud. "Okay, then. It's settled. You have to promise me one thing, though." He held up one finger at the kids.

"What's that?" asked Jonda, concern filtering onto her face.

"Yeah, Daddy. What's that?" Satchel added.

"You have to promise me that you'll save a piece of cake for me. Is that a deal?"

A look of relief washed over Jonda. "Sure, Mr. Macintosh, I can only eat one piece. Mom won't let me eat anymore. She says it's bad for little girls to eat too much pie or cake. Bobby and Josh can eat a lot. They can eat three or four pieces. I've seen them do it. Come on Satchy, let's go see if there's anything under the stands." And without another word, Jonda and Satchel scampered off towards the bleachers.

The catcher smiled widely. "Her attention span is about as big as a cricket."

Artemis looked up from his bucket. Bobby stood in front of him rolling the baseball over the tips of his fingers onto the back of his hand where he'd balance it a few seconds and quickly twist his hand and catch it in his huge palm. He then rolled it back over his fingertips to see if he could balance it longer. Bobby was a born pitcher. Artemis realized this the first time he'd seen the young man heave a ball towards home plate. He was lean and long-armed up top with thick muscular legs down below: the perfect power pitcher. And he had the head for it, too. Nothing seemed to bother him. If he gave up a hit or if someone made a mistake behind him, Bobby just shrugged it off. He possessed a short-term memory, a pitcher's best friend.

"You've got quite a sister, there. I bet she's a lot of fun."

Bobby nodded. "Yeah, she is. She's a corker. I hate to see her grow up. I hate to see her change. I like things the way they are."

Artemis noticed Bobby looking beyond him, at the bleachers. He stood, and the two men, side-by-side, trekked to the dugout.

# 22

As soon as the ball zipped across home plate, the catcher popped from his haunches and fired it to third base. The third sacker had already caught the ball and was in the process of chunking it to the second baseman by the time the umpire barked, "stee-rike three!" Bobby turned and watched his infielders throw the ball around. Josh, trotted from his catching position halfway to the mound and exhorted everyone to keep it up, they were doing great.

Bobby agreed. It was the seventh inning, and they were beating the Eastside Dodgers 2 to 0. Bobby had allowed only a single base runner while Josh was the hitting star with a home run and an RBI double.

Bobby caught the underhanded toss from Artemis, who was playing first base, and winked at his fellow pitcher. Artemis nodded, jogged back to his position. As was his habit, Bobby sauntered behind the mound and rubbed the ball. He picked up the resin bag and batted it around in his palm, ridding himself of the hot, late-afternoon sweat. He was glad he was doing well and not just because Runt Marr was in the stands with contracts in his pocket. Sure, he wanted to impress the baseball scout. Of course, it would be nice if he were offered a big, fat contract. Absolutely, it would be great if he and Josh could play baseball for money. Nevertheless, as mean spirited as it sounded, he was thoroughly enjoying beating the Eastside boys. He loved whizzing the ball past them. He enjoyed the look on their faces when they popped up to the infield or bailed out on his newly acquired curveball as the umpire called them out on strikes. They might be wealthy. They might have more education and drive nicer cars, but today he was their superior. Today, he was in charge. He felt great.

Bobby fought the urge to smile as the next batter trooped to the plate. It was the Eastside's pitcher. A fellow named Adamson. He was a college player at the city's private university. Bobby looked over at Artemis, but the first sacker had his back to him holding up his fingers and yelling "two outs" to the right fielder.

Josh, in his squat, held down two fingers between his legs. Bobby shook his head. He didn't want to throw a curve. Josh frowned. He didn't like Bobby shaking him off. Next, Josh signaled for an outside fastball. Bobby nodded then shook his head.

Josh vigorously shook his head at his brother.

Bobby smirked, and again showed his disagreement.

From the mound, Bobby could see Josh sigh as if to say 'okay' and signaled for an inside fastball.

Bobby agreed. Heartily.

It was payback time. In the third inning, Artemis's first at bat, the Dodger's pitcher plunked the Frisco's first baseman squarely on the shoulder. In the fifth and again in the seventh inning he'd knocked Artemis down with near-miss inside fastballs. Artemis said nothing. He'd simply gotten up off the ground and continued playing. Now, it was Mr. Adamson's turn to taste dirt.

Bobby went into his windup and let fly with a high and tight one or as Satchel Paige would have said, a barber-pitch because he was going to shave his opponent's whiskers. The ball headed straight for the opposing pitcher's chin and would have smacked him if he hadn't jerked backwards; the batter over-reacted. Instead of simply pulling his mug out of the way of the oncoming ball, his feet completely left the ground. He flailed through the air like a tightrope walker high above a stunned crowd whose lost his balance and knows he's doomed. Adamson's rear end smacked the ground hard. It sounded like a dropped sack of potatoes on a linoleum floor. The bat fell from his hand and rolled towards the plate. He looked towards the mound as if he had no idea why Bobby had done this. Bobby stared back at the fallen man, contempt and satisfaction exuding from his visage.

The visiting team's dugout erupted. Catcalls laced with profanity issued from the pitcher's enraged teammates. The Dodger's coach stomped from the visitor's side and began jawing nose-to-nose with the umpire. Several of the Dodgers raked bats across the chain-link face of their dugout and kicked the bottom of it with their metal cleats as if the fence had done them wrong.

Bobby stood in front of the mound. He continued glaring at Adamson, still prostrate in the dirt. The opposing pitcher acted as if he couldn't get up. His legs had no strength.

"How's it feel, sucker? It's a lot easier to throw at somebody than it is to take it." Bobby snarled. He noticed that Josh had come out from behind the plate and was glowering at him. Bobby turned from his brother and strolled behind the mound. He didn't need eyes in the back of his head to know his brother was making his way to the mound. He could feel him.

"Way to go, slick!" Josh hissed. "The game was going great. No trouble. We're winning. And then you go and do a boneheaded thing like throw at one of them. You're lucky the whole team didn't charge the mound and take you apart before I could pull 'em off. And believe me, I wouldn't have been in a hurry."

"Come on, Josh. Lighten up. That twerp's been throwing at Artemis all night. I'm just giving him some of his own medicine. Besides he's not gonna do anything. Look at him. He's just now getting off his duff."

The brothers twisted their heads and watched as Adamson cautiously rose to his feet and dusted his pants. He reached to the ground and picked up his bat and bumped it against his cleat in a feeble effort to imitate Ted Williams.

"He is kind of a wimp. Isn't he?" Josh agreed; his voice lost its edge.

"You even took a little off your heater, didn't you?" Josh risked a quick grin at his brother. "He easily should have been able to avoid such a slow pitch."

"You're right. I didn't throw ole number one the way I normally do, but it's still faster than anything he's got."

By this time, the entire Frisco infield had gathered around the pitcher's mound. The Eastside manager, although still yelling at the home plate umpire, appeared to be winding down, his face no longer the color of an engorged strawberry. At long last, the Dodger skipper finished his diatribe and huffed back to his dugout. During the entire return trip, he glowered at Bobby as if he wanted to tear the limbs from his body and eat them barbequed alongside an order of slaw.

"I wonder what's up his crawl?" Bobby snickered. "You'd think I chunked the ole cowhide at his plump little buns instead of that worthless pitcher of his."

"Uh, that pitcher just happens to be his boy." Larry Timlin, Frisco's new shortstop said. "That's Judge Roy Adamson. He runs traffic court. And our umpire tonight is a cop. Didn't you wonder why the ump was taking so much guff from their coach?"

"Well, I'll be a monkey's uncle," Bobby said. "Who woulda thought?"

"Hey, Bobby," Simmons, the second baseman, chuckled. "You better hope you don't get pulled over by a cop any time soon. You'd probably wind up in the state pen doin' twenty to life for nothing more than running a stop sign."

"Well, live and learn," Bobby rubbed the back of his neck, spit on the ground. "Boys, it just don't matter. I'd have done it, even if I'd known their fat little coach was none other than Judge Roy Bean himself."

"I guess the fun's over, guys," Josh said. "Let's finish this game and quit horsin' around."

The players dispersed to their positions. Josh turned to go back behind the plate.

"Hey, Josh."

Josh stopped, trooped back to his brother.

Bobby wet his lips. He was no longer smiling. "I'm gonna throw two heaters on the inside part of the plate …"

A frown flashed on Josh's face.

"Don't worry. I'm not gonna throw at him again. These'll be for strikes. He won't touch 'em. Anyway, after that I want to get him with the number three."

Now Josh looked confused. "You want to try the blooper pitch on him? What if it gets away from you? That thing's hard to control."

"I can do it. It looked good during warm-ups. It's about time I threw it in a game."

Josh pulled his wire-cage mask over his face. He popped his mitt with his fist. "Okay, but if you hit him don't expect me to defend you." Josh turned and jogged back to home plate.

Bobby watched his brother squat and give him the signal for another inside fastball. He knew he wasn't going to hit Adamson. Bobby also knew that if he did, Josh would be the first one at his side.

Josh struck out the opposing pitcher exactly the way he said he would — with the number three pitch. Satchel Paige's famous blooper ball worked perfectly.

\* \* \* \* \*

When Bobby reminded him about Artemis finishing the game, Josh didn't like the idea. Bobby had the Eastsiders eating out of his hand. He was dominating them. Why would a manager even think about switching pitchers under those circumstances? However, when Bobby nodded at the bleachers towards the stubby scout furiously penciling notes in a worn little pad, Josh understood. Bobby wanted Artemis to have a chance to shine in front of a Major League scout. Josh couldn't have agreed more.

The eighth inning was uneventful. Artemis struck out two of the three hitters to face him – both on that nasty curve of his. He got the third batter to ground weakly to second base

The Frisco squad was also anemic in their half of the inning, mustering a solitary walk out of four hitters. This took the game into the ninth and last inning.

Josh jogged to his position behind home plate and began warming up the pitcher. Artemis leisurely lobbed a couple of balls and motioned to Josh that he was ready. Josh yelled "balls in' and chunked Artemis's last warm up to second base to begin the final throw around. Josh trotted to the mound and joined the rest of the infielders who were touching gloves with their pitcher and telling him the game was in the bag.

Josh held out his mitt to Artemis. Artemis slapped it with his and winked. "Let's finish it in style." Josh nodded lustily.

Before taking his position, Josh rolled his head trying to rid himself of any hidden tension. He pulled the wire cage over his face, adjusted his shin guards with his free hand, and squatted directly behind home plate. He popped his fist into his glove twice as the Dodger's leadoff batter and their fastest runner took his place in the batter's box.

Josh signaled for the curveball and the speedy batter punched a routine grounder at the shortstop. As he sprinted to back up first base, Josh knew there was going to be trouble before it happened. Timlin, normally a second baseman who was filling the vacancy at short created when VanDeaver left the team, charged the ball like an enraged bull at a matador.

The shortstop fielded the ball without a hitch. However, his forward momentum was so great that he was unable to stop or get his feet under him before throwing to first base. He made a lunging, awkward throw at the bag that sailed high and wide and into the outfield. The runner rounded first base and thought about going to second. Thank goodness Bobby, now in right field, had been backing up the play. He quickly retrieved the ball and fired it to second. The runner, realizing he had no chance to advance, returned to first base.

Josh glanced at his pitcher. Nothing. There was no trace of anger, frustration, impatience, aggravation, irritation, annoyance, or exasperation on Artemis's face. His face was as free from expression as if all the muscles had become paralyzed. Timlin, whose charge carried him even with the mound, angrily kicked at the earth and apologized to his pitcher.

Now, Artemis showed expression. He flashed the boy a fatherly smile, walked over to the dejected player and swatted his rump. "It's okay Larry; you'll get the next one."

As if fulfilling prophecy, the next batter smashed a sizzling ground ball at the Frisco shortstop.

Timlin fielded the ball perfectly and executed a beautiful crossover with his feet and threw a strike to first base. One out.

Josh banged his mask against his shin guards. He stared at the shortstop as if the man had done some egregious wrong. He had -- at least in Josh's mind! The hard-hit grounder was tailor-made for a double play. There should be two outs and nobody on base instead of the lone out and a runner atop second. Josh said nothing. Nobody did. You didn't do that to your teammate during a game. It was one of those unwritten rules.

It didn't look like it was going to matter, anyway. Artemis struck out the Dodgers' three-hole hitter on the ole number three -- the change up. Or as Artemis, and increasingly Bobby, liked to call it, the Blooper. One more out and it was time to talk with Mr. Runt Marr of the St. Louis Cardinals Baseball Club.

Cameron VanDeaver strode to the plate. He batted cleanup for the Eastside squad. Josh knew the powerful hitter could tie the game with one swing. He wasn't going to let him do it. He would pitch very carefully to the slugger.

The first pitch was a down and away curveball. Artemis hit the spot with pinpoint accuracy. Cameron didn't bother to swing. Strike one.

Next, Josh signaled for an inside fastball. Artemis threw it as hard as he could and the ball whizzed right at Josh's mitt. Cameron swung, connected, and walloped the ball out of the park and into the pecan orchard -- five feet foul.

"Whew," Josh whistled, standing behind the plate watching as the ball arced foul. "That was close. Oh well, it's just another strike in the scorebook."

Cameron, also watching the ball miss being a home run by less than a body, twisted his head and snarled. "The next one's going to go even further and straighter."

"I hope not," Josh puffed. "We can't let you tie up the game, or we'd have to pay the umpires overtime! We can't afford that; so sorry. We'll have to get you out."

The umpire chuckled.

Cameron grunted and dug his cleats into the dirt.

Josh signaled for a low, outside curve like the first pitch. Artemis painted the corner of the plate like he was Michelangelo in the Sistine Chapel.

Cameron lunged at the pitch, afraid of letting it go by unchallenged. Somehow he got bat on ball and blooped a soft twisting drive into right field. Josh could immediately tell that it was going to fall in for a single, which would score the runner from second slicing Frisco's lead in half. It was a lucky hit. Cameron had been totally fooled by the pitch but, in desperation, had slapped at the ball and made contact.

Then horror widened Josh's eyes. Bobby was trying to catch the fluttering hit. He was sprinting at the sinking, slicing ball like he was Joe DiMaggio at Yankee Stadium. He wasn't going to make it. Josh could plainly see this and hoped Bobby realized it too, but . . . Bobby wasn't pulling up. He wasn't going to let the ball fall harmlessly in front of him and hold the batter to a single. He was determined to catch it!

Josh watched with disbelieving eyes as his brother tried to make a diving catch. Bobby extended and knifed through the air like he was a P51 Mustang strafing the enemy. His lanky body glided above the green below as if he were meant to be airborne, his outstretched arm on an interception course with the evasive white sphere. Unfortunately, Bobby miscalculated. Not by much. Only a little. His reaching glove missed the ball by less than an inch.

"Oh my goodness," escaped Josh's mouth.

The ball struck the ground and began rolling towards the right field corner. Josh quickly glanced at Mike Goselin in centerfield and saw to his added shock that the centerfielder had failed to back up the play. As if feeling his catcher's eyes boring into him, Goselin took off after the ball. Bobby too, bounced from the ground and dashed after his mistake.

Meanwhile, Cameron rounded first base and was halfway to second. The first runner had already scored and stood behind Josh and the umpire jumping up and down like a cheerleader at a pep rally.

In an instant, Josh realized there would be a play at the plate. He positioned himself beside home plate on the third base side, effectively blocking the precious base from the runner. He silently prayed that Bobby would get to the ball before Mike Goselin; Bobby possessed a much stronger arm.

Bobby reached the ball, which had rolled to the fence, just as Cameron rounded third base. Josh's brother heaved the mischievous orb towards home. Timlin, the cutoff man, caught the perfectly thrown ball a few feet beyond first base, turned and fired it home.

Josh braced himself for the inevitable collision. He caught the ball almost simultaneously as Cameron VanDeaver, all two hundred pounds of him, crashed into him. Then everything went black.

*****

Everyone in the bleachers was on their feet. They watched with mixed feelings as the play unfolded. The Dodger fans waved their arms and urged Cameron to run faster, faster, while the Frisco faithful shouted for Bobby to hurry and get the ball and then for Timlin to throw it quickly to Josh.

Both sides became eerily quiet moments before the collision. Eyes opened wider; hands covered gaping mouths, and women instinctively pulled their children close to them as the two powerful men butted body against body. They could see clearly as if the tragedy were happening in slow-motion; the throw from the cutoff man flew a little – not much, but it didn't have to be far off the mark to cause disaster – high and up the third-base line. Their hearts beat faster as the catcher turned towards third base and reached his mitt into the air to catch the errant throw. They grimaced as the runner, head down, shoulder extended like a fullback ramming into the goal line, flung himself against the exposed catcher. Several gasped when air whooshed from the catcher as the determined base runner drove him into the plate.

Then, there were shouts of joy, shouts of excitement. Of relief. At least from half the crowd when the umpire jerked his arm into the air and proclaimed the runner out. The catcher, despite being barreled over and slammed against the ground, held onto the ball. The precious ball was still firmly in his mitt.

Frannie, too, felt relieved and excited that Josh had made the play. The game was over, and Frisco had won.

Her visage slowly changed. Trepidation etched its way across her cheeks and pushed her upraised lips downward. She felt her bottom lip quiver. Josh was not moving.

The catcher lay across home plate, his arms and legs extended as if he were about to make snow angels in the dirt. Both teams slowly gathered around the fallen player. For several seconds, no one bent down to help him. All was complete silence.

Sprinting from his position in right field, Bobby reached his brother and pushed through the gathering crowd. He stooped and spoke. From the stands, Frannie could not hear what Bobby said, but it was obvious to everyone that Josh did not answer.

A sweltering fear pushed through Frannie's body. Her breathing became wispy; water rushed into her eyes. Methodically, zombie-like, never taking her eyes from the fallen player, she made her way down the bleachers and towards the swinging gate and onto the field. As if knowing that she belonged, the crowd parted enabling her to approach the injured man unobstructed.

Bobby held his brother's upper torso in his arms. His mother swabbed her oldest son's face with a plain, white handkerchief and quietly, soothingly told him he was going to be all right. Josh's eyes remained closed. Frannie knelt beside Cora and whispered, "is Josh going to be okay?" Cora turned slightly, smiled and nodded. She turned back to her boy.

The next few minutes lasted an eternity. At first, everyone was quiet. Soon, susurrations and then chatty conversations erupted from the milling people. Everyone wanted to know how badly the player was hurt. No one knew the answer.

The sirens sounded as if they were in another county, their resonance no louder than the high-pitched humming of a woman hanging her laundry on the clotheslines. Gradually, the sirens neared. As they did, the shrill became louder and louder until it resembled a dying cat begging for someone to save it.

The screaming unnerved the spectators and players; the crowd broke up. Several people sprinted to the parking lot like they were the welcoming committee. Not a few covered their ears. The faithful: Bobby, his mom and sisters, Frannie and the preacher, remained close to Josh. Without looking up, they could tell when the ambulance screeched into the parking lot. Cora audibly sighed, and with her hand, brushed the hair from her son's forehead.

Whether it was the tender touch of his mother's hand or the hubbub of the jostling ambulance attendants, she never knew. But Frannie was the first to notice when Josh opened his eyes. At first, he looked straight ahead as if seeing nothing, then his bloodshot eyes fluttered left and right as if trying to figure out what in the world was going on. When Josh's eyes settled on hers, she smiled as deeply as her trembling mouth would allow. Josh closed his eyes, opened them again and smiled. It was as sweet a smile as she'd ever seen in her entire life.

Frannie nudged Cora, who'd turned to watch the attendants unfurl the stretcher. Josh blinked at her, too.

"I told you, you were going to be all right," Cora soothed.

"'Well, look who's awake," Bobby chirped. He patted his brother's hand.

"He's going to be fine," Frannie said to no one and everyone.

Josh opened his mouth. He tried to speak.

"Hold on partner. You don't need to talk. There'll be plenty of time to talk later," Bobby said.

Josh, ignoring his brother, began moving his lips. A throaty, barely audible sound emanated. "Wuzz he owt?"

Bobby grinned at his brother, at his mother and Frannie, then at his two sisters and Rev. Alex. "You bet your britches he was out. There was no way a brother of mine was going to drop that ball. You got him out, and we won the game. It was a great play! An absolutely great play!"

Josh attempted another weak smile. It faltered. "Tha's good," he husked. He grimaced and closed his eyes.

Frannie prayed silently that Josh would be okay. She didn't know what she'd do if he wasn't.

# 23

Cora didn't want to leave her son's side, even though the young nurse promised she'd stay with him. She kissed her eldest on the cheek and trudged down the emergency room corridor to the waiting room.

The doctor had left the tiny curtained cubicle that passed for a room at St. John's Hospital less than five minutes earlier. The tests were back, and he'd come to explain the injury to Josh and his mother. Now, it was her duty to relate what the doctor said to the rest of the family and friends.

She whisked through two wide swinging doors, and went from a quiet, sterile, white, environment to a world that buzzed with a cacophony of noises and exploding color. The expansive waiting room was jammed with groupings of people talking, hugging, and eating cheap snack food from one of the numerous vending machines.

She found her knot of baseball players and fans and began wading through the throng of nervous, anxious people. She saw Jonda's blonde head bobbing in the middle and quickened her pace.

"There's Cora," someone called out.

"That's Josh's mom," someone else added.

Cora halted on the fringe of the group, and took a deep breath. She knew practically every person in front of her. Sarah, Jonda, and Alex emerged from the crowd and hugged her.

"How is he? Is he gonna be alright?" Mike Goselin, one of the players asked.

Cora forced a smile. "Yes, he's going to be fine."

A collective sigh spread through the room.

She continued, "He suffered a pretty bad concussion when his head hit the ground; the doctor said he'll have a headache for a few days. . ."

"Josh always did have a hard head," someone chirped. Everyone laughed. Cora faked a chuckle.

". . . but that's not the worst thing he did."

Cora felt everyone edge closer as if she wasn't speaking loud enough.

"Josh dislocated his right shoulder and in the process tore every tendon and ligament near it. When the swelling goes down, they're going to operate. They're moving him to a room as we speak. "He'll be okay in a few weeks," she hastened to add.

"What about baseball? When is he gonna be able to play baseball again?"

The question came from below her. It came from Jonda. Of all the people who she thought might ask her that, she would have never guessed it would come from Josh's little sister. She gulped. Her tongue was as dry as an autumn leaf. Her lips trembled. This was the part she dreaded most.

"No, he'll never play again. The doctor said he won't be able to throw a ball past the pitcher's mound let alone all the way to second base. He won't even be able to swing a bat without a lot of pain."

"Does he know?" The question came from the edge of the crowd -- from Bobby.

Cora gazed at her son. He looked lost, disoriented. His eyes had a vacant look as if he were in shock.

She nodded that he knew.

\* \* \* \* \*

Bobby listened to his mother with disbelieving ears. This couldn't be happening. This couldn't be happening to Josh.

When she emerged from Josh's room, Bobby wanted to rush to her side. Something held him back. Something forced him to remain near the wall away from everyone else. He knew what it was, and as disgusted and revolted as it made him feel; he couldn't keep it at bay. He was happy. No, he was thrilled beyond belief. He was so excited and energized that not even his brother's terrible injury could keep the feeling submerged. This uncontrollable ecstasy made him angry. Angry at himself for being selfish. Because if Josh weren't lying in a hospital bed, everyone would be congratulating him. He'd be surrounded by his friends and teammates wishing him luck in his new endeavor.

It was simple. Runt Marr thought he was a good pitcher and thought he could make it in the Big Leagues. Runt Marr wanted to sign him to a professional contract.

How could he do it now that Josh was hurt? How could he go off and play professional baseball and leave his brother here, his life-long dream destroyed by a freak accident in a meaningless semi-pro game?

He didn't think he could do it. His family was more important than a stupid game. His brother was more important than baseball.

# 24

The nurses didn't like it, and voiced their disapproval in no uncertain terms. Everyone ignored them. They crowded into Josh's room standing shoulder-to-shoulder from the head of his bed to the threshold of the open door and spilled into the hall. It seemed as if everyone was there. His fellow ballplayers, still in uniform, and their wives or girlfriends lined the wall and doorway. Josh's mother sat in a high-backed vinyl chair pulled close to the bed. Behind her stood Alex and beside her stood Jonda, Sarah, and Bobby. On the other side, close to his head, stood Frannie. She held his hand tightly with her left, and continually patted and stroked the back of his hand with her right.

"Well, here we are," Josh said sounding a little woozy.

"We're here for you, Son," Cora replied. She pushed some sweat-matted hair from his brow.

Josh continued in the nonsensical vein, "I wish I could get up and shake your hands. But if I could do that, you wouldn't be here, would you?"

Several chuckles erupted from the packed throng.

"We just wanted to make sure you realize how much we care," Larry Timlin spoke up from the doorway. Heads nodded all over the room.

"Great! I believe you," Josh smiled. "Now that I know how much you care don't forget that my birthday's coming up in August."

The whole room broke out in uproarious laughter. Josh figured the nurse would soon come barging in ordering everyone to leave. She didn't.

Josh scanned the packed room. Best he could tell every single Frisco player was present. Of course, the long, lanky, chocolate-colored body of Artemis stuck out like a tiger in a lion cage. When Josh's eyes landed on his teammate and friend, Artemis nodded his bare head, poked a smile at him. Josh was glad he'd come. Of everyone, excepting his family, he was the most glad Artemis wanted to come to the hospital.

After scanning the room, his eyes landed and stayed on his brother, Bobby. He pushed himself higher onto his pillow. He needed to sit up. Pain pushed him down, pain and his mother's and Frannie's hands. "Don't you go and try to sit up, young man," his mother chided. "You'll get your head throbbing again."

"Too late," Josh slid down the sheets. "It's killing me."

"The nurse said you couldn't have another pain shot until nine. You'll have to be still and tough it out until then."

Josh didn't hear his mother. He was concentrating on Bobby. "Hey, Bobby, you didn't happen to talk with Runt Marr after the game did you?"

Bobby looked at him sheepishly. His head drooped like a scolded dog.

"Come on, Brother. I can tell you talked to him. What did he say? You know you're going to have to tell me sooner or later. Right now's as good a time as any."

Bobby looked at Josh. He still felt guilty about staying at the field and talking to a scout while his brother was being rushed to the hospital. He wet his lips, nodded. "They want to sign me. Mr. Marr said he'd give me a $500 bonus to sign with the Cardinals. Said I'd probably start out with their team in Carthage."

"Carthage, Missouri? That's great! Heck, that's not very far. We could all come see you play there."

Bobby perked up. He bit his bottom lip and allowed a brief smile to form. "Mr. Marr said I probably wouldn't be there very long, though.

He said two or three weeks at the most, just enough time for them to evaluate me and place me at the appropriate level. After that it's up to me to work my way up to the Majors. I'm hoping they start me out in "A" league, but even if it's "B" or "C" I can handle it. I'm hopin' I can be playin' in St. Louis in four years; five years tops."

"Shoot, I think you oughta start in Double-A, myself. You're the best pitcher in Tulsa. Heck, in Oklahoma."

"And you'd better calm down, Son," Cora warned. "Or else they're going to have to give you some morphine, and you don't want that, do you?"

"No, ma'am, I don't."

"You'd better do what your mother says," Frannie joined in. She reached down and, in front of everyone, kissed him lightly on the cheek.

Josh lay quietly. He was alone. The nurse finally had her way and forced everyone to leave. However, he was not asleep as the nurses thought. His eyes were wide open as he lay in the dusky light of the early evening. He stared at the narrow strip of wall directly above the closed door. There was nothing on the wall. It was simply a white wall. Josh's eyes remained transfixed on the blank nothingness. They did not move. They rarely blinked.

Behind his eyes, his mind raced. And everything he thought about was bad.

His life was over. He didn't care if he ever got out of bed again. He didn't care if he ever left the hospital. He had nothing to go home to. He had no future. Maybe the surgery would go awry; perhaps he'd get an infection and die. That was fine with him. He didn't care. It would be to the good.

The doctor said he'd never play baseball again, at least not at a competitive level. The doctor laughed and said not to worry; he could still play at church picnics and family reunions. Josh had not laughed.

Then Bobby gut-punched him, walloped him without meaning to. Bobby had gone on and on about how Runt Marr wanted him to sign a contract, said he wanted to give him $500 just to ink his John Henry on the dotted line. Said he'd probably be pitching in the Bigs in less than five years. Said he was the best prospect he'd seen in two years. Runt Marr had told his brother he was a can't-miss player.

And not a word about him.

Bobby said Marr had not so much as mentioned Josh's name -- other than to tell him he was sorry his brother got hurt on the last play of the game. The almighty scout said nothing about signing him! And this was before anyone knew the extent of the injury!

Josh gritted his teeth. He glared at the plain white wall, the stupid, idiotic, white wall! Why didn't they have some kind of picture on the wall? What was a patient supposed to look at? This hospital was stupid! The doctor was stupid! His arm probably wasn't even hurt that bad!

But Josh knew he was hurt. He knew his injury was every bit as bad as the doctor said. He couldn't move his arm without jolts of pain that felt like someone was sticking a serrated knife into his shoulder and wiggling it around. It was amazing how something that took about a second to happen could so completely change your life. In that tiny minuscule component of time, his dreams of being a big-league baseball player were destroyed. The thing he lived for was forever gone. He'd never don a uniform again. He'd never strap on the worn, dirty leg guards or pull the sweat-covered mask over his face. The days of squatting behind home plate and signaling for an inside heater or an outside yanker were over. History. Nothing more than memories and a bunch of snapshots his mom had taken over the years.

Josh began to cry. Huge sobbing tears surged down his face onto the warm blanket snuggled against his chin. Still, he cried. The tears flowed and flowed and flowed. He didn't care. He did not so much as try to wipe them away with his unhurt hand.

\* \* \* \* \*

Artemis said little on the drive home from the hospital. He said less at the kitchen table while he and Claire snacked on cheese slices and saltines. Little Satchy lay asleep in his room, but Satchy wasn't the reason Artemis was so quiet.

Claire got up from her chair and poured them some more tea. She sat back down and sipped hers. She looked over at her husband, then reached across the small round table and grasped his hand.

"I know it wasn't my fault. You don't have to tell me again."

"I wasn't going to say a word," Claire defended.

"You don't have to; your face says it all."

"I thought you liked my face?"

"You know what I mean. Quit messin' with me. I told you I know it wasn't my fault. What else do you want me to say?"

"Nothing. Just drink your tea and look at my pretty face."

Artemis did as he was told -- for a few seconds. "It's just . . . it's just that Josh is such a good guy. . ."

"I know he is," Claire agreed. "But it wasn't your fault. That's baseball."

"I know; I know. It's just that he's the first white guy to ever really care about me. Claire, he treated me good. He treated me as if I was like everybody else. Like I was just another player. I hate it so much that he got hurt, and now it's gonna cost him a professional contract."

"And what about you, Artemis Macintosh? You should have been playing for the Yankees or the Dodgers or for somebody twenty years ago. You were plenty good enough. It didn't happen, and you're doing fine. We're doing fine. That's the way the cookie crumbles. That's baseball. That's life. Josh'll have to figure things out, is all. He's young. He'll bounce back."

Artemis nodded. "I'm sure he will. But, it doesn't make it any fairer."

Claire covered her husband's hand with hers. She tried to get him to look at her; he wouldn't, and she didn't' force the issue. "Honey, I thought I saw that scout talking to you after the game. What did he say?"

Artemis continued looking at the cracker crumbs sprinkled on the tabletop. "Oh nothing, really. He told me he could tell I was a good pitcher, and if I were ten years younger, he'd offer me a contract, too."

Claire Macintosh pushed her chair back, and went to her husband. From behind, she put her arms completely around his tight, still-muscular chest and hugged him harder than she'd ever hugged him before.

# 25

The birthday cakes turned out beautiful. They smelled scrumptious. Cora meticulously placed eighteen blue candles on the white cake bearing Bobby's name. Next, she turned her attention to the chocolate cake that was Jonda's. The fudgy smell of the icing wafted into her nostrils overwhelming and replacing the previous vanilla scent of Bobby's favorite flavor. Jonda loved chocolate, Bobby vanilla. Thus, two cakes.

Cora didn't mind. She liked both. She picked up the seven pink candles she'd laid on the table and arranged them in the shape of a smile on the dark-brown cake under the *Happy Birthday Jonda*.

"There," she proudly proclaimed. "I like that."

Cora picked up Bobby's cake and placed it in the middle of the table. She put Jonda's next to it and stood for several seconds, hands on her hips, admiring her handiwork.

Bobby and Jonda's birthdays were three days apart. Other than Jonda's first birthday, they always celebrated them together. It was cheaper and more fun.

A sudden stab of melancholy jolted Cora. She realized this could be the last birthday party her son and daughter might celebrate together. It was unlikely they'd ever do it again, or at least, not for a very long time. Bobby was leaving in two days. Leaving for the big city of Houston where he was to begin his baseball career. Houston was so far away. There was no way she would be able to go see him play. He'd originally been scheduled to play in Carthage, Missouri. However, they,whomever 'they' were, decided to skip the evaluation period and send him straight to the Texas League.

Everyone told her it was a great opportunity for her son. Eventually, he might get to play in St. Louis. St. Louis was a long way off, too. Why couldn't he be satisfied with playing in Tulsa? They had a professional team, the Oilers. Why didn't he play for them? She didn't understand why her son wanted to leave the family to play baseball.

Actually, she did. Josh had explained it to her many times. It'd been Josh's dream first. Still, it didn't stop her from wishing her boy could stay home.

Cora walked to the cupboard and began removing their best drinking glasses from the shelves. She glanced again at the closed bedroom door. She didn't hear anything. Nothing. It'd been that way all morning and into the afternoon. Josh was in there, hopefully sleeping. She doubted it. He was probably lying on his bed looking at the walls. Looking at that darn photo of those two Major Leaguers he'd watched play a few years back. She couldn't remember their names; one of them was called 'Pepper,' she thought and the other one? She couldn't remember.

Apparently they were pretty good players, because Josh all but worshipped the picture.

Cora knew Josh was still depressed about not being able to play baseball anymore. He was devastated when Doctor Jenkins told him the bad news. Even then, he'd held out hope. Sadly, after the surgery, the doctor informed him the injury was worse than he expected. The reality of his situation set in. Josh became morose and self-pitying. She worried about him.

Then last week when she and Alex announced their engagement, he sank even lower. As soon as she finished telling her kids the good news, he abruptly left the room.

Cora filled the sink with hot soapy water. She picked up four glasses and immersed them in the near-scalding mixture. She began scrubbing non-existent grime from her best glassware. She looked out the window at the neighbor's willow tree swaying in the afternoon breeze. It was an old tree and had, no doubt, been through many storms. She rinsed the soap from two of the glasses and dried them with her dishtowel. An old church hymn filtered into her mind, and she began softly singing the familiar tune as she prepared for her children's party, *"then sings my soul, my Savior God to thee . . ."*

\* \* \* \* \*

Bobby let Jonda blow out her candles first. He always did. Her birthday was three days before his, plus there was no way she was going to wait and go second. Naturally, she made a big production out of the whole thing. Before blowing them out, she stuck her finger in her mouth and pretended to be deep in thought over her birthday wish. Then, like always, she wanted to tell everyone her wish before blowing out the candles. And, like last year and the year before and the year before, Mom had to remind her that her wish wouldn't come true if she told anyone.

"Then how will anybody know if I get my wish?" she asked – just like last year.

"You'll know, honey," Mom patiently replied – just like last year. "God will know."

"Well, if it's okay for God to know why can't you? Why can't Josh and Bobby?

"And Sarah," Mom added.

"I don't care if Sarah knows or not. She's a patooty!"

"Jonda Lynn Braun, if I have to, I'll spank you right here, right now, at your own birthday party in front of the whole family and all your friends!"

Jonda dropped her head, when she raised it she was wearing an all too familiar impish grin. She looked at her sister. "I'm sorry, Sarah. I'm sorry you're a patooty."

Before her mother could chastise her again, Jonda blew a huge gust of air at her cake. The candles flickered, and one by one began to extinguish. Jonda continued blowing, but exhausted her air supply with one candle left. Her cheeks turned purple. She refused to give up. The candle flame swayed, refused to go out. Sarah, standing next to the table, bent and with a quick gust, blew out the recalcitrant blaze.

"There, I knew I could do it," Jonda announced, totally ignoring the help she'd received from her sister. "Now, I'll get a bicycle for Christmas, a pink one with a basket and a horn."

"Oh brother," Bobby standing with his back against the wall shook his head. His little sister never ceased to amaze him, probably never would. He sincerely hoped not.

It was his turn. Jonda always helped him, and this year would be no different. She stood at the ready across from the cake loaded down with eighteen sky blue candles.

Bobby approached Jonda and the cake. He knew this might be the last birthday party he would share with his sister for a long time. If he were successful with baseball, he'd be away every summer playing for money. The thought of being a professional player still overwhelmed him. *Why was he, the brother who didn't worship the game the lucky one? Why was he getting the opportunity to make it his career? Sure, he liked the game, but not the way Josh did. Josh lived and breathed baseball.* He'd initially decided to turn down the contract, was determined to refuse the offer. At the hospital, Josh talked him out of it. His brother told him he'd be a dang fool not to play baseball for a living, told him he'd better sign or go look for another place to bunk because he wasn't rooming with a guy who'd throw away the chance of a lifetime.

The thought of Josh depressed him. He was sad to be leaving his brother. His big brother was everything to him. It was depressing to think that while he was in Houston playing ball, his brother would be stuck here with his arm in a sling waiting to go back to work at the hot, dusty railroad yard. It wasn't fair. They should be going together.

When Mr. Marr approached him about signing with the Cardinals, he'd been thrilled, ecstatic, on cloud nine. He was still happy. He now wanted to be a baseball player. Josh was right. He could do it. Or could he?

Because on top of feeling sad about Josh, Bobby was scared. Deep down, something gnawed at him; something poked at him telling him he wasn't good enough; that he was nothing more than a semi-pro chunker who'd gotten too big for his britches.

Bombarded by these emotions, Bobby stepped to the table. Jonda was all set. She hovered over the flaming candles ready to pucker and let fly. Bobby hesitated. He looked to his left. Sarah stood at the end of the table next to her emaciated, freckled boyfriend. Her mouth opened in a wide smile. Sarah wasn't really a girl anymore. She was almost grown. Life had seen to that.

"I want you to help me, Sis," Bobby said.

"Me?" she squeaked. "Jonda usually helps you blow out the candles."

"Today I want both my sisters to help me. After all there's more to blow out this year."

Sarah stepped to his side. Bobby couldn't help but notice that she and skinny boy had been holding hands. That was okay too.

Bobby counted to three and the trio easily blew out the eighteen candles.

"What'd you wish?" Jonda squealed. "Come on, you can tell us."

Bobby gripped his chin with thumb and forefinger as if deep in thought.

"Come on, out with it," Jonda pleaded. "God don't care if you tell."

"I wished . . ." Bobby began. "I wished for another little sister so you could realize what Sarah's been going through for the past seven years." He laughed. Everyone joined him.

\* \* \* \* \*

"Excuse me, Mr. Macintosh, can Satchy go outside with me and play with Sinbad? Momma won't let him come inside, and if I don't pet him, he's gonna get real sad. We're havin' a party without him and he doesn't like it."

Artemis looked down at the little blonde girl holding his son's hand. She flashed a toothy smile at him, nudged Satchy, who did the same. Artemis couldn't help but chuckle.

"I guess it's okay if you promise not to leave the yard. Satchy doesn't know the neighborhood, and he might get lost.

Jonda looked puzzled. She scratched her head. "Lost? How's he gonna get lost? I'm gonna be with him, and I know my way around. I live here. Besides, Momma won't let me leave the yard either. She said you never know when a masher might come and get you."

Artemis patted her blonde head. "You two go ahead and play with your dog. He looks friendly enough. Say . . ." Artemis pointed at her bulging pockets. "Whatcha got stuffed in your pants?"

Jonda stepped back as if wanting to run for the door. She let go of Satchy's hand and crossed her arms like a little pink Buddha. She shrugged. "Nuthin'. I ain't got nuthin' in my pockets."

"Oh, don't tell me that. I can see plain as the nose on my face that you've got something in them." Artemis bent to the little girl in a conspiratorial manner. He looked both ways as if making sure no one was listening. Satchy, realizing something big was about to happen, scooted closer to his dad and friend.

"You can tell me," Artemis whispered. "I won't tell a soul."

Jonda pulled her lips in and then she, too, looked around the crowded room of chattering, eating people. "You promise? You have to promise you won't tell my momma."

Artemis crossed his fingers. "I promise on pain of a thousand lashes with a wet noodle if I tell."

Jonda giggled. "I never heard that one before. That's a good un."

Satchy looked from Jonda to his dad. He too laughed.

"Okay," she whispered and pushed her head ever closer to Mr.

Macintosh. "I got birthday cake in my pockets. Sinbad likes cake, but Momma won't let him have any. I got chocolate in this pocket," she touched her right pocket, "and vanilla in this one." She pointed to her left pocket. "I don't got a lot, but it's all my pockets would hold. Do you care if Satchy puts some in his pockets?"

"Uh, yes I do care. Satchy is not to put cake in his britches."

"Oh," Jonda looked crestfallen. She quickly recovered. "That's okay. I got enough for Sinbad." She grabbed her friend's hand, and they snaked through the crowded living room to the waiting, hungry dog.

"She's a mess, isn't she?"

Artemis straightened. He continued watching the kids weave through the partygoers. He thought Claire was going to stop them when they whisked by her, but she was deep in conversation with Josh's girlfriend, Frannie. He turned to the familiar voice: "Yes, she is. But in a good way. She's got a lot of spirit, and I hope nobody ever tries to destroy it."

Bobby grasped his friend's shoulder. "Sorry I haven't got to talk to you till now. Aunts, cousins, my grandma, you know how it is at these things. Thanks for coming, though. It was sure nice of you."

Artemis smiled at the younger man. "I wouldn't have missed this for anything. Birthday and wedding cakes are my favorites – especially the icing."

Bobby lowered his hand. He looked at the floor as if he'd lost a penny.

"Are you ready for Monday?" Artemis asked.

Bobby raised his head. "As ready as I'm ever gonna be."

"It's kinda scary, ain't it? You ever been away from home?"

"Nope. To tell you the truth, I hadn't even thought of it that way."

Artemis cocked his head. He wasn't sure what Bobby was getting at. "Well, you'll be homesick. There's no two-ways about that. What else is bothering you? Is it your girl? Afraid she won't wait for you?"

"Maundi?" Bobby harrumphed. "She's already dumped me. Told me there was no way she was gonna leave West Tulsa. What she meant was there was no way she was going to leave her mom and dad. No, that's not what's concernin' me."

"What is it, then? Is it your brother?"

Bobby dropped his head, nodded.

"Well I'll be a cooter's grandpa. You can't let that stop you. Don't you realize you've just signed a professional baseball contract?"

Bobby's voice rose. "Seems like that's all I know. I hear it twenty times a day. You'd think I been elected governor or something."

"Shoot! The governor only wishes he could throw the pill like you. He'd leave that big ugly mansion in a minute if he could.

"It's just . . . It's just that it shoulda been Josh. He should be the one goin' off to play ball, not me." Bobby stared deep into Artemis's eyes without ever flinching. "Or it shoulda been you. You deserve it more than I ever will. Both you and Josh love the game more than anything. It's not fair."

"Young man," Artemis's voice changed to that of a father's. "Life's not fair. It's not fair that your father died in a foreign land in the prime of his life. It's not fair that my father wasn't allowed to go to school because the only school close to their farm was for white kids only. It's not fair that your mother has to work seven days a week to feed her family. Yeah, it's not fair that Josh got hurt and society wouldn't let my kind play a silly game like baseball because of the color of my skin. But, I've had a good life. Looking back, I wouldn't change a thing. Your brother will be fine. Don't fret over him. Bobby, you've got a great opportunity. Yeah, it's an opportunity Josh and I would have given anything to have. Just because we weren't as lucky doesn't mean you should fritter yours away. Now, listen to me and listen good." There was a charge in Artemis's voice, his face looked like a judge ready to pronounce judgment on a hapless defendant. "You'd better go down to Houston and play your heart out. Don't you come running back here in a few months, your tail between your legs, complaining it was too hard or the manager was too mean. You go down there and represent your family and your friends like a man. We're all up here rooting for you. Do you understand?"

Bobby gulped. He'd never seen Artemis like this. He felt ashamed. Here he was the luckiest guy on earth, and he was whining. He was making excuses because the bottom line was: HE WAS SCARED! He was afraid he would not succeed and have to come back home a failure.

"Thanks, Artemis. I think I needed that. I think."

Artemis softened; his beaming smile returned. He slapped Bobby on the back.

"You do know," Bobby continued, "I couldn't have done it without you? If you hadn't taught me the Blooper and curve, I'd still be a two-bit thrower instead of a real pitcher. You're one of the big reasons I'm getting this chance."

Artemis's smile broadened. His eyes gleamed with joy. "Thanks, kid. I know I needed that."

The two men simultaneously stepped towards the other. They wrapped their arms around each other, and hugged unashamedly in front of the gawking, puzzled birthday guests.

# 26

The party buzzed all around him. People joked and laughed and ate second helpings of birthday cake. His mother couldn't seem to keep her hands off the preacher. She constantly draped her arm across his shoulder, pinched his tricep, held his hand. You'd think they were a couple of teenagers. His brother went from one guest to the next getting his back slapped as if he'd won the lottery. Sarah sat in the corner with her beau, Mr. Skinny Legs, while Jonda, well, Jonda was being Jonda. He sat on the end of the couch, by himself. He was quite happy to be left alone.

He'd successfully fought off numerous attempts to join the festivities. They didn't understand he wanted no part of the affair. He didn't want any cake. He didn't want any punch. He didn't want any mints or nuts or pretzels or butterscotch rounds. He wanted to be left alone, and that was all. He wouldn't be in the front room taking up space if his mother hadn't thrown such a guilt trip on him. Yeah, yeah, he was glad it was Bobby's and Jonda's birthday party. They were a year older. Happy Birthday Bobby! Happy Birthday Jonda! Whoop-tee-do!

It was no different than any other birthday party they'd ever had, except this one was also serving as a going-away bash for the star of the family, the golden boy, the one, the only baseball hero: Bobby Lee Braun, pitcher extraordinaire!

Even Frannie had tired of him. She was on the other side of the room visiting with Artemis's wife, who'd broken the news that she was going to have another baby. Good riddance! She was too chirpy, anyway. Oh well, she'd be going off to college soon. Sure, she was only going to good ole Tulsa U., but with classes, studying, pep rallies, football games, basketball games, sorority parties, fraternity get-togethers, late-night astronomy projects, and who knows what else they do at college, he might never see her again. Just as well. They were too different. He realized that now.

"Can I get you anything? I'm headed to the kitchen for a refill," Brother Alex held up his empty punch glass, "I can bring you back some cake or punch?"

Josh waved him off with his good arm. "No. I don't want anything. I'm perfectly fine sitting here enjoying this wonderful party."

"No?' The preacher waggled his head. His eyes told Josh he didn't believe a word of it. He moved into the kitchen.

*Good riddance to you, too*, Josh thought. His mom and Reverend Alex Thomas were getting married in the fall. That meant his mom, Sarah, and Jonda would be moving to the fancy parsonage in West Tulsa, leaving Garden City. Leaving their home. That was okay. He was staying. He would live alone in their house, their home. He just hoped his mother didn't take all the pictures on the wall. But why would she? Most of them had Dad in them. Brother Alex wouldn't want any photos of their father in his big house.

Bobby walked past, didn't so much as look at him. *Too busy being the big man of the house. Too busy being the star. Figures. Bobby always liked acting like a hotdog. He'd always enjoyed the limelight. Well, let him go be a hotshot in Houston. Who cares?*

Watching Bobby prance across the living room reminded Josh once again, for the ten-thousandth time, of the collision at home. Automatically, his teeth began to grind. His jaw tightened. He felt perspiration bubble up on his forehead and arms; his neck grew warm. In his mind, he could see the throw coming in from right field as if it were happening all over again. He could see and feel Cameron bearing down on him, lowering his shoulder. He knew the play was going to be close. He knew he was going to be hit. Still he would not move. He refused to leave the plate unguarded.

Josh shivered as if standing in a meat locker. He'd done it again, relived the play, the moment, two weeks ago when his life, for all practical purposes, ended. He'd promised himself he would stop thinking about it, would no longer dwell on that terrible day. But his mind would not stop. His mind, no matter where he was or what he was doing, kept going back to that fateful afternoon and the jarring crash at home plate.

At first, he'd been angry – no, furious – with Cameron VanDeaver. Hated him was more like what he'd felt. That first night in the hospital, he'd wanted to kill the smart-alecky college boy. If Cameron had not bowled him over, had not rammed his shoulder into the ground, he might be packing to leave for Houston. It might be him with the $500 bonus money in his pocket and a signed contract in his dresser. It might be him with the adoring relatives and bright future.

The amazing thing was; he'd do it again. He knew that now. The more he thought about the play, the more certain he was that if it happened all over, he'd again block the plate. And the more he thought about it, the more he also realized that Cameron had done nothing wrong. He was just trying to score. He was playing the game the way it was meant to be played, hard and tough. If roles had been reversed, and Josh had been storming towards home with the tying run, and he spied the catcher blocking the plate, he'd pound into him, too. It was that simple. It was baseball.

Josh got up from his sanctuary and walked outside. No one stopped him. No one said anything to him.

\* \* \* \* \*

"Care if I sit with you?" Frannie asked in a soft, subdued voice.

"Whatever you want," Josh answered as if he didn't care one way or the other.

Frannie sat down on the porch swing near the middle, but not directly against Josh. He pushed off with his feet, and the swing began swaying in the afternoon heat.

"Whew! It's warm out here. I didn't realize it was this hot today."

Josh looked at Frannie as if she were a moron. "It's June. It's Oklahoma. What'd you expect? We don't live in Vermont or Maine or ice-covered Alaska. We live in the great state of Oklahoma, home of cowboys and Indians and all kinds of interesting snakes. Not to mention coyotes and buzzards and armadillos that like to dig in your yard. Oh, we can't forget bugs! We've got plenty of those, especially the kind that bite you and sting you. What a great place to live. Oklahoma! Where the wind comes sweeping down the plains. Oh man, don't get me started on the wind!"

"I think you got yourself started. All I said was it's hot today."

Josh turned and glared at Frannie. He didn't say anything.

Frannie continued looking straight ahead. She gently asked, "When are you going to quit feeling sorry for yourself? When are you going to be Josh again?"

Josh pushed the swing harder. They zipped back and forth like a couple of kids on the playground trying to outdo the other.

"You're scaring me," Frannie practically yelled. "Slow down before this thing flies off the porch."

Josh complied bringing the swing to a complete stop.

"Thank you." Frannie readjusted her bottom in the swing. She edged closer to Josh. "Now that we've satisfied your male hormones, can we talk?"

Josh remained silent, as stoic as Marcus Aurelius. He fiddled with the strap on his sling.

Frannie turned until she faced Josh. She looked into his eyes. He stared back; she wasn't sure he was actually seeing her. She breathed deeply, wet her lips, and with as even a voice as she could muster tried to talk to him. "Josh I know you're discouraged. I know you wanted to be a ballplayer more than anything in the world. I'm so sorry this happened to you." She covered his right hand with hers. He dropped his head.

Feeling more confident, she decided to tackle another subject she knew was bothering him. "Please don't be upset about your mother wanting to get married. She's young. She should get married again."

Josh raised his head and angrily frowned at her. She pulled her hand from his, shrank back.

"She didn't have to marry the preacher!" he spat. "He was my dad's best friend, too. It's almost like they planned it or something. But what do I care? I'm nothing but a railroad man with a bad wing!"

Frannie couldn't believe what she was hearing: the self-pity, the irrational thinking, the self-loathing. How could someone so intelligent, so motivated, so happy, change overnight? Her mind shot back to the game and his injury – or change in an instant?

"Josh, Josh, listen to yourself." She took a deep breath. Which problem did she tackle first? "Were you planning on living with your mother the rest of your life? What about your sisters? Don't you think someday they'll marry and leave home? Do you want your mother to be alone when she gets old?"

"She could always live with me, even if I do get married."

"That's not the same. She needs someone to talk with at night, someone to share her feelings with. She can't do that with you; you're her son. Josh. Your dad's been gone seven years. She needs somebody else. I think he would want her to remarry. And the fact that Reverend Thomas was your dad's friend makes it even better. He's someone your dad liked and trusted. Isn't that better than a complete stranger?"

She didn't know how Josh would respond. At first, he sat there; head bowed, not moving. Slowly, he raised his head, nodded. "Perhaps you're right. Mom probably does need somebody." Then he shook his head. "It just doesn't seem like seven years."

Frannie returned her hand to his; she squeezed.

"Ouch! That's my bad arm."

"Sorry," she apologized. "I forgot your finger bones connect to your arm bone."

A wisp of a smile appeared on Josh's face. "It's okay. I overreacted."

"And," she barged ahead. "You're not a railroad man with a bad wing. You're a very intelligent, sweet man with a great future. Furthermore, I might add, a pretty good lookin' feller, too. That is, when you smile."

It was almost as if Josh was trying hard to smile, but couldn't. His lips seemed unable to curl upwards. He again shook his head. "I have no future. It's gone. This is as good as it's going to get."

"Quit feeling sorry for yourself, Joshua Braun. No, you're not going to be a baseball player. Yes, that was your dream. Sometimes dreams don't come true. Or as your mother would tell you, perhaps baseball wasn't what God had planned for you. Maybe you should ask Him what He wants for your life. Then, with His guidance, you can create a new dream. Make new plans. That's what my dad did. He wanted to be a stupid baseball player too, just like you. But he wasn't good enough. So, what did he do? He went back to school and now's he's an attorney. It's not his dream, and I guarantee you he'd rather have played baseball instead of go to law school, but he's making do. And you can too, as soon as you stop your pity party and start planning for the future."

"But your dad's smart. He's been to college. I don't even have a high school diploma."

"He didn't go to college until after he gave up trying to play baseball. Not until they kicked him off the team because he wasn't good enough. Josh, you're still young. You can start over. You can do or be anything you want. That is if you're willing to work hard and not give up."

Josh rolled his tongue across his lips. Frannie felt hopeful. A thought crossed her mind: *Maybe she should major in counseling?*

He bit his lower lip. He didn't smile at her; he didn't frown either. "Frannie, do you really think baseball players are stupid?"

*He's coming back*, she thought. *The old Josh is right around the corner.*

# 27

The words of the song filtered into his head and slowly woke him. Still he refused to open his eyes. The song got louder, closer. The singer's high soprano voice missed a couple of notes, but never a beat: *"Then sings my soul, my savior God to Thee. How great Thou art. How great Thou art."*

The second 'How great Thou art' bounced off his cheek like warm cat's breath. Without opening his eyes, he knew who the kitty was. "Jonda, leave me alone," Josh mumbled through closed lips.

"Get up, sleepy head. Time for church."

Still not opening his eyes, "I'm sorry, Jonda. I can't go to church. My arm hurt all night, and I hardly got any sleep."

"But you promised. I'm singing today. The junior choir's singing in the big church in front of all the grown-ups."

Josh finally looked at his sister. He expected her to be standing with her arms crossed, blowing gusts of anger through her bangs. She wasn't. She stood beside his bed in her white and pink Sunday dress looking like a confused puppy dog. Her big brown eyes bore through him, not in anger, but in disappointment. She was on the verge of tears.

"I'm sorry, Sissy; I can't go. Not today. My arm is still hurting."

Jonda nodded her head rapidly. Without another word, without another plea, she scooted through the half-open door, gently pulling it closed as she left.

Josh groused as he shaved. He grumbled as he struggled to button his shirt with one hand and gave up after the fourth attempt trying to knot his tie. He shouldn't be having to do this. He shouldn't be going to church when he was hurt. He should be lying in bed resting his shoulder. But do it, he would. He would do anything to get his sister's teary-eyed face out of his mind; anything to make her happy again.

Josh stayed in bed until the family left. He expected Jonda to return and plead her case one more time. She didn't. His mom, brother, and sisters drove off without even a 'good-bye' or a 'so-long.'

He got out of bed ten minutes later and hurriedly got ready for church; at least, as fast as his arm would allow.

It was as if he were attending Tabernacle Baptist for the first time instead of returning to the place of his baptism; the place where he'd spent so much of his childhood. The parking lot was the same narrow graveled strip, and the building looked exactly as he remembered. But it was also different, almost foreign.

Josh climbed the steps of the entryway and pushed open the door of his youth. The scene before him was as if he'd entered a time machine. Everything was the way it had always been. The old brown pews they'd bought from the Methodist church were still in use. The concrete block walls were the same whitewashed color. Josh shook his head. *I guess they still don't have money for paneling.* Lining the walls, as always, were photos of missionaries from places like Ethiopia, Rhodesia, New Guinea, Burma, Thailand. Josh scanned the small auditorium. Still no carpet on the floor. He shook his head. *This is probably the only church in town that hasn't carpeted their sanctuary.*

And the people. The members of Tabernacle Baptist. They all looked the same, yet Josh knew many of them were different. His mind and eyes searched for memories, both rested on the back pew. There sat Mr. and Mrs. Jackson in the exact spot they occupied when Josh was a little boy, and likely would occupy until one or both died. He continued searching the sanctuary. The church was filled with people Josh knew, or used to know. All were hard-working, good, honest people. People you could trust in a pinch. People you could call if you needed help.

Josh located his family on the second pew; the same pew he'd sat in most of his life. He waited until the congregation began singing *When The Roll Is Called Up Yonder*, before making his way to the front. The song leader, who owned a shoe repair shop in downtown Tulsa, waved his stained fingers to the beat of the music and sang as if God would be calling his name that afternoon. The congregation of a little over a hundred people lustily joined him, and sounded like three hundred. Josh scooted past a startled and bewildered Bobby, and edged between his two sisters. His mother, standing beside Sarah, smiled and mouthed the words, "thank you," at him.

The junior choir director asked the children to line up on the platform for their special where they sang three songs before the sermon. It might have been Josh's imagination, but he was certain Jonda, standing in the middle of about a dozen kids, sang the loudest and the prettiest. He could hear her soprano voice easily above everyone else.

The rest of the service flew like a whirlwind. Brother Alex preached on the grace of God and His many blessings. At first, Josh felt himself becoming angry. What did he have to be thankful for? Slowly, his mind filled with images of his family; he replayed the past seven years and how close they'd become in the aftermath of their father's death. He felt a solitary tear slide down his cheek, then a second, and a third. He realized, sitting in the church of his father, how unbelievably selfish he'd been the past few weeks; how he'd subconsciously wanted Bobby to turn down the professional contract; how he'd wished it'd been Bobby, who'd gotten hurt instead of himself. He thought about how nice everyone had been to him, and how they'd waited on him hand and foot, while behind their backs, he ridiculed their efforts.

Josh felt a tiny hand slip into his. He felt short thin fingers clutch his big callused paw. He squeezed back.

Why couldn't he go to night school this fall and get his diploma? Why couldn't he go to business school or who knows, maybe even college and make something of himself? He could do it. Now that he was where he was supposed to be; he could do anything.

# Epilogue

The locker room was everything Bobby expected : the carpeted floor, the freshly painted walls, the hustle and bustle of trainers, attendants, and players getting ready for the day's game. It was so different, yet so similar to the six years he'd spent in the minors.

*Had it really been six years?*
*Was he really almost twenty-four?*
*Had he really made it?*

Bobby sat down in front of his locker and began untying his street shoes. He pulled them off and placed them in the bottom of the wooden locker. His eyes glanced to the nameplate above – Braun 23. That was him. Braun, number 23. This was his locker. Yes, he'd finally made it.

A shiver raced through him as he realized what he would be doing in less than two hours. He would be pitching for the St. Louis Cardinals. He'd be on the same field, on the same team as Ken Boyer and Red Schoendienst and Stan Musial. In fact, if Bobby twisted his body sideways and leaned back, he could see the great one sitting at his locker. Musial was pulling on his sanitary socks and chatting with an older man in a gray suit and black fedora, probably a sportswriter. Who knows? Maybe the reporter would talk with him after the game? It might happen. He hoped so.

Bobby reflected on the six long years he'd spent in the minors. Six years of grueling bus rides, bad food, little money, and dashed hopes. Twice he thought he was going to be called up to the Majors, especially two years ago when he'd pitched a no-hitter and thirty-one scoreless innings in a row. But they didn't need him. So, he'd kept trudging along.

Only this winter he'd wanted to quit and would have if Josh hadn't talked him out of it. It was during Christmas, and he was depressed because he didn't seem any closer to the Big Leagues than when he started. Meanwhile, Josh had married, had a son, gone through business school and had a good-paying job as an accountant. He seemed on top of the world. Josh told him to give it one more year. He reluctantly agreed.

Now, here he was. Finally getting his chance.

Bobby stood and slowly slipped on the white uniform like it was a sacred vestment. He buttoned the jersey and smoothed any wrinkles in the woolen material. There was a brand-new cap in the locker hanging from a hook, and he put it on. It felt good, a perfect fit. He looked at himself in the small mirror next to his locker. He'd always liked the blue and red Cardinal cap. He smiled and struck a bubblegum-card pose. Hey? An exciting thought entered his mind: *How would he pose for his baseball card? And when would they be taking the picture?* He felt the nervous jitters all over again.

He sat back down and laid the pristine cap next to him. His eyes darted to the rumpled paper bag on the floor. He knew what was in it. He'd brought it. Or rather he'd gotten it from Josh last night when he visited his family at the motel. "Hutch," Fred Hutchinson, the Cardinal Manager had given him permission to wear it today, so why was he anxious about putting it on? He retrieved the bag from the floor and reverently opened it, lifting the ancient, sweat-stained cap from the sack. He held it in front of him several seconds just looking at it as if it were about to speak to him. He ran his fingers across the embroidered "StL." He sighed deeply.

"Hey kid, when you're finished admiring the headgear, we need you to warm up. In case you've forgotten, you're pitching today."

Bobby bounced from the chair. He jammed the cap onto his head, grabbed his mitt. "Right skipper, I'm on my way." Bobby brushed past the Cardinal's manager and headed for the ramp leading to the field.

"Kid." Bobby put on the brakes, turned, and looked back. Fred Hutchinson looked him over, smiled. "I know this is easier said than done, but you need to relax. Try to remember that this is the same game you've been playing since you were five years old."

Bobby nodded at the wizened manager. He took a deep breath. "Gotcha, Skipper. I'm trying really hard." He turned again to go.

"Kid, one more thing." Bobby skidded to a stop, faced the old man once again. Hutchinson had an even bigger grin on his face. "Do you think you might want to wear your cleats on the field? You might want some socks, too. The uniform looks better with shoes and socks."

Bobby closed his eyes and gulped. He didn't even have to look. He knew he was standing on the locker room floor in nothing but his bare feet.

\* \* \* \* \*

"Come on, you've admired the ballpark long enough. Let's find our seats. Here, it's your turn to carry Johnny."

Josh accepted his son from his wife and trooped after her. The rest of the group followed behind in a daze.

Sportsman's Park, or Busch Stadium as it was now called, was magnificent. The double-decker stands and the huge scoreboard in leftfield were what first attracted Josh's attention. He'd never seen anything so big. Of course, it was his first Major League park to visit, but he didn't care. He couldn't imagine a finer structure, not even Yankee Stadium could be this grand! As their group neared the field (somehow Bobby had gotten them box seats), his eyes automatically locked onto the playing field. 'Oh my goodness," he exclaimed.

"What?" asked Jonda, standing next to him, playing with the baby.

"Have you ever seen such green grass?"

"It's just grass," she replied. "We've got plenty back home."

"Not like this," her step-dad said. Alex Thomas appeared equally dazed; just as overwhelmed as her brother. She didn't get it. It was just a ball field where guys played baseball.

They found their allocated seats and plopped down, the men barely taking their eyes from the field and the group of players hitting pepper directly in front of them.

"Hey, Artemis," chirped Josh. "Isn't that Kenny Boyer on the far right?"

Artemis looked at the player, then at Josh. He grinned. "I do believe it is. And there's Walker Cooper over there." Artemis pointed down the left-field line where a player lay on the ground stretching.

"You men are impossible. You're acting like little boys in the middle of opening up your Christmas presents," Cora laughed.

"We are," her husband replied. "With all due respect to God above, when I walked through the turnstiles I felt like I was entering Heaven."

"Amen brother," Josh agreed. "And we didn't even have to pay to get in."

Everyone laughed. They were having a great time.

Josh leaned back in the green wooden seat. He was so glad Artemis, Claire, Satchel, and little Jackie Robyn had been able to come with them. It made everything that much better. So much had happened since Bobby left to play ball. He could hardly believe it himself. If you'd told him six years ago, after his baseball injury, that he'd be working as an accountant, living in a nice house, married to a beautiful woman and have a son, he'd have laughed in your face.

So much had changed.

Sarah was married and pregnant. That's why she couldn't make the trip to St. Louis. Of course, Josh kidded her incessantly about having a red-headed niece or nephew. However, Sarah was too happy to come back at him. She had wanted so badly to come, but knew she shouldn't; it was the only disappointing thing about the whole trip. His mom had settled in nicely as a pastor's wife and, despite getting close to fifty, looked as pretty as ever. Josh couldn't remember the last time he'd missed a church service and in January, he'd been elected deacon. Two of the church's new trustees were George and Vernon Delaney. They'd tired of gang life, realizing nothing good was going to come from drinking every night and hurting people for the fun of it. On a whim, they visited the church. After much coaxing by Brother Alex, Josh had accompanied his pastor on a visit to the Delaney's and watched in utter amazement as both hoodlums accepted the Lord as their personal savior. Vernon quickly found he had a gift for teaching young boys, while George joined the choir and became their best tenor.

And Gibbo Ross?

Unfortunately, he'd finally gone over the edge and killed someone. He was locked in the state prison waiting to visit the gas chamber next summer. Josh had accompanied his pastor and the Delaneys twice on visits to the former gang leader, but Gibbo refused to soften his heart and repent of what he'd done.

Josh motioned at a hawker to come over. He bought everyone a Coke and peanuts. "You can't watch a game without Goobers," Josh exclaimed. Of course, the vender agreed with him.

Josh passed a bag of nuts to Artemis.

He and Artemis remained fast friends. He believed they would be for the rest of their lives. Artemis had gotten into church as well. He and Claire attended an Assembly of God church near their house. Artemis still worked at the school, and during the evenings and on Saturdays coached Satchel's little league team, the South Haven Redbirds. Josh helped him when he could. The team was good; they'd lost only two games this year. Artemis's little girl, Jackie Robyn, was quite the athlete, too. She went with them to every practice and was already a better player than any boy her age.

Over the public address system, the announcer began broadcasting each team's lineup. He started with the visiting Pirates. Josh couldn't help but notice their entire row become quiet when the announcer began listing the Cardinal players. They held their collective breaths when he said in a clear strong voice: "And pitching for the Cardinals, and making his Major League debut, number twenty-three, Bobby Braun."

They all clapped for Bobby as if he'd struck out the last batter of the World Series. Josh looked past Frannie at his mother; there were tears of joy in her eyes. He glanced at his beautiful sister, next to him; she was beaming. When he looked at the end of the row, at Artemis, he saw his friend nodding to him. Josh nodded back.

The players ran to their positions, with the pitcher being the last to take the field. It was tradition. When Bobby emerged from the dugout and headed to the mound, Josh immediately noticed the cap. It was old and worn, and from his seat, he could see the sweat rings. He couldn't believe they'd let him wear it. He couldn't have been prouder that Bobby wanted to.

\* \* \* \* \*

Bobby finished his warm-up tosses, went behind the mound and resined his sweaty hand while the infielders threw the ball around. He glanced about the ballpark not really seeing anyone, only a mass of moving humans. That is until his eyes landed on the box he'd reserved for his family. He could see them plainly, as if they were sitting ten feet from him: his mom, Alex, Jonda, Josh and Frannie and his nephew, Johnny, little Satchel, who wasn't little anymore, Jackie Robyn, Claire and Artemis. They'd all come to see him play. Driven all the way from Oklahoma.

His eyes returned to Josh and saw his brother beaming. *Good*, he thought. *I'm glad he's happy.* Then Bobby looked at Artemis, his friend, his mentor. Now it was Bobby's turn to smile.

"Whatcha grinning about?" Red Schoendienst asked. The infielders had gathered around the mound to wish the pitcher luck.

"Yeah, kid, what's the deal?" asked Boyer, the third baseman.

Bobby looked at his teammates, realizing again where he was. "I'm just happy to be here."

"Well, don't get too star-struck," Schoendienst warned. "We've got a ballgame to win, and we're countin' on you to throw strikes." Schoendienst slapped the young pitcher on the back and jogged to his position. The others did the same.

Bobby walked up the pitcher's mound, placed his foot on the rubber, and looked at the catcher for the signal. The black-capped hitter waved his bat menacingly at the rookie.

Walker Cooper flashed a solitary finger for the fastball.

Bobby shook him off.

The catcher stuck down two fingers and patted his right leg for an outside curve.

Bobby again shook his head 'no.'

Cooper frowned, held down three fingers and twirled them.

Bobby, knowing he was right where he was supposed to be, nodded his agreement.

The End

# About the Author

Phil Smith is a fanatical baseball fan whose office is wall-to-wall with old baseball memorabilia worth practically nothing. During his life he has worked as a sacker in a grocery store, night clerk at a funeral home, lumber man, janitor, security guard, computer operator, assembly line worker, letter carrier, soldier in the US army, and high school softball and basketball coach. He is currently employed as a professor of American history at Tulsa Community College. He is still married to the girl he began dating at the age of sixteen, and together they have two children.

CPSIA information can be obtained at www.ICGtesting.com
Printed in the USA
LVOW08s2325190814

399990LV00003B/130/P